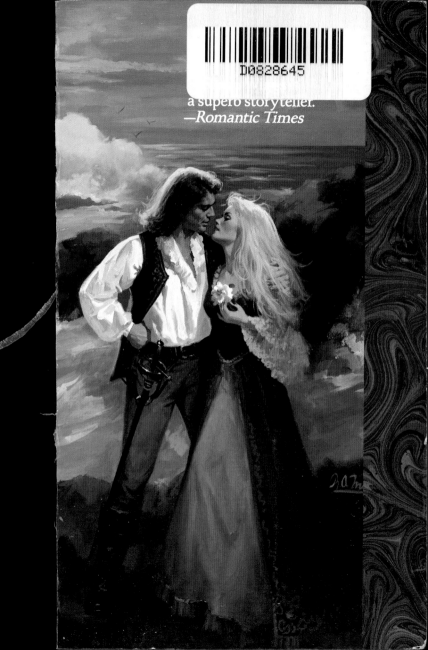

Stolen Treasure

Her words meant nothing, for the shadowy rhythms of her speech captured him, and the secrets that haunted her eyes beckoned mystically.

"Caitlin MacBride, you do ply strange arts upon a man."

"I do no such thing." She drew away and started walking again.

Wesley knew he could not trust her. Yet at the same time he admitted to himself that he had never met so compelling a woman. Heather and moonglow colored every word she spoke. Fierce conviction molded every move she made. She plundered his heart like a bandit after treasure.

A dangerous thing. For the plundering of hearts was supposed to be Wesley's specialty.

Also by Susan Wiggs

The Lily and the Leopard
The Raven and the Rose
Embrace the Day

Available from
HarperPaperbacks

Harper
Monogram

THE MIST AND THE MAGIC

SUSAN WIGGS

HarperPaperbacks
A Division of HarperCollinsPublishers

HarperPaperbacks   *A Division of* HarperCollins*Publishers*
10 East 53rd Street, New York, N.Y. 10022

Copyright © 1993 by Susan Wiggs
All rights reserved. No part of this book may be used or reproduced in any manner whatsoever without written permission of the publisher, except in the case of brief quotations embodied in critical articles and reviews. For information address HarperCollins*Publishers,*
10 East 53rd Street, New York, N.Y. 10022.

Cover illustration by R.A. Maguire

First printing: January 1993

Printed in the United States of America

HarperPaperbacks, HarperMonogram, and colophon are trademarks of HarperCollins*Publishers*

❖ 10 9 8 7 6 5 4 3 2 1

Dedicated with affection to my former teaching partners: Marion Barren, Diane Brown, Barbara Miller, and Charis Smith. Ladies, it's been some party!

Acknowledgments

Heartfelt thanks to Joyce Bell, Alice Borchardt, Arnette Lamb, and Barbara Dawson Smith for performing tasks that would try the saints.

To Irin Barakat, for the Gaelic lessons, *Dia do bheatha*.

With gratitude and green envy, I thank Mary Dodson Wade for sharing her Irish experience with me.

Cead mile buiochas to John and Alberta Lloyd-Evans, my favorite semipermanent residents of Ireland. I've kept your books so long, they're starting to look like mine.

Special thanks to Laurel Natale and Gretchen Gay for their proofreading skills.

Prologue

Tyburn Hill, 1658

The executioner wondered why so many women had come to watch the priest die. Were the ladies of London so bored, then, that the spectacle of a poor wretch being tortured to death lured them from their bowers?

Thaddeus Bull scratched his head through his black hangman's hood. He had never understood the fascination of the Londoners. Give him a pint of ale, a joint of mutton, and a smiling maid; that was all the entertainment he needed.

Strangely, these women represented every layer of society. Masked noble ladies in boxy coaches held pomander balls to their noses. Country maids in faded dresses moved their lips in silent prayer. Tradeswomen and merchants' wives whispered behind their hands.

A bevy of seasoned Southwark whores brayed at one another in their sharp, rough speech. One of them elbowed a path toward Bull, tossed him a coin, and said, "Please, sir, be merciful!"

Bull ignored the plea and the coin. Only in lean times would he stoop to accepting a bribe from a whore. Thanks to Lord Protector Cromwell, present times were not lean.

Through the black rim of his woolsey hood, Bull caught a flash of silver from a woman's throat: a crucifix or a Lamb of God, no doubt, worn in defiance of the ban on popish idolatry.

Guards flanked the road leading to the gallows where the priest would hang. Like Bull, Cromwell's soldiers seemed struck by the presence of the women. Their hard gazes roved over the throng, resting on a comely maid here, a buxom gentlewoman there.

Thaddeus Bull heard the unmistakable scraping noise that heralded the arrival of the prisoner. He glanced at the noose, swinging in the brisk spring wind. Thick hemp for this one, the sheriff had ordered. Thin rope strangles a man instantly and spares him the agony of the drawing and quartering.

The authorities, Bull knew, wanted Father John to feel every moment of slow strangulation, every stroke of the sword. Bull's gaze moved to the blade of his huge knife. Specially wrought in Saxony, the weapon was designed to slit a man cleanly from gullet to crotch. He had honed the edge parchment thin, for he was no butcher to hack away at a poor sod, priest or not.

A familiar feeling coasted over Thaddeus Bull. He was a simple man, but he knew guilt when he felt it. He could almost taste it in his mouth, like a knobby piece of mutton gristle.

Bull cleared his throat. He wished he could spit on the ground but the hood prevented it. Meting out justice was his job and he was paid well to do it. Many of the condemned, eager to secure a place in paradise, gave him gold coins as tokens of their absolution—

not as bribes. But he would accept no inducements today, for this priest was to die hard.

The crowd hushed. Between the beats of the dirge-like drum rhythm came the sliding sound of the wattled hurdle.

Amid the ranks of soldiers rode the sheriff. Behind him plodded a massive horse, its great lower jaw yawing at an iron bit. Harnessed to the beast was the hurdle, a plastered oaken beam dragged along like a narrow sledge.

The prisoner rode with his back aligned on the length of wood, bound at his hands and feet and waist.

The three-mile journey from Tower Hill hadn't been easy, Bull observed. Bumping over the cobbled streets of cheapside, through the mud puddles and horse dung of Holborn, and being dragged through the ripe garbage of the Strand had taken its toll. Father John's face, hair, and robes were covered in filth.

The eerie silence drew out. Bull waited to hear the customary jeers, but none rang from the perfumed throng.

A plump doxy broke through the ranks of the soldiers. Before they could stop her, she dropped to her knees beside the priest and used a damp white cloth to cleanse his face and beard and hair. A soldier dragged the woman away.

Father John raised his clean face to scan the onlookers.

Then the weeping began.

Never had Bull heard the like: great, heartfelt sobs, high-pitched wails, ragged hopeless sounds that seemed wrenched from the very souls of the weepers.

Bull adjusted his hood, the better to see the priest. His long hair was a greasy, matted mane the indeterminate hue of London mud. The beard straggled several inches below his chin. Blast, thought Bull. Beards were a nuisance.

The priest's deep-set eyes were as blank as polished stones. The face bore the ravages of a course of torture that, according to Tower rumor, hadn't drawn so much as a word from Father John. His silence had defied the rack, the wheel, the iron maiden. One interrogator swore the priest was a practitioner of the black arts who was capable of slipping into a trance-like state. Others said he had lost his mind.

Bull heard a whisper, light and feminine, as sweet as a psalm sung by an angel. "Wesley. Oh, Wesley, no . . ."

Who the devil is Wesley? Bull wondered.

John Wesley Hawkins, formerly a king's cavalier and presently a condemned Catholic novice, hoped no one of consequence had heard the whisper of his true name. For six years he had kept his identity a secret known only to England's underground Catholics and a few well-placed royalists.

How ironic to be discovered by the authorities now.

But he just might be. For he heard the name Wesley being hissed from woman to woman.

He was surprised and a little dismayed at the size of the crowd that had come to witness his launch into eternity. It was daunting to have to face so much desperate grief all at once.

Save it, he wanted to say to them. I'm not cut of the cloth of a martyr, never was.

Some men craved the fate that awaited Hawkins. They prayed for the day their tormentors would put their wills to the test and their souls to rest. They envisioned a glorious death and, afterward, elevation to sainthood.

Sainthood had a certain lofty appeal, but it wasn't

strong enough to make John Wesley Hawkins crave death.

Not just death, he reminded himself morbidly, but choking until death kissed his soul; then, still alive, he would be cut down and his body sliced open, his insides drawn out and his heart carved from his chest. Then the beheading and quartering, his parboiled parts displayed publicly to warn off those who dared practice the Catholic faith. A costly commodity, this sainthood.

He hoped he would lose consciousness at the first stroke of the knife, but he had never been a squeamish man and couldn't count on fainting. At Worcester, he had survived a sword wound that would have killed most men. As a further taunt to death, he had stitched the gash with his own hands.

In the Tower, he had refined his ability to resist pain. He remembered little of the rack and less of the hot irons; the burns and bruises only tormented him later.

Someone removed the ropes. Blood charged to the tips of his fingers and toes, so swift and hot that it hurt. But what sweet agony! His very blood had taken up the refrain he had been trying—and failing—to ignore: I want to live. I want to live.

But his fate was here, on this infamous hill surrounded by green fields and budding trees and weeping women.

As soldiers hauled him to his feet and shoved him toward the hangman's cart, he allowed himself a last look at his mourners.

All those women. Some harkened back to his misspent youth. Others were devout followers who had embraced his later cause. There were pretty women and plain ones, rich ones and poor ones, women he had liked and women he had merely lusted after.

Good Lord, he thought. How quickly they had all discovered his identity. He suspected only a few had actually known him; the rest had been drawn by rumor and improbable tales that grew larger with each telling. Gossip through the Catholic underground flowed as swiftly as a river during flood season.

Yet despite their grief, he could summon no sentiment toward them. Torture had scoured all emotion from John Wesley Hawkins.

Until he thought of Laura.

Oh, God, Laura. The very thought brought a shimmer of light into his soul. A sense of loss made the impending horrors seem no more threatening than a stroll through Bartholomew Fair.

Sweet Jesus, keep her safe. It was as close to true prayer as Hawkins had ever uttered, despite his vocation. Priesthood had been a foolish choice, one made in haste and desperation and a yearning simply to *belong*. He was glad Laura's appearance in his life had stopped him from taking his final vows, forever binding his life to the church.

His mind coursed over the plans he had laid for his motherless—and soon to be fatherless—child. Only hours before his arrest, he had paid a widow named Hester Clench to pass Laura off as her niece and speed the three-year-old to safe obscurity. Now the widow Clench possessed the only person who truly mattered to him.

He pictured Laura's round baby face, the profusion of rose-gold curls that gave her the look of a cherub. The memory of her childish laughter stabbed at his heart, for he would hear that sound no more.

Ah, the pain of it. Never to exclaim over his child's first lost tooth, never to see her grow tall and willowy and beautiful, never to play the stern papa evaluating her suitors.

Heat prickled in his throat. He fought the tears. If his death were to have any meaning at all, he must die well.

He was a king's man to the end, he wanted people to say. If he could coax admiration from this hard London crowd, jaded by so many executions, his death might make a difference after all.

Goaded by the hangman, Hawkins stepped into the two-wheeled cart hitched to a mule. So this was where his life would end. No more saying mass in barns and cellars, always one jump ahead of the priest catchers. No more whispered messages to royalists, always looking over his shoulder for Cromwell's hunters.

At the back of the crowd, a man in an opulent high-collared robe dismounted and tried to jostle forward. A felt hat, with the brim tilted up at one side and held in place by a golden clasp, shadowed his face.

He seemed to be shouting, but the wailing of the women and the beating of drums drowned his cries. Recognition niggled at Wesley's torture-numbed brain, prodding a memory.

The executioner stepped up beside him. The cart groaned under the giant's solid weight.

Good, thought Hawkins. The undersized weaklings make a sloppy job of it. The big lout should be able to put him out of his misery quickly.

A cleric arrived. He wore a black cloak unrelieved by ornamentation, and a hat with a round, flat brim. Wesley wondered which sect was in fashion at the moment. Puritan, Anabaptist, Leveler...he couldn't keep all the Protesters straight.

"You've a dire sentence hanging over you," said the cleric.

Hawkins shot a wry glance at the noose. "So it seems."

"Recant, sir, and spare yourself from the sword."

Wesley allowed a hint of wistful regret to soften his features. "My good friend, I cannot."

Impatience tautened the cleric's mouth. "You're as insincere a priest as they come. Why play the martyr?"

"Better to die a martyr than to live a traitor."

"Then you'll suffer the full agony of the sentence. I shall pray for your everlasting soul."

"Do that, and you'll surely send me to hell." Wesley turned to the executioner and sketched the sign of the cross. "For what you are about to do, I forgive you."

"Aye, sir, you'll not trouble my sleep." The hangman had a deep voice muffled by the hood, and an East London accent. Wesley wondered what the man thought about, what he did with himself when he wasn't torturing people to death. Did he stop off at the Whyte Harte for a pint of the plain, rocking back in his chair and regaling his cronies with morbid tales?

The giant removed Wesley's filthy cloak and shirt. Cool air tingled over his bare chest and arms. Sighs gusted from the women, whether at the scars from the lash or at the hard musculature of his stomach and chest, he couldn't tell.

The hangman flung the garments out of the cart. Feminine hands grappled for the clothing. As his wrists were tied behind his back, Hawkins winced at the pain. He heard the sound of rending fabric, shrill voices arguing. Each scrap of his cloak and shirt would be sold off as a holy relic.

Saint John Wesley Hawkins. It had an interesting ring. He would be made patron of something, but what? Liars and cheats? Gamblers and skirt chasers? Defrocked priests?

Through the slits of his hood, the hangman eyed

Hawkins's belt. The tooled leather, several layers thick, had ridden at his waist for many years. It was a beautiful piece, but that had little to do with its value. Inside the belt were several slim compartments, waterproofed with wax, in which he carried falsified documents, secret messages, and money when he had it.

The belt was empty now. "It's yours if you want it," said Wesley.

The giant shrugged. "Wouldn't span me gut." He took hold of the noose.

Thick rope pressed on Wesley's shoulders; twisted hemp scratched his neck. The hangman stepped down from the cart. Wesley's thighs tightened. He expected the mule to bolt any moment.

The executioner raised his hand to slap the beast and urge it forward. But he didn't strike the brown flank yet.

Four women Wesley remembered from his cavalier days sidled close to the cart. He knew their intent was to rush forward and hang on his legs, speeding the strangulation so the rest of the sentence would be performed on a corpse.

Near the rear of the crowd he spied five masked and mounted men. Cromwell's own, judging from their buff coats and hooked halberds. For too many years, those evil hooks had buried themselves in the chests of royalists and men of reason and justice. Wesley tried to hate the Roundheads but couldn't. They had supported the Commonwealth out of genuine concern for order and fairness. But in just ten years, Cromwell had made butchers of them.

The cloaked man, who had been wrestling his way through the throng, had been waylaid by the sheriff. They argued heatedly, their arms making sharp, angry gestures.

Hawkins inhaled the tang of springtime: the fragrance of new leaves and freshly mown fields, the heavy scent of blossoms wafting from the orchard beyond the hill, the smell of Tyburn Creek, so fresh compared to the sewage stink of the Thames.

Even the most vociferous weepers quieted during the drawn-out moment. Somewhere, a bird chirped and bees hummed. A baby cried and fell silent. A horse grunted, a sound like a man clearing his throat. A sound of impatience.

The time had come to speak.

He had rehearsed a lofty tirade for days. Before this mass of thousands he would utter truths so profound that the Londoners couldn't help but be moved. His words would go down in history.

For the life of him, and it did come down to that, Hawkins could not remember a word of his wonderful speech.

That was the moment panic set in, a beast leaping out of the dark and clawing at his soul.

A whisper in the back of his mind rescued him: *Say what is in your heart.*

"God save England!" His voice had been the envy of Douai seminary. The bell-like clarity, the deeply resonant tones, and the beautifully rounded vowels were those of a gifted priest.

"God save England," Hawkins repeated. "And God save Charles Stuart, her rightful king!"

Gasps exploded from the crowd.

Thaddeus Bull's hand swung sharply downward.

Laura. Wesley clasped the thought of her to his heart. *I love you, Laura. Will you remember me?*

Bull's palm clapped against the mule's flank.

And John Wesley Hawkins, former king's cavalier and reluctant Catholic cleric, felt the cart lurch out from under him.

1

Castle Clonmuir, Connemara, Ireland

"He's thrown me out!" Magheen MacBride Rafferty's wail keened through the great hall, startling lazy hounds and drawing stares from the castle folk. "'Tis a mad and cruel man he is. My husband of only a fortnight has cast me from his house!"

Caitlin MacBride folded her hands on the blackthorn tabletop and regarded her sister. "What do you mean, Logan's cast you out?"

Magheen spread her arms. She reminded Caitlin of a young willow, albeit one with a temper. "Sure amn't I here?" Lifting the back of her hand to her smooth brow, she sank to the bench opposite Caitlin. "I would rather fall down ice cold and eternally dead than come to you, but he left me no choice. You must help me. You must!"

"Why did he send you home?" Caitlin asked, her voice low because of the avid listeners. Tom Gandy, the steward and self-styled bard, looked on with the interest of a bettor at a cock fight. Rory Breslin, who

served as both armorer and marshal, set aside the
harness he was braiding. Liam the smith put his finger to his lips to shush the brood of children who
cavorted with the shaggy wolfhounds at his feet.

Only Seamus MacBride, chieftain of the sept and
Caitlin's father, paid no heed to the drama at the
round blackthorn table.

"He sent me home because I refused to share his
bed," Magheen stated loudly.

"And you blame him for sending you back?" called
Rory Breslin. The other men chuckled in agreement.

Magheen gave a magnificent toss of her head.

Caitlin pressed her hands hard on the table and
prayed for patience. "Why, Magheen? I thought you
loved him well."

"I do! What woman wouldn't? The fault's upon
your head, Caitlin. You should have told me what
Logan demanded as dowry."

"I didn't think you'd be interested," Caitlin said
calmly.

"You knew I'd be affronted," Magheen shot back.
"Twelve head of cattle and a booley hut besides! Sure
that's the price a man demands to take a lesser woman
to wife. Logan should be satisfied with me alone."

"Logan Rafferty is a great lord and a man of business," said Caitlin. "Even for you, he asked a dowry."
And he was a blessed fool to divulge the amount, she
reflected.

Magheen buried her face in her slim white hands.
Her lacy shawl slipped back, revealing a sleek blond
braid coiled over her head. She was as comely as a
primrose, as demanding as a queen.

"Did you ask him to waive the dowry?" Caitlin
inquired with a twinge of hope. She had pledged
more than she could afford to Logan and despaired of
paying it.

"Of course. But he won't listen to me. You've got to put reason in that big thick knob of his, Caitlin."

"The problem is between you and Logan."

"Then the MacBride must settle it," said Magheen.

Caitlin glanced at Seamus, who gazed with feverish concentration at his book of hours. "Daida can't."

"You're as cold as Connemara stone," Magheen snapped.

"Magheen, *deirfiur*, I—"

"You don't know what it's like to love a man."

Ah, but I do, thought Caitlin, closing her eyes for a moment. Ah, I do . . .

"Caitlin MacBride!"

She opened her eyes to see a familiar figure striding toward her. Light from the yard outside limned his broad shoulders, narrow hips, and mane of curly black hair. Spurs jangled like discordant bells with every step he took. His long beard, parted and braided, brushed against his massive chest.

"Eek!" Magheen leaped to her feet and hitched up her skirts. "Stay away from me, Logan Rafferty!"

"Sure I wouldn't have you for thirteen head of cattle and two booley huts!" Logan shouted.

"Well!" Magheen planted her hands on her hips. "You won't be having me at all." She started toward the privy apartments at the rear of the hall.

"Don't you dare leave, Magheen," Caitlin said.

"I'll not be after suffering the insults of this greedy *spalpeen*." Magheen walked down the length of the lofty hall, hips swaying, looking over her shoulder in blatant defiance.

Logan watched with longing and regret on his face, but he stood his ground.

From the women's corner, spinning wheels whirred to a halt. A sense of waiting hung in the peat scented air.

Shoving aside an inquisitive wolfhound, Logan reached the table and stopped. Caitlin inclined her head slightly. "Logan." Although he was her overlord, she addressed him informally. To do otherwise would have seemed strange, for she had grown up in his shadow, hitting short of the mark when she could have hit dead center, losing horse races she could have won, stumbling over poems she could have recited perfectly—all to save the vast male pride of Lord Logan Rafferty.

She had grown accustomed to deferring to him. But she would never grow accustomed to the bitter taste of it.

He eyed Magheen's slowly retreating figure. "A handful, that one." His gaze drifted to her derriere. "Two hands full."

Caitlin faced him squarely across the table. "You've come about Magheen?"

"Ah, it's all business you are. You're twenty-two years old, Caitlin MacBride. You'll wither on the tree like an unplucked rowanberry."

His sympathy was as insubstantial as the mist over the mountains. Logan cared not a dram for her unmarried state.

Unmoved, she said, "I know I owe you Magheen's dowry and that I'm in arrears." She slid a glance at her father, who sat poring over his book and looking lost, as he had since the castle chaplain, Father Tully, had mysteriously disappeared just after Magheen's wedding two weeks earlier.

Help me, Daida. She tried to convey the silent message to him, but he continued his quiet study.

"Logan, please. Can payment wait until the calving?"

"I've been waiting, Caitlin. And Magheen won't give herself to me on credit." Mirth rose from the men at the hearth. "My people have gone without

Clonmuir milk and meat since Easter." Looking for accord, he glared at the men. "And I've gone without my husbandly privileges."

Caitlin drew a deep breath. Drastic troubles called for drastic measures. "I've the best stable of ponies in Connemara," she said. "Will you accept a mare and a stallion?"

"Faith, the Clonmuir ponies do tempt me, Caitlin. But I'll not be taking them. They're only more mouths to feed." Logan leaned toward her. His black beard brushed the table. "And what are you doing with so much fine horseflesh, eh?" he asked softly.

She prayed he would not guess her secret. "The stable has been the pride of the MacBrides since the time before time. I'll not be turning them out because of a few lean years."

His thick eyebrows clashed. "You're putting the welfare of Clonmuir horses before that of your own dear sister."

She pressed her lips together, thinking of Magheen, of her other people, women and babies— sweet Saint Brigid, so many babies!—who depended on her. "Give me a week, Logan. I'll send you a bullock as a token of my good intent."

"What of my good intent, Caitlin?" Exuding the proprietary air he had been born with, Logan put out a hand and caressed her cheek. "I've offered a solution if you would but agree."

"Have a spark of sense. You're married to my sister!"

His coal black eyes kindled with annoyance. "By Christ's holy rood, I have no marriage with Magheen!"

She glared at him through the light fog of peat smoke. "You could have, if you'd reduce your demands."

"Never," he stated. "A lord can ask no less."

"And I can do no better until the calving." She

gathered up her papers. "One healthy bullock. Conn will bring it to you."

His fist crashed down on the table, hammering for attention. "It's not a bullock I want, Caitlin, but a wife!"

"You'll have her, I promise. But she's nearly as unreasonable as you."

The wail of a baby laid siege to any reply Logan might have made. The quality of the cry was unmistakable. Only hunger could give that earsplitting edge to a child's cry.

Yet another family of starvelings had reached Clonmuir. Forgetting Logan, Caitlin hurried to welcome them.

Magheen was already there, cradling the baby in the crook of one arm and motioning urgently with the other for someone to fetch milk. Worrying the brim of his caubeen with his fingers, a man approached Caitlin. "You are lady of the keep?"

No one ever mistook her for an underling. Wondering why, she said, "Yes," and smiled reassuringly. "Welcome to Clonmuir."

"Talk is, your hearth is open to such as us."

Caitlin nodded. Behind her, she heard the sounds of plates and utensils. The scenario had been repeated so many times that the servants needed no instructions. "Warm yourselves by the fire," she invited.

As the family trudged past, she looked into their nearly senseless eyes. In the hollowed depths she saw suffering beyond imagining, sorrow beyond bearing, horrors beyond believing.

And she knew, with a painful twist of her heart, that these wretches were the lucky ones.

The unlucky ones lay in ditches, prey for wolves or—aye, she'd heard it said—starving Irish.

Damn the English. The curse trembled silently through her. "Still taking in strays, are you?"

She turned to Logan. "And what would you have me do?"

"I'd have you meet my price, Caitlin MacBride, or the marriage is off for good." With that he strode out into the yard, whistled for his horse, and rode toward his home of Brocach, twenty miles to the north.

Caitlin rubbed her temples to soothe away a dull throb of pain. Unsuccessful, she went to see to the needs of her guests.

Ten minutes later a youthful voice called from the yard. "My lady!" Hoofbeats thudded on the soddy ground.

"Curran," she said, picking up the hem of her kirtle.

She rushed down the long length of the hall, past the women at their spinning, past her father, past a group of children playing at hoodman blind. Not one of them, she knew, felt the pounding sense of trepidation that hammered in her chest.

She felt it for them as she always had. They never feared news from Galway, even in these dangerous times. In every sense save the formal one she was the MacBride, chieftain of the sept, and she wore their fears like a postulant wears a hair shirt.

A fast ride and a sharp wind had whipped up color in Curran Healy's already swarthy face. He swung down from his tall, muscular pony and bowed slightly to Caitlin.

"What news, Curran?" she asked.

"I've been to the docks," Curran said in a strained tone. He was but fourteen and lived in dread of his voice breaking.

"Devil admire you, Curran Healy, I told you never to stray to the docks of Galway. Why, if a healthy lad like you fell into the hands of the English, they'd geld you like a spring foal."

He shuddered. "I swear not a soul marked my passing. I saw merchants—"

"Spanish ones?" she asked on a rush of air. Anticipation thrummed through her so sharply that it hurt. Months, it had been, since she had heard from him. . .

"English." He rummaged in his satchel. "My lady, and the great God forgive the sin upon my head, but I stole this."

She snatched the sealed parchment from his hand. "This is a bonded letter." She whacked the youth on the chest with the packet. "Great is the luck that is on you, Curran Healy, for I should have you flogged for endangering yourself."

He pulled at the pale sprouts of hair growing on his chin. "Ah, my lady, sure there's never been a flogging at Clonmuir."

Defeated by his logic and her own curiosity, Caitlin opened the letter. "It's from Captain Titus Hammersmith to . . . " She bit her lip, then spoke the hated name. "To Oliver Cromwell."

"What's it say, my lady? I don't read English."

She scanned the letter. On feet of ice, apprehension tiptoed up her spine. *I shall extend every courtesy to your envoy who is coming to solve this great matter . . .The covenant of this mean tribe of Irish is with Death and Hell! By the grace of God and with the help of this excellent secret weapon, the Fianna shall be as dust beneath the bootheel of righteousness . . .*

"What's an envoy?" asked Curran.

Fear tugged at her stomach. She forced a smile. "It's something like a toad."

"Can't be. Legend is, that if you bring a snake or toad to Ireland by ship, the creature will flop over and die."

"No doubt Cromwell's toad will do just that."

"And if he—it—doesn't?"

She shook back her heavy mane of hair. There had not been time to plait it this morning. There was never time to behave like a lady. "Then the Fianna will have to ride again."

"What of this talk of a secret weapon?"

She laughed harshly. "And who—or what—on this blessed earth could possibly defeat the Fianna? We'll see that happen when the snakes return to Ireland!"

2

"You're one lucky man," said a cultured, nasal voice. Very proper. Oxford or Cambridge. The clerics at Douai would be surprised to know St. Peter was an Englishman.

Wesley tried to lift his eyelids. Tried again. Failed. Exasperated, he used his fingers to pry them open. Blue sky and billowy clouds. Dull white wings stretched against the wind. Had he somehow escaped Satan's horseman after all?

"What's that?" His voice rasped from a throat scoured raw by the hangman's noose.

"I said," came St. Peter's voice, "you're a lucky man."

Wesley frowned. Why was St. Peter talking like a Gray's Inn barrister? A cool shadow passed over him. He blinked, and the shape came into focus. A high-collared cloak, not an angel's robes. A face he recognized, and it wasn't the face of Saint Peter.

"God's blood!" he said. "John Thurloe! Are you dead, too?" "I wasn't the last time I checked."

Wesley propped his elbows against hard wood and

struggled to rise. Pain? No, pain couldn't follow him into the light, where the sky shone blue and distant and his heart beat vibrantly in his chest. "By God, I used to hate you, sir, but now you're as welcome as the springtime."

Wesley heard a creaking sound, the groan of thick rope straining against old wood. Canvas luffing in the wind.

"Jesus Christ, I'm on a ship!" said Wesley.

Thurloe bent his legs to absorb a swell that rolled the narrow deck. "You must keep your popish confessor busy, priest, with all the swearing you do."

The sin was minor compared to others Wesley had committed. "Last I remember, I was swinging from Tyburn Tree." He touched his stomach and chest through the shirt he wore. The executioner's sword hadn't so much as split a hair.

Thurloe's features pinched into a frown. "And your various parts would be spiked on Tower Gate and London Bridge if not for the tender mercies of myself and our Lord Protector."

The cobwebs began lifting from Wesley's mind. He remembered himself moving, as if he were galloping toward an eternity of regrets, of half-finished business. The terrible journey had taken him past the fair-haired child he had left behind, past words he should have said, past a crown he had tried to defend.

He asked, "Cromwell arranged a pardon?"

"A stay of execution."

A memory flashed through Wesley's mind: the hooded giant, the weeping masses, the jolt of the cart. His feet kicking at empty air, the wheel of green leaves and blue sky overhead, the burn of the rope around his neck.

After that, a muddle of pain. His body dragged to

the block, the black hood looming into view, a blade glittering against the clear sky, steel slicing toward his bare flesh.

Then a shout: *Hold thy stroke!*

An ugly blur followed: horses' sweaty hides, soldiers' buff livery, clenched fists, and muttered curses. Questions, protests, speculation spoken over his limp body. A dark robed man arguing with the sheriff at Tyburn.

"It was you, wasn't it?" he asked Thurloe. "You stopped the execution."

"I did."

"I can't say I'm fond of your timing. You might have come earlier." Wesley cocked an eyebrow at Thurloe. The wind plucked at his wispy brown hair arranged in a tonsure around the balding top of the man's head. "Just a stay?"

"That will depend on you, priest. Or should I say Hawkins?"

Damn! "Who's Hawkins?" he asked.

"Don't be lame, sir. Several of the ladies present called you Wesley. Lucky for you, I quickly deduced the truth." Thurloe spun in a shimmer of dark velvet and brass buttons. He set a hat on his head. Wesley recognized the tipped brim fastened with a palm sized brooch. "Come with me."

Wesley dragged himself up on wobbly legs. The ship strained at her cables. His vision swam, then resolved into a view of a narrow deck and an aftercastle rising beyond a web of rigging.

To his left the sea swelled out endlessly. To his right, a small town huddled a stone's throw away.

"Milford Haven," said Thurloe.

"Milford Haven! My God, that's two hundred miles from London," said Wesley. Lost miles, during which he had imagined being borne to hell in the devil's chariot.

"You see, we've not even left port."

"Why not?"

"Because not all of us are going with you, Mister Hawkins."

"Going where?"

Thurloe made no response, but led the way down a hatch and through a companionway that smelled of wet timber and moldering rope. Two men descended on Wesley with soap and a razor. Fifteen minutes later, he found himself thrust before the Lord Protector of England. The sight of Oliver Cromwell freshened Wesley's fear that he had gone to hell after all.

Framed from behind by a bank of diamond shaped stern windows, Cromwell stood at a burl writing desk. Reddish brown hair, cropped to his shoulders, framed a bold-featured face ornamented by a curling mustache and pointed beard. The Lord Protector's eyes had the gleam of ice-coated rock.

"Bit of an improvement." His gaze sharpened on Wesley. "Ah, Mister Hawkins. I've got you at last, after all these years."

In the wells of the desk sat an array of crystal ink bottles with silver stoppers. The gilt-edged blotter and the straight-backed chair bore an imprint of the lions of England. The trappings of royalty.

Wesley planted his feet on the red Turkey carpet of the stateroom. "What ship is this?"

Cromwell's lips tightened as if he found the question impertinent. He drew himself up proudly. The pose looked faintly ridiculous on the Lord Protector. His plain cloth suit appeared to be the work of a country tailor. "It used to be called *Royal Charles* but it's been rechristened *Victory*."

"And where are we going?"

"*You* are sailing west as soon as I've given you your instructions."

"You're sending me into exile?"

Beneath the legendary ruby nose, a controlled smile tugged at Cromwell's mouth. "Exile? Too easy for the likes of you, Hawkins."

"You obviously want something from me, else you'd not have spared my life," Wesley reminded him. The truth hit him suddenly, a swift blow to his empty belly. He was alive! Laura. Laura, darling. The thought of her clasped him in an embrace of both joy and dread.

"You royalists are always so astute," said Cromwell, his voice sharp as an untuned víol.

Wesley ignored the taunt. He had been astute enough to elude Cromwell for six years.

"Sit down, Mr. Hawkins."

As the Lord Protector lowered himself to the richly carved chair, Wesley took a three-legged stool opposite him. Thurloe poured brandy into small glasses.

"The Irish problem." Cromwell pressed his palm to the map before him. The chart depicted the island, with stars drawn at the English-held ports and hentrack markings tracing the route of Cromwell's dread Roundhead army.

Ireland? Wesley frowned. Perhaps the pressures of his office were weighting Cromwell's reason.

"I know nothing of Ireland," said Wesley. Almost true. A hazy memory came to him, filtered by the years. His parents' stern faces and cold eyes as they informed him that England was not safe for Catholics. His banishment to Louvain on the Continent, where Irish friars had put him to work printing outlawed books in Gaelic. The kindness of the brothers had almost filled the void in his heart. And the strange, lyrical language of the Gaels had lingered like a never-to-be-forgotten song in his mind.

"You stand to learn more than any civilized man ought to know." Cromwell jabbed a thick finger at the map. "Dublin, Ulster, all the major ports belong to us. The Pale is ours. We gave the rebels a choice of hell or Connaught, and most of them made the mistake of choosing Connaught. And that's where the problem lies."

The west of Ireland. Wool, peat, herring . . . what else? He could not think of a commodity that would induce Cromwell to risk his men. But that was the Lord Protector: all-powerful, enigmatic, consumed by ambition, and unwilling to explain his motives.

"Galway," said Wesley, deciphering the upside-down word near Cromwell's finger.

"Aye, and the entire coast of Connemara. I've garrisoned troops at Galway. The Irish were driven out of the city long ago. But we've had resistance."

The Lord Protector looked as if he could not comprehend this defiance. Why, Wesley thought ironically, wouldn't the Irish wish to give up their age-old way of life, their tradition of self-rule, and their Catholic religion in order to embrace a revenue-hungry Protestant conquest?

Wesley realized he knew more about the Irish than he had thought. He took a drink. The brandy dropped like hot lead in his empty stomach.

"The heart of the resistance," said Thurloe, "is a band of warriors called the Fianna. Do you know the legend?"

"No." Wesley suspected it had to do with dark magic, fey folk, and shadowy deeds.

"It's a medieval order of warriors, bound by blasphemous pledges and initiated in pagan rites. They fight like devils. Our captains swear the villains hold their horses under a spell, so fierce are the beasts."

One corner of Wesley's mouth lifted in a half smile. "I think your captains have been in the bogs too long."

"They do God's work," Cromwell retorted.

"The Fianna use antique weapons," Thurloe continued. "Broadswords, slings, cudgels, crossbows—and violate every rule of war. They strike like a sudden storm in the dark: swift, unexpected, devastating to men who pursue victory with honor."

"And where do these warriors come from?" asked Wesley.

"Some are Connemara men. We know this because of the unique horses they ride. The Irish call them ponies, but the beasts are as large and thick as cavalry horses. Other warriors might have been recruited from the exiles of Connaught to the north."

"And your army can't contain them?"

"My army has righteousness on its side," Cromwell insisted. "But they're not trained in dirty, sneaking, bog-trotting tactics."

And you think I am, Wesley silently observed. He took another sip of brandy. Resurrecting an ancient order was, he decided, an act of political genius, a clever way to remind the despairing Irish that they were the sons of warriors.

"They have a weakness," Thurloe said.

Cromwell picked up a quill pen and brushed it over the map. "They have a blind, pagan devotion to their leader."

Thurloe nodded. "The man has already achieved the status of legend. Our soldiers hear ballads sung about him. His Fianna will follow him to the very gates of hell and beyond."

"Who is he?" asked Wesley.

"No one knows." Thurloe's sharp, Puritan features drew taut with chagrin. As master of protectoral intelligence, he prided himself on knowing the business of every last mother's son in the Commonwealth. He resented the elusiveness of the Fianna. "We suspected the hand of popish priests in this, but we've culled every cleric from the area, and still the rebels ride."

Cold distaste turned the brandy bitter in Wesley's mouth. England was not the only dangerous place for the Catholic clergy.

"I want the devil taken." Cromwell's ruddy fist crashed down on the leather blotter. Crystal ink bottles clinked in their wells. "I want his head on a pike on London Bridge so all England can look upon an Irish thief and murderer."

Wesley winced at the contempt in Cromwell's voice. "He's only a man fighting for his life and his people."

"Bah! Honest Englishmen lived for years among the Irish, who enjoyed equal justice from the law. The rebels broke that union, just when Ireland was in a state of perfect peace."

"Or perfect suppression," said Wesley.

"I did not bring you here to debate questions of justice. I can drastically shorten your stay of execution."

"Sorry."

"Once this chieftain is taken," Thurloe continued, "the Fianna will disintegrate." A tight smile played about his mouth. "The Irish are sheep who lose their way without their shepherd."

"Then from Galway we'll take all the coastal districts of Connemara," Cromwell stated with an air of finality. "We'll put a noose around the rebels in Connaught."

Wesley no longer wondered why Cromwell had cut him down from Tyburn Tree. He knew.

"Mister Hawkins," said Cromwell, "do you value your life over that of a murdering outlaw?"

I'm a Catholic, not a madman, thought Wesley. "Absolutely, Your Honor."

"I thought so," said Cromwell. "You're to find the chief of the Fianna and bring his head to me before the year is out."

The ship's timbers creaked into the silence. The smell of brine and mildew pervaded the air.

"Why me?" asked Wesley. "I'm a king's man, and one of the few left in England who's not afraid to say so."

"Where's Charles Stuart now, eh?" Cromwell sneered.

"Helping the man who helped him escape Worcester?" He planted his elbows on the table. "He's wenching on the Continent, Mr. Hawkins, and doesn't give a damn about you."

Wesley wouldn't let himself rise to the taunt, wouldn't let himself think of the night spent in an oak tree with a frightened young prince. "What makes you think I'm your man?"

"I've learned much about you. Your parents sent you overseas for rearing among papists. You returned to England to become a thief taker, growing rich on bounties and blood money."

Tightening his muscles, Wesley fought to govern his emotions. Few knew of his parents or of the deeds he had done, tracking thieves, hauling them kicking and screaming to justice.

"Then you threw in your lot with the royal tyrant," Cromwell went on. "We lost track of you. But we knew you were in England, spreading sedition and popish idolatry."

"I seem to have been a busy man," Wesley said wryly.

"It's your reputation for tracking that put the idea on us," said Thurloe. "Men swore you were capable of finding the path of a snake over stone, or a bird's flight through a cloudy sky."

"I think that's overstating my talents a little."

"In your time, you were the most successful thief taker in England."

"But there are others who have given their loyalty to you."

"True, but you're fluent in Gaelic. From your training in Louvain."

Wesley made no reply. Thurloe was conscientious indeed.

"Ah, and one final thing." Cromwell smiled, the drawn-back grin of a viper about to strike. "Your success with women. Even as a postulant you couldn't resist."

Wesley went cold inside. He wondered how much the Lord Protector actually knew of his lapse.

He found out when Thurloe presented him with a letter. "From William Pym," the Secretary of State announced in a voice hot with venom. "You seduced his daughter, and she died three years ago birthing your bastard."

Wesley closed his eyes as shame scoured his soul. Here was his penance. He forced his eyes open. "I comported myself poorly. How will that help me corner an Irish outlaw?"

Thurloe produced another letter. A whimsical script danced across the page. "There is a reference to the Fianna in this, from a woman of Connemara to a Spanish gentleman in London."

"You intercepted it?" Wesley asked.

He nodded. "The woman's name is Caitlin MacBride. She's mistress of a coastal stronghold called Clonmuir."

"An excellent place to start," Thurloe put in. "The attacks of the Fianna began not long after the English burned the fishing vessels of Clonmuir."

"If you can sweet-talk your way into her bed as easily as you did into the beds of English ladies," said Cromwell, "you'll be able to coax secrets from her." He chuckled with pleasure.

"You're enjoying this, aren't you, my lord?" asked Wesley.

The Lord Protector lifted his glass. "An unenviable task. Irishwomen are Amazons—dirty and ugly—and this Caitlin MacBride will be worse. She's twenty-two and unmarried despite her holdings. But you'll put up with her barbaric ways. Knowing you, you'll probably find them interesting."

"I cannot seduce a woman," Wesley stated with a rush of guilt. The appearance of Laura in his life had made him swear off women.

"You'll do as I say now, my friend," said Cromwell.

"And if I fail?"

Cromwell smiled grimly. "You won't. My commander in Galway is Captain Titus Hammersmith. I sent letters ahead, explaining what is expected. You are to cooperate with him in every way."

"I can't work with Roundheads breathing down my neck."

"Believe me, Mr. Hawkins, you won't have to."

An arrow of suspicion embedded itself in Wesley's mind. Cromwell was too confident. Something rang false. "So what's to stop me from losing myself in Ireland?"

Cromwell waved a summons at someone standing outside the door. Wesley heard the sound of approaching feet, one pair heavy, the other light and rapid. The back of his neck began to itch. He rose from the stool and turned toward the door.

"Papa!" A tiny girl burst into the stateroom.

Wesley's legs wobbled. He dropped to his knees. She leapt into his arms and pressed her warm, silky cheek to his.

"Laura, oh, Laura." He kissed her, then pressed her face to his chest.

"Papa, you sound funny," said Laura. She touched

his throat. "What happened to your neck?"

"I'm all right," he whispered. Tears needled the backs of his eyelids but he conquered them. Think. Cromwell had the child. Wesley raised his eyes to the woman who stood wringing her hands. He held Hester Clench captive with the furious thief taker's stare he used to employ on recalcitrant prisoners.

The truth shone brightly in the woman's frightened face. She had told Cromwell everything.

Every blessed detail she'd vowed to take to the grave.

"Damn you," he said quietly.

She had dark eyes and a handsome face he'd once thought kindly. Her chin came up, and she said, "It's best for the child. Lord Cromwell swore he'd keep her safe and save her immortal soul from your popish training."

Wesley held Laura away from him, for he feared to crush her with his rage. "You lied to me," he said in a low, deadly voice.

"For the sake of this innocent child I had to," the woman said with conviction. At a nod from Cromwell, she withdrew.

Wesley's faith in human mercy withered. Cromwell had outbid him for the loyalty of Hester Clench. He buried his face in Laura's peach-gold hair and inhaled her fragrance of sea air and sunshine. Her soft curls bobbed against his face, and then she pulled back, regarding him through gray-green eyes that were mirrors of his own.

"Auntie Clench said I'd never see you again, Papa."

"We're together now, sweetheart." But for how long?

"I cried and cried for you. So Master Oliver promised he'd let me see you again." Laura peered over her shoulder. "Thank you, Master Oliver."

The words of gratitude knifed Wesley through with fury. But his arms were gentle as he cradled his child, treasured her, felt his heart spill over with love for her.

"Look, Papa," said Laura, holding out a silver bauble on a ribbon. "Master Oliver gave me a locket. Isn't it pretty?"

Fury stuck in Wesley's throat.

While Cromwell and Thurloe conferred over their maps and their plans, Wesley and Laura shared a meal of biscuit, small beer, hard cheese, and grapes. She chattered with the blithe innocence of untroubled childhood, and he listened with a smile frozen on his face. It would serve nothing to let her glimpse the black hatred that gripped his soul, to confess the loathsome thoughts that claimed his mind. To Laura this was all a great adventure. She'd had them with him before, fleeing priest catchers and Roundhead huntsmen, sleeping in haylofts, and bolting down meals in rickety farm carts. She had no idea she was a pawn in Cromwell's deadly game.

At length the rocking motion of the ship lulled her; she settled her head in his lap and tucked her tiny hand in his.

"I love you, sweetheart," he whispered.

As she fell asleep in his arms, Wesley felt the walls of the stateroom pressing on him, squeezing at his will. Cromwell had trapped him in a prison more confining than the dank stone walls of Little Ease in the Tower of London.

The Lord Protector broke Wesley's reverie by calling out an order. Two burly sailors appeared in the doorway.

Wesley drew his arms more protectively around Laura.

"Restrain him," said Cromwell.

Big sea-hardened hands grasped Wesley by the arms while Cromwell pried the sleeping child from his lap.

A roar of protest rose in Wesley's chest but died on his lips. If he awakened Laura now, she might forever be plagued by the nightmare of being wrenched from her father's arms. The less she knew of the sinister plot, the better chance she had of surviving the ordeal.

Cromwell held her in the crook of one arm. He looked so ordinary standing there, an indulgent uncle with a favored niece. Except for the stone-cold glitter in his eyes.

"You know, Mr. Hawkins, it would be beneath me to harm a child. But have you ever considered the fate of foundlings in London?" Without waiting for a response, he went on, "Lost children become virtual slaves." He gazed tenderly at Laura, smiling at the way her golden eyelashes fanned out above her freckled cheeks. "This one is pretty and could escape the drudgery. It's said that dwarves and children are used to serve people in brothels because they're too short to see over the edge of the bed. Then when she grows too tall . . . we can always hope she'll stay as pretty as she is."

The implied threat hit Wesley like a cannonball. "No, goddamn you—" He strained against his captors. The muscles in his arms braided into taut, trembling cords. Hard fingers bit into his flesh.

"If you succeed in bringing the Fianna to heel by year's end, you'll win your own life, and that of your daughter."

"You'll have to put that in writing," Wesley snapped, his mind galloping ahead. Seeing the expression on Cromwell's face, he gave a bitter smile. "Aye, you've been offered the throne. You'd best guard your reputation like the crown jewels. I want your sworn and witnessed statement that if I do as you bid, neither I nor my kin will be harmed."

Reluctant admiration glinted in Cromwell's eyes. "The Lord Protector always keeps his promises. You'll have your statement. But if you fail . . ." His voice trailed off and he backed toward the door, pausing in a flood of sunlight through the hatchway so that Wesley could have a last glimpse of his beloved child.

"You accursed son of a—"

"Year's end," Cromwell repeated. "Don't fail, Mr. Hawkins."

She had failed again. Caitlin had searched the high meadows for the bullock she'd promised Logan Rafferty. But the shaggy beast had vanished like St. Ita's stag beetle.

Now Caitlin would have to endure more of Magheen's strident complaints. Stabbing a shepherd's staff into the loamy ground, she made her way back to the stronghold.

Springtime blew sweet upon the heaths. On the morrow would come the feast of the planting, and Seamus MacBride had decreed it a high holiday. But what sort of holiday would it be without food?

She found her father in the kitchen, a vast stone room connected to the great hall by a narrow passageway.

"More sage, Janet," he said, peering over the cook's shoulder into a bubbling iron pot. "Don't skimp, now. It's a feast to be sure we're having tomorrow."

"Daida." Caitlin rubbed her palms on her apron. "Daida, I must speak to you."

He looked up. Vague shadows darkened his eyes,

his mind off on another of his mysterious quests. Then he smiled, giving her a glimpse of the handsome lion he had been in his youth. A lion with the heart of a spring lamb.

"Caitlin." He spoke her name suddenly, as if he'd just remembered it. "Ah, 'tis a grand day, and praise the saints."

"Yes, Daida." Although Curran's warning hovered like a bird of prey over her thoughts, she forced herself to smile and nod toward the door. "If you please, Daida."

They stepped outside to the kitchen garden. The tops of Janet's turnips and potatoes reached desperately for the weak rays of the spring sun. The sight of the sparse planting depressed Caitlin, so she looked out across the craggy landscape, the rise of mountains skirted by stubbled fields and misty bogs coursing down toward the sea. The late afternoon sun gilded the landscape in a rich mantle.

Seamus's gaze absorbed the view. "Devil so lovely a day as ever you've seen, eh, Caitlin? Isn't it grand, the broadax of heaven cleaving the clouds, and the great skies pouring pure gold into your lap?"

Why was it, she wondered sadly, that the splendor of the land moved him to poetry, while the privation of his people affected him not at all? "Daida, about tomorrow—"

"Ah, it'll be fine, will it not, colleen? And isn't it we Irish that are brewed from God's own still?"

She rested her hand on his arm. The muscles lay flaccid, the flesh of a man who shunned hard work as a monk shuns women.

"Tom Gandy says you've invited everyone in the district."

"Tom Gandy's a half-pint busybody, and a sorcerer at that."

"But you did, didn't you?"

"Of course. Your mother—St. Brigid the holy woman keep her soul—always planned the grandest of feasts. Now that she's gone, 'twould be a sad and cruel thing for us to do less."

"Daida, since the English burned our fishing fleet, we can barely feed our own folk. How can we—"

"Ach, *musha*, you worry too much. We be under the sacred wing of providence. We'll feast on fresh meat, see if we don't."

Suspicion stung her. "What do you mean?"

He spread his arms in a grandiloquent gesture. "I've had Kermit slaughter that young bullock."

Caitlin pressed her fists to her belly to keep her temper in check. "Oh, Daida, no! We needed that bullock for Magheen's dowry. Logan won't have her back without it."

Seamus dropped his hands to his sides. "But won't it be grand, the sweet taste of it and all our neighbors and kin toasting the MacBride. Think of it, Cait—"

"That's just it, Daida," Caitlin cut in. She had been raised from the cradle to honor her sire, but she had learned on her own to speak her mind. "You never think!"

She stalked off toward the stables. It was wicked to speak so to her father but she couldn't help herself, any more than she could quell the impulse to run free along the storm swept shores.

In the dim fieldstone stable, the black stallion waited in anticipation, muscles gleaming, nostrils flaring. Sunlight bathed his hide in gold as if he had been singled out by the gods to ascend to the heavens on wings of mist.

Caitlin walked between the stalls past the large strong-limbed ponies. For generations untold, Connemara horses had borne heroes to victory. But the stallion was different.

His velvet lips blew a greeting to her.

He had no name. He was as wild and free as the kestrels that combed the clouds over the mountains.

Black he was, the color of midnight, the shade of eternity, as beautifully formed as nature could manage.

"There, *a stor*," Caitlin crooned, slipping a soft braided bridle over his ears. She used neither bit nor saddle. When she mounted him they became one mind, one soul, one will. Her bare legs against his bare hide formed a pagan bond of two spirits which, though as different as human and beast, melded into unity. The black needed no more than a touch of her heel to urge him out of the stable and across the rock-strewn fields.

The smells of the sea and of dulse weed enveloped her; the scent of greening fields should have reassured her, but didn't. The Roundheads could, at any moment, swoop down and destroy the tender plants and subject Clonmuir to a starving winter.

Caitlin rode west, into the shattering colors of the sunset, toward the surging iron-gray sea. She let her hair fly loose, free as the mane of the black, free as the mist in a windstorm.

Her troubles lay behind her, an enemy she had left in her dust. Her swift rides renewed her spirit, made her feel capable of confronting and besting any problem that arose. So Seamus had wasted the bullock. She had faced troubles before. Despite the danger, she knew where she could get another.

The black's gallop gave her the sensation of flying: a lifting glide that made the air sing past her ears. She abandoned thought and surrendered to the pulse of hooves, the rush of wind through her hair, the tang of salt on her lips.

They reached the coast where cliffs reared above

the battering sea. Riding the wind, the black sailed over a ravine, then tucked his forelegs in a daring descent that made Caitlin laugh out loud.

On the damp sandy beach, she gave him his head. He arched his neck and leapt with breath-stealing abandon. He crashed through the surf, a black bolt of living thunder, full of the rhythm and mystery of Connemara's wild, god-hewn coast.

The English claimed the coast from the shore to three miles deep. Caitlin scoffed at the notion. This land belonged to forces no human could claim.

The sun had sunk lower when the black slowed to a walk. Deep bronze rays winked like coins upon the water.

Caitlin dropped to the sand, the chill surf surging around her ankles. She patted the stallion's flank. "Off you go," she said. "Come back when I whistle."

His tail high, the horse trotted down the strand. Tears stung her eyes at the sheer beauty of him. He was as full of magic as the distant lands of Araby, as handsome and noble as the man who had given him to Caitlin, the man who claimed her heart.

Alonso Rubio.

Come back to me, Alonso, she thought. I need you now.

"Sure there is a way, you know," said a sprightly voice, "to summon your true love."

Caitlin spun around, her gaze darting in search of the speaker. A chuckle, as light as the land breezes, drew her to a spill of rocks that circled a tangled, forgotten garden. Once this had been a place of retreat for the lord and lady of Clonmuir, a place of welcome for travelers from the sea. But time and neglect had toppled the rotunda where her parents had once sat and gazed out at the endless horizon.

"Tom Gandy," she said. "Blast you, Tom, where

are you?" Tidal pools were reclaiming the garden, and she stepped around these, lifting the hem of her kirtle. Crab-infested seaweed draped the stone blocks, and gorse bushes grew in the cracks.

A brown cap with a curling feather bobbed behind a large boulder. A grinning, leather-skinned face appeared, followed by a thick, squat body.

Glaring, she said, "You're a sneak and a busybody, Tom Gandy. Cromwell would have you burned as a witch if you were worth the faggots."

"No doubt he'd be after doing that if he could lay hands on me." Tom climbed over the rocks and dropped beside a clump of briars near Caitlin. Even with the lofty feather, his head barely cleared her waist. Like the rest of him, his fingers were stumpy and clumsy looking, but he reached out and retied her straggling apron strings with the grace of a lady's maid.

"Ah, but it's a sight you are, Caitlin MacBride. Ugly as a Puritan. When was the last time you took a comb to that hair?"

"That's my business." She tossed her head. "Yours is as steward of Clonmuir, and you'd best see to your duties."

"What duties?"

"Finding another bullock for Logan MacBride, to start with."

"We know where to find plenty of healthy cattle, don't we?" She ignored the suggestion. "Perhaps I'll banish you to Spain. I've heard king Philip employs dwarves as playthings for his children."

"Then we'd both be playthings for Spaniards," he observed, shaking his head. "Twenty-two years old and still not married."

"You know why," she said. "Though I still don't know how you found out about Alonso's pledge."

"Pledge! You little *oinseach*—" He tilted his head back to gaze up into her face. "A hot young man's promise has as much substance as the dew in summer. But we're not here to discuss that. You wish for your true love—"

"How do you know what I wish?"

"—and I'm here to tell you a way to summon him."

Caitlin regarded the little fellow warily. Some swore Tom Gandy was endowed with fairy powers. But not Caitlin. She had seen him bleed when he scratched his finger on a thorn; she had nursed him when he lay weak with a cough. He was, despite his extraordinary appearance, as human as she. If he possessed any gift, it was only the ordinary sort of magic that allowed him to come and go soundlessly and unexpectedly; his powers were those of a wise and wonderful mind that allowed him to see into peoples' hearts as a soothsayer sees into a crystal.

"And how might that be?" she asked teasingly. "It's the eve of a holiday. Have you a pagan sacrifice in mind?"

"Horror and curses on you, girleen, 'tis much simpler than that. And all you'll have to sacrifice is . . . Well, you'll find that out for yourself." Tom swept off his hat and bobbed a bow. "Sure I've been furrowing my poor brain with great plows of thought, and I've found the answer. You simply pluck a rose at the moment the sun dies, and wish for him."

"Pluck a rose, indeed!" She swept her arm around the tangled garden. "And where would I be finding a rose in this mess?"

A mysterious smile curved his lips. "You'll find what you need in your heart, Caitlin MacBride."

She rolled her eyes heavenward and spoke to the painted sky. "Such nonsense as that . . . " She looked down again, and her words trailed off. She stood alone in the bramble-choked garden. Without a sound, without a trace, Tom had vanished. A few moments later she saw the stallion vault back up to the cliffs, enticed back to the stables for a measure of fodder from Tom.

"Odd little imp." Caitlin plopped down on a rock and stared out at the gathering mists of evening. "Pluck a bloody rose indeed."

She drew her knees to her chest and sighed. Once, this garden had been a necklace of color and grace. The fallen rocks had been terraces dripping with roses. Her mother, the lovely Siobhan MacBride, had tended her flowers as if they were children, nourishing them on rich, lime-white soil and keeping back the weeds like a warrior staving off an invasion.

But the garden and everything else had changed when the English had claimed the coast in a choke hold on Ireland. The garden seemed to be eaten up by the pestilence of disorder and conquest. Weeds marched over the delicate plants, trampling them just as Cromwell's legions trampled the Irish.

I will rebuild my home, she vowed. Alonso will come. He promised . . .

Tall grasses, ugly and dry from winter, rattled in the wind. The sea crashed against rocks and slapped at the shore.

The wind shifted and its voice changed, a sigh that seemed almost human. A shiver scuttled like a spider up Caitlin's back.

Deep inside her lived a dark, Celtic soul that heard ancient voices and believed fiercely in portents. As a haze surrounded the lowering sun, the secret Celt came awake, surging forth through the mists of time. On this night, the gates stood open to the fey world. Unseen folk whispered promises on the wind.

A curlew cried out, calling Caitlin back from her reverie. She blinked, then smiled wistfully. The world was too real to her; she knew too many troubles to escape, as her father did, to realms where bellies were full, grain yields bountiful, and cattle counts unimportant.

Still, the charged air hovered around her, heavy as the clouds before a storm, and she remembered Tom Gandy's words: *Pluck a rose the moment the sun dies, and wish for him.*

Foolish words. Fanciful beliefs. There wasn't a rose within miles of this barren, windswept place.

You'll find what you need in your heart, Caitlin MacBride.

The sun sat low, a golden seam between earth and sky. A single ray, powerful and narrow, aimed like a spear of light at Caitlin's chest. She felt it burning, the heat of it pulsing. She stood and stepped back so that the sunbeam dropped to her feet.

And there, smiling up at her, straining through the thick briars and reeds, grew a perfect rose.

Caitlin dropped to her knees. She would have sworn on St. Brigid's well that no rose could grow in this unkempt bower, nor bloom so early in spring. Yet here it was, white as baby's skin. Secreted within the petals were all the hues of the dying sun, from flame pink to the palest shade of a ripe peach. Painted by the hand of magic, too perfect for a mortal to touch.

The breeze carried the scent of the rose, a smell so sublime that a sharp agony pierced her. All the years of waiting, of struggle, seemed to wrap around her heart and squeeze, killing her hopes with exquisite slowness.

The sun had sunk to a burning sliver on the undulating chest of the dark sea. Day was dying. A few seconds more, and—

Pluck a rose the moment the sun dies, and wish for him.

Without forethought, Caitlin grasped the stem of the flawless rose and squeezed her eyes shut.

A thorn pierced her finger but she didn't flinch. She gave a tug and the plea flew from her lips. "Send me my true love!"

She spoke in the tongue of the ancients, the tongue of the secret enchantress buried in her heart.

Caitlin clasped the rose to her chest and repeated the plea. She touched the petals to her lips, anointed it with her tears, and spoke three times, and her voice joined the voice of the wind. The incantation flew on wings of magic to the corners of the earth, from her heart to the heart of her true love.

The sudden chill of twilight penetrated the spell in which, for the briefest of moments, she had been beguiled, helpless, wrapped in an enchantment against which she had no defenses.

She opened her eyes.

The sun had died in flames of glory, yielding to the thick hazy softness of twilight. The last purpling rays reached for the first stars of night. The mist had rolled in, carried on the breath of the wind, shrouding the rocks and sand and creeping toward the forgotten garden. Long-billed curlews wheeled black against the sky. Caitlin stood rooted, certain beyond all good sense that the spell had worked. She searched the desolate garden, the cloud-wrapped cliffs, the hazy shore.

But she stood alone. Utterly, desolately, achingly alone.

The wind dried the tears on her cheeks. The hopeful sorceress inside her retreated like a beaten horse.

Blowing out a sigh and an oath, Caitlin glanced down at the rose. It was an ordinary plant, she saw now, as common as gorse, pale and lusterless in the twilight.

There was no more magic in Ireland. The conquering Roundheads had stolen that as well.

She opened her hand and drew the thorn from her finger. A bead of blood rose up and spilled over. Furious, she flung the flower away. The wind tumbled it toward the sea.

Abandoning whimsy, she turned for home.

A movement on the shore stopped her. A shadow flickered near a large rock, then resolved into a large human form.

A man.

3

Caitlin stood rooted, unable to move, to think, to breathe. Thick fog swirled around the man, tiny particles of moisture catching the brilliance of the new stars and bathing him in the hero-light of legend. Huge and unconquerable, aglow with an unearthly radiance, he strolled toward her.

Wild and primal urges pulsed through Caitlin, reawakening the slumbering believer deep inside her.

The stranger seemed more myth than human, the Warrior of the Spring from Tom Gandy's ancient tales, a champion with the aspect of a pagan god.

Still he came on, walking slowly, and still she watched, suspended in a spellbound state woven of whimsy and desire.

She thought him beautiful; even his shadowy reflection in the dark tidal pool that separated them was beautiful. He was strong-limbed and cleanly made, his body pale, his hair aflame with the colors of the sunset, his face shapely and his eyes the hue of moss in shadow. Caitlin felt no fear, only the awe and enchantment that flowed like a river of light through her.

Above tall black knee boots, he wore loose breeches cinched at his narrow waist by a broad, highly ornamented belt. A blousy white shirt draped his massive shoulders, the thin fabric wafting with the subtle undulations of the well-conditioned muscle beneath. His clothing and his astonishing mane of hair appeared slightly damp as if kissed by the dew.

With his deep, shadow-colored eyes fixed on her, he skirted the tidal pool and came to stand before her.

He gave her a smile that she felt all the way to her toes.

Caitlin gasped. "Heaven be praised, you were sent by the fey folk!"

"No." The smile broadened. His unearthly gaze shimmered over her, and she felt herself vibrate like a plucked harp string. "But I'd swear you were. God, but you catch a man's soul with your loveliness."

He spoke softly, his vowels and *R*s as light as the mist, his stunning compliment a breath of spring wind on her face. He was so strange, so different . . . And then realization struck her. He was foreign. English!

The spell shattered like exploding crystal. Caitlin reached for her stag-handled hip knife. Her hand groped at an empty sheath.

Crossing her fingers to ward off evil, she stepped back and looked around wildly. The weapon lay on the ground a few feet away. Had she, in her trancelike state, set it down? Or had he, by some evil witchery, disarmed her by will alone?

Catching her look, he bent and retrieved the knife, holding it out to her, handle first. "Yours?"

She grasped the knife. He was a *seonin*, an English invader. In one swift movement she could plunge the weapon to the haft in his chest. She should.

But the tender sorcery of his smile stopped her.

She slipped the knife into its sheath, leaving the leather thong untied. "And who the devil would you be, I'm wondering?" He touched a hand to his damp brow where dark red curls spilled down. "John Wesley Hawkins, at your service," he said. "And you're . . ."

"Caitlin MacBride, and I'm at no Englishman's service," she snapped. "What might you be doing here, Mr. Hawkins?"

He plucked a twig from his hair. "I was shipwrecked."

She lifted one eyebrow. "A likely story, indeed. We've had no reports of a shipwreck."

"Alas, you wouldn't have. I was the only survivor." He lowered himself heavily to a flat rock. "Bound away from Galway, we were, on a trading mission. No, not guns, don't glare at me like that. A squall whipped up. Next thing I knew, the decks were swamped and we'd capsized. Everything was lost. Everyone."

"Then how did you survive?"

"I'm a strong swimmer and managed to stay afloat. A big rowan branch happened by and I clung to it. It carried me here, and—" He slid her a sideways glance. "You don't believe a word of this, do you?"

"No."

"I'd rather hoped you would."

"You weren't really on a trading vessel, were you?"

"It was a very small ship."

"How small?"

He hesitated. "A coracle."

In spite of herself, Caitlin felt a glimmer of humor. "Then I'm after thinking you were the only one aboard."

"Aye." Unexpectedly, he reached for her hand. His was damp and cool from wind and water. "Sit beside me, Caitlin MacBride. I've had a close brush with death and it's unnerved me."

She didn't think a howling banshee could unnerve him. Pulling her hand away, she settled herself on the rock a careful distance from him. The sky had melted into a rich indigo tapestry shot through with points of silver. The waves glowed as they curled toward the shore, crashing on sand and rock.

She thought suddenly of the letter Curran had stolen from Galway. Could this man have something to do with Cromwell's new plan? Best to find out. "Well, then, John Wesley Hawkins, I'm waiting for the truth. Why are you here?"

He took off first one boot, and then the other, pouring out the water and then putting them back on. "I'm a deserter."

She blinked. "From the Roundhead army?"

"Aye."

"Why did you leave?"

"I don't hold to killing innocent folk just to make an English colony of Ireland. Besides, the pay—when it came—was poor."

"Where were you bound for, then?"

"I'd planned to sneak into Galway harbor and find my way onto a trading vessel. Unless you've a better idea."

"I can't be doing your deciding for you, Mr. Hawkins."

"Wesley," he said. "My friends call me Wesley."

"I'm no friend of yours."

"You are, Caitlin MacBride." The evening light danced in the color of his eyes. She saw great depths there, layers of mystery and passion and pain, and an allure that drew her like a bit of metal to a lodestone.

"Didn't you feel it?" he persisted. "The pull, the magic?"

She laughed nervously. "You're moonstruck. You're more full of pixified fancies than Tom Gandy."

"Who's Tom Gandy?"

"I expect you'll meet him shortly if I can't find a way to get rid of you."

"That's encouraging." He took her hand again. A tiny bead of blood stood out on her finger. She tried to snatch her hand away. He held it fast.

"You're bleeding," he said.

"A thorn prick, no more," she stated.

"I didn't know fairy creatures could bleed. I always fancied them spun of mist and moonlight, not flesh and blood."

"Let go."

"No, my love—"

"I'm not a fairy creature, and I am surely not your love."

"It's just an expression."

"It's a lie. But 'tis no high wonder to me. I'd be expecting falsehoods from a *Sasenach*."

"Poor Caitlin. Does it hurt?" Very slowly, with his eyes fixed on hers, he put her finger to his lips and gently slipped it inside his mouth.

Too shocked to stop him, she felt the slick inner warmth of his mouth, the moist velvet brush of his tongue over the pad of her finger. Then with an excess of gentleness he drew it out and placed her hand in her lap.

"I think the bleeding's stopped," he said.

But something else had started inside her, something dark and fearsome and strangely wonderful. She retorted, "And I think you're an English *spalpeen* through and through. You haven't answered my question. What do you intend doing with yourself?"

"That depends on you, Caitlin MacBride. Will you take me in and succor me, then send me on my way with a fine Irish blessing?"

She needed another mouth to feed like she needed another sister like Magheen. "And why should I be extending the hand of friendship to an Englishman? You *Sasenach* take what you please without asking."

"Caitlin. I'm asking."

Ah, there was magic in the man, in the warm, beguiling honey of his voice, in the comeliness of his face, in the layers of world-weary appeal in his eyes. But there was magic in wolves as well, dangerous magic.

She felt at once angry and confused. She had cast a net of enchantment and managed to land a shipwrecked Englishman. And how had he managed so quickly to lure her thoughts from Alonso? An enemy on the loose was a greater threat than an enemy under one's roof. She resigned herself. "Come along, then." She glanced about as she stood, glad that the black horse had followed Tom home. She did not want the stranger to see her treasure. A plundering Englishman would think nothing of stealing her horse.

And as for the sasenach, she would watch him like a wolfhound eyeing the barn cat.

"Where are we going?" asked Hawkins.

"To Clonmuir. This way."

Dark triumph surged in the heart of John Wesley Hawkins. The ugly business would be over before he knew it. He had made a rendezvous with Titus Hammersmith, the harried Roundhead commander who could not best the Fianna, and already he had gained the acquaintance of the maid of Clonmuir.

But God, he thought, his eyes riveted on her as he climbed over brambles and rocks to the top of the cliffs. The last thing he had expected was this. Cromwell had painted a daunting picture of a half-wild barbarian woman. Thurloe swore she was well past marrying age, but Wesley couldn't believe it.

This, he thought, still gazing at her, is something a man might believe in.

The moon had started its rise, and pale, watery light showered her. She had skin as smooth as cream. Her tawny hair and eyes gave her the fierce beauty of a tigress, while the soft edges of her full mouth and the delicacy of her features reminded him that she also possessed an excess of feminine assets. Caitlin MacBride was a formidable yet irresistible mixture of implacable will, wily intelligence, and endearing Irish whimsy.

And she could lead him to the Fianna.

For a week, Wesley had combed the woods and dales west of Galway where the Fianna had last struck. But heavy rains had washed away any sign of the warriors' retreat. Then he had scouted about Clonmuir, watching the comings and goings. He had observed no wild warriors, but fishermen and farmers. No mail-clad berserkers, but an old man chasing a shaggy black bullock. No host of heroes, only small bands of half-starved exiles.

Odd that he'd seen no priest.

We've culled every cleric from the area. The memory of Thurloe's words swept like a chill wind over Wesley.

This evening he had watched a girl streak across the heaths on a beautiful black horse. He had followed her to the remote beach and had seen her speaking with a stocky dwarfish fellow.

When the dwarf had vanished, Wesley had initiated the encounter. His story of shipwreck was as weak as watered claret, but the lie about being a deserter from the Roundhead army had gained him a small measure of sympathy.

Sympathy was a useful tool indeed.

They walked across a boggy field. The earth felt springy beneath his feet. The girl beside him was silent and absorbed in thought.

He noticed the forthright manner in which she walked, a purposeful stride mitigated by the slightest of limps. The flaw was subtle but his tracker's eyes took note. He burned to ask her what unhappy accident had hurt her. He held his tongue, reluctant to provoke her quick temper.

The night wind swept up the dark honey waves of her hair and fanned them out in a thick veil. Her bare foot caught a rock and she lurched forward. Wesley's first impulse was to put out a hand to steady her, but he drew back.

Pretending not to notice the stumble, he asked, "Your father is the lord of Clonmuir?"

She hesitated a moment, then said, "Yes. He's the MacBride, chief of our sept."

"So Clonmuir is your ancestral home?"

"Yes. Since Giolla the Fierce became the servant of St. Brigid. And until the cliffs beneath it crumble and the keep falls into the sea."

He started to smile at her vehemence, but realized his amusement would not sit well with her. "Cromwell claims the entire coast of Ireland, three miles deep, for the Commonwealth."

Her chin came up. Her eyes flashed in the moonlight. Her body went as taut as a drawn bowstring. "I spit on Cromwell's claim."

"You're very devoted to your home."

"And why shouldn't I be?" She spread her arms, embracing the broad sweep of the rugged landscape. "It's all we have."

Wesley caught his breath and wondered at the ache that rose in him upon hearing her speak, on watching the reverential and possessive way she walked across Clonmuir land. The mood of the sere wind-torn grasses racing up to meet the broken-backed mountains, the spirit of the misty wide sky crowning the craggy jut of land, flowed in her very bloodstream.

Something about her called to him, and the yearning he felt discomfited him thoroughly. He had made a vow, broken it, and gotten Laura. Her appearance in his life had compelled him to renew his oath of celibacy. Like a drowning man, he had clung to that oath, turning aside invitations that would have brought a smile to Charles Stuart himself.

So how could he be feeling this heart-catching tenderness for a wild, barefoot Irish girl? Damn Cromwell. And damn Caitlin MacBride, for Wesley could not help himself. He stopped walking, touched her arm.

"Caitlin," he said urgently. "Look at me."

She stopped and eyed him warily.

"Caitlin, what happened to us, down there on the strand?"

"I don't know what you mean."

"You do. Don't deny it."

"Moonstruck English fool," she murmured. Her words meant nothing, for the shadowy rhythms of her speech captured him, and the secrets that haunted her eyes beckoned mystically.

"Caitlin MacBride, you do ply strange arts upon a man."

"I do no such thing." She drew away and started walking again.

I cannot trust her, thought Wesley. Yet at the same time he admitted to himself that he had never met so compelling a woman. Heather and moonglow colored every word she spoke. Fierce conviction molded every move she made. She plundered his heart like a bandit after treasure.

A dangerous thing. For the plundering of hearts was supposed to be Wesley's specialty.

They passed a great, brooding rock that sat on the upward-sloping lip of a cliff. Tiny facets in the granite winked in the moonlight. Wesley paused, passed his hand over the surface of the stone. "There are symbols chiseled here," he said, and the rough whorls beneath his fingers made him shiver.

"So there are." Sarcasm edged her voice. "Pagan runes."

"Who put them here?"

"Probably the first MacBride to leave his cave and proclaim this the Rock of Muir, his throne. Come along, Mr. Hawkins. We're almost to the stronghold."

Clonmuir crouched like a great beast on a cliff overlooking the sea. Its west-facing walls resembled a set of teeth bared at the snarling breakers. To the east rose rocky hills that disappeared into the haze of the night. In the distance, moonlight glimmered around the high gable of a church topped with a heart-shaped finial.

They entered the stronghold through the main gate and walked across a broad yard of packed earth, empty save for a few weeds straggling along the walls and chickens roosting in nests of dried kelp. Wesley could make out the humped shape of a small forge barn and several thatched outbuildings, a cluster of beehives, and a cloistered walkway leading to a kitchen.

"Wait here." Caitlin left him standing by an ancient stone well while she crossed to a long, low fieldstone building with a stout door. She opened the door and a chorus of equine noises greeted her. The famed ponies of Clonmuir, Wesley realized.

A man's voice spoke in Gaelic and Caitlin replied in low tones. Wesley strained his ears but could not hear the words. A small girl with long braids crept around the side of the stable, gaped at him briefly, then darted back into the shadows. The years of conquest, Wesley realized, had taught all Irish to be cautious, even in their own homes. A flash of shame heated his face. He had come here under false pretenses to coax secrets from Caitlin MacBride—secrets that could force her to forfeit her home. The idea sat like a hot rock in his gut.

She rejoined him in the yard. "Come along," she said briskly. "We deny hospitality to no one—even an Englishman." They made their way to the donjon, a tall, rounded structure with walls pierced by arrow loops and tiny windows. She pushed the heavy main door open.

Sharp-scented peat smoke struck Wesley in the face, stinging his eyes. A translucent gray fog shrouded the scene in layers, from the woven rushes on the floor to the blackened ceiling beams. The great hall had no chimney, only a louvered opening in the roof to draw out the smoke.

Children cavorted with a lanky wolfhound in a straw-carpeted corner. A group of women sat knitting skeins of chunky wool on fat wooden needles. Most of them conversed blithely in Irish, but the youngest was silent, sulky, and dazzlingly beautiful.

At a round table a group of men drank from horn mugs and cracked nuts in their bare hands, throwing the shells to the rush mats. The eldest wore a knitted cap on his head and had a waist-length white beard. Beside him sat the dwarf Wesley had seen with Caitlin. The fellow spoke rapid, colloquial Gaelic and swung his legs as he talked, for his feet did not reach the floor.

Caitlin headed for the table. Wesley watched her face but she held it set, the pure, sharp lines of her features scrubbed clean of sentiment. "We've a visitor," she announced.

A dozen inquisitive faces turned toward Wesley. He wondered if these rough-hewn Irishmen belonged to the Fianna. On the heels of that thought came a sudden, sharp ache. Too many years had passed since he had enjoyed the company of good friends.

He tried to take in their expressions all at once, but got caught on the dwarf. His face was a picture of such pure delight that Wesley couldn't help smiling, even as he wondered why his appearance so pleased the man.

"He says his name is John Wesley Hawkins," Caitlin explained. "He's English."

Gasps and grumbles colored the smoky air. Large hands closed around knife handles. Women gathered small children to their skirts. Wesley carefully kept his smile in place.

"Is he an idiot?" a big man asked in Gaelic. He had hair the color of West Indies yams and a face that resembled a well-cured ham. He held his horn mug in two great, red-furred paws. "Look at that grin," the giant said, tossing a nutmeat into his maw. "I say he's an idiot."

Wesley made no indication that he understood the foreign, lilting tongue. He was not here to challenge a taunt, but to infiltrate the Fianna, to find out their secrets, and to capture their leader.

"You could be right, Rory," said Caitlin. "But he's our guest, and we'll give him a meal and a place to sleep. Lord knows, Daida has made certain there's plenty to eat."

"And why should we be opening hearth and home to a *seonin*?" Rory demanded. "It's the business of his kind to take the very food out of our mouths."

Caitlin's shoulders stiffened. "I didn't know having an Englishman under the roof frightened you, Rory."

He shook his shaggy head. "'Tis not that, Caitlin, but—"

"Then we'll treat him as a guest."

Enmity blazed in the huge man's eyes. "If he makes one false move, I'll put that gawm of an Englishman right through the wall with one great clout."

Wesley kept a courteous smile on his face when every instinct told him to lunge for the door.

"You're such a Goth, Rory," grumbled the dwarf.

"He doesn't look like an idiot to me," the white-bearded man said in English. "He looks properly Irish, save for that naked face of his."

"Don't insult us," said another man, dark-haired and nearly as large as Rory. "An English bastard would never fill the fine, wide boots of an Irishman."

A roar of agreement thundered from others. Horn mugs banged on the tabletop. "Well put, Conn," shouted Rory, then turned to the man on his other side. "What think you we should do with our guest, Brian?"

Brian had a quick smile, merry blue eyes, and a deadly looking shortsword at his hip. "I say we give him the same reception Jamie Lynch gave his son in Galway all those years ago."

Shouts of approval met the suggestion. James Lynch Fitzstephen, Wesley remembered with a chill, had hanged his own son from the window of his house.

Caitlin waited for the uproar to subside. Desperately Wesley searched her face for some hint of mercy. He saw unadorned beauty and strong character, but no sign of whether or not she would let the men do their will with him.

The room quieted, and she spoke in a voice that trembled with grief. "Has it come to murdering strangers, then?" Her soft words captured everyone's attention. "Have we learned to hate so much?"

"I suppose we might see what he's about," Rory grumbled into his mug.

Only when he let out his breath with a whoosh did Wesley realize he had been holding it. Squaring his shoulders, he approached the table and held out his hand to the eldest man. "I assure you, sir, I am English, but I don't necessarily regard that as a virtue." He clasped the man's hand briefly, and their eyes met. The Irishman was handsome, with unusually soft skin and strongly defined facial bones. His eyes were light, the color of damp sand. "You're the MacBride?" Wesley guessed.

"Aye, Seamus MacBride of Clonmuir, by the grace of God and several high st.s. You are welcome by me, although I cannot speak for the others."

"Devil admire me, but I like him," piped the dwarf, bobbing his head. "Fortune brought him here."

Caitlin's gaze snapped to him. "And what would you be knowing that you're not telling us, Tom Gandy?"

Tom Gandy's eyes rounded into circles of innocence and he dropped to the floor. In his beautiful green doublet, silk pantaloons, and tiny buckle shoes, he would not look out of place in a portrait of the Spanish royal family.

Disregarding Caitlin's question, Tom said, "Don't we all know that it'd bring the bad luck on us to treat a stranger ill?" Rory slapped his forehead. Caitlin rolled her eyes.

Wesley looked back at Gandy only to find that the man had vanished. "Where did he go?" Wesley asked.

"He can go to the devil for all I care," grumbled Rory. He scowled up at Caitlin. "You went off alone again. How many times must I tell you, it's dangerous."

"You are not my keeper, Rory Breslin," she replied.

"Not for want of trying," said Brian with a knowing wink.

Wesley observed the tension in her body, the pause no longer than a heartbeat during which she looked to her father. But Seamus MacBride didn't notice; he had lifted his gaze to the patch of star-silvered sky visible through a high window.

Suddenly, Wesley understood her problem. He didn't know which to credit—his experience with women or his experience as a cleric—but he had insights into female hearts, and he was rarely wrong.

Caitlin MacBride wanted her father to be a father, not an old man reminiscing over a mug of rough brew.

Furthermore, Seamus MacBride was completely unaware of his daughter's needs.

Interesting, Wesley thought. And perhaps useful.

He paid close attention as Caitlin introduced some of the others, rattling off names like a general calling roll. Liam the smith, as wide and thick as an evergreen oak; young Curran Healy whose eyes spoke the hunger of a boy longing to be treated as a man; a surly villager called Mudge; and a host of others united in their loyalty to Clonmuir and their suspicion of their English visitor. In addition, there were wayfaring families who huddled around the fire and ate with the avid concentration of those who had known the ache of hunger.

Wesley told them he was a deserter from Titus Hammersmith's Roundhead army.

The men of Clonmuir told him they were fishermen and farmers, shepherds and sawyers.

Wesley thought they were lying.

They thought he was lying.

"Our visitor's got a thirst on him," Conn O'Donnell announced with a wolfish grin.

To Wesley's surprise and pleasure, it was Caitlin herself who held out a mug. Their fingers brushed as he took it. The contact sent a shock of heat through him. He sought her eyes to see if she, too, had felt the quick fire.

Her momentary look of confusion told him she had. She drew her hand away, tossing her head as if to shake away the spell. "Drink your poteen, Mr. Hawkins."

He sniffed suspiciously at the contents of the mug. "Poteen, is it?"

Taking a mug of her own, she dropped to the bench beside him. An almost-smile flirted with her lips. "It's not usually fatal to drink the poteen."

Still Wesley hesitated. "What's it made of?"

"'Tisn't polite to be asking," she retorted, taking a slow sip from her cup. Her lips came away moist and shiny. "Just barley distilled over slow-burning peat. Savor it well, Mr. Hawkins, for you English have burned the barley fields since we brewed this last batch of courage."

Goaded by the reminder and by the gleam in her eyes, Wesley lifted his mug and drank deeply.

The liquid shot down his gullet and exploded in his gut. A fire roared over the path the poteen had taken. Tears sizzled in his eyes. An army of leprechauns bearing torches paraded through his veins. "Barley, you say?" he rasped.

"Aye." All innocence, Caitlin took a careful second sip. "Also pig meal, treacle, and a bit of soap to give it body."

Wesley quickly learned the art of judicious sipping. Avoiding questions, he took supper in the hall, then retired with a cup of tame ale to the hearth. The meal of stale bread and something gray and soupy he dared not inquire about cavorted with the poteen in his stomach. He thought longingly of the sumptuous suppers he had enjoyed with England's underground

Catholics and royalists. White-skinned ladies had delighted in teaching Laura her table manners. His former life had been fraught with danger, but he had known occasional comforts.

As the men spoke of an upcoming feast, Wesley expected Caitlin to withdraw to the women's corner. But she stayed at the central hearth, staring from time to time into the glowing heart of the turf fire as if she saw something there that no one else could see. Wesley wondered what visions lurked behind those fierce, sad eyes. Someday he would ask her.

"What are you looking at, *seonin*?" asked Rory. He and Wesley stood in a thatch-roofed outbuilding at Clonmuir. Rory held a broken cartwheel in one hand and a vise in the other.

"Your arm," said Wesley, eyeing the intimidating bulge of muscle beneath Rory's tan hide. Lord, they grew men big and tough in these Irish parts. He wore a broad silver armlet engraved with Celtic knots. From elbow to shoulder ran a long, shiny scar. "How did you hurt yourself?"

Rory tried to work a stave around the wheel. The iron hoop slipped. Patiently he set it back in place. "I cut it while sharpening a plowshare."

And my mother's the Holy Roman Empress, thought Wesley, propping his elbow on a stone jutting from the rough wall. It was a sword cut if he'd ever seen one, and he had seen plenty, some on his own body. He must remember to ask Titus Hammersmith if he recalled wounding one of the warriors of the Fianna.

Rory Breslin was certainly big enough to make a formidable fighting man. But Welsey doubted he could be their fabled leader. Though strong as a bullock, Rory was also as simple as one of the shaggy beasts that used to graze over the hills of Ireland. He didn't possess the guile to lead men into battle and out so successfully, time and time again.

"Why don't you drive a nail into the stave to hold it while you secure the other end?" Wesley suggested.

Rory's thick eyebrows lifted eloquently. "I'll not be needing your English advice."

"I wonder," Wesley said carefully, "why you and the men aren't out fishing. It appears Clonmuir could use the food."

"Because the *Sassenach* burned our fleet," Rory snapped. "Every vessel's gone save a curragh and the leaky hooker."

Hearing the pain in the big man's voice, Wesley flinched. "I don't hold with such practices."

Rory gave a dissatisfied grunt and went back to his work.

"Why aren't you at prayers with the rest of them?" Wesley inquired.

"You ask a lot of questions, English."

"Very well, I'll leave you to your chores." Wesley stepped toward the door.

"Wait a minute. I'm supposed to be—" Rory broke off. "Keeping an eye on me," Wesley said with a breezy grin. "Don't blame you a bit, my friend. Seems you've ample cause to distrust an Englishman." He gazed out the doorway. Beyond the walls lay the tiny village of thatched huts clustered shoulder-to-shoulder around the church, bleached white by the wind. Behind them the land rose up, hills scored by deep clefts and clad in budding heather.

No one had invited Wesley to prayers. They assumed that he, like most Englishmen, protested the Catholic faith.

They had no priest to sing mass. He wanted to ask

where the cleric had gone, but wasn't certain they knew. Admitting he was Catholic and had studied at Douai would have wrung some sympathy from the Irish, but Wesley held silent. Something sinister was happening to the priests of Ireland; all he needed was an overzealous bounty hunter after him.

The church bell clanged with the dissonance of aged iron. A few minutes later, Caitlin MacBride and her entourage streamed up the road toward the stronghold.

The sight of her struck Wesley with a fresh bolt of yearning. His hand gripped the door frame, and his eyes devoured her. She wore a clean kirtle and apron. Her loose blouse and skirt molded a form similar to those he had heard described in the confessions of notorious skirt chasers. Suddenly he felt every minute of his three years of self-imposed celibacy.

She walked beside an exceedingly pretty girl with sleek blond hair and pale skin. He remembered her from the night before; she had been sulking in the women's corner.

"Who is that with Caitlin?" he asked Rory.

"'Tis Magheen, Caitlin's younger sister."

"So there are two MacBride sisters."

"Magheen's not a MacBride any longer. She wed not long ago." Rory scowled in disapproval. "She came back home because Caitlin failed to make good on the dowry."

Wesley eyed the voluptuous younger sister, a blooming Irish rose who lacked the savage appeal of Caitlin. "What man would turn such a beauty out?"

"You'll see." Rory returned to his chore.

And Wesley did see, later, at the feast. People swarmed to Clonmuir from the countryside. They came on foot or crammed into carts, or by sea in *pucans* and curraghs—large, loud families who brayed greetings to one another and ate and drank as if the meal laid out on tables in the yard were their last—or their first in many days.

A high whistle pierced the noise. Heads turned toward the main gate. A large man on a handsome mare came clattering through, followed by two sturdy-looking retainers. He wore a long tunic woven of heather wool and studded with polished stones. His mane of black hair flowed around a face fashioned of strong, clean lines and draped with a long, braided beard.

The quintessential Irish lord, thought Wesley as the man dropped lithely to the ground, tossed his reins to a boy, and strode toward Caitlin and Magheen. He might have ridden off the tongue of a gifted bard.

Putting down his mug of ale, Wesley moved closer to the lord's table to await the approach. Above his white beard, braided with brass bells for the occasion, Seamus MacBride's face was florid, his eyes sparkling, and his mood blissful from drink.

Caitlin sat beside him, silent and watchful, her plate of spit roasted beef untouched.

"Logan Rafferty!" Seamus spread his arms. "'Tis well come you are to our feast!"

Rafferty aimed a thunderous glare at Magheen. She moved closer to Caitlin and peeked demurely at him from beneath her long golden lashes.

Logan tossed back his inky hair. "And while the lot of you makes merry, Hammersmith is on the move again."

"Hist!" said Caitlin, her amber eyes wide and fierce. In rapid Gaelic she added, "Have a care with that tongue of yours, *a chara*. We've an English visitor."

Wesley stood with one hip propped on the table edge and an easy smile on his face. Inside, he seethed like the Atlantic in a gale. Surely this arrogant lord

was the leader of the Fianna. Why else would Caitlin
have been so quick to silence him? And who else
would know the plans of Titus Hammersmith? For
that matter, why had Hammersmith decided to go on
the offensive so quickly? Damn the murdering
Roundhead! Only a week ago they had agreed he
would wait for a report from Wesley.

Rafferty subjected Wesley to a long perusal punctuated by flaring nostrils and glowering black eyes.
"English, you say?"

"John Wesley Hawkins." He lifted his mug. "My
friends call me Wesley."

"My inferiors call me Logan Rafferty, lord of Brocach." "I'll do my best to remember that." Wesley
pulled himself to his full height. The two men stood
as equals, eye to eye, each broad of shoulder and narrow of hip.

"What do you intend doing with yourself,
Hawkins?" Rafferty demanded.

I'm here to take your head off, thought Wesley.
Aloud, he said, "I'm for Galway tomorrow."

Rafferty hooked his thumbs into the band of his
trews. "Galway, is it?"

"Aye." Wesley had just made the decision. With a
stab of loss he realized he no longer needed to seduce
Caitlin MacBride in order to coax secrets from her.
"If I manage to give Hammersmith the slip, I'll take
ship to England."

"The sooner the better," muttered Rafferty. Turning his back on Wesley, he said to Magheen, "The fid-
dler's playing a reel, *agradh*."

She gave him a beautiful, false smile. "Why, thank
you for telling me so. I was just thinking, our English
guest might like to learn the steps."

Wesley found himself pulled into the center of the
dancers. Magheen danced like a shadow on a breeze,

light and graceful, conscious that the movements of her willowy body attracted every male eye in the yard. Although she smiled up at Wesley, her gaze kept straying to Logan Rafferty.

Wesley was curiously unresponsive to the lovely woman on his arm. Again and again his attention strayed to the golden-skinned girl who stood with her father and Logan Rafferty by the table.

"It's generous of you," said Wesley, "to give an Englishman this dance when your husband's obviously such a great lord."

"My husband's a great fool," she retorted. "I'm using you to show him so."

Wesley could not suppress a grin. "All men should find themselves so used." The pattern of the reel brought them near the table. Like a she-wolf guarding her cubs, Caitlin watched their every move. Feigning casual interest, he remarked, "Rafferty must be a busy man, times being what they are."

"Aye. He expects me to sit and warm the hearth-stones while he—oh!" Magheen lurched against Wes-ley. He whipped a glance over his shoulder in time to see Caitlin drawing back the foot she had stuck in her sister's path.

The deliberate interruption convinced Wesley that he had guessed correctly about Rafferty.

When they passed the table a second time, the lord of Brocach reached out and grasped Magheen's arm. "Get some manners on you, wife," he ordered.

Magheen tossed her head. "I'll not be your some-times wife, Logan Rafferty. 'Tis a full partner I'll be or none at all."

His spine stiffened. The people nearby hushed, the better to hear the quarrel.

"I came here to make a bargain," said Logan. To Wesley's surprise, he addressed not Magheen or Seamus, but Caitlin. "I've decided to reduce the dowry, out of the goodness of my heart."

Magheen's face blossomed into a smile that might have set the mountains to singing.

"The betrothal papers specified twelve healthy cows," said Rafferty. "You offered one bullock as a token of good faith. I'll take that, and call us even."

While the onlookers gasped, Magheen buried her face in her slim white hands. Seamus hid behind the wide rim of his mug. Caitlin closed her eyes, nostrils thinning as she tried for patience and lost the battle.

"You picked the wrong time to let reason come on that great fat head of yours, Logan," she burst out. In one swift movement she picked up her untouched wooden trencher of beef and thumped it down on the table in front of him. "There's your bullock, and welcome to it!" Leaping up from the table, she stormed across the yard and disappeared up a crumbling flight of stairs to the wall walk.

Christ have mercy, she seethed, her bare feet clapping against age-worn flagstones. "Will nothing go right with me these days?"

She had made a brilliant marriage for her sister only to have the two fighting like Roundheads and Irishmen. She had cast a spell for her lover and had conjured a renegade Englishman. And to cap all her woes, Hammersmith was on the march again.

She paused at a wide break in the wall. Her gaze traveled down the sheer drop of Traitor's Leap, where the sea hurled white-bearded breakers at the pointed rocks. Back in the Tudor queen's time, a member of the MacBride sept had tried to adopt English policies. His efforts had driven him to this spot; his guilt had hurled him over.

Her thoughts circled round and round like a flock of gulls after a fishing boat, and came to rest on John

Wesley Hawkins. She should feel relieved that he had decided to go. And yet a hidden voice in her heart whispered that he must stay, for there was unfinished business between them.

"I'd been wondering why you wouldn't touch your meal," said a smooth, golden voice.

She spun around. There stood Hawkins, smiling that heart-catching smile, transfixing her, backing her against the rough crenellated wall.

"I take it that roasting the bullock wasn't your idea," he added.

"My father's." She swung back to look over the wall. Waves exploded against the shore but farther out, the waters lay dark and calm. How many times had she stood here, gazing at the flat empty line of the horizon, seeking a glimpse of a tall ship coming toward her, bearing her heart's desire?

"It's a good harbor," Hawkins said.

He stood very close to her, so close that her shoulder grew warm. "Yes." She took a step away from him. The natural harbor had a narrow entrance leading to a deep, horseshoe-shaped cove.

"Cromwell is determined to have Clonmuir in Hammersmith's control, isn't he? So he can have a port of his own, a port capable of accommodating deep-draught vessels."

"Yes," she said again. "That's why we're so determined to hold it for our own."

"Cromwell's army exceeds the entire population of Ireland," said Hawkins. "He has enough men and guns to lay waste to every stone of Clonmuir. How will you stop him?"

"We'll—" She clamped her mouth shut. How careless this disarming man made her. "You'd be surprised, Hawkins, what a few deeply committed warriors can accomplish."

"No," he said with an odd, wistful shimmer in his shadow-colored eyes. "No, I wouldn't be surprised. And you're to call me Wesley."

"It's such an English-sounding name."

"That it is, Caitlin MacBride. A man can't change what he is."

How true, she thought. It was that very truth that had led her, again and again, to forgive her father's follies. If she and Hawkins had been other than they were, they might have been friends.

"Tell me about Logan Rafferty and your sister." He had moved closer again, a brush of heat against her arm.

She knew she should retreat, or better yet, push him away. Yet the commanding beauty of his face, the obvious ease with which he held himself, kept her in a thrall of curiosity. She knew she shouldn't confess the turmoils of Clonmuir to an English stranger, but where was the harm in it? She had no confidant save Tom Gandy, and her steward's habit of speaking in riddles was more vexing than satisfying. Despite Hawkins's intimidating good looks and blatantly English character, something about him put her at ease. Just looking into his eyes gave her a feeling of peace, like the rocking motion of a boat on a calm sea.

"Logan comes from an old and illustrious clan," she explained, "although he's taken on some English ways. That should please you."

"So far, nothing about the man has pleased me."

Caitlin held back a smile. "He should have chosen a wife of higher rank but . . . well, you've seen Magheen."

"She's very pretty."

A tiny ache flared in Caitlin's chest. Pretty was a word that could never apply to her. Tall and gawky, wild of hair, her face made up of harsh lines, she was not one to escape men's attention. But it was not the soft, poetic devotion of smitten swains. Instead she commanded soldiers who had no choice.

Images of Hawkins dancing with Magheen harried her thoughts. He had moved with animal fluidity, a perfect foil for Magheen's winsome grace. In looks, Hawkins was her masculine equal. She wondered why he wasn't paying court to her now instead of pursuing Caitlin.

"Magheen's not merely pretty," she said. "She's bright and amusing and wise in . . . important ways. She's had many suitors, but would settle for no less than Logan. But nothing is simple. Because of her lower station, he demanded a large dowry. I tried to hide the sum from Magheen, for she would have been outraged."

"I take it she found out."

"She did." Reluctant amusement tugged at the corners of Caitlin's mouth.

"So what did she do about it?"

"She refused to share his bed until he reduced his demands."

"Ah. Your little sister has some of your defiance in her."

Caitlin erected a wall of defense around her emotions. "We've been without a mother for six years. You've seen . . . our father. We don't have the luxury of behaving like conventional ladies." She sighed. "The matter might have been settled this very day. Logan would have had a live bullock, not one turning over a cookfire."

"Your father's doing?"

"Aye. So now I must find another means to appease Logan."

His eyebrows lifted in surprise. "You? You alone, Caitlin?"

"Aye."

"It's a heavy burden for a young girl." His large hand came up. Like the brush of a feather, it coasted along her jawline.

Caitlin was so surprised by his touch that for a moment she stood unmoving, hearing the crash of the sea and the dull thud of blood in her ears. Her skin tingled where his rough knuckles caressed her. Pulled by a force woven of longing, loneliness, and magic, she leaned toward him, staring at his strange English-made shirt and the thick belt he wore at his waist. St. George's cross was stamped into the leather.

The patron st. of England brought her to her senses. She drew back quickly. "You mustn't touch me."

Very slowly, he lowered his hand. "You need to be touched, Caitlin MacBride. You need it very badly."

She girded herself with denial. "Even if it were so, I would not need it from an Englishman."

"Think again, my love. We're easy with one another despite our differences. Remember our first meeting—the shock of it, the *knowing*? We could be good for each other."

"And when, pray, has an Englishman ever been good for Ireland?"

A lazy grin spread over his face. "Even I know that, Caitlin. St. Patrick himself was English born, was he not?"

"But he had the heart of Eireann."

"So might I, Caitlin MacBride. So might I."

Ah, that voice. It could coax honey from an empty hive. She wondered at his cryptic words, at the look of yearning in his unusual eyes. Beating back the attraction that rose in her, she laughed suddenly. "You *should* be Irish, with that head of red hair and that gullet full of blarney, Mr. Hawkins."

"Wesley."

She stopped laughing. "Go down and enjoy the holiday while you may, Mr. Hawkins. You've chosen to leave tomorrow." The words, spoken aloud, hurt her throat like the ache of tears.

He put his finger to his lips and then touched hers. "As you wish, Caitlin." He ambled off along the wall walk and joined the throng in the yard.

The phantom brush of his fingers lingered like a tender kiss on her mouth. Caitlin faced back toward the sea. Just a few minutes ago her thoughts had fixed on Alonso. But like a high wind chasing the surf, Hawkins had scattered those thoughts. Worse, he had awakened the slumbering woman inside her—the woman who yearned, the woman who ached.

Dusting her hands on her apron, she scuttled the emotions that threatened to overwhelm her. She had no time to be thinking of either man. If Logan was right about the movements of the Roundhead army, she had best be after sending Hawkins away.

The task proved harder than she had anticipated. Early the next morning they stood together at the head of the boreen, the skelped path that wound through the village and looped over the mist-draped hills to the southeast.

The rich colors of the rising sun mantled him, picking out pure gold highlights in his hair and softening the lines of his smile. She would always remember him this way, with his back to the sun and its rays fanning out around him.

"Seems we'll not be seeing each other again," she remarked, forcing lightness into her tone.

"So it seems."

"Have a care, then, Mr. Hawkins, for Hammersmith doesn't like to be kindled by des—" Appalled, she snapped her mouth shut. Mother Mary, why couldn't she govern her tongue in the presence of this man?

"You speak as if you know him."

"And what kind of fool would I be if I made no effort to know my enemy?" she retorted.

He stood very still, his eyes never leaving hers. "You are no fool, Caitlin MacBride. I could wish—" He stopped and drew a deep breath of the misty air. He seemed as reluctant as her to speak freely.

"Could wish what, Mr. Hawkins?"

"Just . . . have a care for yourself, Caitlin. Hammersmith is a powerful man. A dangerous man. If he gets close to Clonmuir, promise me you'll flee."

She laughed. "Flee? Not likely, Mr. Hawkins. Clonmuir is my home. I'd defend it until the last stone is torn from my dying hands."

His mouth thinned in disapproval. "I was afraid of that."

"Don't fear for me. 'Tisn't necessary." She glanced at the angle of the sun. "You'd best be on your way."

But he continued to stand still, gazing at her while larks and sparrows greeted the day. Against her will, she remembered that other parting, the tears that had flowed as freely from her eyes as the pledges that flowed from Alonso's lips. Somehow, this tense, dry-eyed farewell hurt more.

"God, I don't want to leave you," Hawkins burst out.

Stricken by his vehemence, Caitlin dove for the haven of formality. "The blessings of God be on you, Mr. Hawkins. And may your way be strewn with luck."

He lifted his arm, reaching for her but not touching her. Caitlin understood the unspoken question. He wanted her to take the next step, to come into his arms.

But with the self-control bred into her by generations of warriors, she stood her ground. For if she stepped into his arms now, she knew she would never leave.

4

Footsore and grubby from the long trek to Galway, Wesley reflected glumly on his visit to Clonmuir. He had found no barbarous Irish rebels, but men dedicated to preserving their lands and their very lives from English invaders. Caitlin MacBride was not the uncivilized harpy Cromwell had warned him about, but a fascinating woman with a heart big enough to embrace all of Clonmuir and Irish refugees as well.

A heart big enough to believe the lies of John Wesley Hawkins. She had believed him when he'd told her he meant to sneak back to Galway and stow away on a ship. She had given him a sack of provisions from her meager stores. She had consecrated his journey with the poetry of an Irish blessing.

An image of her rose in his mind. Like yesterday, he remembered Caitlin, her skin colored by wind and sun, her features stamped with remarkable character, her hair a waving cloud the color of wheat at harvest time. Most vividly of all he recalled her eyes, soft as honey one minute and hard as amber jewels the next.

And filled, in unguarded moments, with a look that almost made him believe in magic.

Pushing aside the thought, he gazed down the street to the wharves. The English Commissioners for Ireland had promised that Galway would become another Derry, open to Spain, to the Straits, to the West Indies and beyond.

But no new world port took root in Galway. Galway's marble palaces had been handed over to strangers, her native sons and daughters banished. The town had become a ruin, a host to a few hulks full of plundering soldiers and Roundhead field artillery.

Wesley wished he could descend into the blind emptiness that had claimed him when he had faced torture, but the comforting oblivion eluded him. Everything he had done since Cromwell had seized Laura went against his unusual but rigid code of honor. If he thought too hard about capturing Logan Rafferty and delivering his rebel head to Cromwell, he would not be able to live with himself.

Heartsore, Wesley picked through pitted streets and neglected buildings to the house in Little Gate Street where Capt. Titus Hammersmith kept his headquarters. The good stone town house had two chimneys, a neat kitchen garden on the side, and a guard posted on the stoop.

Where was the family Hammersmith had turned out in order to set himself up in comfort? Probably wandering in exile, possibly begging a meal and shelter at the gate of Clonmuir.

A sergeant-at-arms let him in and led him down a dim corridor. The house was overheated—Hammersmith complained loudly about the damp Irish cold—and smelled of burning peat and cooked cabbage. Wesley entered a well-lit library. Hammersmith stood at the desk, poring over maps spread out before him.

The Roundhead commander turned, his well-fed bulk filling the space between the desk and wall. It would be a mistake to assume him soft, though. In the middle of his thick body dwelt a heart as cold and immovable as Connemara marble. His one vanity was a profusion of glossy brown ringlets that gave him the look of a cavalier rather than a Roundhead.

"Ah, Hawkins," he said. "You're back." His gaze slid from Wesley's drooping hat to his damp boots. "Hard journey, was it?"

"I had to walk."

"What happened to that little coracle I gave you?"

He had given the sailing vessel to a down-at-the-heels fisherman in the Claddagh who had lost his own boat to English thieves. "Battered on the rocks," he said.

Wesley studied the maps. They were copies of the ones Cromwell had shown him, but these had been crisscrossed by battle plans. "So it's true. You are planning an advance."

"How did you know?"

"I heard at Clonmuir."

Hammersmith's jowls quivered. "You were at Clonmuir! But you've been gone less than a fortnight."

"I told you, I work quickly."

"You're living up to your reputation. I'm surprised that mad MacBride woman didn't roast your bald parts on a spit."

She did worse than that, thought Wesley. She stole my heart.

"How'd you get out alive?"

"I overwhelmed her with my personal charm," said Wesley.

Hammersmith's eyes narrowed. "Are your papers still in order?"

Wesley patted his stomacher. The wide belt was stiff from the inner pouch of waterproof waxed parchment. "I still have my safe conduct from you, and my passport and letters of marque from Cromwell." He frowned down at the maps. "You shouldn't have planned to march without consulting me. An advance at this time would be ill-advised."

Danger speared like a shaft of light in Hammersmith's eyes. "And why, pray, is that?"

"I told you. They know about it at Clonmuir."

"Impossible! It was in the strictest of confidence that I—" Hammersmith clamped his mouth shut. "They can't know."

"They do."

"What else did you find out at Clonmuir?"

"The identity of the leader of the Fianna."

Hammersmith's eyebrows lifted, disappearing into the lovelocks that spilled over his brow. He held himself still, waiting, a snake about to strike. "And . . .?"

"Logan Rafferty, lord of Brocach."

The eyebrows crashed back down. The cruel face paled. "Impossible!" he said again.

"I'm fairly certain," said Wesley. "He has great influence in the district, and seems a man made for fighting. He's also married to a daughter of the MacBride."

"Is that all you offer me?"

Wesley recalled his dance with Magheen, the conversation interrupted by Caitlin's well-placed foot. "His wife practically admitted he's involved."

"Then she was having you on."

"I can find out for certain quickly enough," said Wesley. "I know where Rafferty's stronghold is. With a small party of—"

"I can spare no men." Slamming the subject closed, Hammersmith gestured at the sideboard. "Will you have something to chase away the chill?"

Wesley hesitated, trying to see past the guarded look in the soldier's eyes. "Please."

As Hammersmith went to pour, Wesley lifted a corner of the map and scanned the sea chart. Inishbofin, an island off the coast of Connaught, was marked with a crudely drawn cross. Putting down the map, he turned his attention to what appeared to be a bill of lading half hidden under the leather desk blotter. Instead he saw that it was a list of women's names and ages, each followed by a number. A census roll? Wesley wondered. Common sense told him that it was; the finger of ice at the base of his spine warned him otherwise.

Quick as a thief, he snatched the paper and slipped it into his belt. It would bear pondering later.

At the sideboard, Hammersmith splashed usquebaugh out of a crystal bottle. The bottle had a silver collar bearing the *claddah*, two hands holding a heart, oddly surmounted on a badger.

Accepting the large glass, Wesley took a long drink. The amber liquid slid over his tongue and down his gullet, heating his stomach.

Seeing the expression on his face, Hammersmith gave a satisfied nod. "Mild as new milk, eh? The Irish make good whiskey and comely women."

Wesley was disinclined to pursue the topic. "Why do you insist on marching now? Wouldn't it be safer to take Rafferty first?"

Hammersmith slapped his hand over the papers by the map. "New orders. I tell you, you're wrong about Rafferty, and I can spare you no men. Cromwell's son, Henry, wants that port now."

For God's sake, Wesley thought, isn't the entire east of Ireland enough?

"We're to garrison an abandoned stronghold on the western shore of Lough Corrib," said Hammersmith. "After that's established, we'll march up from the south and take Clonmuir in a pincer movement."

Crushing Caitlin MacBride's home like a grape in a winepress, raping the women, and turning the battle-maddened survivors out to starve.

"Damn it!" Wesley slammed his empty glass on the desk. "Rafferty's your man! Take his stronghold instead."

Lifting an eyebrow up into his lovelocks, Hammersmith studied his guest. "What is it about Clonmuir, Mister Hawkins, that fires your passions?"

Wesley immediately saw his mistake. Never show you care, he reminded himself. He should have learned that lesson with Laura. He evaded the question with one of his own. "Have you been sent reinforcements?"

"No."

"Then what makes you think your march will succeed this time?"

Hammersmith's smile was the cold curve of a brandished blade. "Don't be modest, my friend. This time, I have you."

"Pissing Irish weather," muttered Edmund Ladyman, a soldier riding beside Wesley.

A clod of mud flung up by a horse's hoof struck Wesley on the knee. "I'm with you there," he said as the mud slid down into his cuffed boot.

The roadway had been churned up by hundreds of hooves and the iron-bound wheels of supply carts. A thick mist surrounded the plodding army, turning the woods into a dark, dripping prison of lichened trees. Since the reign of Elizabeth, Englishmen had set themselves to the task of deforesting Ireland. But even the most greedy of shipbuilders hadn't yet made a foray into the untamed western lands.

Galway lay miles behind them, but the difficult part of their march still loomed ahead, in the crags of Connemara where secrets wafted on the wind and wild warriors hid in the fells.

Wesley disliked Ladyman, a thick-lipped, foul-mouthed Republican from Kent. Wesley found that he disliked most of the English soldiers. But they had their uses. "Were you on the last march, Ladyman?" he asked.

Ladyman tugged at the towel he wore beneath his helm to keep the rain off his neck. "Oh, aye. And the four bleedin' marches before that as well."

"So you understand the way the Fianna works."

"Aye. Bastards always go after the supply carts, that's why we're riding behind them. They won't be expecting that. Pillaging natterjacks. Stealing the food from our very mouths, they are."

"Probably because they're starving."

"That's the whole idea, eh?" Ladyman peered through the damp green gloom. "We're safe here-abouts, 'deed we are. They never strike in daylight, sneaking bloody kerns." A drop of rain gathered on the tip of his nose. With a curse, he wiped it on his sleeve.

"So why do you carry on?"

Ladyman regarded him with astonishment. "The friggin' booty, what else?"

"Any booty to be had in these parts has surely been picked over by now."

"I'm speaking of Clonmuir," Ladyman replied. "There's a treasure in that castle worth a king's ransom."

"Who told you that?"

"It's all the talk, has been for years."

Wesley shook his head and stared downward. Between his aching thighs, the sodden body of his cavalry mare plodded with patient stupidity. A shame he could not reveal that he had been at Clonmuir.

Ladyman had been deceived, as had every other man who believed the tale. The advantage to Hammersmith was obvious. By enticing the men with the promise of rich spoils, he kept interest high and the desertion rate low.

Ladyman rode with the careless ease of a professional soldier. The fool. There was no treasure at Clonmuir.

Ah, but there was, he corrected himself. There was Caitlin MacBride. More precious than gold, she was a fiercely beautiful woman desperate to protect her own.

He didn't want to think about her. He had deceived her about his purpose. Now he was marching toward her home with an army. He couldn't afford to harbor tenderness toward her.

But thoughts of her dogged his path each day and plagued his sleep each night. In fact, he was dreaming of her one night as he slept in his damp bedroll near the banks of Lough Corrib. She stood on the strand amid a tumble of rocks. Proud and vulnerable, a look of stricken wonder on her face, the breeze blowing her tawny gold hair in billows about her shoulders. Her loose blouse seemed exotic in its simplicity; her feminine lines needed no molding by stays. He could sense her need, her desire, because within him burned an answering need of equal intensity.

She lifted her arms and stepped toward him, reaching, smiling, as if he were the answer to her most cherished wish. He brushed his lips against hers, just so, increasing the pressure until she surged against him and cried out—

"Guards!"

Wesley sat straight up and blinked into the darkness.

"Guards!"

Scattered campfires burned low, throwing the

huge shadows of hurrying men against a wall of woodland.

"Guards!" The furious shout came from Hammersmith's command tent. "Smith! Bell! Lamb! Front and center!"

By the time Wesley reached the tent, the commander had lined up the night watch outside and was pacing in front of them, a quirt slapping his thigh. "Not one of you heard anything?"

"Not a sound, Captain." "I swear it, nary a peep. Naught but the whir of bats' wings."

"Then how, pray," said Hammersmith sarcastically, "do you explain this?" Between his thumb and forefinger Hammersmith dangled a freshly picked shamrock.

"Why, these grow like weeds in Ireland, sir."

"Not on my chest while I sleep they don't!" Titus Hammersmith roared. "Some sneaking Irish left it as a sort of sign, or—or—"

"Warning?" asked Wesley. He moved toward the rear of the tent, which faced the rock-rimmed lake. He touched the canvas and saw where it had been slit with a knife. A grown man could never fit through the opening.

Puzzled, Wesley entered the tent through the front. Torchlight from outside threw eerie shadows on the canvas. Hammersmith's cot stood several feet from the opening. It was not simply a matter of reaching inside, then.

"Here's where the intruder entered." Wesley indicated the sliced-open canvas. "Was anything else disturbed?"

Hammersmith gave a cursory glance around. "No, I—" He tugged distractedly at a sausage curl. "Cut!" he roared, making Wesley jump. "By God, the Irish devil has cut a lock of my hair!" He stumbled back as if he'd been mortally wounded. "I've heard the old Celts use human hair in their spells."

"It could have been worse," Wesley murmured. "The intruder could have slit your throat." But he was beginning to understand the Irish character. They were warriors, not cold-blooded murderers.

"Jesus, Captain," said his lieutenant. "D'ye think one of 'em's havin' ye on?"

"Shut up," snapped Hammersmith. He whirled on Wesley. "Find the devils. Find them now."

Wesley led a score of mounted warriors northward. The darkness hung thick around them, and the urge to light one of the pitch torches they had brought along was voiced by more than one soldier.

Like the troops of cavalry, Wesley wore a buff coat of thick leather over back and breast armor, and the menacing iron headpiece which gave the Roundheads their name. In addition to the torches, they carried swords, pikes, and pistols.

The latent sense of decency that had driven him to the seminary at Douai tiptoed up behind him and tapped him on the shoulder. With an effort, he shrugged it off. Now was no time for scruples.

They came to a great spill of rocks that rolled down toward the lake. The horses balked and had to be led around the rockfall. Wesley paused to search for a sign. Squinting in the gloom, he studied the dead grass that grew in the crevices.

Before long he discovered a barely discernible depression in the mud, made by a small, broad foot. Christ, had the Irish enlisted children now?

An owl hooted a breath of song into the night. A badger rooted in the damp leaves.

"We're going the wrong way," muttered one of the men.

Wesley leaned down to inspect a gorse bush. One branch had recently been broken. "No, we're not," he said.

The hill rose to a ridge along the lake. The rocks formed a bowl around a small clearing, sharp peaks thrusting through the mist with a weird, stark beauty that captivated Wesley. For a moment he fancied himself gazing at a castle fashioned by giants. The lake lapped with a steady swish at the reedy shores.

And over all hung a thick, pervasive, unnatural quiet that Wesley didn't like in the least. As he reached up to pluck a swatch of flaxen fabric from a low-hanging branch, he understood why. He straightened and turned, apprehension clutching at his belly.

His gaze darted over the area. Most of the Roundheads had descended to the clearing. Moonlight threw their shadows against the wall of rock opposite the lakeside. Directly ahead grew a thick forest, nearly as dark and impenetrable as the granite.

The wind keened across the lake, carrying the smell of fresh water and something else, a faint animal scent. Guiding his horse down from the ridge, he joined his companions.

"Well?" asked Ladyman.

"The trail's too obvious," said Wesley.

"Not to me," said another soldier, scratching his brow beneath his round helm.

"They *want* us to follow them."

"But why the devil would the bastards want that?" Ladyman demanded.

Another Roundhead uncorked a bottle and took a drink of beer. "Hammersmith's nervous," he said. "He's starting to believe in all those heathen Irish superstitions."

"I mislike this darkness," a third man said, grabbing a bundle of torches and striking flint and steel.

"Douse that!" Wesley ordered furiously. "For God's sake, you'll give away our pos—"

But it was too late; the torch flared high, filling the air with the smell of pine pitch.

Ladyman reached for the beer bottle. "Let him comfort himself with it. I say the captain's imagining things."

"Did he imagine the shamrock?" Wesley challenged. "The shorn lock?"

Ladyman shrugged, his armor creaking. "I have a keen nose for the stink of Irish. I don't think there's an Irishman within miles of this place."

"Fianna! Fianna e Eireann!"

The full-throated bellow burst from the darkness.

A rumble of hoofbeats pounded, the sound of a stampede out of control, coming at them from all sides. The man who had lit the torch fell, an arrow protruding from his neck. The bundle of torches caught fire, sizzling on the damp ground.

"Jesus Christ," whispered Ladyman, wheeling his horse back toward the ridge. "Jesus Christ!"

Wesley gripped the hilt of his sword. The blade hissed from its scabbard.

As one, the party started back in the direction they'd come. A company of black-clad horsemen blocked the way.

"To the woods!" Ladyman yanked his horse back around. He disappeared into the darkness. The other Englishmen drew swords and pistols.

"We're surrounded!" Ladyman's desperate cry drifted across the field as he reappeared.

The men on the ridge stood sentinel, fists raised, horses blowing mist into the moonlit night.

"Fianna!"

The shouts and hoofbeats drew nearer. An almost forgotten feeling rose inside Wesley. In a flash he recognized the taut sense of anticipation, the feel of the sword in his hand, the cold sense of purpose that closed over his soul.

John Wesley Hawkins was ready to do battle. At the seminary at Douai, the priests had taught him to abhor violence. Yet all those values were scrubbed away by the dark, pounding thrill of impending action.

For the past five years his battles had been fought in secret against an enemy he could not meet face-to-face. His only weapons had been words and deeds done in shadow. Now he rode with that very enemy as comrade.

But now, oh, now, he was about to pit himself, sword to sword, against a flesh-and-blood foe. That he had no particular quarrel with the Irish mattered little. His daughter's life depended on defeating these wild warriors.

And defeat them he would. Unthinkingly he sketched the sign of the cross.

Ladyman gasped. "What the bloody hell—"

His words drowned in another flood of Gaelic shouting and galloping horses. Wesley's gaze snapped from shadow to shadow at the fringe of the clearing. Their numbers too small to match the English, they had culled away this search party, ringing them on three sides and the ice-cold lake at their backs.

The Irish came like nightmares borne on a foul wind, black-clad and licked by firelight, their old-fashioned helms bobbing with the rhythm of their horses. All wore breastplates emblazoned with a golden harp, and many had veils flowing from their helms.

The Englishmen scattered. Gaelic shouts boomed across the field. The Irish ponies were more fleet and agile than the cavalry mounts.

A large Irishman on a thick-limbed pony galloped to the fore. Rafferty? Wesley wondered, admiring the man's skill.

The warrior guided the horse with his knees alone. In one hand he held a short-handled ax, in the other, a large hammer. He swung the weapons with the ease of a reaper wielding a scythe. The hammer clapped against an English helm. The ax rived into an English breastplate. A hoarse bellow of agony rolled across the chill flat water.

Wesley rode toward the aggressor. If it were Rafferty, he must be stopped. Leaderless, the Fianna would scatter; lives would be spared.

The huge warrior on his dark horse spied Wesley. Sawing at the reins, he galloped across the uneven ground.

"Oh, my God," Wesley whispered. His sweat condensed inside the round helm, flooding him with the rusty iron taste of fear.

The ax swung toward his head. Wesley ducked. "Jesus!" he yelled, wrestling his helm back in place.

Wheeling the horse, the warrior charged again. Wesley swerved. The motion carried him out of the saddle and onto the hard ground. His horse ran away in panic.

The warrior drew rein and turned for another charge.

Wesley grasped one of the torches. Running backward, he ducked the ax and hammer and retreated toward the lake.

Panting hollowly inside his helm, the warrior followed. Wesley waded in to his waist, his tender parts shrinking from the icy water. The bloody ax blade arced toward Wesley's head.

At the last possible moment, in that cold slice of time that determines whether a man lives or dies,

Wesley thrust the flaming torch at the horse's face.

The beast skidded, splashing to a halt. The heavy rider pitched over the horse's head and into the water. Wesley heard the dull snap of a breaking bone. The Irishman's helm fell into the lake. In a blur, Wesley saw a mop of earth-colored hair. So his opponent hadn't been Rafferty after all.

The horse sidled away, its reins trailing. Wesley vaulted into the saddle. Leaving the Irishman floundering in his heavy armor, Wesley galloped the horse out of the lake and into the fray.

Some of the Roundheads had retreated into the water. Others made desperate attempts to flee into the woods. Two lay motionless on the ground. Those who remained had long since discharged their pistols and muskets, then flung them down, for they had no time to reload.

The Irish fought with lusty vigor, howling and singing in their ancient tongue.

Wesley rode toward them. An arrow buzzed past his head. Across the clearing sat a small man on a pony, nocking another arrow in a short bow. Wesley recalled the slit in Hammersmith's tent; he'd lay odds he had found the culprit.

Several yards away, another Irishman fell. With relief and astonishment, Wesley realized the Gaels were flagging. For all their fierce bravado, their numbers were small.

He reined the horse toward another pocket of fighting. A motion caught his eye. He turned to see a warrior on a sleek horse sail across the clearing. Centaurlike, he rode with both hands free; one wielding a sword and the other a mace.

Wesley sensed a strange power in the horseman. Perhaps it was a trick of the uncertain firelight, but an aura seemed to hover about the warrior, drawing the eye and evoking a feeling of awe mixed with dread. The very sight of the warrior brought fresh war cries springing from the enemies' throats.

Bending low over the horse's neck, Wesley charged.

Lithe as a dancer, the leader of the Fianna guided the beautiful horse in an expertly carved loop. Wesley's swinging sword hissed through empty air. The iron-spiked mace crashed against his shoulder.

Ignoring the numbness that spread down his arm, Wesley aimed the big Irish pony head-on at the willowy stallion. The beat of hooves kept pace with each quick-drawn breath. The smell of damp metal made his eyes water.

In a trick that had served him well in his cavalier days, he waited until the animals were nearly nose to nose, then hauled sharply on the reins.

The horse stopped while Wesley vaulted forward, wrapping his arms around the warrior, ripping his opponent out of the saddle and flinging them both to the wet ground.

The warrior had a small man's quickness, twisting lithely beneath him, bringing his foot up toward Wesley's groin.

Deflecting the strike with his own leg, Wesley grasped a flailing arm. Who *is* this? he wondered. Surely not the heavyset, broad-shouldered Logan Rafferty.

They tumbled and rolled, breath rasping and hands grappling for discarded weapons. Nearby, the pitch fire had risen to a roaring blaze. Heat lapped at Wesley's back and singed the ends of his hair. Irish shouts and running feet sounded behind him, coming closer.

He slammed his opponent against the ground. A rush of breath flowed from behind the helm. The silk veil snagged on Wesley's gauntlet. He heard a ripping noise and a metallic clatter as the helm came off and rolled away.

Wesley lifted his hand. One chop to the windpipe and—

"Good God Almighty!" The words burst from him on a flood of astonishment. Lying beneath him, awaiting the death blow, with tawny hair framing a savagely lovely face, was Caitlin MacBride.

5

She stared at him, frozen by awe and disbelief. Her eyes were mirrors of fury, reflecting the blaze of the fire. Her mouth worked soundlessly; then a furious cry burst from her: "Seize him!"

Strong arms jerked him backward. A blunt object clubbed his hand. Dull, cold pain shot up his arm. Fingers gripped his hair and yanked his head back, baring his throat.

"Move back, my lady," someone said, "else you'll soon be soiled by English blood." A blade flashed in the firelight.

The tendons in Wesley's throat stretched to the point of snapping and tickled in anticipation of the slice of the blade.

"No!" Caitlin scrambled to her feet and grabbed the drawn-back arm. "We'll spare this one. For now." Bending gracefully, she retrieved her helm and shook out the veil.

The pressure on Wesley's neck eased, enabling him to take in the scene. The English had been routed. A few floundered in the lake. Three sprawled on the ground. He recognized Ladyman, horseless, melting into the shadows. The rest, presumably, had fled. Some of the Irish moved across the firelit field, gathering discarded weapons, catching riderless horses, and stripping the corpses of their valuables.

"Spare him?" asked Wesley's captor. It was Rory Breslin; Wesley recognized the deep rumble of the Gael's voice.

"Why the devil should we be sparing an English spy?" the big warrior asked. "We never have before. And this *Sassenach* stole into our stronghold and tried to learn our secrets."

Caitlin tucked her helm under her arm. Her endless legs, lovingly hugged by tight leather trews beneath a short tunic, took her on a wide, unhurried circle around Wesley. She regarded him like a trader sizing up an inferior bit of horseflesh.

"He interests me," she stated. "I should like to know why he entered my household under false pretenses and lied to us."

"But the man almost killed you. It's the closest anyone's ever come to—"

"Nevertheless, perhaps he's of more use to us alive than dead. A spy as bold as this one might be worth something to Hammersmith."

Someone tossed the reins of the black to her. "Bind him and give me the rope," she ordered. Then, for the first time, she spoke directly to Wesley. "You've a long march ahead of you, my good friend." Her very words made a mockery of the moments they had shared at Clonmuir. "I do hope you'll cooperate."

As Rory bound his wrists so tightly his fingers went numb, Wesley resisted the impulse to wince. He made a parody of a courtly bow. "My lady, your wish is my command."

She curled her lip in distaste. Yet in her firelit eyes

he saw a brief wistfulness. "I knew there was no more magic in Ireland," she whispered, more to herself than to him.

An ache of regret flared in Wesley's chest. He had come to Ireland to romance secrets out of Caitlin MacBride and to destroy the chieftain of the Fianna. Instead, he had managed to get himself captured. And in unraveling the tangle he had made of things, he would have to hurt her.

If she didn't kill him first. She swung into the saddle. He had never seen anyone, male or female, move with her grace, her movements as fluid as a mountain stream spilling over rocks. Her center on the horse was faultless, her posture perfect, all the more astonishing because he knew he had bruised her badly.

"God forgive me for hurting a woman," he muttered.

She jerked the rope that bound him. "What did you say, Englishman?"

"I never would have attacked you if I'd known you were a woman."

"English chivalry," she snapped. "You'd not skewer a woman with a sword, but you'd steal our land and leave us to starve. More fool you, because I would not have hesitated to kill you."

"You nearly succeeded." A lingering sense of disbelief thrummed in his voice. "But thank you for sparing my life."

"Don't thank me yet, Mister Hawkins. Before long, you may be wishing you'd died a quick death among your friends." She nudged the sleek horse with her knees and started into the woods. The rope pulled taut. Wesley lurched forward, stumbled, then regained his footing. Half running, he forced himself to keep pace with the trotting horse. A jagged stitch seized his side, and his breathing came fast and harsh.

Caitlin's warriors surrounded them, some ahead,

others bringing up the rear. Wesley tallied no more than a dozen men. A dozen, yet Cromwell swore the Fianna had the strength to best legions of Roundheads.

To draw his mind from discomfort, Wesley concentrated on the extraordinary woman dragging him through the wild woods. He still reeled with the shock of his discovery. Beneath the tunic her armor, which must have been cast especially for her, molded her lithe form with delicate artistry. She rode with a dogged will that a cavalry captain would envy.

Tripping over rocks and ducking under branches, he tried to equate this new Caitlin with the vulnerable woman he had met on the strand. Even then he had guessed at the substance of her character, but never could he have anticipated this. He remembered wondering about the visions that lurked behind her fierce, sad eyes; he had meant to ask her.

He didn't have to ask her now.

Caitlin MacBride, the leader of the Fianna. She was Joan, the martyred Maid of Orleans, incarnate. A century before, that young woman, crude of manner but possessed of an abiding dream, had led men to victory and laid waste to English claims on the French throne. Men thrice her age and thrice her size obeyed her smallest order. Such a woman was rare and dangerous, he realized with a shiver. Men followed her, enemies feared her, and Wesley had to stop her.

"Well?" she said over her shoulder. "You're quiet as a sleeping saint, Mister Hawkins. Saying your prayers, are you?"

Her fury had subsided. Yet he felt no easier about his situation. "You've given me much to ponder, Caitlin MacBride."

"Ah. And just what would you be pondering?"

"Joan of Arc," he said, trying not to pant.

"Joan of Arc? And who would she be? Your lady love?"

"You don't know?" He leapt over a knotted tree root.

"That's what I said, Mr. Hawkins."

"I'll tell you about her some day. It's a long story."

"You might not live long enough." Her laughter cut him like a knife.

They jogged along in silence for a time. Wesley felt the distrustful stares of the others pricking at him. God, what tortures did these men have in store for him?

He had escaped being tortured to death at Tyburn, he told himself. He would escape this disaster, too.

For Laura. Her image, sweetly gilt by a halo of paternal love, drifted through his fading consciousness. God knew what Cromwell would do with the innocent child if Wesley failed. If he failed. If he failed . . . .

The thought kept brutal pace with his every painful footfall. Caitlin refused to slacken the punishing pace. The woods grew thicker with spiny underbrush and rocky ground. Wesley's foot slammed into something hard and jagged. White-hot pain shot up his leg and coursed like fire through his body. Brilliant light exploded behind his eyes. He was aware of his feet moving, his legs pumping, his pride overcoming the urge to flop to the ground. He felt his mind moving away from the pain, sliding deep into a familiar abyss of warm, white comfort.

He focused on the inner light. His breath slowed to match the rythmical cadence. Always it happened like this, brilliance pulsing all around him, a burning shield against pain and suffering.

"Mr. Hawkins? Mr. Hawkins!" The strong melody of Caitlin's voice penetrated the moment.

The blindness peeled away in layers, like living flesh being skinned from a hide. Clenching his jaw against the tearing pain, Wesley opened his eyes. The strange thoughts swirled away before he could grasp them.

The war party had stopped. Reeling with agony and exhaustion, he became aware of his surroundings. They had climbed the foothills west of the lake. Shallow caves, hidden by reedy dry grass and bushes, dotted the cliff sides. Wisps of smoke puffed from one of the larger caves. Caitlin dismounted. A girl scurried forward and took the reins.

"Thank you, Brigid." Caitlin unwound Wesley's rope. "See that my horse gets sweetened oats and a fine brisk rub."

Wesley fell gasping to his knees.

Brigid regarded him with awe and fear. "Is it a *Sassenach*, my lady?"

"Aye," said Caitlin, pointedly eyeing Wesley's blousy pantaloons. "A regular tight pants."

"I've never seen a Roundhead before. But where are his horns and his tail?"

Caitlin laughed. "You've been listening to Tom Gandy again."

Brigid clasped the reins to her chest. "Oh, my lady, he tells such wondrous tales. I do so want to ride with you."

"Perhaps one day you will, *a storin*. See to my horse. Off with you, now."

Glancing over her shoulder, the child led the horse away.

Caitlin plucked a cork out of a leather flask and thrust it at Wesley. "Drink slowly, now," she said, "else you'll puke it all back up."

Even through his agony Wesley's pride rose up. He did not want her to see him puke. He sucked slowly at the flask, letting the cold, sweet water trickle down his parched throat.

"How far have we come?" he asked in a faint, hoarse voice.

"Some ten miles, I'd say." Dawn had broken, and the rose-gold light of the rising sun gave her the look of an angel. But the gleam in her eyes reminded him of a fairy demon. "I'm pleasantly surprised by your stamina, Mr. Hawkins. I expected you to collapse after a mile." A strange softness came over her implacable features. "What a pity you aren't one of us."

"Aye." Fatigue crept up to claim him. "A great pity, indeed." With that, he pitched forward where he knelt.

Throughout the day, Caitlin kept a surreptitious eye on her captive. Not that there was any need. Rory had tethered Hawkins's bound hands to a tree, and besides, the man slept the sleep of the dead.

Still, she could not keep her gaze from wandering to the large Englishman lying in the shade of a sycamore tree. She had never taken a prisoner before. Least of all a deceitful *Sassenach* who had tried to worm his way into her heart.

"I doubt he bites," said Tom Gandy.

"And what makes you believe I was wondering about that? Don't you think we'd best have a meeting and plan our next move?"

Tom took out a chunk of beeswax and drew it carefully along his bowstring. "Aye."

Careful not to betray her weariness, Caitlin walked with Tom to the largest of the caves where the men lounged, some of them sleeping, others quaffing ale and dickering over the meager spoils of the skirmish.

"We're in luck," said Tom, sitting back on his heels.

"The Irish are always lucky," said Rory.

"A fine thought, that," muttered Caitlin, "if only it were true."

"I've spied out Hammersmith's army. He's well supplied with flour and lard. Some livestock, too. He thinks to fool us by putting his train in the vanguard rather than the rear."

"We'll take it," Caitlin said decisively. "Without supplies, our friend Titus Hammersmith will run back to Galway."

"And you'll have a fine fat bullock for Logan Rafferty," said Rory.

"That would be a blessing," said Caitlin. "Although it would take a bit of explaining to tell him where we got it."

"Shall we topple the powder and shot into the lake?" asked Rory.

"Yes," said Caitlin. "It's of no use to us, anyway, since we have so few guns."

"We'll have to get our hands on that food," said Conn. He rubbed his bandaged side, cursing the cut Hawkins had dealt him in the fight.

She closed her eyes and drew a deep breath. Refugees, turned out of their homes by the Roundheads, came in a steady stream to the western provinces, bringing sickness, despair, and starvation to the very gates of Clonmuir. "I have an idea," she said. "Hammersmith's expecting an attack by land. So we'll approach—and leave—by water."

The men broke into smiles as she explained her plan. Under cloak of night, archers would harry the vanguard while the rest crept up from the banks of the lake and toppled the supply carts into the water, seizing stores and stowing them in the swift, light curragh.

"You make a fine chieftain, Caitlin MacBride,"

declared Brian. "I only wish you had an army of thousands following you."

Her gaze moved around the circle of her friends. Broad of shoulder, straggly of beard, in threadbare tunics and battered armor, the men resembled a band of pirates. Yet their loyalty enclosed her in an embrace of camaraderie that made her glad she was alive.

A thickness rose in her throat. "Nay," she said, her voice trembling with emotion. "Many's the time I have considered begging Logan Rafferty for his men-at-arms, or enlisting the Irish soldiers banished to Connaught. But we don't need them, don't need their hunger for plunder and revenge, their quarreling factions and their prejudice against following a woman. The Fianna alone can hold its own against the English dogs."

She lifted a chipped horn cup and saluted them all. "I swear to God, I do not need a single man more. Except perhaps a priest, but they are all gone now." She drank the bitter ale and smiled through a veil of tears. "Sleep now, my friends, for we've hard work ahead come nightfall."

She stole a nap from the quiet afternoon hours. Visions of Hawkins haunted her sleep, and she awoke feeling groggy and strangely off center. At twilight, the men gathered on the slope below the caves. Caitlin checked on Hawkins. He slumped against a tree, still asleep. The uncommon appeal of his face raised a disquieting clamor in her heart.

She and her men prayed together, ancient blessings uttered in the tongue of their grandsires. Then they formed a circle, extending their right arms into the center so that their fingers touched. The moment hummed with magic, the energy of the group so overwhelming that it seemed all things were possible.

Caitlin studied their strong, rugged faces, drew a deep breath, and shouted, "Fianna!"

"Fianna!" they echoed, and began girding themselves for the raid. "Fianna!"

The shout brought Wesley awake. Every muscle in his body, from his scalp to his toes, came alive with a fiery ache.

"Accursed Fianna," he muttered. It hurt to move his lips.

"What's that?" Tom Gandy sat on the ground an arm's length away.

"Nothing," said Wesley. "Just a nightmare."

The band rode off, hooves and boots thudding on the sodden ground. Caitlin rode at the head, her slim body encased in armor, her veil fluttering like a banner over her hair, the golden harp on her black cotte flashing in the waning light.

"She cuts quite a figure," said Tom.

"Indeed she does."

"I'm to stay back as your guard." Tom opened a wicker basket. "Not that you need guarding, the way Rory bound your hands."

Wesley tried to flex his bloodless fingers. "I won't tax your skills," he said.

"Good." Tom dug in the basket. "For I'm no match for a great hulking fellow like you—at least, not physically." Pausing, he drew something from the folds of his belt.

Wesley gasped. It was a lock of Titus Hammersmith's hair. "I consider myself forewarned," he said.

Tom smiled, tucked away the prize, and handed Wesley a crumbling biscuit. The morsel was mealy and gray, probably from the potatoes that had been added to stretch the flour.

The biscuit dropped from his numb fingers. His stomach contracted with a pang of hunger. "I can't eat with my hands so tightly bound," he said.

Tom helped himself to a biscuit. "You know, the

Irish prisoners seized at Ballyshannon were made to eat off the ground with their hands tied behind their backs."

"No, I didn't know," said Wesley.

"Lucky for you, I'm a compassionate man." Tom's thick fingers pried at the knots.

Wesley tensed in readiness to attack. He didn't relish the idea of pitting his own strength against a dwarf but his situation was desperate.

"Ah, but you mustn't even think of that," said Tom Gandy, aiming a glance over Wesley's shoulder.

Wesley craned his neck. Several yards away sat a thick-set man idly swinging, as if it were a shepherd's whistle, the largest sledgehammer Wesley had ever seen. His other arm was in a sling.

The man tugged a curly black forelock in a mock salute.

"That's Liam the smith," said Tom. "I believe you broke his arm last night."

"How do you do?" Wesley called.

Liam scowled at his bad arm.

"Lucky for you, he's mute," said Tom, "or you'd hear a fine stream of curses from him."

Resigned, and not a little worried about Liam the smith's thoughts on guarding the man who had wounded him, Wesley sat still while Tom loosened the rope. Hot blood fed the tips of his fingers. The stinging pain reminded him of the day he had been drawn on a hurdle from the Tower to Tyburn.

How far he had come since that day. Yet he seemed no closer to his goal. Laura remained Cromwell's hostage. The blade of his cruelty hung over her tender neck, ready to fall the moment Wesley failed.

He ate several biscuits and drank some rough beer. Wiping his mouth on his sleeve, he said, "What makes her think a dozen men can defeat Hammersmith's legions?"

"A dozen less two," said Tom. "She's done it before. And it's not a matter of defeating them, but of outsmarting them."

"Was the Fianna her idea?"

"Saints, no." Tom laughed. "'Twas the idea of Finn MacCool, in the time before time."

"But was resurrecting it her idea?" Wesley asked.

"Aye. The notion came on her when the *Sassenach* burned our fishing boats. They'd already stolen most of our cattle, so there was no leather for making new curraghs. There was nothing for it, she decided, but to go to war."

"Not a common accomplishment for a young woman."

"My friend, there is nothing common about Caitlin MacBride."

"I know."

"Don't ever forget it."

"I doubt she'll let me. But why is she the leader?"

"You've seen her in action. Men follow her like lemmings over a cliff."

With a prickle of apprehension, Wesley realized that Tom Gandy was parting easily with his answers. Which could only mean they had no intention of letting him go. "Do you happen to know what she has in store for me?"

Tom rocked back on his heels and let out a hoot of laughter. "Faith, if I told you that, you'd never believe me! Neither would Caitlin." He jumped up and scurried away.

Wesley lay back, staring at the clouds rushing over the moon. He was wet and sore, a madwoman's prisoner, and yet for reasons he couldn't fathom, a sense of peace invaded his soul.

His gaze picked out little Tom Gandy, who was having a one-sided conversation in Gaelic with the blacksmith.

The man must be a witch, thought Wesley, beginning the slow glide into slumber. Something niggled at him, a voice speaking secrets in his head, a plan of sorts . . .

"You care nothing for my feelings!" Magheen tossed back her silky hair. "If you did, Caitlin, you'd find some way to make Logan see reason."

"Blessed angels, I have tried," said Caitlin. She was weary from the campaign. They had been back at Clonmuir only a day. Magheen had started haranguing her the moment she'd stepped through the gates. "I offered him a share of the new stores, but he refused."

"I've half a mind to tell him where the provisions came from," Magheen threatened.

"You wouldn't! Magheen, please—"

"Ah, Caitlin." Magheen laid a hand on her arm. "'Tis my temper speaking for my mind. I've seen you feed half the district on English victuals. I'll not interfere, I promise. Are you sure he wouldn't settle for a nice barrel of salt beef?"

Caitlin eyed her beauteous sister meaningfully. "Logan wishes a more lasting dowry, not one that could be consumed in a few meals."

"But what about me?" wailed Magheen, drawing the attention of everyone in the hall, including Hawkins, who lounged near the central hearth. He might have been a visiting lord, so relaxed and comfortable did he look—except for the sixty-pound cannonball soldered to a chain and shackled to his left foot.

Caitlin turned a gaze of longing to the untouched

meal on her trencher. "I'm trying my best, Magheen," she said evenly. "But I've yet to see *you* try."

"What the devil do you mean by that?" she demanded.

"Do you love Logan Rafferty?"

"St. Brendan's sprits'l, you know I do."

"Then if that's so," said Caitlin, "why do you refuse him your bed?"

"It's a matter of pride, Caitlin. You know that. The price Logan demanded for me was humiliatingly grand. If you'd told me before the wedding, I never would have married him. I shouldn't need a dowry at all. He ought to be grateful to have me alone."

"Your portion is paltry even if we abide by the old laws, which Logan has ceased to do." Her point made, Caitlin picked up her knife. Before she could spear the piece of meat her stomach had been screaming for, Curran's shrill whistle shrieked from the gate tower. With a sigh, she set down her knife and went to greet the newcomers.

They were heartbreakingly familiar: a fisherman from Slyne Head and his rag-clad family. The English had burned the man's fishing boat and driven the family from their home.

His wife had a hollow-eyed look Caitlin recognized. The unspoken horrors she had seen were somehow more vivid than if she had described them in detail.

"Took the lay priest, too," the fisherman lamented. "Bagged him like a partridge and carted him off to God knows where."

Smiling through tears of pity, Caitlin welcomed the family and offered them food and shelter. Weariness plodded with her as she returned to her seat at the round table. Her meal would be cold, but she was past caring.

Just as she seated herself, an argument erupted at the end of the hall. "It's mine, I tell you, I seized it fair and square!" Conn tugged at the long English musket Rory held.

Exasperated, Caitlin pushed away from the uneaten meal.

"Only after I slew the peeler it belonged to," Rory retorted. "Take your hands off my spoils."

"Stop it, both of you," said Caitlin. From the corner of her eye she saw Hawkins sit forward in frank interest. Discomfited by her prisoner's attention, she pried Rory's fingers from the musket and set the gun aside.

"I nearly got myself killed battling the devil," said Rory. "The musket's mine by rights."

"I clapped eyes on it first," Conn said heatedly.

"How could you, when it was aimed at my own head?"

Caitlin looked from Rory's fierce red-bearded face to Conn's equally fierce dark one. Over the months since she'd organized the Fianna she had learned one unassailable truth of leadership. Be decisive. Never let them see you at a loss. Or in a mistake. Hawkins had been her blunder.

Yet her mind was a blank. The problem with Magheen, the new refugees, the details of dividing up the spoils of the raid, her father's blithe indifference, and especially Hawkins's bemused scrutiny all seemed to swamp her like a storm-driven tide.

"Well?" asked Rory, glaring at Conn.

"Well?" asked Conn, glaring at Caitlin.

"I . . . really, you're two grown men. Sure it's unbecoming to bicker and—"

"The musket's useless," said a smooth quiet voice.

Caitlin swung toward Hawkins. "Not that it's any of your business, but just how would you be knowing that?"

He shrugged and reached for his mug of poteen. "The firing pan's missing, the bayonet's broken off in the plug, and the barrel's bent."

"'Tisn't bent," Rory grumbled.

"Look closer, my friend. The first time a man attempts to fire it, it'll blow up in his face."

Scowling, Rory took the musket from Caitlin and sighted down the barrel. "Damn." He rubbed his shoulder. "The English devil did wallop me right smart with it."

Caitlin found herself suppressing a grin. Rory Breslin was one of the few men whose shoulder could do damage to iron. With a chagrined expression, he passed the gun to Conn. "It's yours if you want it. I'll stick with my hand ax. No danger of that ever blowing up in my face."

"No, thanks." Conn set aside the musket.

"Give it to Liam the smith," said Hawkins. "Maybe he can use the parts for scrap."

Tom Gandy giggled drunkenly and swept his arm toward Hawkins. "Sure isn't he full of brains."

"Hasn't he the knob of the world on his head!" Rory added.

"The high learning be at him, praise be to St. Patrick and St. Dympha!" Conn thumped Hawkins none too gently on the back.

With undenied pleasure, Caitlin watched a flush sweep over the Englishman's face. He had out thought two warriors, and they would be long in forgetting it.

"Caitlin!" Darrin Mudge, a smallholder from the district, called across the hall. "This English wine is spoiled. Won't even make a decent vinegar, while the *cruiskeen* you gave Duffy is smooth as silk."

She folded her lips with displeasure. Mudge was the last remaining neighbor to possess sheep and cattle, which he prized with the possessiveness of the sidhe with a dead soul.

" 'T'ain't fair, I say! What good be raiding if we get no decent spirits?" Mudge persisted.

Heaving a sigh, Caitlin realized she'd not have a chance to eat her meal tonight. Each time she finished settling one dispute, another came chasing at its heels.

God in heaven, she thought. Will not one person let me savor my victory?

To her utter astonishment, Hawkins raised his mug in a blatant salute. He said nothing, only looked at her with knowing eyes, offering her a momentary haven from the myriad demands that claimed her. He of all those present asked for nothing. Not that he had any right, but still, for the instant that their gazes were locked, she felt an odd sense of peace.

One corner of his mouth lifted in a smile that caused her heart to thump loudly in her ears.

No. She couldn't soften just because he had a pretty face and a way of reading her emotions. He was her prisoner, her enemy. Soon she would have to decide what to do with him.

She returned to the table and sat down. Just then her father stood, dashing her last hopes of eating her supper. How magnificent he looked, with his beautiful white beard plaited, and the tumbled stones on his tunic gleaming in the rushlight. His face was smooth and ageless, for the years did not trouble Seamus MacBride. When Siobhan had been alive, she'd done his worrying for him. After that, Caitlin had.

He banged his mug on the table.

Now what? Caitlin wondered.

"MacBride!" someone shouted, and others joined the salute. "MacBride, Clonmuir, and Ireland!"

Just as if, Caitlin thought with a twinge of annoyance, Seamus himself had led them to victory.

Acknowledging the salute with a regal nod of his head, Seamus cleared his throat. "My friends, my family. Ach, *musha*, but you do me honor. Soon, the Lord and his angels be willing, I will attempt to return that honor."

Murmurs rippled through the hall. Feeling conspicuous, Caitlin moved to a nearby bench. Her father had that stubborn light in his clear eyes, the look that told her he had set himself on a path from which he would not swerve.

"Ill tidings have come from Slyne Head," said Seamus. "And it's not the first we've heard. A great scourge is sweeping over Eireann and taking our most precious treasure. Our men of God."

Heads bobbed in grim acknowledgment.

"Our priests are disappearing." Despair tore at Seamus's voice. "God alone knows what is happening to them. Some run before the sword of the English scourge, hiding out in bogs and secret dales. Others abandon their raiments for common disguises. But those are the fortunate ones. Too many are caught, informed upon by cursed bounty hunters. I know not if they are transported to England and tortured, set adrift to drown at sea, or exiled to Spain."

"The *Sassenach* tortures them," Rory stated.

"And eats their parts for breakfast," Brian added with a shudder.

"A notion is on me." Seamus clasped his hands to his chest. "They are not all dead. God would not be so cruel. I believe these priests who have been seized are collected at some spot and held like convicts."

Fists shook in outrage. Caitlin felt her attention drawn to Hawkins. He listened avidly, curiosity burning in his eyes.

"By the silver hair of my honor," Seamus declared, "I vow I shall find these misplaced men of God."

Caitlin slumped on the bench while all around her, people exclaimed in admiration. She alone understood the ramifications of Seamus's decision. Men obeyed her because she was the daughter of the MacBride. Without his presence, her authority would disintegrate. Her men would erode into warring factions, relax their vigilance, and become easy prey for the English.

She was as sympathetic as the next person to the plight of the Irish priests, but sacrificing all she had accomplished was too great a price to pay.

"And so," Seamus continued, "in order to proceed on my holy quest, I must abdicate as the MacBride."

Just as incredulous looks passed among the listeners, the main door burst open. His color high from a fast ride, Logan Rafferty strode into the hall. Magheen flashed him a venomous look, but he didn't notice. His gaze settled on Hawkins. "I thought you'd gone on your way, Englishman."

Hawkins grinned. He wasn't used to the powerful effects of poteen, and had drunk more than his fill. "How could I stay away?" he asked blithely, drawing his knee up to his chest.

At the sight of the chains, Logan's eyes widened, then narrowed. "What the devil's this?"

Caitlin held her breath. With a word, Hawkins could betray the Fianna to Logan. Then the prideful lord would forbid her activities. Please God, don't let him tell, she prayed silently. Hawkins spread his hands.

"Clonmuir hospitality. Hard to resist, eh? But enough about me. You've interrupted an abdication."

"A what?" Logan turned to Seamus.

"Aye, it's true. I'm off to find the priests of Ireland."

"But you have no successor," Conn called out. "No son, nor even a nephew to take your place."

"And a grandson seems highly unlikely." Logan pointedly eyed his wife across the room.

"So I must name a successor."

The crowd inhaled a collective breath; then the speculation began. Rory Breslin squared his shoulders. He was a giant of a man and a master of pitched battle. But Rory was made to carry out orders, not conceive battle plans.

Tom Gandy planted his feet and set his hands on his hips. Not a soul at Clonmuir would dispute his wily intelligence, his blade-sharp wit tempered by a humanity that endeared him to all. But he was, despite his gifts, afflicted by dwarfism and suspected of dabbling in the black arts. Caitlin didn't believe it for a moment, but some did. Every drought, every famine, every contagion would be blamed on him.

Her gaze, in concert with everyone elses's, finally and reluctantly settled on Logan Rafferty. Full of a swaggering confidence that dug at her pride, he stood with his arms akimbo and his head thrown back.

Lofty of rank and a MacBride by marriage, young and strapping, and charming when he wished to be, he would carry out the duties of the chieftain with alacrity.

But he didn't know about the Fianna. Fear trembled inside Caitlin, for she knew all would be lost. Logan was too cautious to lead raids on the English.

A protest leapt to her lips, but died unspoken. No woman had ever been in on the decision before. But she was Caitlin. She was different. "Daida, please—" Then she stopped herself. Please what? There was nothing she could do, no words she could speak, that would sway the men.

"If I choose you," said Seamus to Logan, "will you rule by the old law?"

Logan's spurs clinked as he approached the high table. "Has it not always been so at Clonmuir?"

Sighs of relief gusted from the listeners. But Caitlin studied him closely. A guarded look shadowed his eyes, and suddenly she knew with sick certainty that he was lying. Once chieftain, he would rule in English fashion, collecting tithes, parceling out tenantry, claiming ownership of lands that had belonged to no one but the immortals since time began. It was all she could do to keep from leaping up and blurting out her fears.

Alonso, she thought. I need you now. I need a man who believes in me. A man whose voice will speak my heart for me.

"What about Caitlin?"

The hall reverberated with the strong English voice of John Wesley Hawkins. With gaping mouths and astonished eyes, all turned to face him.

A strange heat rose to stain Caitlin's throat and cheeks bright red.

Logan spun around, his black eyes flashing. "Dare you speak, Englishman?"

Hawkins shrugged. "Someone had to, for she won't speak for herself."

"This is none of your concern," snapped Logan. Addressing Rory, he said, "Kill the fellow and be done with him. Faith, he's just another mouth to feed."

But Hawkins's words took root in the fertile minds of the men who had ridden with her to triumph. She could see the idea begin to blossom in her father's eyes and in Tom's knowing smile.

"Look, she runs this household and leads—is served by brave men." Hawkins stood, hefting the iron ball in one hand. "What are the qualities of a chieftain?"

"He must put the needs of the clan before his own," said Seamus.

Hawkins gestured pointedly at her uneaten meal. "While you were stuffing your gullets, she was settling disputes."

"He must be able of mind and body," said Rory Breslin.

The Englishman smiled. "Show me a weakness in that woman, and I'll eat my ball and chain."

"He rules by sacred trust," said Tom Gandy.

"Here I stand in bondage," said Hawkins, "and yet I trust her."

"Damned meddling Englishman," Logan spat. "You only want a woman as chief so you can wheedle your way out of those chains. Turn him over to me, I say."

Hawkins ignored him, facing Seamus instead. "You had to ask Rafferty if he would rule according to tradition. Would you even have to ask this of Caitlin?"

"No, of course not, she—"

"Need I say more?" Hawkins took a sip from his mug.

"It could work, by God," said Seamus. "Aye, she's her mother's daughter and has been the strength of this sept these six years. I'm not too proud to admit it."

People began to murmur, heads to nod. Frozen on the bench, Caitlin felt a sick hope building in her, rising, reaching. She could be the MacBride. She deserved to be. She had given her heart and soul to Clonmuir. No one cared as much as she. No one knew these people as she did. She fought for them, wept when they grieved and rejoiced when good fortune came to them.

Ah, sweet Jesus, I want this, she thought. More than anything, I want to be the MacBride.

Hawkins sat with an indulgent smile on his face, the smile of a man capable of manipulating a crowd. The smile of a man with a secret motive. She'd worry about that later.

"Can you do it, Caitlin?" Seamus seemed to be calling to her across a great distance. "Can you take up the white wand of the MacBride?"

She rose to her feet. Now was no time for feminine modesty. Her gaze locked with Logan's, and they waged a silent battle.

I've bowed to your wishes all my life, she told him. A hundred times, I've let you best me when I could have won. This time I'll not sacrifice my people for your pride. It's time I showed you my true abilities, time I had what is mine by right.

"Daida," she said, "every person in this room knows I can. But it's more than that. I know that I must."

"This is madness," Logan burst out. "No clan or sept can have a female chieftain."

"Oh, no?" Magheen asked. "Where is it written, Logan? You show us, and I'll see that my sister bows down at your feet."

He looked as if he'd eat her for supper. "You bow at my feet and I'll—" Reining in the thought, he said churlishly, "It doesn't have to be written. It's tradition and common sense."

"What of Scathach," Magheen challenged, "the warrior goddess who tutored Cuchulainn in his skills?"

"And then there was Aife," Tom Gandy added in his loud bardic voice, "another woman chieftain. I remember me, too, of Queen Macha Mong Ruad, who reigned—"

"You'd all be fools to follow the rump of a misguiding woman," Logan hollered. "Sure doesn't the herd led by a mare stray and perish."

"And sure don't the heifers grow big where there are no bulls," Magheen countered.

Hawkins eyed Logan up and down. "The job calls for more intelligence than physical strength."

"And you've got more cheek than common sense," Brian muttered as Logan shot a lethal look at the prisoner.

"The law calls for a vote," said Tom Gandy.

"A vote?" roared Logan. "Get some wits on you, little man. It's the *brehons* who do the electing, and there are no *brehons* here."

Tom smiled bitterly. "Because the English have outlawed our law-givers. But here there be men of good heart and sound judgment."

"Aye," said Seamus, "and hasn't that been the quality of the *brehons*? Let each man who would have Caitlin for his chieftain light a flame to signify his allegiance."

Uncertain glances passed among the men. Caitlin's heart pounded with dread.

Tom took a torch from a wall bracket, thrust the end into the central fire, and held it aloft. "MacBride!" he yelled.

Curran Healy shuffled forward and lifted a flame of his own. Conn O'Donnell followed suit. After him came Liam the smith and Brian. Rory Breslin hesitated, then strode forward and lit his flame. One by one, every other man present cast his vote.

The hall blazed with light and loyalty. Only Seamus and Logan remained. Caitlin held her breath. Involuntarily, her gaze sought Hawkins. He lifted his mug and mouthed the word "courage."

Seamus screwed his eyes shut, muttered a prayer, and lit a torch. Snorting in disgust, Logan turned his back on them.

With her nose in the air, her hips swaying, and a

look of defiance on her beautiful face, Magheen walked past her husband.

"Where are you going?" he demanded.

"To cast my vote."

"Women have no right to vote."

"Maybe that will change once Caitlin's the MacBride." Magheen picked up a torch.

"If you so much as go near that fire," Logan warned in a low, deadly voice, "I'll never take you back."

Magheen kept her eyes trained on him. Her face paled, but her arm was steady as she lit the torch and shouted, "MacBride!"

Seamus lifted his glass. "Good health to us all," he proclaimed. "And may we be seven thousand times better in health and happiness this time again!"

Pride rushed like a fresh wind over Caitlin. Her heart lifted and she spread her arms, wishing she could embrace every man, woman, and child in the room.

Even Hawkins. Especially Hawkins.

People pressed around her, bestowing good wishes and blessings. At length Logan came close. He bent and clasped her hand in customary fashion.

Caitlin had no time to feel relief, for in the next instant his words gave the lie to his actions. "I'll not be forgiving you, Caitlin MacBride," he whispered. Each word was a drop of poison, stinging her heart and flooding her with doubts.

But when Logan moved away, there was Hawkins. Her enemy, her prisoner, her champion. He, too, took her hand. His was calloused, abraded by rope burns and hard labor. Caitlin shivered slightly at his touch.

In his gaze she saw dreams and mysteries, secrets she longed in spite of herself to unlock. He had the strangest eyes. In the flickering torchlight, she fancied, just for a moment, that she saw two souls locked behind the cool gray-green prisons of his eyes. The Roundhead scoundrel and the man of mercy.

"You've still not had your supper," he said.

"I'm not hungry anymore."

"Come out in the yard with me, Caitlin, away from this crowd."

"You're a prisoner, no longer a guest." Still, she felt drawn to him, enticed by the unknown like a sailor chasing a phantom horizon.

"Very well." He started to lug his iron ball away.

"Wait," Caitlin heard herself saying. He turned back. Lord Jesus, but he was broad and well favored. "I . . . could be using a breath of air."

They stepped into the cool of the evening. A harrying wind stirred the stunted evergreen oaks, scraping crooked branches against the walls. From the stables came the mutter of horses settling in for the night. From the hall came the sound of Tom Gandy's voice weaving a tale that promised to hold his listeners spellbound for hours.

"Why did you put forth my name?" she asked.

"Because you wouldn't speak for yourself. And you wanted to, Caitlin MacBride, so badly. I could see the need flaming through you, burning in your eyes. What surprises me is that none of your own seemed to notice."

His words had magic in them. A powerful force told her to believe him and to thank God and all the saints that he had voiced her deepest desire. But he was a liar, she told herself.

"English never do a thing without the possibility of gain," she said. "You want something and hope to get it from me."

"Of course I do," he agreed readily.

"Your freedom?"

"That's correct." But his eyes told her there was more to his wants than simple freedom.

"I can't give you that. You've proven yourself treacherous and I cannot trust you."

His eyes flashed in the darkness. Anger? Hurt? His moods were as hard to read as the moon on a cloudy night. "Very well, Your Highness," he said. "Why do *you* think I wanted you elected?"

"You think things will be easier for you with me in charge. You think putting a woman on the seat of the MacBride will weaken us."

His lip curled in a sardonic smile. "Let's see. You dragged me for miles at the end of a rope, left me bound and helpless while you raided an army's supply train, and soldered me to a cannonball. I've known battle-hardened generals who treat their prisoners easier."

A twinge stung her insides and touched her in the small secret place where her womanly pride dwelt. She made no sign that his words hurt. When Alonso came, he would set the woman inside her free.

"What are you going to do with me, Caitlin?" Hawkins asked.

"I don't know yet. Are you worth a ransom from the butcher Cromwell?"

Fury iced his handsome features. "Don't send me to Cromwell. You'd be a fool if you did."

She sensed real desperation behind the cold façade. Apparently Cromwell showed no compassion for men who managed to get themselves captured. "There must be some use for you."

His expression warmed suddenly. Reaching out, he stroked her beneath the chin. "I could be very useful to you, Caitlin MacBride. I could give you what you need."

His words had layers of meaning that she refused to ponder. "What I need," she said, drawing away from his disconcerting touch, "is some answers from you, Mr. Hawkins." She paced the yard, aware every moment that his compelling stare dogged each step. Bracing herself against the well, she stopped. "Don't the English punish deserters with death?"

"I believe that's the usual punishment."

"Then you're no deserter, and never were one," she snapped. "You came to spy on us, didn't you?"

Gazing across the yard at her, Wesley drew a deep breath of the salt-sharp air and stood silent, pondering the events that had brought him to this moment.

Fate, was it? he wondered. No, a folly of his own making. To find the beginning, he let his mind travel back in time.

Priests were so rare in England that, though only a novice, he'd performed the duties of an ordained cleric. The nomadic life had been hard, the temptations many. And in High Wycombe he had strayed from his path and bedded a woman named Annabel Pym.

Months later he had returned to the town to be confronted by the lady Annabel, her belly great with his child, her face a mask of censure. Annabel died giving birth. Her parents, furious with grief, had thrust the baby into Wesley's arms and summoned the priest catchers.

Those early months on the run passed through Wesley's mind in a blur of frantic action. Engaging a slovenly, illiterate wet nurse, then dismissing her as soon as Laura could tolerate cow's milk. Passing Laura off as a foundling when people demanded to know what a cleric was doing with a child.

And finally, holding her close at night and breathing in the scent of her, which planted a seed of paternal tenderness so deep that nothing could touch it. The seed had flourished into strong, vigorous, protective love.

"Well, Mr. Hawkins." The rollicking rhythms of Caitlin MacBride's Irish speech crowded into Wesley's thoughts. "I'm waiting for an answer. Are you a spy, then?"

Wesley hesitated another moment. He had found the chief of the Fianna as he had been sent to do. But her identity—and the fact that he was her prisoner—changed everything. He would have to negotiate this conversation cautiously, a man testing new ice on a pond. He would have to lie through his teeth.

"Aye."

She stiffened as if he had jabbed her with a pointed weapon. "For the love of God, why?"

A sadness welled up in him, a sense of futility that tugged at his purpose. "Our nations are at war, Caitlin. War makes men commit acts that go against their principles."

"Ah." She shoved away from the well and planted herself in front of him. "So war—and not yourself—accounts for your treachery."

He wanted to trace the cool curve of her cheekbone. He wanted to taste her lips which, even in anger, were soft and full. He wanted to knead the tightness from her shoulders and recapture the magic of their first meeting. Instead, he aimed a sardonic grin at the iron ball shackled to his ankle.

"Thanks to you, Caitlin MacBride, my treachery amounts to nothing." But not for long, he thought, wishing it were otherwise. Before long, he would have to make his escape. And when he left Clonmuir, he would not be alone.

6

The wild rhythm of tambours and *bodhran* drums jostled Wesley awake. The tingle of bells and the twang of a harp stabbed at his aching head and jolted him to a sitting position. His pillow, a flea-infested wolfhound named Finn, growled in protest.

Wesley rotated his shackled ankle. The chill of the hall invaded his bones. Above the cacophony of the music, the wind howled and the sea crashed ceaselessly at the gray crags of Clonmuir.

He blinked into the predawn dimness. Men snored on pallets, and a few boys slumbered amid the hounds around the low-burning peat fire.

The lack of privacy at Clonmuir appalled Wesley. The men of the household lived as they had hundreds of years ago, crowded around a fire that lacked even the simple invention of a chimney.

Wesley's joints creaked as he rose to his feet. The distant rhythm thudded at his temples with blurry pain. Poteen. The stuff was pure poison.

"Where d'you think you're going?" Rory Breslin's voice rumbled from the darkness.

"To the privy," said Wesley.

"Can't hold the poteen, eh?" Rory said in Gaelic. He snickered unpleasantly and cupped his groin.

Wesley forced himself to pretend ignorance. "What's that racket?"

"That . . . *Dia linn*!" Rory scrambled to his feet and kicked the man next to him. "Up with you, Conn. It's time."

Conn groaned. "My mouth feels like the bottom of a cave."

"Time for what?" asked Wesley.

"The inauguration, if it's any of your concern."

Lugging his iron ball, Wesley went outside and used the privy. Despite the crudeness of the stronghold, its facilities were impressive, with a long shaft in the wall that swept the waste into the sea far below.

The yard was empty and soft with the first pale shimmer of daylight. He eyed the forge barn, a low hive-shaped stone building across from the stables.

It was tempting. Inside lay tools with which he could strike his chains and be off into the woods within five minutes.

But where was the use in escaping? He had found the chieftain of the Fianna. He knew what he had to do.

The question was, did he have the heart to carry out the plan he had made for Caitlin?

The instant he had pulled the helm from her head, he'd realized that he could not perform the task Cromwell had set for him. He could not lop off her beautiful head and toss it at the feet of the Lord Protector.

Nevertheless, he had to take her away from Clonmuir and the Fianna so the raiding would cease. His pained thoughts drifted to Laura, innocent victim in a deadly struggle. Wesley knew he would travel to hell and back to save his daughter.

He rubbed his bristly face and pondered his dilemma. His task was threefold: gain Caitlin's trust, spirit her away, and then . . . he could barely force himself to think of what must come next. It was too awful. He had never done such a thing. It went against vows he had sworn before God.

Scratching their beards, their heads, and their crotches, the men of Clonmuir came outside, one by one. A dozen distrustful glares stabbed into Wesley.

Contriving a breezy grin, Wesley waved. He received muttered Irish curses in response.

With a shrug, he stripped off his shirt and doused himself at the well with icy water, then shook out his hair and put his shirt back on. He longed for a razor, but these hairy Irishmen seemed to have no more use for razors than for chimneys.

Women poured out of the keep. They looked curiously at Wesley but concluded that a gray-faced Englishman shackled to a sixty-pound cannonball posed no threat.

"Come along, *seonin*." Rory shook his shaggy head like a wolfhound just out of a river. "Can't be trusting you alone."

Wesley walked through the gate. He sought Caitlin, but saw her nowhere. Led by the band of musicians, a small procession marched toward the church. The pipes whistled a wild, discordant tune underlaid by the vaguely ominous thump of the goatskin *bodhran*. The gathering crowd, the ancient music, the tension in the air, all added up to the eerie suspicion that something important was about to take place.

"Thirty years it's been since we last seated the MacBride." Conn O'Donnell cuffed young Curran in the head. "Look lively, now. It's your first inauguration and a proud day for Clonmuir."

"'Twould be prouder still if we had a priest to sing a high mass." Tom Gandy trotted up on his pony. He eyed Wesley. "Aye, a priest would be good right about now."

A prick of guilt stabbed at Wesley. These people put great stock in priests. As a former novice, he could bring some comfort to their souls, but he held his tongue. He strongly suspected a traitor at Clonmuir, for their own chaplain had disappeared. But in their faces he saw only simplicity and strength and faith; he could not imagine who would inform on a priest to gain a bounty.

The only obviously treacherous man among them, he reflected, was John Wesley Hawkins.

The music stopped. The people passed through the church doorway, carved with Celtic and Christian symbols. The mysterious perfume of incense struck Wesley with vivid memories of other masses, other ceremonies. Candlelight danced with the shadows of the north wall, where half columns framed a bank of unglazed windows. The chancel arch opened over a simple stone altar.

Wearing battle gear and chewing on a heel of bread, Seamus stood in front of the altar. Magheen sat on a kneeler turned backward. Arrayed like a princess in a gown of blue linen so fine it was called Irish silk, she glared across the middle aisle at Logan Rafferty, who glowered back.

Seamus brushed the crumbs from his beard and breastplate. Dented and rusted in places, the joints creaking hollowly with each movement, the tarnished armor was a sad reminder that Ireland had been at war for generations.

Seamus wore a long broadsword with a bold tracery of Celtic knots etched along the blade. A single unfaceted garnet winked from the hilt.

Seamus turned to mount the steps to the altar. His broadsword slammed against the rail. His rusty armor groaned. He nearly fell on his face.

"Girded to rescue the priests of Ireland," remarked Tom Gandy. "What think you of our crusader, Mr. Hawkins?"

"He'd be perfect for the role of Don Quixote."

Gandy scratched his head. "Donkey who?"

"A Spanish knight in a drama by Cervantes. He treated whores as ladies and went tilting at windmills. But he was wise, in a mad way. Wiser than most."

"Ah, the perfect role for our Seamus," said Tom.

"Where's Caitlin?"

Tom jerked his head to one side. "In the Lady chapel."

Candlelight illuminated a slim, kneeling figure, her back turned and her head bent in prayer. The flames winked off a statue of a serenely smiling Virgin.

Neither serene nor smiling, Caitlin rose and turned, walking across the front of the church toward the altar.

She wore a long white robe several sizes too large for her. Intertwined Celtic symbols adorned the cuffs and hem. Her head was bare, her hair loose in a shimmering fall of colors ranging from sun gold to deep tawny amber. A quiet power fired the look of determination in her eyes, the clenching of her fists at her sides.

Wesley wondered if he had been mistaken to suggest electing Caitlin as the MacBride.

It was a good move, a wise move, he told himself. Perhaps now Caitlin would have no time to lead the Fianna on more murderous rampages.

"She's been here all night," said Tom. "Praying."

A strange ache lodged in Wesley's throat. Caitlin would carry the weight of Clonmuir on her shoulders.

But she was only a girl, he reminded himself. A girl.

The musicians struck up a new tune as the congregation filed out of the church. Wesley waited on the ancient porch. When Caitlin passed by, she paused before stepping down onto the road.

The look on her face struck him like a blow from Liam's hammer. Never had he seen such pure, savage purpose. And yet sadness lurked in the shadows beneath her eyes. Her youth—even the small portion of it she had enjoyed—lay behind her. What lay ahead, he knew with a vicious twist of guilt, was heartbreak.

"Ah, Caitlin," he whispered, "I'm sorry."

She lifted her eyebrows in surprise. "For what?"

"For proposing you as chieftain. 'Tis too great a burden."

"Nonsense, Mr. Hawkins. I only pray I'm worthy to bear it." She went to mount the black horse. Behind her rode Seamus on a tall, tough-looking white pony. Then came Tom, Rory, and Liam, Magheen riding astride with her gown hiked up, followed by a surly Logan Rafferty.

Behind them tramped the inhabitants of the stronghold and village.

Full of a gut-deep, unnameable dread, Wesley joined the march toward the rocky coast.

They came to a cliff topped by the Rock of Muir. Tumbled stones, hewn by ancient hands, circled the broad, grassy area.

"The Giants' Round," Tom Gandy informed Wesley. "Faith, it's no accident that the boulders form a perfect circle around the throne of the MacBride. How do you reckon they got here?"

"I suppose you want me to say magic."

"Don't you believe in magic, Mr. Hawkins?"

"No."

Gandy grinned. "What a careless mortal you are then, my friend."

Caitlin stepped to the center of the circle. Sea mist swathed the scene in silvery mystery. Wesley felt like a spectator at a pagan drama, enacted in a world in which he didn't belong.

He set his jaw; he should be accustomed to the role of outcast. And yet today the sense of crushing aloneness weighed heavily on his spirits.

Caitlin turned to her father. Her unconventional beauty riveted Wesley. Even Magheen's delectable comeliness faded in comparison.

Seamus held out a slim white stick. "My daughter," he said, "you are the hope of Clonmuir. Take thou the throne of the MacBride."

She grasped the white wand. Acting as the *ollam*, Tom recited the laws she would swear to uphold. She held herself like a queen, her head and feet bare, the wind tossing her hair into a froth of gold and amber. The newly risen sun shot through the mist and bathed her in radiance. She seemed to absorb the light, a precious opal filled with the colors of magic.

As Caitlin approached the rock, the rhythm of the music quickened. A stiff wind skirled down from the granite heights. Her slight limp was the only evidence that she breathed as any other mortal, that she was a woman who could be hurt.

Wesley nearly called out to her to stop, to turn back, to abandon her burden. But he held his silence. She was a woman to run toward danger, welcoming it, embracing it.

When Caitlin reached the rounded crest of the rock, the music stopped, giving way to a breathless silence disturbed only by the crash of the sea and the lonely cry of a cormorant.

Caitlin turned. The white robes parted to reveal a

black tabard emblazoned with a golden harp. She lifted the wand toward the blazing dawn sky.

"This is the symbol of the MacBride," she called in clear Gaelic. *"Is treise tuath no tighearna!"*

"A people is stronger than a lord!" the others echoed.

The primitive ceremony chilled Wesley to the bone as Caitlin turned in a slow circle, viewing her domain.

And it was hers, Wesley realized. Aye, the English might claim the land, but Caitlin MacBride owned its soul. He saw the truth in her fierce eyes, in the protectiveness of her regard, in the strange stillness that gripped her despite the swirling, howling wind.

The sense of unreality persisted. Caitlin MacBride was the dawn star, her incandescence undimmed even by light of day. Long after her delicate bones were dust, Caitlin would shine forever in the sky of eternity.

"MacBride!" shouted Seamus, his voice strong above the battering sea.

"MacBride!" The entire gathering, save a glowering Logan Rafferty and a gape-mouthed Wesley Hawkins, took up the inaugural cry. It carried in a thundering wave across the land.

With all the hopes and promises of her people glowing in her eyes, Caitlin descended from the Rock of Muir. Tears streamed unchecked down her cheeks. She passed close to Wesley but did not look at him, only stared straight ahead at an eternity hidden to him. She seemed spellbound, her remarkable mind filled with thoughts he could not imagine.

Never, ever, had Wesley felt so drawn to a woman. It was a fever in his body and a madness in his mind, a fire out of control. Shocked at himself, he remembered his plan.

For Laura's sake, he must get Caitlin to London. For her own sake, he must . . . . Again, the sharp wanting brought him up short. He would do what he must.

When she awoke the day after the inaugural celebration, Caitlin felt drained. For the hundredth time, she asked herself what devil had goaded her into taking the mantle of the MacBride. For the hundredth time, she forced herself to admit that her motivation had been composed of equal measures of desperation, devotion, and raw ambition.

Holding a large, wooden-bound book, she stood in the yard with the rest of the household to say farewell to her father.

She would miss his wonderful smile, his blithe conversation, even his moments of sheer lunacy.

And she would worry about him. Brian, whose sword arm made him formidable and whose ready wit made him good company, would ride with Seamus as both bodyguard and companion.

Hawkins leaned against the well in the center of the yard, one leg cocked and his booted toe pointed at the ground, the cannonball lying at his feet. His cavalier's pantaloons and white shirt, parted at the collar to reveal his muscular neck, flapped in the breeze. He gave her a jaunty smile and a wave.

Why, she wondered in annoyance, must I struggle so hard to look away from him? An aura of allure hovered about the Englishman, a curious quality that arrested the eye and tweaked the imagination. Perhaps it was the unexpected vibrance of his red hair, or the unusual hue of his eyes, the color of moss in shadow. Or the smile that caught at her heart and never let go.

She tore her attention from her prisoner and clutched the heavy book to her chest. Like the musty smell of the pages, the ideas contained within the tome lingered in her mind.

Seamus came out of the stable yard mounted on his tall pony. Brian followed on his own mount, leading a smaller pack horse. Caitlin felt a twinge of sadness at the sight of her father. He was a man of great heart and farseeing vision, yet that very vision obscured the everyday problems right under his nose. Deaf to the quarrels of his men, immune to the melancholy of his daughter, he embraced larger purposes most men gave up as lost causes.

"I'm off to find the priests of Ireland," he announced grandly. "Where is the *deoch an dorais*?"

Rory came forward with a pewter mug. "Here is your parting drink, *a chara*. Keep you well."

Weeping, Magheen ran forward and kissed her father.

He straightened and turned to Caitlin. "Sure and it be yourself who is the MacBride now. Protect this place from Cromwell," he said. "He is a great, bad man."

Caitlin nodded gravely. "God speed you on your way, Daida."

He passed the mug to Rory, then lifted his arms as if to encircle the entire household. "A hundred thousand blessings on your heads, friends of my heart," he shouted. "And a hundred thousand more this time again!"

Caubeens and handkerchiefs waved. Men shouted encouragement, and women called blessings. Seamus MacBride rode out through the main gate.

"There goes Donkey Hote," remarked Tom Gandy.

"Who?" Caitlin asked distractedly.

"Donkey Hote. A character in a drama by somebody's servants. Hawkins told me about him. And speaking of our prisoner, have you decided what you're going to do with him?"

The prisoner was sitting on the iron ball and showing Janet's youngest son how to whistle using a blade of dried grass. Other children, even shy Brigid, gathered round to watch. Enraptured, the youngsters seemed as caught up in the Englishman's magnetism as Caitlin was.

She tapped the book. "I've been studying the question."

"Ah. The Tree of Battles."

She nodded. "The MacBrides have followed its rules of combat for three centuries."

"And what does the book advise?"

She sat on her heels and flipped through the thick parchment pages. The text was handwritten, each page embellished by scrollwork and illumination. "Here," she said, pointing.

"'A prisoner rightly seized in combat is subject to the rules of war,'" Tom read aloud. "'Conversely, the captor must follow a suite of action that will retain his honor and preserve him from the censure of his peers. The prisoner shall be lodged in a room furnished with a goodly pallet . . . meat every other day . . . wine rations . . .'" Frowning, Tom skimmed a passage of minutiae. "Lord love us," he murmured, "this would have us treating him better than we do our own folk."

"It can't be helped," said Caitlin. "I intend to follow the rules to the letter. It must never be said that the MacBride mistreats prisoners. Those are Roundhead tactics, not ours."

"Indeed." Tom peered over her shoulder. "Let's see . . . we must offer the prisoner a chance to give his parole. If he does, he's to be given free run of the keep so long as he stays within the walls."

"I dispute that part," said Caitlin. "He's a lying,

cheating Englishman. He'd swear on his damned Protestant soul that he'd not attempt escape. Then he'd flee the moment our backs were turned."

Tom's face creased in a puckish expression. "All the same, you vowed to follow the letter of the law."

"I did. And I shall," Caitlin said resolutely.

Tom read on. "Ah. Here's something interesting. 'The prisoner shall be bathed and garbed in clean raiments by the ranking mistress.' What say you to that, my lady?"

"Let me see." She scowled at the page. Bathe Hawkins? Her stomach made a queer twist at the idea of touching his body, feeling his skin warm beneath her fingertips. Magheen, she thought. Magheen could do it. As quickly as the notion came to Caitlin, she discounted it. Logan was furious enough with his errant wife; if he found out she had bathed an Englishman, he would probably double his demands.

"All right," she said, blowing out a sigh of resignation. "To do any less would bring us dishonor. We shall follow the time-honored rules."

Tom's eyebrows lifted to the brim of his hat. "Starting with the bath?"

She heaved another great, heartfelt sigh. "Aye. Starting with the bath."

Guarded by Rory, watched with amusement by Tom, and propelled by Caitlin MacBride's firm, impersonal hand, Wesley stepped into the kitchen of Clonmuir. He blinked through the dimness at a vaulted stone-and-plaster ceiling, begrimed by cooking grease and black smoke. A hearth as wide as an armspan and taller than a large man blazed with a well-stoked fire.

To one side stood a folding screen. An ominous-looking array of iron utensils hung from hooks above a stout block table: a scissorlike apparatus with crimped ends, a long sharp spike, a screw-top clamp.

Apprehension stole like a sickness through Wesley's gut. He had an urge to cross himself, but the iron ball in his arms and common sense stayed his hand.

"Wait here." Caitlin moved the folding screen aside.

Wesley drew in his breath. At the hearth sat a giant wooden half barrel with steam rising from the surface.

"Oh . . . my . . . God," he whispered, the words tumbling from his lips on a wave of panic. He bolted for the door, yanked it open.

"Not so fast, *spalpeen*." Rory Breslin slammed it shut again.

Frowning, Caitlin tucked a ribbon of tawny hair behind her ear. "What is it?"

But Wesley barely heard her soft query, barely noticed the flicker of firelight on her starkly beautiful features. A familiar blindness descended over him, shadows alive with shapeless horrors. The innocent peat fire blazed into a furnace of agony. The steam twisted like dragon's breath over the caldron, waiting to sear his skin, to invade his lungs with poison.

"I wondered when you'd get around to torture." The hard, flat voice sounded alien on his tongue. "You're not so different from Oliver Cromwell yourself."

"What's that?" she asked sharply.

Lost in a maze of terror, Wesley felt the room close in on him, the smothering wings of the angel of death. And then he was gone, tucked away by invisible comforting hands in some unseen haven where the pain could not touch him, where he could retreat into the blinding light . . .

A hand jerked at his sleeve. The impatient touch raised him up out of the darkness. "God's mercy, Mr. Hawkins," said Caitlin, "have you lost your senses? What are you babbling about?"

He stared into her golden firelit eyes and wondered at her confused expression. "Babbling? I was babbling? But I said nothing, I—"

"Must be your odd English speech." She released his sleeve. "For a moment I fancied you were reciting the Twenty-third Psalm. In Latin."

Wesley knew he'd never be so incautious. He forced a grin and avoided staring at her instruments of torture. "Aye, your ears deceive you, indeed. The English pray in the vernacular, not in Latin."

"And do they always pray before a bath?"

"A bath?" Wesley's knees began to wobble. He nearly dropped the cannonball on his foot. "But I thought . . ." His gaze riveted on the coil of rope, the long knives, the pincerlike instruments.

"Blessed Virgin Mary," said Caitlin, her voice breathy with disbelief. "You thought I meant to torture you, didn't you?"

He held himself completely still, said nothing.

"You did," she persisted, her voice a low, musical throb, the echo of a plucked harp string. "Sweet Jesus, Mr. Hawkins, what's been done to you to make you believe such a thing?"

You don't want to know, Caitlin MacBride. I barely know myself.

"I'm just startled," he said, injecting blithe insouciance into his tone.

"I see." He heard skepticism in hers. "I suppose I'd best explain."

Carefully he set the cannonball on the floor. "Please do."

"These utensils you regard so fearfully are for

making the *drisheen*. It's been a long time since we've had sheep for slaughtering, but Janet keeps the tools for crimping the sausages."

He gestured at the tub. "And that?"

"I intend to follow the formal rules of combat, Mr. Hawkins. You are to be treated as a prisoner of rank. I shall bathe and clothe you. Tom Gandy, my steward, has drawn up a document to govern your conduct."

"I need no piece of paper to—" Wesley stopped himself. If it would put Caitlin more at ease with him, all the better.

". . . strike your irons," she was saying.

The possibility snared his attention. He moved his right foot. The shackle chafed painfully around his ankle. "You mean I'm to be rid of this?"

"Yes. So long as you fulfill one condition."

"Anything. God, the very surety of my soul, if need be."

She gasped softly. "I'd never ask that, even of my worst enemy. I merely require your parole—your sworn oath that you will not attempt to escape."

"You have it," he replied without hesitation. "I swear I will not try to escape."

Her eyes narrowed. "Not good enough, Mr. Hawkins."

"Caitlin, a man sitting in a bathtub is not in a position to do much damage."

A smile tugged at the corners of her mouth. "True, but Tom and I discussed what it would take to trap an Englishman's honor." She groped in her voluminous apron pockets and removed several objects, laying them on the table. "Here's the cross of St. George, England's patron," she said. "It was part of a banner Rory seized in a skirmish on Beltane last. And this—it's a coin cast in the image of the devil's butcher, Cromwell. Since he claims your loyalty, I'm not averse to your swearing on it. Oh, and this." She laid down a Bible with a cross on the cover. Bits of plaster clung to the wood. "I pried off the figure of Christ. You Protesters seem to find the representation of our Lord offensive, and prefer your crosses bare."

"You've done much thinking about an Englishman's heart, Caitlin MacBride."

"Englishmen have no hearts," she retorted. "But a few of you do still possess a wee sense of honor."

"And you think I'm one who does?"

"No," she said simply. "I'll strike your irons, but you'll be watched every moment. I sincerely hope you have no strange privy habits, for you'll find yourself embarrassed."

"I don't embarrass easily." He stared at the floor to hide the laughter in his eyes.

"We shall see about that. Lay your hands on those objects that be sacred to all Englishmen, and swear your parole."

Wesley moved to the table. He placed his left hand on the torn silk depicting the cross of St. George and his right on the Bible.

"The coin as well," said Caitlin.

Wesley moved it to the far edge of the table. "Not that. You ask me to take an oath on sacred objects. Cromwell is not one of them."

"He's not?"

"Not to me."

"Then why do you fight and kill and conquer for him?"

"Because I have no choice."

"Is he paying you, then, Mr. Hawkins? Did you come here hoping to line your pockets?"

"No! My God, Caitlin—" He bit off the protest. "Shall we get on with it?"

"In a moment. We must have witnesses." A grin tugged at her mouth. "Visible ones, that is." Going to the door, she pulled it open. Rory and Tom practically fell into the room.

"I'm surprised you've no splinters from pressing this"—Caitlin brushed playfully at Tom's ear—"to the door."

Rory flushed deep red. Gandy merely shrugged and laid a parchment document on the table.

"Swear it," said Caitlin.

Wesley pressed his hands to the objects on the table. "I swear on St. George and on the Holy Bible that I have given my parole to my captor, Caitlin MacBride, chieftain of Clonmuir."

"Sign it," said Tom.

Wesley used a quill that had seen better times. The nib was split and his signature appeared strange, in double images. Slightly discomfited, he handed the quill to Caitlin. She signed the statement with a swift, sure stroke. Tom Gandy wrote in a beautiful old-fashioned script, and Rory Breslin in a crude one that bent the nib beyond repair.

"That will be all," said Caitlin. "I can handle Mr. Hawkins from here."

"Are you sure?" asked Rory. In Irish he added, "I trust him less than a hungry wolf."

"I don't trust him either," Caitlin replied, also in Irish. "But he's not stupid. We have his sworn oath. He'll behave."

Rory shook his great, shaggy head. "I can't bear to watch." He elbowed Tom Gandy. Tom removed the oath and himself quickly. Rory followed reluctantly. The fire snapped into the silence.

"Well?" asked Wesley. "Are you ready to test my honor, Caitlin MacBride?"

She took a heavy ring from her apron, selected a

large, antique-looking key, and bent to his ankle. He winced as she rotated the shackle. Her accusing eyes glared up at him. "This tore right through your boot. Your leg's rubbed raw."

"So it is."

"Why didn't you say anything?"

"I didn't think my discomfort would move you."

"This is Clonmuir," she said, "not a house of torture." With deft and gentle hands she removed the shackle and then his boots. Enjoying the freedom of movement, Wesley flexed his ankle.

"Now the bath," she said.

A strange thrill shot up his back. Disrobing in front of this ferociously attractive woman held interesting possibilities.

He choked off the notion. Once before, he'd broken his vow of celibacy and had gotten Laura. Losing her to Cromwell was God's retribution. Winning her back, no matter what the cost, would be his penance.

But he had been three years keeping his vow. Since finding Laura, he had ground his lust beneath the heel of obligation. It hadn't been difficult. Until now. Until Caitlin.

He peeled off his shirt and linen chemise. Caitlin's gaze slipped down a notch, then climbed back up. Grinning, he removed his belt and tugged at the laces of his pantaloons.

"Wait." Her voice rose with urgency. She moved the screen between them so that she could see only his head and shoulders.

Wesley chuckled. "Aren't you afraid I'll attack you?"

"Lift a finger to me, and you'll show us the worth of an Englishman's sworn oath. Besides, you'd not be the first *Sassenach* I've fought—and bested."

He recalled vividly her actions in battle, the swiftness of her movements, the certainty of her instincts, the power of her wiles. "I didn't expect a show of modesty from the MacBride."

"I may be the MacBride, but I am also a woman, with a woman's sensibilities."

He studied the set of her shoulders, the way she bent her head very slightly, the bright ribbons of hair that escaped her thick, clumsily woven braid. Suddenly it struck him that she was vulnerable, and in a way she might not realize herself. She accepted the responsibility for Clonmuir, but beneath her soldier's armor beat the heart of a woman. She relied on strength, but she also needed tenderness.

"Ah, Caitlin," he said on a sigh. "Forgive me."

She blinked in startlement; then comprehension bowed her lips into a small smile. "Nothing to forgive, at least, in this instance. Men do be forgetting I'm a woman."

"I'll never forget." His gaze moved over the rounded shapes of her breasts. "I can't forget."

She ducked her head. "Into the bath, Mr. Hawkins."

He sank in up to his chest. The water was a few degrees shy of scalding, and he loved it. The breath left him in a sigh.

"Warm enough?"

"Aye, indeed. I've not had a bath since—" He checked himself. God, but it was easy to talk to this fierce Irish stranger. "Not in a very long time."

She moved the screen aside. In her hands she held a scrubbing cloth and an egg-shaped cake of yellowish soap. She walked in a slow circle around the tub.

"Have you never bathed a man before?" Wesley asked.

"Of course I have. It's been my duty since my mother passed on."

He heard the catch in her voice. "And when was that?"

"Six years past. She had something growing inside her. A traveling barber called it a fistula."

"I'm sorry, Caitlin."

"Two I'm-sorrys in one conversation. You might be a decent man if you weren't a Roundhead, Mr. Hawkins."

Wesley pondered the idea of a mother. It was as alien to him as the New World across the sea. Vague images came to him: a cruel feminine mouth forming words of censure, a remorseless voice dictating his banishment to Louvain. "What was she like?" Wesley asked.

"My mother?"

"Aye."

"And what the devil do you care about my mother?"

"Just humor me, Caitlin. I'm interested."

She plucked absently at a stray curl. "Her name was Siobhan. Her father was a lord. He never spoke to her after she married my father who, as you know, is not a man of any great means. Never even dowered her."

"Then how did they manage?"

"I do think myself, Mr. Hawkins," she said crisply, "that true love graced every day they spent together. It makes the managing easy."

"So you do believe in true love?"

"Of course," she said. "I'm Irish."

She drew a stool to the tub. "The last thing I bathed was Magheen's shoat at fairing time. The poor beast squealed to raise the high saints of heaven."

"I vow I won't squeal," Wesley assured her.

But he could not suppress a sigh of pure pleasure when she slipped the soapy cloth over his shoulders and chest, her strong fingers kneading his muscles and gliding over his slick skin. The hands that were so deadly in wielding a shortsword plied a cake of soap with soothing gentleness. Her swift, sure touch tingled with subtle magic.

A light scent pervaded the air. "Perfumed soap?" Wesley asked, surprised.

"It's wild heather. Our crops might fail, but the heather still blooms. Even the English can't eradicate it, though I don't doubt they've tried. Magheen makes the best soap in the district."

"Somehow I can't picture Magheen boiling soap."

"There's a bit more to my sister than most men imagine, Mr. Hawkins."

"Wesley. Will you please call me Wesley?"

"No. It's too familiar."

"And what could be more familiar than having me naked in the bath?"

Her hand paused on his shoulder, then resumed scrubbing in a soothing circular motion. "It's the task allotted to me. Lean forward, please."

He rested his elbows on his knees. She brushed aside the long ends of his hair. The cloth massaged the back of his neck and lower, between his shoulder blades and—

"Dear sweet Virgin Mary!" she said.

Wesley looked toward the door. He gripped the sides of the tub and prepared to vault from the water. "What?" he demanded. "What is it?"

"You've been beaten."

He ran a hand through his hair. Damn. He hadn't considered her reaction to the scars crisscrossing his back. "That I have," he said breezily. "But your touch makes me forget the pain."

Her hand moved hesitantly down his spine. Absurdly, he imagined that the scars smoothed out and disappeared wherever her fingers roamed.

"Who did this to you?"

"I don't know. My back was turned."

"This is not a jest."

"I didn't think so either at the time." In truth he had not thought anything. The beating belonged to the impenetrable blindness that hid inside him and cloaked his pain.

"Why were you punished . . . Wesley?"

He loved the sound of his name on her lips. "It was for . . . insubordination."

"To whom? Hammersmith? Were you lashed for desertion?" She took his silence for an affirmative. "But these wounds are healed."

"Maybe it wasn't the first time I deserted."

"Was it the last?" she demanded.

"I believe that's up to you."

"You're lying. You always lie, Mr. Hawkins."

"I got these scars back in England." No harm in admitting that, or in letting her draw her own conclusions. If he told her he had suffered for being a Catholic, she wouldn't believe him, and he'd lay himself open to the treachery that had struck the chaplain of Clonmuir.

"Does it have anything to do with why you came to fight in Ireland?" she asked.

"You ask too many questions. This is my first bath in a very long time and I aim to enjoy it."

To his relief, she abandoned the topic and soaped his hair thoroughly. "You wear it long," she commented. "Not all cropped like most Roundheads."

Three months ago, his hair had been a glorious mantle of ruddy waves. Neglect had made it a mass of snarls.

"I'm not like most Roundheads."

"In what way are you different?"

"I'm a royalist."

She dropped her cloth. He grinned, enjoying her astonishment.

"That's another lie. If you were a royalist, you'd be intriguing with Charles of the Stuarts in France or Saxony or wherever he's got to these days."

"Having Charles on the throne might be good for Ireland."

She pursed her lips. Longing to kiss her, he came forward, inches from his goal when she said, "If that's a ploy to win my pledge for the House of Stuart, it won't work. An envoy came last year seeking Irish troops. But when he saw the state Clonmuir was in, he headed straight back across the channel."

"You might think about lending your support to Cromwell's rival," said Wesley.

She blew out a breath. "Ireland will still be under England's yoke. What does it matter if the carter changes?"

"Was there ever so cruel a driver as Oliver Cromwell?"

"An excellent point, Mr. Hawkins. I wonder why you're fighting his battles for him."

"Enough bickering," Wesley said. "Surely your rules of combat forbid you to badger the prisoner." He leaned back, enjoying the steady tingle of her fingers on his scalp. Through half-closed eyes he watched the play of firelight over her face.

The soft glow transformed the warrior into a woman. Her mouth was pliant and mobile, too wide to be called sweet, yet too full-lipped to be called anything but sinfully kissable. Her small nose was straight and rather thin, her chin squarish in a way that harmonized perfectly with the rest of her features. She had a slender neck, long enough for a man's gaze to savor for a while until, inevitably, his attention strayed to the lush swell of her bosom beneath her round-necked blouse.

But most riveting of all were the eyes of Caitlin MacBride. Dark brows and darker lashes framed twin pools so deep and mysterious that he could drown forever in them. The color ranged from rich brown to blazing amber. The irises caught spears of light from the fire and threw back arrows of warmth at his heart.

Madness, he thought. The heat of the water is making my brain soggy. I must not let myself feel for this woman.

Yet Wesley wanted to forget his vows. He wanted to feel her hands on him, everywhere, on the places hidden by the water, on his thighs, his hips, his—

"—foot," she said in an impatient voice.

"Er, what's that?"

"Lift your foot."

"Oh." He did so.

She took it between her hands and he reveled in the lovely slide of her fingers over his flesh. Ah, heaven. What a wise gentleman was that fellow who had set the rules of combat—

"Dear God in heaven!"

Startled again, Wesley grabbed the sides of the tub. "Now what?"

"Your foot is scarred, too."

"Caitlin, I—"

"Someone burned you." She rubbed her thumb over the slick bottom of his foot. "What happened, Wesley?"

"It was an accident. I trod on a campfire—"

"You lie constantly." She picked up the other foot. "Englishmen are stupid, but not so stupid that they'd put both feet in a fire. These burns were deliberately made. Great God, no wonder you took a fright at the sight of this kitchen. Who did this to you? And why?"

"Don't ask me, Caitlin. It's over now."

She folded her lips as if sealing off further questions.

"Thank you," he said.

She cleaned his fingernails and pared them with a small knife.

"Have you a razor?" Wesley asked.

"For what?"

"To shave my beard."

"Irishmen never shave."

"As you have so frequently pointed out, I am not an Irishman."

She pushed away from the tub. "I'll be after seeing what I can find." She spoke to Rory at the door and returned a moment later with a long blade, furry with rust.

Wesley regarded it dubiously. "This doesn't look like any razor I've ever seen."

"It's all Rory could find."

"Ah." He lathered his face with soap. She came toward him with the blade extended.

Hastily Wesley took the razor. "I'll do it. You don't have any experience at this sort of thing." Slowly, painstakingly, he used both hands to draw the instrument down his cheeks, across his chin, beneath his nose. The razor pulled at his skin, nicking him. The sting of soap made him flinch.

Caitlin MacBride put her hand over her mouth and giggled.

Wesley gave her his sternest priestly look, but she only laughed harder. As quickly as he could, he ended the ordeal of shaving and sat pressing a cloth to his bleeding face.

By then Caitlin was laughing uproariously, clutching at her sides and gasping for air.

"What the devil is so amusing about watching a man shave?"

"It's not a razor, but a scrape we use in the sheep shearing."

"I appreciate your telling me." He dropped the instrument in disgust. "After I've finished."

"I've never understood why Englishmen scrape their faces naked," she said. "Sure it seems a lot of trouble."

"When a pitiless wench gives me a shearing tool, it is." He scowled. "Beards are a lot of trouble." His knees rose like pale atolls in the tepid water. "One is always dropping food into them."

"Only if one is a pig—or an Englishman."

"Then you hold my entire race in contempt," said Wesley.

"You hold *my* entire race in bondage," she said. "Are you through bathing?"

"If I stay in here much longer, I'll be a pickled herring."

She put a pile of clean clothes on the stool and a pair of boots and trews on the floor. "Those are Rory's things," she said, dragging the screen into place. "You two are of a size."

"Parts of us are," Rory called in Irish through the door. "But not the good parts."

Caitlin flushed and pretended not to hear.

Wesley gritted his teeth and pretended not to understand.

"I didn't know you'd noticed my size," he said, oddly pleased. He came out of the tub and dried himself, then dressed in clothing he had seen in tapestries woven centuries ago: thick trews that hugged the legs and hips, a chemise worn soft by years of wear, a white tunic that reached to midthigh, and tall boots of pliant leather that laced crisscross over his shins.

He stepped from behind the screen. Perhaps it was a trick of the wind through the eaves, but he thought

Caitlin's breath caught. Their gazes locked, and they shared a moment like the one that had passed between them on the strand, a moment suspended in time, alive with an emotion too deep to be shared by mere strangers.

"Ah, Cait," he whispered, "why do I feel I know you so well?"

Caught in the snare of his subtle tenderness, Caitlin trembled, trying to shake off the spell. "No man knows me, Mr. Hawkins. Particularly not an Englishman."

"A moment ago you were calling me Wesley." He stepped forward and cupped her cheek in his damp palm. "God, you are beautiful in the firelight."

She stood rooted, too startled to draw away. He spread his caress over the curve of her cheek.

"Your skin is soft," he whispered. "I always thought that it would be, but I wasn't certain until I touched you."

"Brash talk from an Englishman," she chided, but could not make herself pull away. Her eyelashes swept downward. His fingers skimmed to her throat. She swallowed involuntarily. He stepped closer still, his lips finding the silky tendrils of hair that fringed her brow. The warmth of his mouth unleashed a powerful flood of wanting in her.

"There is something between us, Caitlin MacBride." Aware as she was of the listeners outside, he kept his voice low. "Something vital and important and magic. We'd be fools to ignore it."

"No." She reached up to touch his face, caught herself, and curled her fingers into a fist. "You're more full of blarney than an—" She stopped and bit her lip.

He touched her mouth with his finger, gently releasing the fullness of her lip. "Than what, Caitlin? Than an Irishman?"

She jerked back, as stung as if he'd slapped her. The drowsy warmth of enchantment fled to be replaced by cold conviction. "You are no Irishman, Mr. Hawkins."

She turned on her heel, marched to the door, and jerked it open. Tom and Rory stood staring at the ceiling and whistling as if they had not been straining to hear every word.

Wesley held himself still, fighting to govern his anger. The cold lash of Caitlin's temper had a decided sting.

Tom smiled pleasantly as he inspected Wesley. "Now, that's an improvement. We'll make a civilized man of him yet. But why'd you shave your fine red beard, Mr. Hawkins?"

"Call it a sudden urge to shear a sheep," Wesley said wryly.

Caitlin hastened toward the great hall, speaking over her shoulder. "Rory, see that the curragh is mended. We'll be needing what the sea can give us if people continue to arrive at this rate. And Tom, do something about that family in from Killaloe. I swear, the children look as if they'd not had a bite of meat in a year. See that they get plenty of the good salt beef."

English beef, thought Wesley, and English flour. She was no better than a common thief, stealing from men who could hardly afford to lose rations. Still, he couldn't resent her for feeding empty stomachs.

"You may go to the hall, Mr. Hawkins," she said. "The rules state that you're to have meat every other day. Janet will serve you." And then, in a swirl of threadbare skirts and with a toss of her tawny braid, Caitlin MacBride was gone.

7

Life was hard at Clonmuir, Wesley quickly discovered. The Roundheads had burned most of the crops, and the bread consisted of a coarse mixture of stale chaff and potato. Since the English had destroyed the fishing fleet, the harvest from the sea was meager. The watered beer tasted more of cask than of hop.

The people of Clonmuir viewed him as a curiosity, not a man to be feared but not one to be respected, either. They rarely solicited his opinion, but when he spoke, they listened politely. He felt alone in a tightly knit community, a feeling as familiar to him as the *Ave Maria.*

Several times each day the thought of escape crossed his mind. But he had given his parole. He had thought of a way to spare Caitlin's life and gain Laura back, and in order to carry out the plan, he must stay at Clonmuir.

His ear for Irish sharpened and he listened to conversations not meant for his ears, but he heard little of value. He tried his best to draw Caitlin to him. He used looks and smiles that had worked like love potions on Englishwomen. But she kept her distance, seemed unmoved by his subtle efforts. Maybe he had lost his touch.

He might have had some luck prizing information from Magheen if he'd thought it worth the effort. But, as self-absorbed as she was pretty, she paid no heed to the workings of Clonmuir.

He came upon her of an evening when she sat with Aileen Breslin and the other ladies in the hall, the fiction of a skein of wool in her lap. She looked up. Her flame-blue eyes studied him hungrily, and her lips parted. She was, Wesley realized, a woman who appreciated a man's looks. Yet he was seized by the certainty that she wished he were someone else.

She inclined her shining head. "Mr. Hawkins."

"Good evening, my lady."

She winced as if the courtesy were a stitch in her side. She had the eyes of the women who used to confess to him—secretly, in barns, haylofts, abandoned carriage houses—eyes haunted by burdens too heavy to bear alone. Some priests thrived on accepting the pain of others. They grew stronger from bearing a stranger's sins. But the compassion these troubled souls wrung from Wesley always left him weakened, sometimes gasping for breath.

"I suppose you're going to point out that our spinning is illegal," she said tartly. "The English outlawed it to force us to pay to have our wool spun by *Sassenach* hands."

In response, he bent to Magheen's spinning wheel, which she treadled halfheartedly. "Look," he said. "The treadle is rubbing against this shaft, like so . . ." He adjusted a pin and tested the treadle. It moved smoothly, with a whisper of sound.

Magheen gave a small smile. "Thank you, Mr. Hawkins."

He stood to leave.

"Mr. Hawkins?" It was Rory's mother, Aileen. "I've been having the same trouble with my own wheel. If you don't mind . . . ?"

"Of course." He quickly made the adjustment.

"How can we be thanking you, Mr. Hawkins?"

"You can start by calling me Wesley. And you can finish by telling me about Caitlin."

The two women exchanged a glance. Aileen lowered her eyes and resumed her work. Magheen said, "Caitlin . . . is Caitlin. What more do you need to know?"

"Why has she never married?"

Magheen twisted a piece of wool from the spindle. "And why should I be wondering about a thing like that?"

"She's your sister."

"Caitlin doesn't need anyone. She's the MacBride."

Aileen tucked a lock of gray hair under her kerchief. "Sure I always thought her under a love spell. Perhaps she pines for a man she cannot have."

"Oh, bosh." Magheen gave her arm a pat. "Caitlin would never pine for a man."

But the idea seized Wesley's thoughts. Logan Rafferty? he wondered. Aye, it made sense, indeed it did. Rafferty was too handsome by half and a great lord at that, well-heeled for these parts. Did Caitlin yearn for her brother-in-law?

But with Logan, Caitlin had been cool, businesslike, unemotional. If she harbored feelings for Rafferty, she hid them well, no doubt out of loyalty to both Magheen and to the Fianna.

"Bedad," said Aileen, "her head's full of clan matters. She can't see the nose in the middle of her face."

Magheen giggled. "Sure you mean she can't see Rory staring calf-eyed at her every day."

"My Rory's a fine block of a man, brave and strong. What more would the girleen be wanting?"

Magheen sighed. "True love."

"True love! Bah! As if it were something to be sprinkled down on a body like fairy dust. Why, I never even clapped eyes on my Paddy until I stepped up to the church porch on my wedding day. I didn't know I loved the blighter till the day I laid him to rest, may the sweet breath of heaven blow upon his soul. Love's something that grows with the seasons. Some years the harvest is poor, but all told . . ."

Wesley excused himself and moved away. They could tell him little about Caitlin. They never wondered what lay in the depths of her soul. But Wesley did. Constantly.

Leaving the hall, he went to the stables and paused while his eyes adjusted to the dimness inside. He absorbed the warm scents of hay and horse and sweetened oats. Caitlin's lovely crooning voice drifted to his ears. As always, the sound stopped him dead, then lifted him up and swirled him back across the centuries, when Ireland glittered like an unconquerable jewel.

He found her crouched in the last stall with the black stallion. An oil lamp hung from a rafter. On the floor in front of her lay a detailed map.

At Wesley's approach, the horse made a grunt of warning. She looked up, startled, and swept the map to her chest.

"Do you always sing while contemplating battle plans, Caitlin?" he inquired.

"The only plan you need concern yourself with is how Hammersmith will react if he hears I've captured you. Do you think he'll beat you again?"

"Would that bother you?"

She shrugged. The uncertain light from the lamp

infused the motion with liquid grace. "Beating one's own men seems foolish and contrary to one's goals." She tucked the map in her apron pocket and stood.

Wesley studied her face, the shadows beneath her eyes, the fullness of her lips. She practiced no feminine wiles. She didn't have to. "You can't tell him you've taken me," he stated.

"I can. I'm the MacBride." Her body stiffened unconsciously as she spoke, and her breasts thrust against the fabric of her blouse.

Wesley's blood heated. "But you won't. You can't have me bearing tales about who you are or what you're about."

She pushed a finger at her lip. "I realize that. I've given great combs of thought to the problem."

"Then you agree that you should keep me." With the smug satisfaction of an argument won, Wesley propped his shoulder against the stall door.

Caitlin's eyes picked him over as if he were a carved goose on a table. "Aye, I'll have to either keep you . . . or kill you."

"I vote for keeping me."

A glint of humor shone in her eyes. "I was after thinking you would. And so I shall keep you, Mr. Hawkins, so long as you behave yourself."

"And if I don't behave? If I try to escape?"

"I'll hunt you down and kill you." The conviction in her voice chilled him, and yet he felt something else, an ache of pity that a wonderful creature like Caitlin MacBride should be compelled to have the heart of a murderer.

"Then you leave me no alternative," he said lightly. "I shall stay. Think of it, Cait, we'll grow old together. We'll walk on the strand and watch the sunset, and you'll sing songs to me in that lovely voice of yours." Caught up in his own fantasy, he took her hand and brushed his lips across her knuckles. Even so slight a caress delved deep to the center of him. God, he was mad for her.

She extracted her hand from his. Faint color graced her cheeks like the first flush of ripeness on an apple. "I'm afraid you don't understand, Mr. Hawkins."

"Wesley. And I do understand you, Caitlin MacBride. I understand why you're so strong and yet so vulnerable, why I sense a woman's longing in your eyes and a warrior's hardness in your heart."

She pulled her hands protectively to her chest. "And haven't you got the brains of the world, Mr. Hawkins. Tell me how you came to these understandings about myself."

"You're defending your home. And it's a tragedy, in a way. Circumstances have forced you to bury your femininity."

"Circumstances?" she lashed out. "What a pretty word. You English have made me what I am, stolen my dream of having a husband and fam—" As if aware that she had revealed too much of herself, she picked up a currycomb and turned to the black. "Go on back to the hall. I'm busy."

Wesley decided to retreat from the subject—but not from her. The horse's glossy hide contracted at Caitlin's touch, and it made a contented grunt. In silence Wesley watched the play of light and shadow over the stallion's musculature. One of the thieves Wesley had taken years ago had stolen some art collected by Henry the Eighth, and he thought of those drawings now.

"You know," he said, "I once saw a drawing of a horse by a Florentine master, Leonardo da Vinci."

"Did you now?" she asked over her shoulder. Uninterest flattened her voice.

"They were rendered in rust-colored pencil on parchment. The most magnificent horses I'd ever seen. I was certain they were idealized pictures. The musculature was too perfect, the proportions too precise, to represent a real animal. But I was wrong," Wesley concluded. "This horse surpasses even da Vinci's vision."

"Or anyone else's," Caitlin added, running her hand over the smooth bulge of the horse's cheek. A soft, dreamy expression crept over her face.

"Caitlin, could you not sell some of these horses to feed your people?"

She gave a short laugh. "The Irish are butchering their horses for food. The only ones who need horses anymore are warriors, and there are so few of us left. I've heard that some Irish traitors sell their horses to the English cavalry." Her gaze encompassed the interior of the stables. Slyness crept into her expression. "Sure wouldn't they love to get their hands on these?"

"Caitlin, they would kill to get their hands on your horses. You'd best be damned careful."

"I'm careful."

Wesley scowled at the black. "What is his name?"

"He has no name." Her hands skimmed the arch of the horse's neck. "To give him a name would be to make him ordinary."

He stepped up behind her. Without touching her, he measured her waist with his spanned hands. Just as he had thought. Slim as a sapling. "Where did you get him, Caitlin?"

She leaned her cheek against the black's neck and drew her hand slowly over his throat, up and down, up and down, in a motion that made Wesley quicken with raw yearning.

"He was a gift."

"From whom?"

"Ah, that I'll not be telling you, Mr. Hawkins."

"From Logan Rafferty?" he persisted, bracing himself for her response and his jealousy.

She burst out laughing. The sound made him admire her spirit, to be able to laugh in the midst of hardships.

She wiped her face with a corner of her apron. "Sure Logan Rafferty wouldn't give me the gleanings from his fields, much less a horse like this."

"Then who—"

"Never you mind, sir. I talk too much around you as it is."

"Not nearly enough," he said. "I could listen to you until the snakes came back to Ireland and still not weary of you."

"I daresay you'll become weary of me before long, Mr. Hawkins." She drew the currycomb slowly over the black satin withers.

"You're very devoted to the beast," he observed.

"And well I should be. He's seen me through many a battle."

Wesley pictured her riding in the dark of night, her hair and veil flying on the wind and her sword held tightly in her small hand. A fresh pang of concern jabbed at him. "Caitlin, have you ever considered that one day your luck could fail?"

"I have a superior horse, loyal men, and people who depend on me. I can't afford to be harrying myself about ill luck."

"But if the Roundheads ever captured you . . ." His voice trailed off as he pictured her home overrun by soldiers, her men killed, and Caitlin splayed out beneath a lusty Englishman. Wesley severed the thought with a shake of his head. He would not allow himself to think of that. Besides, if his plan worked, she would be safe from the Roundheads soon.

"Don't you ever tire of fighting, Caitlin?" he asked.

"I can't say it would matter if I did." Her movements as she groomed the horse became quicker, more agitated.

"Don't you grow weary of killing?" Wesley asked.

"Killing whom?"

"Killing anyone."

"English are the only breed I hunt."

"Well, do you ever tire of it?" he persisted.

"Of course not." She moved to the high hips of the horse, brushing smartly. "Do you?"

"Eternally," he admitted, remembering the bloody battles of the Civil War, the resultant crushing guilt and sense of aloneness that had driven him to take vows at Douai.

"That's because you don't know what it's like to fight for your home, Mr. Hawkins." Passion underscored every word she spoke. "For the very food you eat."

A response rose in his throat, and he wanted to shake her, tell her yes! Yes, I do know. I have had to leave my home. I have suffered torture, had my beloved daughter wrenched from my arms and held hostage.

But the urge to confess was overpowered by the need to guard his secrets. "Cait," he said softly, his hand covering hers and slowing the motion of the comb. "Put that down and look at me."

She stiffened. "Don't be touching me, Englishman."

"I don't think I can help myself."

She tossed her head, and her downy hair rippled across his chest. He smelled its wild, fresh fragrance. "Scared, Caitlin?"

"Never," she swore.

"Then turn around."

Exasperated, Caitlin pivoted sharply and found herself pinned between Hawkins and the horse. Hard muscle behind her, hard muscle in front of her. It wasn't fear, but confusion that made her bite her lip and ask, "Why do you keep after me, Mr. Hawkins?"

"That's another thing I can't help." His finger came up and skimmed her cheekbone, tracing the line of her jaw. "I understand you better than you think. Better, perhaps, than anyone at Clonmuir. You claim that your lot is poor, that you are forced to fight, yet you still have your home and family."

"Aye, praise be to the high saints of heaven." Solemnly she studied his face. "And do you have a family, Mr. Hawkins?"

"I—my parents sent me away for schooling when I was very young. They're dead now. I had no brother or sisters." Seeking to distract her from further questions, he bent and blew lightly into her ear.

She shivered. "This horse bites, you know."

"I think he likes me. Almost as much as you do, Cait."

"I don't like you. How can I like you? I don't even know you, for you refuse to answer my questions."

He stroked her upper arms. "It's just that there's so little to say. You have Clonmuir, and that makes you far richer than I." He gazed over the horse's back, where a patch of sunset shone through a barred window. Even the warmth of her pressed against him failed to melt the ice of aloneness. "Sometimes I don't think I belong anywhere."

The idea drew his mind to Laura, and a sense of urgency gripped him. What if Hammersmith reported to Cromwell that Wesley had been killed? What would become of Laura then?

"Mr. Hawkins?" Caitlin's voice interrupted the terrible thoughts. "Are you all right? You look green-sick of a sudden." She glanced down at his hands on her arms. " And you're holding on too tight."

He forced himself to ease the pressure on his fingers, but secret fears still pounded at him. He had best do something about his situation, and soon. But what?

In June, a sudden unseasonable chill whipped across Connemara. The wind off the Atlantic grew claws, raking them over the desolate cliffs. The greening fields faded once again to the drab hues of death—gray and lifeless brown, the sea painted the shade of a polished gun barrel, the sky watery and with no color at all.

Magheen refused to return to her husband until he reduced his dowry demands to a mere token.

Logan refused to alter his demands until Magheen returned to his hearth and home. And his bed.

She professed to despise him, and each night she cried herself to sleep.

He swore he couldn't bear the sight of her, and each day found a new excuse to ride the twenty miles to Clonmuir.

Liam the smith's broken arm healed slowly. Aileen Breslin made poultices for him while Tom Gandy spun tales by the hearth.

And off in Galway, Titus Hammersmith complained about the pissing Irish weather and raged about the fact that, once again, the Fianna had raided his stores, this time right out from under his nose, off a ship in Galway harbor. The crew had been put in tenders and set adrift while the plundering Irish had pirated flour and meat and sailed northward in a swift, uncatchable curragh.

The families of the district began arriving at dawn to claim their shares of the booty from the latest raid. Wesley stood in the yard next to Tom

Gandy and Caitlin, who oversaw the distribution.

"Take an extra ration of flour, Mrs. Boyle," Caitlin urged a quiet, thin woman who kept her eyes focused on the ground.

"Ah, that I couldn't," the woman murmured. "'Twouldn't be fair."

"Come on, now," said Caitlin. "You're expecting again, aren't you?"

The woman drew her shawl tighter around her. "Aye, that I am. Seems I scarce wean one of them and another gets started."

"It doesn't just happen all of its own accord," Caitlin chided her gently.

"Ah, that I do know."

"Mickleen Boyle should be more careful with you, less demanding."

Mrs. Boyle gave her a smile of startling sweetness. "And who's to say it's him doing the demanding?"

Caitlin laughed appreciatively. The Irish, Wesley reflected, spoke openly and candidly of matters the very mention of which would send most self-respecting Englishwomen into a dead swoon.

From the wall walk, Curran's whistle shrilled a warning. The thud of hoofbeats hammered on the road outside the gates. Like ants whose hill had been disturbed by a giant foot, the people of Clonmuir snatched up the fresh stores and scurried off to hide them.

Into the yard rode Logan Rafferty, flanked by four burly retainers.

Despite the weather, Magheen dropped her shawl and, with a spicy sway of her hips, minced past him on the pretext of admiring Aileen Breslin's newly knitted hood.

Making a great show of ignoring her, Rafferty dismounted. His big, well-fed body was a marked contrast to the condition of the people of Clonmuir.

To Wesley's constant amazement, no one ever questioned Rafferty, ever wondered why he flourished while others starved.

"Still playing host to the enemy, I see," Logan boomed, glaring at Wesley.

"My business," Caitlin reminded him.

"But that could change," said Logan. "I've a new proposal to bring my wife to heel."

Across the yard, Magheen went completely still, listening.

"Oh?" asked Caitlin.

"Give me the Englishman."

"What?"

"Instead of the dowry, I'll take Hawkins."

Wesley marched forward. "Now, just a bloody minute—"

"So simple," said Rafferty, ignoring him. "Magheen could be back where she belongs by nightfall."

"At the cost of a man's life?" asked Caitlin. "For that is what it would be, would it not, Logan?"

"And how many Irish lives has the scoundrel taken?" Logan demanded.

"This breaks the rules of combat," said Tom Gandy.

Rory Breslin clapped a paw over Gandy's mouth. "Pipe down, you whey-faced imp!"

"Combat?" Rafferty's thick eyebrows clashed. "What's this to do with combat?"

Wesley sharpened his attention on the big Irishman. By God, Rafferty truly didn't know about the Fianna. And from the closed look on Caitlin's face, she didn't want him to.

"We're at war," she said. "Sure that's all Tom meant."

"All the more reason for me to be taking the *seonin* in hand," said Logan.

Wesley decided he would rather be taken in hand

by a banshee. Yet he felt a twist of sympathy when he saw Caitlin's face, pale and strained with torn loyalties. She glanced from Magheen to Logan, and back again to her sister.

An idea smacked Wesley on the head. Before he could talk himself out of it, he planted himself in front of Rafferty. "Suppose we make a wager. If you win, I'll go with you and Magheen comes too. And if I win—"

"You'll not have your freedom, wager or no," said Tom, hiking up his pants.

"Nor will I be agreeing to change my demands," Logan said.

"Then I'll settle for a forfeit from Caitlin."

She took a step forward. "What forfeit?"

He let a smile glide across his face. "Something that's well within your means to give me."

"But—"

Tom put his hand on her sleeve. "Hush, perhaps the *Sassenach* can help us solve our problem."

"Those are your stakes," said Rafferty to Wesley. "What is your game?"

"A horse race," said Wesley.

Logan threw back his head and guffawed, joined by his men. "A horse race, you say? I accept."

"No," said Caitlin.

"You think I can't best a tight pants?" Logan demanded.

"I'm the MacBride, and I say no."

"I proposed an honest wager," Wesley told her softly. He wished he could reach out to her, cradle her head against his shoulder, kiss away the lines of strain on her face.

"You've no right to offer yourself as part of the stakes," she retorted. "You belong to me."

His grin widened slowly. "Then you'd best pray I win, sweetheart."

While appreciative laughter rose around them, she blushed like the summer dawn. Wesley drew her aside, out of earshot. "Look, it's a way to put Rafferty in his place."

"No one puts Logan in his place, especially on a horse. His mother swears he came into the world screaming for a mount. No one can outride him, no one but—" She bit her lip.

"No one but Caitlin MacBride," he finished for her.

She scuffed her bare foot at the hard ground. "I have never beaten Logan in a race."

"Because you couldn't? Or wouldn't?"

Her silence gave him the answer. He did understand this woman, her frustration and the delicate balancing act she performed. "Let me best him for you, Caitlin."

"His horse is superior to any you could ride."

"Not so."

"What the devil do you mean? Our ponies can't best the mare. They're bred for endurance, not speed."

"I'll ride the black."

"What?"

"I said, I'll ride the black."

"No." She drew back, her eyes as hard as topaz stones. "No one rides the black. No one but me."

"It's the only way," said Wesley. "The black's my one chance."

"But he's mine, he—" Her mouth snapped shut, and pain glimmered like unshed tears in her eyes. He longed to know how she had come by the animal and why it meant so much to her. But now was not the time for discussions of the heart.

"I must ride the black," he said.

"I don't even know that you can ride."

He remembered the battle at Worcester, remembered outriding a troop of Parliamentarians by leaping a series of hedgerows. The memory brought with it a surge of self-confidence.

"I can ride," he said simply.

"The black will kill you." The cold wind snapped over her, brushing strands of gold hair across her lips.

"And what is one less Englishman to you?"

"An excellent point." She called over her shoulder, "Brigid! Fetch the black and saddle him."

Rory stood arguing loudly with Rafferty. "We can't let him ride. Sure he'll just seize the opportunity to escape."

"If the black doesn't wrap him around a tree, I'll be after bringing him in line," Logan said.

The thought of escape burned across Wesley's mind like a streak of lightning through a midnight sky. But he doused it with a flood of rationalization. He had to carry out his plan for Caitlin and set his daughter free from Cromwell.

Rafferty's swaggering confidence boded well for Wesley. The Irish lord was too sure of himself, too sure by far. Wesley knew how to exploit overconfidence.

But when the black arrived, bridled and saddled, with fire in its eyes, Wesley felt the first uncomfortable twinge of doubt. The beast was as wild as the breakers hurling themselves at the rocks of Connemara. Its long, slender legs danced over the hard packed surface of the yard. The wind tossed its mane, and its nostrils flared. The horse jerked its head around, spied Caitlin, and seemed to settle somewhat.

Wesley held out his hands for the reins. The black yanked back its head and sidled away.

"There now, my pretty lad," crooned Wesley. "It's

all right. You're for a ride now, aren't you?" The black stood still, head hanging in false submission that could, at any moment, explode into revolt. With his eyes on the tense withers, Wesley took hold of the saddle. The old, well-oiled leather creaked in the waiting silence.

Wesley put his foot in the stirrup. Before he could even swing his other leg over, the black sidled again, sending him bouncing to the ground.

"So it's a game you're playing." Wesley ground his teeth against the bruising pain. He tried again, and this time anticipated the horse's direction, landing squarely in the saddle. "The stirrups are too short," he said. "Brigid?"

Suppressing laughter, the girl came forward and lengthened the stirrups. Wesley sat transfixed by the feel of the horse beneath him. Never had he felt such fine, strong bones, such beautiful form, the coiled speed evident in every tightly knotted muscle.

Brigid retreated. Everyone, from the youngest child to the oldest man, edged back and watched.

Wesley's legs tightened around the black ever so slightly.

The stallion jolted into motion. Its four hooves left the ground at once. Its back arched like a bow and then snapped. Wesley felt himself flung like a rock from a catapult, propelled into the cold gray sky.

He fell fast and hard as if a giant fist pounded him into the ground. His bones compressed. His lungs emptied of air.

Breathless, with lights winking before his eyes, he heard distant, raucous laughter. White heat flashed in his mind. His soul shivered. "Not now," he muttered, but it was too late. He felt himself swirling away toward a familiar blinding nothingness.

Caitlin rubbed her eyes. It had happened so quickly, so predictably. The seemingly docile behavior of the black, then the wild detonation of motion. Hawkins had fallen like a rag doll; now he lay unmoving and not breathing, in the dust. She had been prepared for the reaction of the stallion. She had been prepared for the laughter that sifted through the cold breeze.

The one thing she wasn't prepared for was the fear that streaked through her.

She dropped to her knees beside him and turned his face to her.

A pallor lay over his cheeks, the flesh taut over a bone structure that, in repose, she found achingly beautiful. "Mr. Hawkins," she said. "Mr. Hawkins, can you hear me?"

He opened his eyes. The unusual gray-green irises reflected the clouds flying in the wind. She sensed a difference in him; a distant glazed look made him more of a stranger than ever.

"The pain has gone," he said. It was the same wonderful voice but the round tones sounded even richer, even deeper, even more compelling. The words he spoke struck her with their oddness. Then he took her hands, and the glowing heat of palms warmed her fingers. She gazed into his eyes, seeking answers to questions she could not voice. Hawkins put her hands aside and stood, staggering only slightly as he walked toward the black.

"The fall's stolen his wits," muttered Rory.

Grinning, Logan reached for Magheen. "Come along, wife. Let's go home and find our bed."

Magheen wrung her hands, torn between being won honorably by her husband and regretting the cost of it.

Oblivious to the mutterings, Hawkins walked directly to the black, which stood trailing its reins in the dust. Its withers trembled with wildness.

Hawkins laid his palm on the horse's large head. The stallion's rolling, white rimmed eyes seemed too calm, and Caitlin wondered if the animal, too, felt the strange heat of the Englishman's touch. "You are a beast of the earth," Hawkins said quietly, "a creature of the wind. And I am your master."

The black dropped its head. Hawkins took the reins and mounted in a graceful leap.

And, to the gaping astonishment of everyone present, he rode the horse out the main gate and walked it at a leisurely pace to the head of the boreen. A few of the onlookers discreetly chewed their thumbs in the old sign against sorcery.

"Damn!" Logan mounted and tore after the Englishman while the others hurried to the gate.

Aileen twisted the fingers of both hands into crosses. "The devil admire him! He's put the beast under an enchantment."

"Nonsense, woman," Tom Gandy snapped. He slid a sidelong glance at Caitlin. "Hawkins has a way with wild things."

The wind stirred little dust eddies over the skelped earth of the boreen. Breathless, Caitlin gazed at the church a mile distant. Then, half frightened of the *Sassenach*'s alien speech, she looked at Hawkins.

Like an awakening dreamer, Hawkins shook his head. Amazement shone on his face, and he sent Caitlin a lopsided grin. "That was easier than I'd expected."

A feeling of relief gentled the rhythm of her heart. So, he was back to his jaunty English ways. The mist seemed to have lifted from his eyes. He sat the stallion—the mad widowmaker—with ease. Man and horse moved as one, muscular thighs wrapped around muscular hide, and the unmistakable anticipation of speed evident in Hawkins's face. He held his wrists loose and easy, his back supple, ready to bend with the motion.

Ah, Logan, thought Caitlin, you're in for it now.

"Easy?" she said. "The beast tossed you off like a load of seaweed."

The smile lingered about his lips. "Did he now?" Reaching down, he snatched her hand. "A kiss for luck, then, Caitlin?"

She flushed at the thought of kissing him. She snatched her hand away. "Remember your parole, Mr. Hawkins."

"And remember the wager, Caitlin." His easy grin was full of promises she could not fathom. The certainty in his tone made Caitlin shiver—not with fear or cold, but with a feeling she dared not put a name to.

Logan galloped up and slid his horse to a halt. "Ready, Englishman?"

"To give you a mouthful of my dust?" asked Hawkins. "Certainly."

Caitlin stepped aside, her back to the press of excited onlookers. The Irish took horse racing seriously. And when the race pitted Irish against English, and the stakes determined the fate of the beauteous Magheen, the contest took on the importance of a high holiday.

Tom Gandy lifted an alderwood staff. "Take your marks," he shouted. "You'll go to the church and back."

Hawkins's gaze focused on the distant steeple. Logan's knees tensed. The staff sliced through the air. "Go!"

Both horses shot forward in an explosion of speed. Sand sprayed over Caitlin. Dragging strands of wind-blown hair from her eyes, she knew what the outcome would be. The black's gallop sang in a rhythm as inevitable and unfaltering as a heartbeat. The chase to the steeple belonged to him and him alone.

Hawkins rode with far more style and grace than one would expect from a Roundhead horse soldier. He bent low over the black's straining neck, his ruddy hair bright against the ebony hide. Over the thud of hooves, Caitlin heard Hawkins let out a wild yelp of sheer exuberance. That yell spoke to the soul of her, for she, too, knew the exhilaration of a fast ride.

The mare had the great unfailing heart of the Irish-bred horse and strove to the last inch of her ability. But Caitlin knew, as she had known from the moment Hawkins had bewitched the stallion into obedience, that all the mare's efforts would be in vain.

Magic flowed in the black, born of centuries of breeding for beauty and speed. The sight of him in full gallop brought forth thoughts of the mysterious land that spawned the extraordinary breed, and still more thoughts of the man who had—

"He's going to break and run!" bellowed Rory.

Hawkins reached the church ahead of Rafferty. Horse and rider disappeared behind the bleached stone building.

"The treacherous devil!" Rory raked Caitlin with his furious eyes. "See how it is with the *Sassenach*!"

Caitlin pressed her hands to her chest as if to keep the heart from being torn out of her. Mother Mary, why had she trusted him? Why—

Hawkins appeared on the other side of the church. He doffed an imaginary hat to his sputtering opponent, then galloped back to the gate. Logan made a valiant final effort, but finished four lengths behind Hawkins.

Indecision held the spectators silent and still. If they cheered Hawkins, would it seem disloyal to the Irish lord? Yet if they hissed at the winner, would it seem disloyal to the MacBride?

Only Tom Gandy let loose with sheer exuberance.

"A grand, fine show!" He grinned at Caitlin and danced a little jig. "Now, what do you suppose our guest will have as his forfeit?"

Caitlin watched breathlessly as Hawkins and Logan trotted their horses to the strand where they would let the mounts walk off the tension of the race. The sea rushed up to meet them on the sandy beach.

They were so alike, the Irish lord and the English soldier. Both more handsome than any man had a right to be. Both powerful and forceful. They might have been friends had they found themselves on the same side of a conflict. Ireland might have a chance if they were allies.

Absurd. Logan Rafferty was determined to have Magheen at the price he demanded, and John Wesley Hawkins was an English invader. Neither cared a dram for the security of Ireland.

Hawkins rode to Caitlin's side and dropped to the sand with a quiet thud. Handing the reins to Brigid, he took a step toward Caitlin.

She looked anywhere but at him. She noticed the bellowslike heaving of the black's sides, the sleekness of its hide in the noonday sun, the sharp imprints of its hooves in the sand. The crowd pressed close, their unspoken curiosity pounding louder than the surf. A rook sang out as it swirled through the crags.

His rough, cold hand grasped her chin. Her heart jolted as she gazed into his moss gray eyes.

"You owe me a forfeit, Caitlin MacBride," he said. The breeze plucked at strands of his hair, curling them against his windburned cheeks.

She jerked her head away. "Just what is it you want, Mr. Hawkins?"

"A kiss, Caitlin MacBride. I'll have a kiss from you."

The breath left her chest in a rush. Inhaling slowly, she drew in the cold salt air. "That's your forfeit?"

"Yes. A taste of you."

"I declare to my soul, this is getting interesting," whispered Aileen Breslin.

"It's an outrage," Rory snapped.

Caitlin challenged her prisoner with a furious stare. "I'd rather kiss a natterjack."

"You'll have to settle for me instead."

She should be grateful. In truth the request was modest enough. Yet her nerves rattled like dried reeds in the breeze. She asked, "Why?"

His laughter flowed like warm mead from a crystal goblet. "Do you really have to ask?"

"I'm asking."

"Because I want to know if the MacBride tastes like a woman, or a warrior."

Her face heated. "That's absurd."

"It's my request and my prerogative to be as absurd as I please. You knew the stakes. Will you have it said that the MacBride breaks her word?"

Her patience snapped. She wanted nothing more than to have done with the affair and be off about her duties. The spoils of the last raid needed to be tallied and stored. And Magheen was no doubt girding herself for a major row.

"Very well," Caitlin snapped. Placing her hands against the wall of his chest, she lifted up on tiptoe and brushed her lips over his cheek. "There's your forfeit, Mr. Hawkins."

She pivoted and marched away, praying all the while that people would think the color came to her cheeks from the bite of the wind, not from embarrassment.

His large hand clamped down on her shoulder, and he pulled her around to face him. "You call that a kiss?"

"And what would you be calling it?" she flung at him.

"I've found more pleasure having corn pecked by a chicken from the palm of my hand."

In spite of herself, Caitlin burst out laughing. "The English have strange tastes."

Sounds of mirth drifted from the gathered crowd. Some tried to sidle closer. Tom Gandy made a shooing motion and kept them back.

"Caitlin." Hawkins touched her cheek. "That wasn't quite what I had in mind."

"Oh, for heaven's sake," she burst out, "do you not see how silly you're being?"

"It's only silly if you continue to shy from me like a maiden. You're the MacBride. You've done worse than kiss an Englishman." His hands held her fast at the arms, and he bent to whisper in her ear. "I won the forfeit." His breath caressed the curve of her ear. "I want to feel the fullness of your lips with my own. I want to slide them open with my tongue and taste the dark inner sweetness of your mouth. I want to feel your body pressed to—"

"That's enough, Mr. Hawkins!" Summoning the last of her composure, she said, "You've made your point."

His hands lifted to her shoulders. "Well? I'm waiting."

She suppressed a shiver. Kissing in the manner he shamelessly described was so . . . so intimate. It was surrendering a part of herself she held close and inviolable. "No," she said.

His fingers trailed up and down her arm, the motion at once soothing and unsettling. She clutched her shawl around her shoulders.

"You're afraid," he said, the amazement of sudden revelation lighting his face. "By God, Caitlin, I never thought I'd find the one thing you fear."

"I'm not afraid," she said.

"You've never been kissed before, have you?"

She looked beyond him, her vision blurring as memories swept over her. Ah, she'd been kissed. Once. Alonso had kissed her once. He had held both her hands lightly, as if they were fragile crystal. She recalled his handsome face, dark and tender, the tumble of inky hair over his noble brow, the sculpted bow of his mouth. Their lips had met lightly, two butterflies colliding by accident and then winging away.

Caitlin MacBride had lived for four years on that too-brief moment.

"I've been kissed before," she said crisply.

One side of his mouth lifted in a half smile. "We'll see about that, love."

He caught her against him. Far off down the strand, Rory Breslin made a sound of outrage and then fell silent. Caitlin stared at Hawkins. Echoes of the enchantment that had graced their first meeting sang through her mind. A mystical bond tugged her toward him, a bond as inevitable as the pull between the moon and the tide.

His arms closed her against him, bands of strength keeping her in, keeping the world out. She became aware of her breasts against his chest and the scent of wind, horse, and man that clung to him. The steady thud of his heart pulsed against her.

Somewhere in the back of her mind, she knew that one simple cry would bring a troop of warriors down upon Hawkins. One simple cry would set her free. One simple cry would rob her of the wonder she felt in his embrace.

"All right," she said. "The MacBride keeps her promises."

The Englishman's kiss began with a smile. The smile of a gentle sorcerer, the smile that called to the very heart of her. His lips touched her forehead at the hairline and tingled down to her cheekbone. She tried to turn her head away but he caught her chin with his thumb and forefinger and held her still. His caressing kisses danced over her face, as light as the rain in springtime. Caitlin stood spellbound, a stranger to herself.

The wild, fey believer inside her blazed to life. *Let him*, said a voice from another world. *Just for now, do not fight him.*

His mouth grazed hers. It felt nothing like a butterfly's wing. The warm breeze of his breath tasted sharp and smoky with the essence of the usquebaugh he had drunk earlier. He pressed more insistently, sharing the moist secrets of his mouth.

Wonder grew up like a magic forest around her. The people on the strand, even the sea at her back and the sand beneath her feet, floated away in a tide of sensations too new and too baffling to name. She stood alone with John Wesley Hawkins at the very center of the world. An ache started in her neck, for she had bent it back, but she welcomed the discomfort as proof of the vibrant life surging through her.

The endless kiss took Caitlin out of herself and freed the yearnings she had kept bridled for years. She no longer remembered who she was. She had been put on this earth for the sole purpose of drowning in the arms of this Englishman.

True to his word, Hawkins moved his tongue tantalizingly in the channel between her lips. She opened for him, felt the tender plunge of his tongue and the vibrations of the sound he made in his throat. His hands slid up her sides and hooked her beneath the arms, hauling her ever closer while his thumbs made circles beneath her breasts. She felt suddenly and unaccountably soft, sweetly heavy. Womanly.

A heated drowsiness slid through her veins. With tentative curiosity, she put out her tongue, gliding it into the warm home of his mouth. He sucked at it in a rhythm that matched the long pulsebeats of their hearts.

Caitlin rose giddily, a leaf on an updraft of warm air, turning, reaching, beckoned by the diffuse golden light behind her closed eyes. She clutched at him, filling her hands with the artistry of his masculine form. She needed something badly, something that was as vital to her as the air she breathed. Hawkins, with his deft hands and narcotic kisses, dangled fulfillment like a glittering jewel before her. Closer, she wanted to be closer still, with nothing between them save their own heated flesh.

The pressure of his mouth eased. He drew away, holding her at arm's length.

Disoriented, Caitlin found herself drawn into an almost forgotten memory. She had once gotten a long thorn stuck through the fleshy part of her hand. The pain had not started until Aileen had drawn the thorn out.

A pain not unlike the one she felt now.

Hawkins filled her vision, broad shoulders and shaggy head framed by the crags and cliffs of Connemara. He had a look of astonished delight on his face, while dangerous banked fires smoldered in his eyes.

Still gripping her shoulders, he stepped back and said, "Look me in the eye, Caitlin MacBride, and tell me you've been kissed before."

8

In the next week, Magheen sulked more than ever and bossed the servants unmercifully. Rory Breslin wished aloud that Rafferty had won the wager and carried off both Magheen and the Englishman. Darrin Mudge complained that Jimeen O'Shea had stolen one of his pregnant ewes. Jimeen countered by setting fire to Mudge's booly hut. More refugees arrived, a group of old men and young children who reported in dire tones that their womenfolk had been carried off by the Roundheads.

And through all the turmoil and all the arguments pushed the memory of the Englishman's kiss.

Indecent, Caitlin told herself.

Incredible, said the fairy devil inside her.

I would go to confession if Father Tully hadn't disappeared.

You'd not confess the passion you felt during that kiss even under torture.

It's Alonso, Caitlin insisted. The kiss made me forget Alonso. He made me feel like a madonna.

Painted icons never have any fun, countered the

fairy devil. *Hawkins makes you feel like a woman.*

"Don't be kindling me, you great mutton-wit!" Tom Gandy's angry shout carried across the hall to Caitlin.

Sighing in exasperation, she went to the round table to see what Rory and Tom were arguing about this time.

"Look now, you wee schemer." Rory jabbed a finger at Gandy's chest. "And what is it you think you would be up to entirely, using my stout turf cart to be after the dulse?"

Gandy thrust the finger away. "'Tis a high wonder, Rory Breslin, if you are not the dumbest creature God ever put breath into. The dulse is edible and we can gather it right off the fine wide strand."

Rory made a terrible face. "The weed stinks, imp, and I'll not have it in my—"

"Hush, both of you. I'm weary of the yammering!" Caitlin burst out. "Rory, you'll let Tom use your cart and thank God for food the English can't take from us." She threw aside her shawl, stormed out of the hall, and marched to the stables.

"Come along," she said to the black. "We'll have a grand long ride, just the two of us."

But as she led him across the yard, she felt his gait falter and heard a soft thud. One horseshoe lay like an inverted smile in the dirt.

"Blast," muttered Caitlin. She started to call out for Liam the smith. Then she remembered his arm, still healing from the break he'd taken the night they had captured Hawkins.

Her luck had gone bad that night, and showed no signs of improving.

She considered summoning Rory. But his heavy hand with the hammer could damage the hoof. She bent and retrieved the shoe. "On with you, *a stor*," she said. "I'll do the job myself."

"With my help," said the resonant English voice that sounded in her dreams, yet never failed to startle her.

She glared at Hawkins. With his Irish garb and piratical smile, he looked indecently handsome. "And what would you be knowing about the fine art of shoeing a horse?"

"Enough of the smith's craft."

"Smithing is serious business, Mr. Hawkins. Sure didn't the smith refuse to make the nails used at the Crucifixion?"

He tucked his thumbs into his wide, thick belt. "Then who made them?"

"Why, 'twas the lowly tinker, and isn't misfortune on the tinker ever since and the smith a respected artisan?"

"Then I'm in good company," he declared.

"I'd not risk letting a treacherous Englishman lay hands on my horse. One false blow of the hammer and you'd ruin him."

"Caitlin." His big hand stroked the black's smooth cheek. "Does he balk at my touch?" The animal stood still, in calm acceptance. Ever since the race, the black had—to Caitlin's great annoyance—taken to Hawkins. "I don't know where this animal came from or why he's here, but I suspect there's not another like him in the world. God's truth, if I feared any chance of my damaging him, I'd cut off my hand."

The urge to believe him nagged at her, but she said, "Your hand, your head, Englishman. It doesn't matter. None of your parts are worth the sum of this horse."

"I value a good horse as much as you do."

"Come along, then. You may as well earn your keep." She led the black to the forge barn and looped the reins around a stone post outside.

Hawkins stepped inside. Flails and scythes hung on the wall along with an array of horseshoes. Caitlin selected one, laying it on a bench. "This is already forged for the black. Liam always keeps some in supply."

Hawkins placed it on the anvil. "I'll shoe him hot," he remarked, "for a better fit."

"Where did you learn that?"

He picked up a set of bellows and pumped them at the embers. "In the west of England—during my cavalier days."

She pressed back against the stone wall of the building. "You were a cavalier?"

"Aye."

"But you're with the Roundheads now."

"Aye."

"Why? I demand to know, Mr. Hawkins."

He gave her a slow, lazy smile designed to conceal the hooded look in his eyes. "Because Cromwell is Lord Protector of England now, and he has ordered me to stand with the Commonwealth."

She came away from the wall, planting herself inches from him. "Just like that, you'd abandon your loyalty to the Stuart prince?"

"It didn't happen 'just like that,' Caitlin." Heat roared from the furnace, and ashes plumed to the hole in the roof. He set aside the bellows, took hold of the hem of his tunic, and peeled the garment over his head and down his arms. "Believe me, my loyalty to Cromwell runs no deeper than the scars on my back."

Stripped to the waist and gilded by firelight, he made a picture she saw only when she closed her eyes during one of Gandy's hero tales. Muscles ridged his stomach. Red-gold hair gleamed on his chest and came together in a V pointing downward as if indicating something important.

He grinned, pleased by her scrutiny. "You make a hard job easy, Cait. No wonder men follow you into battle." He turned to rummage in the box for tools. "I'll need to forge new nails."

"Make them slender," she said. "I'll have no split hooves."

He thrust a nail rod into the fire. While it heated, he turned to her. "God, Cait, you are lovely as the sunset."

She huffed in disbelief. Her fingernails were chipped from helping the fishermen patch the curragh. Hours ago, she had braided her hair, but most of the tawny strands had escaped to swirl in disarray about her face. Bits of tar smudged her apron, and the hem of her kirtle sagged.

"Blarney," she said. "If your English ladies fall for such praise, more fool they."

He moved closer. She started to step back, but stopped herself. No. She would not give him the satisfaction of intimidating her.

"You wanted to humiliate me in front of my people."

"Perhaps it was a way to get them to view you as a woman, with a woman's needs, instead of simply their chieftain, the settler of their arguments and the hand that feeds them."

"I know what you see," she retorted. "You see an Irishwoman whose home and lands you mean to plunder for Cromwell."

He winced. "I see a woman. A passionate, desirable woman. I cannot call you beautiful, nor pretty, nor comely."

Caitlin hated herself for the lump of disappointment that dropped like yesterday's porridge in her stomach. "No, and I'm not after asking you to."

"You are all of those things, Caitlin," he went on as if she hadn't spoken. "And yet you are none of them."

"Now you *are* talking blarney."

"No, but I'm at a loss. I'm usually glib with words. I know how to say things to women and I know how they'll respond. But you're different. Beauty is a pruned rose blooming on a trellis. Pretty to look at, but ordinary. And you are not ordinary." He moved his shoulders. Mounds of muscle swelled and relaxed with the motion.

"Words cannot give shape to you." He reached out and pulled her against him. She felt his smooth skin warmed by the fire, the undulation of muscles surrounding her, protecting her. The strange feeling passed like a warm breeze through her. No one ever protected Caitlin MacBride.

He bent to whisper in her ear. "Let my tongue not stumble over words, Caitlin. With you, my eloquence is one of hands caressing, like so . . . lips touching, like so . . ."

Stricken to her soul by his touch, his nearness, she stood unmoving while his mouth came down and savored hers with a lingering tenderness as if he were sampling a rare fruit. She became burningly aware of the texture of his lips, the varying pressure on her mouth, the slope of his neck and the raw silk of his hair twined through her fingers.

Only then did she realize she was clinging to him, offering herself with a wantonness that both shamed and enthralled her. With an effort of will, she lowered her hands, pressed them to the heated expanse of his chest, and stepped back.

"Your eloquence is wasted on me," she lied. Her lips felt moist and bruised, her body curiously alive, sensitive and on edge. "It's wrong. Dishonorable."

"Caitlin, no!" He took her by the shoulders, the gentle pressure of his hands unnerving her. "Men and women search for a lifetime to find what we've found together, to feel what we feel for each other. Here we have our destiny dropped upon us like a stroke of fate, and you say it's dishonorable. No, my love, praise all your Irish saints, for it's a miracle."

She turned away, wrapping her arms around her middle. He had to be mistaken. It was Alonso she wanted, Alonso who commanded her heart. She wouldn't succumb to an enemy's sweet embraces and false words of fate and destiny.

"It'll be a high miracle if you can shoe the horse," she said, swinging back to face him.

With his brows raised in challenge, Hawkins drew on a pair of thick leather gloves and set to work making nails. He took a rod of iron and drew it out with strokes of the hammer. Breaking off several nails with a header, he tossed the finished ones into the forge trough. Hissing steam permeated the air.

Caitlin regarded him through the diffuse mist. Steam softened the lines of his face and torso, while fire glow and shadows cavorted over his glistening flesh. His hair fell in a ruddy mane about his face and neck. He resembled an image from a dream, as warm and vibrant as sunshine.

He stopped working and smiled at her. "What are you thinking that makes you look at me so?"

"I'm thinking I'd best do something about you soon, Mr. Hawkins."

"Are you open to suggestions?" Setting aside an iron chisel, he brushed her cheek. The glove glided, hot and rough, on her skin.

She pushed his hand aside. "Not of that sort."

"Ah." He leaned against the bench and crossed his ankles, his booted toe pointing at the earthen floor. "The way I see it, you have few options. You can't send me back to Hammersmith. I'd reveal your identity as the chieftain of the Fianna. You can't set me free to wander, for you can't trust me not to sell your secret to the highest bidder."

"True," she said. "Perhaps I should have given you to Logan."

"That would have been a mistake. In the first place, I don't appreciate being cast in the role of a bride's dowry. In the second place, I'm smarter than Logan, and I'd be compelled to escape."

"You gave your parole."

"To you, Cait." His gloved hand came up again and brushed a tendril of hair from her brow. "Only you. Because I respect you, I'm bound by my word."

"Are you saying you don't respect Logan Rafferty?"

"No more than I respect a man-eating shark. Do you respect him?"

"He's an Irish lord, and my superior."

"That doesn't answer my question."

She hesitated. Logan was arrogant and presumptuous. But he was also her brother-in-law who had Magheen in agony with love for him. "Aye," she said softly. "I respect him."

"Then why haven't you told him about the Fianna?"

"Surely you can guess, Mr. Hawkins."

"I'd rather hear your answer."

"Logan has his own ideas on how to deal with the English, and they happen to differ with mine. The success of the Fianna cuts at his pride. If he knew of my involvement, he'd put a stop to our activities."

"How have you managed to hide it from him?"

"The same way we hide it from everyone else. We strike swiftly and cleanly, like a storm in the night. Logan believes it's the work of exiled soldiers from Connaught. He has no reason to question me."

Finger by finger, Wesley plucked off the gloves. "Do you worry about Magheen telling him?"

She smiled. "For the present, Magheen wouldn't

toss him a rope if he were drowning. And you seem to view my sister as most men do, as a pretty ornament with no more depth than a soup trencher. I know better. Magheen is a MacBride and loyal to me."

He picked up his tunic and pulled it back on over his head.

Caitlin breathed a sigh of relief, for the sight of his bare chest scattered her thoughts and chipped away at her resolve.

"Then that narrows the choices to two," he concluded, the white fabric muffling his voice.

"And what might those choices be, Mr. Hawkins?"

His head emerged from the neckline, his hair gloriously ruffled. He was a fine lion of a man. Not for the first time, she wished his sympathies lay with the Irish rather than Cromwell.

"You can either kill me. Or marry me," he said.

His suggestion slammed into her with the force of a blow. She reeled back. "No!"

He bent and began fishing nails out of the bucket. "No to what?"

"To both choices. I will neither kill you in cold blood, nor marry an Englishman."

"I'm relieved by the former, but you'll have to explain the latter. Why won't you marry me?"

"It isn't obvious?"

An intoxicating smile slid across his face. "Not with the taste of you still fresh as the dew on my lips."

She willed away the blush that heated her cheeks. "I would never marry a man whose aim is to subjugate Ireland, a man who knows I would fight to the death to keep my people free. Besides being *Sassenach*, you could be a—a criminal or an outlaw of some sort."

Something dangerous flashed in his eyes, but the look was so quickly gone that she could not put a name to it.

"What sort of man would you marry, then?" asked Hawkins.

Leaning against the stone wall of the forge barn, she closed her eyes.

A Spanish nobleman as dark and beautiful as a song at midnight. A man who kept the true faith in his heart. A man who set her upon a pedestal and worshiped at her feet. A man who shared her desire to keep her people free.

She opened her eyes. Hawkins stared at her with a stark yearning that caught at her heart.

"Oh, God," he said.

"What is it now, Mr. Hawkins?"

"I would forfeit the very surety of my soul to be the man who brings that look upon your face, Caitlin MacBride."

"That's a high price to pay, Mr. Hawkins."

"It's useless anyway. You've obviously conjured up some hero no mere mortal could ever rival. The man you dream about doesn't exist."

He does, she thought with an ache in her chest. He does. "Let's be about our business, Mr. Hawkins." She went outside.

She needn't have worried about his skill with the horse. The hot shoe bedded into the horn of the hoof. A little cloud of blue smoke arose, neither worrying nor hurting the horse. Hawkins tapped the shoe on with a few swift, sure strokes, then cooled it with water.

A few moments later, they led the stallion across the yard.

"I'm going riding," said Caitlin.

"Let me come with you."

Ah, she wanted him to. They were so easy together, the two of them. Such an ill-matched pair, enemies who spoke together as old friends. "No," she forced herself to say.

"I won't try to escape."

"I have only your word on that. And an Englishman's word has no more substance than spindrift." Grasping the black's mane, she swung onto his back. Hawkins's gaze caressed her bare leg and foot.

"Are you sure you'll be warm enough?" he asked.

"Don't worry about me, Mr. Hawkins."

"Caitlin, I was born to worry about you."

"Fag an bealach!" came a cry from the gate. Children playing in the yard cleared the way.

Perched like a king atop Rory's cart laden with seaweed, and pulled by Curran Healy, Tom Gandy appeared through the main gate. "Got the beast shod again, have you?" he asked.

Startled, Caitlin said, "You've been out on the strand all day. How did you know?"

"A leprechaun told me." Tom tipped his hat, and the cart rolled past, leaving the fishy stench of *dulse* in its wake.

Hawkins scratched his head. "How *did* he know?"

"I've learned not to be after questioning Tom Gandy."

She rode off, but could not ride fast enough to escape the remembered burn of the Englishman's touch, the musical timbre of his voice, and the secrets he guarded in his eyes.

"Dying! I'm dying! Ach, *musha*, *yerra*, and bedad, Jesus save me!"

Alarmed by the pitiful cry, Caitlin sped through the hall, past silent huddled men and women who wept loudly and prayed desperately. In the passage behind the hall were offices and private apartments. She entered one that blazed with oil lamps and reeked of the peat smoke that wafted from a brazier.

On a pallet in the middle of the room lay a small figure, wailing in agony. "God, I'm dying of this cruel griping in me!"

Caitlin dropped to her knees beside him. The sight of his flushed face and glazed eyes filled her with terror and pity. "Tom? It's me, Caitlin. Curran said you took sick after eating the *dulse*."

"I be past sick." His head rolled to and fro on her father's best gullsdown pillow. "It's dying I am, my girleen. Strangled for all time in the big gut. St. Dympha pity me!"

Tears scorched Caitlin's eyes and blurred her view of Aileen Breslin, who knelt on the other side of the pallet. "Here, Tom." Aileen held out a cup. "Have a bit of the senna."

With a grimace, Tom turned his head away. "I'll not touch it, woman. You've put sheep scour in that!"

"Just a wee dropeen of the purgative," Aileen cajoled, "to give the drink strength."

"Please, Tom," said Caitlin. "Just a sip."

"*Yerra*, let me die in peace!" He turned his face into the pillow and doubled himself into a ball of agony. "Aye, 'tis strangled in the big gut I am, and no way to save myself. Soon the sidhe will come to frolic with my poor dead soul."

"Sure the Little People will think him one of their own," Rory said mournfully, stepping into the room.

Tom's terrible cries swept through Clonmuir, echoing in the stone corridors and coiling stairwells. Before long, the entire household had gathered in the sickroom and in the hall outside.

"Dying!" Tom burst out again and again. "I'm

dying, and there is no priest to ease my poor soul into eternity. It's damned, I am. Damned to the high fires for all time."

"That's for the Almighty to decide," Aileen assured him.

"Tom, no," said Caitlin. A devastating helplessness closed over her. Sickness was no enemy she could vanquish with lightning raids. "You're ailing, but you'll recover."

"Ach, *musha*, the end is hard upon me." His fever-bright eyes swam with sorrow and despair. His hot hand clung to Caitlin's. "For the love of God, I need a priest. Caitlin, *a stor*, if ever I've meant something to you, you'll find me a cleric."

"The priests are all gone from Ireland. But we shall pray for you, dear Tom. We'll pray very hard."

A tear slipped down his cheek. "Let them all come to me one last time, Caitlin," he said. "I would look upon the good folk of Clonmuir before I face judgment."

With a bleak and empty heart, Caitlin moved out into the passageway and motioned for the others to enter by turns. Women and children, even some of the men, sobbed with unabashed, heartfelt gusts.

Loudest of all was Rory Breslin, who snorted into a handkerchief and said, "The stubborn little imp. I'm sorry for every foul word I said to him. I never should have let him use my cart . . ."

"A priest," Tom wailed once again. "My soul from the devil, but I need a cleric!"

Her shoulders sagging with sorrow and frustration, Caitlin hurried into the chapel. The alcove nestled in a curve of the ancient curtain wall. Here she had prayed for her mother's soul. Here she had prayed for Alonso's return.

And now she came to beg mercy for Tom. Her hand shook as she lit a candle. Shadows flickered in the corners, uncertain company for her unquiet soul. She knelt before a statue of the Virgin, carved by her great-grandsire many years before.

The musty smells of damp stone and forgotten incense tinged the air. She pressed her palms together. The carved Virgin stared serenely down at her.

"Blessed Mother, help me," she whispered. "My darling Tom is dying, and he needs a cleric to ease his way to heaven. I don't know what to do."

"Is there truly no hope?" Hawkins knelt beside her.

She shot to her feet in a fury. "And what would an Englishman be caring about a dying Irishman? Sure if the Roundheads hadn't burned our fleet and fields, Tom would be feasting on peppered buttermilk and fresh meat instead of choking himself on seaweed!"

Hawkins's face paled. "Caitlin, I feel nothing but shame for what my countrymen have done to yours."

"Tom is leaving me," she snapped, not wanting to hear the sincerity in his voice, "and I cannot even do him the final favor of bringing a priest to cleanse his poor soul."

"Is it really so important, having a cleric?"

She rubbed a finger along the bridge of her nose. "You wouldn't understand, Mr. Hawkins. An Irishman's faith is his most precious possession. We endure a life of toil, but the hardships are bearable because of our faith. Knowing he'll pass on to a greater reward is Tom's only comfort."

Pain and mystery glimmered in Hawkins's shadowy regard. His shoulders sloped downward, weighted by invisible burdens. Her fury subsided into misery.

"Being shriven is important to Tom, then."

How did Hawkins know about the shriving? "Tom Gandy is a good man, but he's human and fallible. He has sinned and must answer for those sins. A final confession will cleanse him. But we have no one. No one." She pressed her hands to her eyes. "Why couldn't Daida have returned? I took wisdom and encouragement from Tom all my life. But I cannot fulfill his last request."

Wesley recognized the desolation in her face, in her posture as she stood before the Virgin. He'd seen the fear of death too many times. And he'd seen the ease the shriving had given to the survivors of the loved one.

His heart ached. He remembered the whispered confessions he'd heard in secret during his travels through England. He felt again the weight of the faith the people had placed in him. But with Caitlin the burden pressed harder, because she was so strong, because he cared so much. Because she needed him.

"Come here." He pressed her cheek to his chest, stroking her hair. She submitted willingly, shuddering a little with a quiet sob. The manipulative rogue inside him told him to seize the moment. She was vulnerable now, vulnerable to the betrayal he had conceived for her. The magic that had bound them from the very start revived the liberating, soul-deep conviction that he was never meant to be a priest. *Come away with me, Caitlin MacBride . . .*

Her need probed a soft spot in him. Despite his dire situation, despite his fear for Laura, he could not let Caitlin suffer. A decision rose within him, pushing through doubt and hesitation.

"Caitlin, if Tom were to be shriven your heart would be easier."

"Aye." Her breath fanned his neck. "Mine, and every other heart at Clonmuir."

It was madness to reveal even a part of his secret to the warrior woman who held him captive. Yet he heard himself saying, "I can help you."

She drew back. The evening sunlight slanted through a high cruciform window and found a warm, sparkling home in her sad eyes. "How?" she asked. "He needs a cleric, and you're obviously not—"

"I am." He took her face between her hands. Caitlin laughing was a sight to delight a man's spirit. Caitlin weeping was a sight to compel a man to sell his soul.

"I don't understand," she said.

"I'm a Catholic, Caitlin."

"Sure aren't we all—" Her mouth dropped open as she apprehended his meaning. "No."

"Aye, and was once a novice of the Holy Faith—"

"You're a hard and cruel liar."

"—trained at the seminary of Douai in France."

She swallowed, her throat rippling smoothly. "Douai. Isn't that where they train English priests to return to England and minister to Catholics?"

"Precisely."

She pulled away, looking him over as if seeing him with new eyes. "Then what were you doing with Hammersmith's army?"

Trying to save my daughter, he wanted to say. But Cromwell's threat hung like a thundercloud in his mind.

"Fighting for the Commonwealth." He tried to draw her back into his embrace.

She jumped away. "You sinner! You've taken sacred vows!"

"That's true."

"And yet you—you hold me and kiss me with lust in your heart. You make a sinner of me!" She fled toward the door.

He followed, grasping her by the arm. "Caitlin, listen to me. I sinned long ago when I chose the seminary, for I had no true vocation. I went to Douai to test my faith, and faith failed the test." He paused, grappling with the words. "Look at me, Caitlin. I am years past the age of a novice. I could not bring myself to make the final submission to the Church." Even if Laura had not appeared in his life and changed it irrevocably, he would not have taken holy offices.

He touched Caitlin's cheek, loving the feel of her soft skin under his finger. "At last I have found what I sought, Cait. Not in the Church, but in you."

"But it's wrong, it's—"

"Ah, the darkness is after me!" Tom's far-off wail swept into the chapel.

Yanking her arm from him, she said, "Can a novice administer last rites?"

"When a patient is *in extremis*, and there is no priest available, it is permitted."

"Can I believe you, Englishman?"

"I have no credentials to give you save my word, and the scars of torture." He touched his back to remind her of the healed lacerations that branded him.

"You were tortured for your faith? But I thought—" More loud wails drifted in through the passageway. Caitlin winced as if Tom's pain had found a way into her heart.

"Where did your chaplain keep his vestments?"

She tensed, hesitating. Another surge of grief keened through the castle. Her features took on the firmness of sudden decision. "This way."

A few minutes later, clad in a white cassock and smoke-colored robes, and armed with vials of holy water and olive oil, Wesley stepped into the sickroom.

For a moment no sound stirred the astonished silence. Then whispers erupted, hisses of outrage and disbelief.

"How dare he profane a priest's vestments?"

"Heresy!" "Blasphemy!" "He should be clifted like a diseased sheep!"

"Hush," said Caitlin. Quickly she related his tale. "We have no choice but to trust in his word." She faced Wesley with fire in her eyes. "The Almighty will exact a price if he's played us false."

Tom Gandy lay weaker than ever on the pallet. His tongue lolled out of his mouth and sweat beaded his forehead.

Wesley stood at the foot of the pallet. The torches and braziers haloed him in warm light.

Tom Gandy dashed the sweat from his eyes. "Ach, *musha*, my prayers be answered. A high miracle, it is!"

Wesley handed a globe-shaped censer to Curran, who had been the chaplain's acolyte. The spicy aroma of incense filled the room.

The sea lapped with a distant swish at the walls of Clonmuir. Rooks called through the twilight, and badgers chittered in the wood. Wesley studied the dying man, and a familiar futility welled inside him. The power and mystery of God beckoned, but dangled just out of his reach. Forbidden fruit.

A leaden weight descended on him. He was charged with accepting a man's sins and saving his soul. He did not know if he had the heart, the strength, to do so. His own soul was soot black with sins.

But for Caitlin MacBride he would attempt the impossible. He breathed in the incense. "We'll need privacy for—"

"Not so!" Tom interrupted. "They've been my friends in life. Would you have them abandon me as I die?"

"Of course not," said Wesley. "Whatever comforts you, Tom."

"Almighty God bless me, for I have sinned." Tom Gandy launched into his confession, his voice gathering strength as he spoke. "All my life I have been a

vain and wicked man, and greedy, too. Why, time
was, Red Niall and I caught seven nets full of herring,
and him with his wife and the wee ones hungering so,
and I did not give up my share."

"The Lord forgives your gree—"

"And God, remember the day old Jamesy went to
his reward? By my black soul, I'm not worthy to be
mentioned in the same day as Jamesy. Back in 'thirty-
six it was, and myself just a snip of a lad with an eye
for his daughter. Beauteous, she was, with her booza-
lums like bladders of fresh cream, and . . ."

"I remember that girl!" Rory Breslin cut in. "Sure
wasn't she the one what run off with a babe in her
belly?"

"Sure wasn't I the one what put it there?" moaned
Tom.

The stories went on and on—cattle raids, petty
thefts, lusty trysts, and sins of pride. Tom Gandy played
the bard of Clonmuir to the very last of his strength,
regaling the folk even with the sickness snatching away
his breath. People gathered close to hear. Some
couldn't keep from grinning; others jabbed each other
in the ribs and exchanged knowing nods of the head.

Twilight slid into deepest night. Wesley's back and
shoulders began to ache from kneeling motionless
beside Tom. He resisted the urge to stretch, to rotate
his neck and stamp some feeling back into his feet.

But the others sat enraptured by the soliloquy. Mugs
of poteen made the rounds, and even the doomed Tom
Gandy found the strength to take a quaff. "Sure and
wouldn't it be a cruel thing," he gasped, "if myself and
the cup should part without kissing . . ."

Wesley felt a yawn coming on. Too late, he put up
his hand to stifle it.

"Ah, the time has come." Tom sighed, interrupting
himself. "Dear Lord, I have told you but a wee bit of

my misspent life, but sure the idea must be upon you. I am ready to receive your blessing."

With the oil, Wesley used his thumb to draw the sign of the cross on Tom's forehead. *"Per istam sanctam unctionem . . ."* He murmured the words while entreating the Almighty to absolve Tom Gandy of his sins and take his soul unto the bosom of heaven.

His orator's voice and smooth Italianate Latin served him well. Tom's friends pressed close, their faces aglow with cautious amazement, then joy, then delight. And finally, heartfelt relief. He realized then how much a priest meant to them, even a failed one. The onus of their dependency sat like a bit of bad meat that upset his stomach.

Disconsolate, Rory shuffled forward to have a closer look. He trod on Magheen's bare foot. She let out a shriek and pinched him hard on the backside. Rory yelped. "Ouch! Just you wait until we have done with the imp, wench, and I'll—"

"Get some manners on you!" Aileen shook a finger at her overgrown son. "Faith, that you're acting like this and God visiting . . ."

While waiting for the squabbling to subside, Wesley slid a glance at Caitlin. She regarded him with equal measures of distrust and wonder. He had lied to her by omission. It was neither the first nor the last time he would do so.

I'm sorry, Caitlin.

Together, the people of Clonmuir and their reluctant shepherd fell to their knees in a vigil for the dying Tom Gandy.

Cold to the bone and stiff in every joint, Caitlin awakened at dawn. She had meant to spend the night in prayer but exhaustion had finally claimed her.

She pressed her palms against the chilled stone floor of the sickroom and blinked to clear her vision. A few others lay about, sound asleep. The smell of poteen and usquebaugh mingled with incense in the air.

Tom Gandy's pallet was empty.

Grief crashed into her with the force of a breaker on Connemara stone. She jumped up and stumbled out into the passageway. Gone! Her Tom was gone! He had died in the night, and she had not been there to mark his passing. Tears scorched her cheeks.

Damn Hawkins—damn them all—for not waking her. She sped through the passageway and burst into the hall.

The peat fire burned low, casting shadows against the lime-washed walls. One shadow loomed tall and broad, the other small and round, a plume nodding lazily above his head.

". . . and after the lady Siobhan passed, we went adrift, Wesley," Tom was saying. "You see, she was our anchor, the voice of all that is gentle in a harsh land." Tom paused to quaff from a large mug. "Pass me that herring, will you? I've a sharp hunger on me. Anyway, the *Sassenach* were on the advance and it only got worse when Cromwell came to power. And then Caitlin—"

"—is going to give your soul to the devil, Tom Gandy!" she hollered, striding toward the hearth.

His smile was brilliant, his color deep with robust health. "Are you now, girleen?"

Belatedly she remembered the tears on her cheeks and scrubbed them away with her sleeve. "I ought to . . ." Adequate threats eluded her. She glared at both of them. "A few hours ago you ripped my heart out, making me think you were dying. Now here you sit, swilling ale and eating herring as if you hadn't a care in the world."

"I was dying. But a miracle occurred."

"Don't you believe in miracles, Caitlin?" asked Hawkins.

"Not when they're brought about by a selfish bard and a lying Englishman!"

Hawkins cuffed Tom on the shoulder. "Tell her, then. It wasn't my doing."

A sheepish grin spread across Tom's face. "'Twas Aileen's sheep scour. My good man here persuaded me to swallow it. Then it wasn't a priest I needed, but a privy."

A sound of disgust burst from Caitlin. She stormed from the hall, pausing in the yard to wash her face at the well. Moments later, mounted on her stallion, she shot out of the main gate and streaked along the rocky fields toward the strand.

She could not outpace her anger. Hawkins had duped her and Tom had enjoyed it.

Before the pounding ride could drive the rage from her, she dropped to the sand and let the black run off at will. A few minutes later Hawkins trotted up on Clonmuir's best pony, a rangy stallion painted white and brown.

"Who gave you permission to leave the keep?" she demanded.

"Your steward." He dismounted and stood before her. The wind caught at his hair and burned high color into his cheeks. He must have washed and shaved, for he looked as fresh and clean as a cleric before Sunday mass.

Lord help me, thought Caitlin, a man has no right to look so appealing this early in the morning.

She was glad he had shed his priest's garb, for the sight of him clad in cassock and robes had stabbed at her conscience. Not that his borrowed tunic, tight trews, and knee boots pleased the eye any less. He seemed made for an Irishman's garb. A wolf in sheep's clothing.

"Well, I'm ordering you to go back," she said. "And no tricks, now. You've given your parole."

As if he hadn't heard her, he took her hand, holding her just firmly enough that she couldn't escape without a struggle. "Come walk with me, Caitlin. It's time we faced the matters that are between us."

She probed his gaze with her own and had a sudden flash of realization. Now she recognized the veiled sadness that always seemed to haunt his eyes. A confessor's eyes, they were, weighted by the sins of others.

He led her down the strand. The damp sand chilled the soles of her bare feet. The sea washed around great jutting rocks that thrust their sharp peaks into the morning sky.

In the distance lay her mother's forgotten seaside garden, overgrown and forlorn with memories. Caitlin bridled. "I won't go there with you."

"You must." He placed his free hand in the small of her back and gave her a gentle push. "It's where the enchantment started, Caitlin. A place for us to explore the magic."

Still she resisted. "Magic? Bah. You're worse than Tom Gandy."

He turned to face her. "What are you afraid of, Caitlin?"

I'm afraid of the way you make me feel, her heart cried out.

"Nothing," she said. "Let's go." Pulling away from him, she marched toward the garden. She skirted a calm tidal pool where the rising sun touched the surface with fire. Gorse and brambles choked the spaces between the rocks. The garden was ugly, barren, a scar upon the shore, all beauty scraped away by the wind from the sea and the turmoil at Clonmuir.

With bleak satisfaction, she said, "You see, there is no magic here."

He caught her against him so swiftly that she gasped. "That's because we haven't conjured a spell yet. But we will, my love."

"No." She tried to ease away but he held her fast. "You are my enemy. And you're pledged to God."

"Not anymore, Cait. Not since—"

"You took a vow of celibacy. Your lust condemns us both to hell!"

"What of your lust, woman?" The words burst from him on a rush of anger. He gripped her shoulders and held her away from him. "Damn it, you like this. You like the way our bodies fit together, and our mouths—"

"That's a lie, John Wesley Hawkins!" To her mortification, fresh tears stung her eyes.

He closed his eyes tightly and drew a long breath as if to calm himself. "Caitlin. Were I your enemy, I'd take this lovely neck of yours . . ." Very delicately, he traced her throat with his finger. "I'd wring the life from you, steal your horse, and hie away to Galway."

She knew he had the power to do so. She also knew, to the very depths of her soul, that he would never, ever harm her. But Lord, how much easier things would be if he were simply a murderer.

"I'm not going to do that, am I?" he asked softly.

"You can't."

"Would you like to know what I am going to do?"

"I have no interest in your plans."

His arms moved around her once again. Despite the chilly bite of the wind, she felt warm and protected and . . . cherished.

"Sit with me, Cait." He took off her shawl and spread it on a patch of sand. He drew her down beside him, and she went without protest, for already the force of the spell defied resistance.

He tucked her head into the lee of his shoulder. She hugged her knees to her chest. His hand moved up and down her arm, up and down, a slow, sleepy motion that made her feel soft inside like an undercooked egg.

"Cait, I want you to know exactly how I feel about you."

"A confession?" She laughed. "Sure you must be tired of confessions after last night."

"It's good to hear you laugh, Cait. I think you'll be surprised at what I say because no man has ever said these things to you."

"I hear nothing but words from a *Sassenach*," she said. "Lies are made of words."

"I know, Caitlin. That's why I'm going to make love to you. Not just with words, for I don't trust my tongue to say what's in my heart. I shall make love to you with my hands and mouth and body—"

"For pity's sake, Mr. Hawkins—"

"—so that you'll truly understand. I'm going to look at your bare breasts and put my hands there, probably my lips as well. I shall kiss you in places you never imagined being kissed, and then I'll slip my hands down your beautiful smooth belly and into your woman's place."

"No." A strange rapture stole the vehemence from her denial.

"You're hot there even now, aren't you, Caitlin?" he murmured. "I want you to think of the feel of my hands, massaging, writing poetry on your skin. When two hearts mesh as ours do, the coupling demands completion and release."

"And who says our hearts mesh? It's the plan of a treacherous blasphemer," she said.

"Shall I go on, Caitlin? Shall I tell you how you'll feel when I'm so deep inside you that—"

"I won't listen to this! You would treat me like a Roundhead's doxy—"

"No, my darling. I'll love the woman you keep hidden inside you. You've led men to battle, but never into your heart. Men respect you, they obey you, but they see you as a warrior. You've never had the chance to blossom."

She pulled back even as her heart leapt toward his honeyed promises. "You took a vow—"

"Even before I met you, I knew my vocation was a façade, a hiding place for a man who'd lost his soul, a man who hungered to belong somewhere, anywhere." He gathered her back into his arms. "Don't fight me, Caitlin. Our love was fated by powers stronger and wiser than mortals." He lowered his mouth gently, tenderly, shaping his lips to hers.

She tried to bolster her will with an image of her beloved Alonso. But the picture in her mind was hazy, diffuse, shrouded in a fog of desire that had nothing to do with the man of her past and everything to do with the man kissing her.

I am faithless, she thought. Where was the strength she was so proud of?

On fire with passion for the woman in his arms, Wesley found his conscience at odds with his purpose. He hated himself for misleading her with lies of love, hated himself even more for the betrayal to come.

But even self-recriminations could not stem the hot tide rising through him. Like the waves on the sand, passion licked at him, slapped down his scruples and made him aware that, even if he had lacked the motivation of Laura, he would move mountains to possess this woman.

She was sweet, the taste of her as fresh as dew, the tang of salt on her soft lips a heady potion. She moved her head artlessly to one side and her tongue brushed his lips, evoking a stab of need as vivid as the sting of a bee.

Battling the urge to plunge into her and stifle her protests with his mouth, he broke the kiss and gazed into her flushed and startled face.

Against his will and his plan to entrap her, he smiled. "I promised I would confess my heart to you."

"I don't want your words or your kisses." But her voice shook. Her eyes flooded with the need he had awakened in her.

"Caitlin, life is short, especially in Ireland. Last night, Tom lay at death's door. Only the whim of fate snatched him back among the living. You live a dangerous life. One day you might ride against the Roundheads and never come back. You would die having never known the fulfillment of being a woman."

"Bold talk, Englishman. I don't want to die at all. But if you think I suffer for wanting your kisses, you're wrong."

He framed her face between his hands. Amber facets flecked eyes so wide and deep that he fancied he glimpsed eternity. Her moist, love-bruised lips parted slightly as if she had been about to speak and had forgotten what she had meant to say.

Taking a deep breath, he prepared to speak the ultimate lie. He had rehearsed the line a hundred times. He knew just the amount of solemn sincerity to give each word. He strove for the same tone that had, many years before, lured duchesses into his arms, the tone that later brought secret Catholics to their knees in rapture.

"I love you, Caitlin MacBride." The words didn't come out as he had planned. For the first time since he was a gawky youth of fifteen, the bronze voice of

John Wesley Hawkins broke. The words sounded raw and raspy. As if he truly meant them.

She wore a look of startlement, wonder, and cautious acceptance.

My God, thought Wesley. It's working. She believes me.

Before the spell could break he rushed on. "It happened the first day I met you. Do you remember? You stood there gaping at me as if I were a ghost. You held yourself so straight and proud, you could have been a graven image. But your finger was bleeding. The instant I tasted your blood I knew you were a mortal woman, and that I would fall in love with you."

"You read too much into a chance meeting."

"No, my love. Open your mind and admit that something happened that night. I thought the feeling would fade but it has only grown stronger. I gave you my parole that I wouldn't leave you, but more than my word binds me to you. It's the feeling that spreads through me when I touch you, the magic of your smile and the certainty that we belong together."

She stiffened in his arms. "No, Wesley."

"My name on your lips is so beautiful to hear, a song from a fairy's harp. Say it again, Caitlin." He pressed a kiss to her throat just below her ear. "Say my name."

"Wesley." Her voice was soft, broken, and full of the need she tried so hard to conceal.

More than three years had passed since he had held a woman in his arms, yet even if it had been yesterday, the present moment would have felt wholly new to him. Caitlin was firm where others were soft, angular where others were curved. She was the brilliant sun while others faded in a sky filled with pale stars.

His long, heartfelt kiss drew an exotic sweetness from her lips and sent the heady essence of her purling through his veins. She was vulnerable beneath her layer of fierceness. He could feel her body trembling with a desire she could not conquer.

"Caitlin. Cait," he murmured. "A thousand times have I seen you in my dreams. Now I would look upon you with my waking eyes, and you'll show me how paltry my dreams are."

Endearments he would have had to force out for any other woman seemed to pour from his lips like sand through spreading fingers. He pulled loose the front lacings of her blouse. She clutched at the fabric. Her eyes flashed a wild, hunted look.

He leaned forward and kissed her, traced his tongue over the curve of her lips and along the ridge of her teeth. At length he drew back and pulled the blouse down over her shoulders.

She wore a rough-spun chemise beneath, laced across her chest. Wesley lowered his head and put his mouth to the cleft rising from the neckline. Ah, she was a dusky mystery there, all shadows and secrets, the taste and scent of her wild and fey, a flower in a dark forest.

His teeth found the lace of her chemise and he tugged at the frayed bow, then let the garment drift downward to pool around her waist.

With a gasp, she clasped her arms across her bosom. She gazed at him for long moments while the waves slid up to stir the sand, and a pair of sea eagles glided to their nest in the cliffs. With resolution hard on her face, Caitlin slowly lowered her arms. "There is something inside me that wants you, but—"

"Then listen to the voice of your heart."

Her breasts were beautiful, soft and full, the flushed tips pulled taut. "Sweet Jesu," said Wesley. "I knew you'd surpass my dreams. By God, Caitlin, your light torches in my blood." As he lowered his hands and head, he realized with a jolt of surprise that he no longer spoke words of idle flattery. His lips and tongue adored her, filled themselves with her.

With a hand so unsteady it surprised him, he lifted the hem of her kirtle and caressed her, his hands big and coarse on the silk of her skin. He slid his fingers over the curve of her hip, past wispy undergarments and downward into the secret warmth of her. Making a wordless Gaelic sound in her throat, she clutched at him.

"Shall I stop?" he whispered.

She covered his hand with hers. "Don't you dare."

He kissed her tenderly, almost chastely, while the movement of his hand was decidedly unchaste. She relaxed with a lovely rippling motion like that of a gentle stream moving over rocks.

The heat of her surrounded him and invaded his body. Her unabashed scrutiny settled on the commotion that strained against his trews. For a faltering moment he wondered if she were indeed a virgin, so direct was her gaze.

"My body has been awakened by women in the past," he confessed. "But never my soul. God, you bewilder me, Caitlin MacBride." He leaned forward to kiss her mouth.

A moan of anguish escaped her as she reached up to push him away. "You force a cruel choice on me, Wesley."

"Is it so cruel to ask you to choose your heart?"

"I'm the MacBride." She pulled her shift and then her blouse up over her shoulders. "The price of dallying with you cannot be borne."

"I ask no price—"

"A man never does." Putting her hands to her lips, she gave a shrill whistle. Wesley saw a glint of pain in her eyes. "For a woman, there is always a price. The MacBride cannot ride nursing a babe at her breast."

A shout sounded from the cliffs above. Caitlin jumped up, snatching up her shawl and shaking it out.

Wesley spat a vivid oath, then lifted his eyes to the huge man on horseback coming toward them.

"There you are," bellowed a deep, angry voice. Iron shod hooves thumped into the sand.

Wesley gave Rory Breslin a smile he did not feel. "Top of the morning to you, Rory. Fine news about Tom Gandy, is it not?"

"Oh, indeed, your reverence." Rory's hard eyes took in Caitlin's tumbled state, and he dropped to the ground. "Are you all right, *a stor*?"

She nodded a bit vaguely, as if that last show of resolve had wearied her. She seemed shaken, confused, a dreamer just awakened.

"May St. Ita's stag beetle give you a pinch," Rory burst out, reverting to Irish. "You can't trust that *Sassenach* with a female oyster. Don't you know better than to go off with the likes of him?"

"Shut up, Rory."

Rory tied her shawl with a firm tug. "Nay, I'll not shut up. You should have listened to me. Should have kept him under lock and key where he belongs. *Musha*, when I think of him . . . and what would have happened entirely if I hadn't come along?"

She had nearly given herself to him. The answer was written on her face as clearly as fresh ink on parchment.

Meeting Rory's fury with a careless grin, Wesley acknowledged that his plan had failed. He had shown Caitlin her own vulnerability; now she would be more cautious than ever.

He would need a new plan to lure her away from Clonmuir.

Three nights later, the solution dropped into his lap.

9

It happened in the deepest part of the night, when even the most vigilant of the wolfhounds lay twitching and snoring among the men and boys in the hall.

Wesley came awake, prodded by a noise so faint he thought he had imagined it. Or dreamed it. But his years as an underground Catholic and royalist had sharpened his senses for the sounds of stealth. He sat still, listening. He heard nothing more, but the hair on the back of his neck lifted.

He tiptoed from the hall, leaving by way of a low side portal designed for escape in times of siege. The yard lay in darkness, the main gate closed fast and the guard at the tower quiet, probably dozing.

With apprehension crawling over his skin, Wesley went to the privy stools in a recess of the western wall. He was about to enter the stone enclosure when a strong arm hooked around his neck, closing off his windpipe. Just before his breath was blocked, he had caught a familiar scent. Aye, he knew the smell of men like this: the dust of the open road and the stink of bad food, memories from his days as a fugitive.

He kicked out behind him while his hand plunged into his belt for the knife that wasn't there. As a prisoner, he was forbidden to carry even a dirk for eating.

Silver stars winked before his eyes. His elbows and knees battered his opponent. Just for a moment, the pressure on his neck eased, and he stole a deep breath. Swearing softly in Gaelic, the assailant said, "Give a hand here. This is the one."

A second man, a hulk who stank of wet leather and strong drink, leapt in front of Wesley. His fist thudded into Wesley's gut. A roar of breath emptied from his lungs.

"You're sure?" the second man asked.

"Aye, 'tis the priest we're after—the one with ruddy hair and clean-shaven face like a Norman."

Priest catchers! And Irish ones at that. Wesley's consciousness had begun to fade, but the realization revived him like a bucket of ice water. He made a strangled sound of fury and lowered his head. The man in front of him doubled his fist for another blow. Inadvertently supported by the man behind him, Wesley drew up his legs, pressed both feet squarely into the broad midsection, and gave a hearty shove. The Irishman fell backward, his knees catching the edge of the privy. His fingers grasped at the empty air.

His body made a muffled crunching sound as he fell down the privy shaft and into the cold sea.

A hiss of horror escaped the man holding Wesley from behind. Wesley seized the moment to twist away and pin the man against the privy seat. A knife flashed; Wesley hammered his assailant's hand against the stone. The blade dropped to the ground with a dull thud. Eyes bugged with fear stared up at Wesley.

He pressed his thumbs to the man's Adam's apple. "Who sent you?"

The man made a gurgling sound. Wesley eased the pressure and heard him say, "Dunno . . . I swear it! 'Tis rumors we hear in the *bruighens*, God have mercy!"

The puling plea sickened Wesley. "You dare invoke God's mercy?" he demanded in a deadly whisper. "You, an Irishman, selling men of faith to the *Sassenach*?" He centered his weight on the heaving body. The man's back bowed over the edge of the privy. "Where do you send the priests?"

The man's face glimmered in the moonlight like damp bread dough. "In . . . Inish . . . Inishbofin! Spare me, I beg you—"

"I'm a Catholic. It's very important that you realize that."

"Aye. Aye, mercy, I do realize—"

"Excellent," said Wesley. Lifting with his legs, he pitched the man over the edge.

Shudders convulsed his body as he put his forearm to his brow and vomited, then sank to the ground. The tide would flush the priest catchers away with the filth. Fish would feast on their rotting flesh. And he, of course, would say nothing of the encounter. Caitlin must not know that her home was vulnerable to sneaking traitors. She had enough to fear already.

Then the horror receded, to be replaced by an idea so scathingly manipulative that he shuddered anew. *Inishbofin*. The isle of the white cow.

Could he deceive these people, these simple folk who put their trust in God and their loyalty in Ireland?

Could he deceive Caitlin, the fierce, committed woman who defended her home against Cromwell?

Laura, he thought. Her helpless image drifted into his mind, and agonizing paternal love twisted through his thoughts. For Laura's sake, he would tell any lie, commit any sin, brave any danger.

"I would have a word with you."

Seated at her writing desk in her privy apartment, Caitlin raised wary eyes to Hawkins. In the instant that she took in his appearance, she remembered every word he had said to her on the strand, remembered every stirring touch of his hands and lips.

Devil take the man. He always looked so clean, so vital, so maddeningly comely. So what? she concluded in annoyance. She was a woman, after all. He had made her experience desire; for that she was grateful. But she wouldn't let him turn passion into a weakness.

"Shouldn't you be after hearing confessions and christening babes, your reverence?" she asked in a cutting tone.

He plowed his fingers through his red mane. "I couldn't tell them no," he said. Weariness dragged at the smile lines around his eyes. Since Tom's recovery, folk had besieged Hawkins with the requests they had stored up since the disappearance of the chaplain, Father Tully.

"I tried to explain that I've disavowed the priest-hood," he went on. "But they're so desperate they'll confess to an imposter."

"More's the pity." She closed her writing desk. She had been penning yet another appeal to Logan Rafferty, asking—nay, begging—him to dismiss the dowry and take Magheen back.

"What is it, Mr. Hawkins?"

His easy smile did nothing to improve her humor. She clung to anger, for it was a safer emotion than the softer ones her heart urged her to feel for him.

"Let's go outside to the wall walk, Caitlin. It's a glorious evening."

A breeze, fresh with the promise of high summer, gusted through the unglazed window and underscored his suggestion. She pushed back from her desk. "Let's see what you're about and be done with it."

They crossed the yard and mounted the steps. The square-topped merlons framed a view of the sea that was as familiar as a psalm, yet as changeable as the clouds scudding in from the west. Great long fronds of sunlight fell over the horizon. Summer days stretched long in Connemara; for hours, the last rays clung tenaciously to the edge of the earth.

"This is the *leim*, Traitor's Leap," she said, propping a bare foot between two merlons.

"I assume there's a story behind that." Hawkins filled the gap with his broad frame, leaning over to inspect the long, sheer drop to the rock-bound seacoast.

"Tom Gandy would say the breakers are the lost souls of Ireland, rising up from this place to snatch men with treacherous hearts." She could not resist adding with a gleam in her eye, "So you'd best watch yourself, Mr. Hawkins."

"I'd rather watch you."

"What is it you wanted to talk to me about?" Caitlin asked.

"I know where the priests of Ireland are."

A succession of emotions leapt in her chest: shock, hope, distrust. "Is Daida back? Did he find—"

"No. The knowledge doesn't come from your father."

She rubbed the side of her hand over the old stone of the wall. "Sure I thought the priests were dead."

He winced. "They're not all dead."

"Why did you wait to tell me?" Her eyes narrowed in suspicion. "Did Hammersmith bid you tell me this lie?"

"Why should I lie about something so easily confirmed?"

"So where are the priests?"

He shook his head. "I'm not a man to give something for nothing. I'll take you there."

"Don't make me laugh. You'll tell me, or I'll assume you're lying."

His wonderful smile awakened a throb of yearning inside her. He said, "You don't give so much as an inch, do you? The priests have been exiled to an island."

She caught her breath, not daring to believe him. "Which island?"

"If I told you, then you'd have no reason to include me on the rescue."

"And how would a Roundhead horse soldier be knowing about this island?"

"This Roundhead horse soldier knows how to keep his ear to the ground."

"I'll have Rory search for the place. If he finds it, the Fianna will attack by sea."

He swept his arm in an arc toward the open water. "How many islands scatter the coast of Ireland? How long would it take Rory to find the right one?"

She bit her lip. What trick was Hawkins about? Would he commandeer the boat and attempt to sail to freedom? No, not the way she would transport him, bound like the prisoner he was.

"Very well, Mr. Hawkins. Rory and Conn will accompany us in the big hooker. And if you're lying, that will ease my decision as to what I'm going to do with you."

Grinning, he caught her against him and kissed her loudly on the cheek. "If I'm wrong, you can feed me to the sharks."

"Don't tempt me, Mr. Hawkins." Pulling away, she stomped down the stairs into the yard.

* * *

"Hold her steady as she goes," called Rory Breslin, who piloted the single-masted hooker. "There's a fair wind for westering. No need to tack."

Patterned after the Dutch-built *hoeker*, the vessel was made to ply along the treacherous rocky coast. The English had burned the fishing fleet, but the hooker had escaped serious damage.

Sitting in the bow with his booted foot propped on an upended tender boat, Wesley glowered at the receding shoreline. Clonmuir reared up, its profile crowning the high crags. Its majesty caught at his chest. God, what a place to call home. No wonder the Fianna defended it so fiercely. No wonder Hammersmith craved it.

His hands, bound behind his back, itched to throttle Caitlin MacBride.

Distrustful Irishwoman, tying him up as if he planned some piracy.

His annoyance grew, for piracy was exactly what he planned.

She had just thrown a bit of sand in the cogs, that was all.

He fixed a polite smile on his face and addressed Conn. "How are you going to find your way after dark?"

Conn laughed. "A foolish English question if I ever heard one. We steer by the stars."

"The sky's clouding up," Wesley pointed out. "Tonight you'll have no stars to guide you."

Conn drank from a clay bottle of usquebaugh. "In that case, I'll follow my nose."

" 'T'would be simpler if you'd be leaving off your games and tell us where we're headed," said Caitlin.

"Not yet," Wesley said stolidly.

Conn propped an elbow on the gunwale and addressed Caitlin. "You don't suppose your father's found the clerics, do you?"

She made a face. "Sure he's probably lost on the road to Dublin."

For the hundredth time Wesley thought his plan through. First he needed to get his hands free. That bit was easy enough. The difficult part would be dispatching Conn and Rory, subduing Caitlin, and setting the Irishmen adrift in the tender.

A daunting prospect. Here he sat, a bound prisoner bent on fighting two armed warriors—no, three. He must remember Caitlin's fighting skills.

But he also remembered the razor-sharp knife in his boot and the stone-cold purpose in his soul.

The sheltering arms of the cove at Clonmuir opened to broad waters. Here, the sea was rough and the wind high. The hooker climbed a swell to stand upright in the trough. The motion slammed Wesley from one side of the cockpit to the other. Without the use of his hands, he bounced about like a freshly landed fish.

Caitlin let out a yell of pure delight and waved at Rory. "A grand day to be riding the high sport of the sea," she cried.

Despite the bruises he had taken from the rollicking motion, Wesley smiled. To Caitlin, the caprices of nature were a blessing. She threw herself into the adventure with the eagerness of a child.

Conn, on the other hand, gave a great agonized moan and lost his supper over the side.

"Is it seasick you are, Conn?" asked Caitlin, bending down.

"Aye." His pale face shone like a full moon. "To the death I am."

"Sure a bit of a sail won't kill you." She gave him a friendly punch on the shoulder.

Conn rolled his eyes to heaven. "Faith, it's the high hope of death that keeps me alive."

Laughing, Caitlin handed him the bottle. "Have some more of this, Conn. 'T'will tame the wildness in your gut."

Wesley marveled at his good fortune. Conn, seasick! Seizing the opportunity, he announced, "I have to take a leak."

Conn swore into the bottle. "Wet your trews, then, *seonin*."

"Good God, man, give me a little dignity."

"As the English have given dignity to Ireland?" Caitlin asked.

"Look, I didn't have to tell you about the priests."

"Very well," Rory broke in, irritated. "Just be sure you stand downwind and watch your aim."

"I'll need my hands undone," said Wesley. "Unless you want to undo my laces and hold my pecker for me."

"God Almighty, anything but that," Rory snapped.

"Damn your Irish hide, you'd have me pitching over the edge to drown."

"That might not be such a—"

"Oh, for pity's sake," Caitlin burst out. "I'll hear no more bickering about . . . about such a ridiculous thing. Just loose his hands, Conn, and stand ready with the rope."

"I don't like it," the Irishman grumbled.

"Just do it." Her movements jerky with annoyance, she climbed toward the bow and disappeared on the other side of the tightly pulled foresail.

At the same time, Wesley moved aft, nearly falling on his face more than once. Rory wrestled with the tiller. Foam rushed past the hull, evidence of their high speed.

He presented his back to Conn. "Would you mind hurrying?"

Conn jerked at the knots. Wesley eyed the main sheet that held the boom in place.

Conn yanked the rope free. Wesley flexed his fingers. "I thought I'd lost my very hands, you had that pulled so tight."

"Just be about your business, Hawkins." Conn belched miserably and clutched at his stomach.

"Of course." Bending his knees to absorb the swells, Wesley turned out to sea. Rory called out a familiar insult in Irish.

Conn stood ready with the rope in one hand and the jug of usquebaugh in the other. He hugged the bottle protectively. "You'll not be getting so much as a drop to drink," he said. "It goes through you too fast."

"I am fast," Wesley murmured as he finished lacing his trews. With lightning speed, he reached down and snapped the main sheet free. The rope sang through the pulleys.

The thick boom swung wildly.

Conn ducked, but not fast enough.

The boom thumped into Conn's shoulder. With a howl of pain, he pitched to the deck.

Wesley shoved him over the side. He made a splash like a geyser, drenching Wesley with cold saltwater.

Caitlin scrambled from the bow. "What the—"

"Duck!" shouted Wesley.

The boom sped toward her. For a sick moment he imagined her brains smashed, her dead eyes staring at the sky. "Caitlin!"

She stooped low. Wesley grabbed the flailing sheet and jerked it back into place.

Conn surfaced, spluttering and cursing.

Caitlin gripped the rail. "Conn!"

Wesley moved to her side. His hand slipped into his boot and withdrew the knife he had seized from the priest catcher. "Can he swim?" he asked.

"Conn! We'll tack around and pick you up," she shouted. Rory was already hauling on the tiller.

"I said, can he swim?" Wesley demanded.

"A Clonmuir man? Of course he can swim."

"Good. Then he can stay afloat until Rory fetches him in the tender."

"Don't be ridiculous. We'll just tack around and—"

"You and I are going on alone, Caitlin."

She gasped as if he'd struck her. She reached for her stag-handled knife. Before her fingers even touched the hilt, Wesley snatched the weapon from its sheath and stuck it into his belt.

Comprehension stormed across Caitlin's features. In Irish, she screamed to Rory, "He's turned on us!"

A bellow of rage blasted down the pitching deck. Rory abandoned the tiller and drew his own knife.

Caitlin lunged for Wesley. He caught her against him. "Ah, Cait," he said, "I've dreamed of the day you'd throw yourself into my waiting arms. I'd hoped you would be in a better mood when it happened."

She kicked and swore. The Irishwoman had more strength than ten English ladies. "Dog!" she yelled. "You kinkish bog-trotting muckworm! You threw Conn overboard!"

"It was you who insisted on bringing him. Good God, woman, will you be still? You'll have us both in the drink."

Rory stood in the middle of the cockpit. The sight of the Irishman with teeth bared and weapon ready daunted Wesley enough to make him throw off the last of his principles.

Very carefully, he placed the blade of his knife against Caitlin's throat.

"You slimy bastard," she hissed.

"A hundred thousand curses on you," Rory bellowed.

Thrashing in their wake, Conn added a hundred thousand more.

"Listen carefully," said Wesley. "I dearly hope you'll do as I say, for I don't want to have to kill the MacBride."

Rory demanded, "What be your will?"

"Get in that tender and go fish Conn out."

Indecision wrenched the big man's features.

"Do it," Wesley ordered.

"But—"

"Either get out of this boat, or I cut the girl." Wesley used the voice that had once set thieves to quaking in their purloined boots. "Now."

"Do it, Rory!" Caitlin yelled.

"Forgive me," he said in Irish. "We'll find a way to save you, see if we don't."

"Go back to Clonmuir," she said, her voice calm and reassuring despite the knife at her throat. "Tell Tom to carry on as best he can until I return."

Rory's fists clenched with terror and rage. Wesley felt a lurch of sympathy. He, too, knew the horror of seeing a loved one threatened by an enemy.

"It's time to go, Rory," he called.

With his massive shoulders slumping in defeat, Rory heaved the tender overboard and jumped in. Within minutes, he'd landed Conn in the hull. Both men gripped the sides of the rowboat, their faces turned to the hooker.

Gazing across the swells at their pained faces, Wesley finally gave vent to sympathy. "I swear by all that's holy, I won't harm her," he said. "We'll be back!"

Caitlin punctuated his promise with an elbow to his ribs. He pulled her more tightly against him, feeling firm muscle and soft curves. "You're making this hard, and it needn't be. Don't fight me, Caitlin."

"I'll never stop fighting you, you leaky-brained coward!"

Wesley sighed, then inhaled the delicious scent of her hair. "I'm sorry to hear that, love." Wrestling her to the planks, he bound her hands and secured the rope to a cleat.

Not once during the binding did she cease cursing him with oaths in English and Irish, layering the invectives as thick as *dulse* on the sand. In bright blue language she cursed the day he was born. She cursed his family back to five generations. She cursed the air he breathed and the space he occupied.

The breeze dried the cold sweat that had formed on his face. Gratefully he put his knife back into his boot and set a westerly course.

Though he sailed alone with Caitlin MacBride on the high seas, Wesley felt no swell of victory. The sense that all the planning, all the maneuvering, was just an elaborate game designed to get his daughter back, drained the emotion from him.

"Now what, Mr. Hawkins?" she demanded with a deadly look in her eyes. "Do you mean to take me out and drown me?" Before he could answer, she laughed bitterly. "No, that would be too much of a mercy to hope for. You English seem to enjoy torturing your captives before murdering them."

Wesley realized uncomfortably that if she did know his eventual plan for her, she might beg for a slow death instead.

He gave her his most engaging grin. "My plans have not changed, sweet Caitlin. We're going to steal us a priest."

"We're lost." Caitlin rubbed her sore wrists and scowled at the rope that bound her. Hawkins knew how to tie a pretty knot. She had probably worn her teeth to the gums working at it.

"No, we're not," he replied.

She pressed her lips together in vexation. The sky was a swinging bowl of stars. They had skirted the rockbound coast of Connemara and entered the surging waters off West Connaught.

"You know nothing about the priests," she insisted acidly.

He sent her a wounded look. "They're at Inishbofin."

"Inishbofin!"

"Aye, in exile at the old garrison there."

"I've heard of the island," said Caitlin. She had been too angry to speak to him during the long, comfortless voyage, but now weariness loosened her tongue. "The Irish held out there until two years back."

"Now it's in Commonwealth hands."

"Is that where you were tortured?" she asked.

"I wasn't tortured at Inishbofin."

"Then how do you know about the priests?" He made no answer, so she turned the subject. "And just what are you after doing once we get there?"

"I told you. We're going to steal a priest." He rummaged in a basket, took out a piece of bread, and handed it to her.

She grasped it with her bound hands and took a bite. "Just one?"

"We can hardly accommodate more in this boat. But it's a start, Caitlin, don't you see? We'll have reconnoitered the garrison. We'll know how it's guarded. One day we'll be able to come back and free them all."

It was odd to hear him speak so, to see his eyes light with noble purpose. "Why would you want to rescue the clerics of Ireland?"

He looked away as if she'd caught him cheating at backgammon. "I was almost one of them. I don't wish to see priests locked up like criminals. Tell me, how did the chaplain of Clonmuir disappear?"

"Father Tully? Sure it was just after Magheen's wedding to Logan. The nuptial feast took place at Clonmuir."

"So he disappeared from Clonmuir?"

"No. There was a processional to Logan's castle at Brocach. Father Tully went along to bless the marriage bed, for Logan hasn't had a chaplain since the *Sassenach* outlawed them. The next day, Father Tully was nowhere to be found."

"So he disappeared while he was under Logan's protection."

"If you have something to say, Mr. Hawkins, then say it. Don't bandy about like a cock in a pit."

"Why is it that, when the Roundheads raid, Rafferty's holdings stay intact?"

"He's chief of the district. Even the Roundheads still show a bit of respect for the Raffertys."

"Then why was Father Tully snatched from his household?"

"Saints and angels, I don't know," she snapped. "But I do know what you're doing, Mr. Hawkins. You're trying to drive a wedge between Logan and me. Well, it won't work. Logan is a fine Irishman. If he's adopted a few English ways, that is only because he judged it the safest means to keep his people from being harassed. *You* are the faithless one, Mr. Hawkins."

He gazed at her for a long moment. From his silence, she knew the argument was over. In spite of herself, she felt relieved, because he raised uncomfortable doubts in her mind. She stared back at him, refusing to flinch and trying to deny the handsome picture he made as he sailed to the west. Iron-gray swells rose at his back, framing him in liquid glory.

"Ah, Cait," he said. "Do you remember the things I said to you that day on the strand, the way we touched each other?"

She recalled every shocking word, every soft caress. "No," she said. "I've put that folly completely out of my mind."

"You have not. I need only to look in your eyes to see that you remember. And it's important that you do remember."

"Why?"

"Because I meant every blessed word. There's Inishbofin," he added, pointing at a line of winking lights in the distance.

Five hours later, in the dark heart of the night, Caitlin was stirred to wakefulness by the shifting of the hooker in its secret mooring in a rocky cove of Inishbofin.

Two shadows stepped into the boat and came toward her. Round helms glinted in the uncertain gloom.

She gasped, wrenching her bound hands and preparing to fight to the death against the soldiers.

One of the Roundheads yanked off his helm. A mass of tight black curls shone in the moonlight. A familiar voice whispered, "Hush, *a stor*, it's me, Father Tully, and our good Mr. Hawkins."

Five hours after that, as dawn broke over the craggy coast, an English frigate hove into view.

10

"*Papers all seem to be in order,* Mr. Hawkins," said Tate, the English captain. "Still, your story's extraordinary. I shall have to keep you under guard until we reach Galway."

From a wealth of secret documents concealed in his thick belt, Hawkins had brought forth yet another paper. Thus far, Caitlin had watched him produce a safe conduct from Titus Hammersmith and a passport authorized by Oliver Cromwell himself.

Ice cold with anger, she was more certain than ever that Hawkins was no mere Roundhead horse soldier.

Seeing the look on her face, Father Tully squeezed her hand.

Tate scrutinized the passport, his thin lips moving silently as he read. A narrow, pointed beard gave his face an unpleasant shape. "Says here you're a special agent of the Lord Protector."

Hawkins started to look at Caitlin, then stopped himself. "That's what it says."

"Would you care to elaborate, Mr. Hawkins?"

"No, thank you."

Caitlin felt a sudden loss of breath, as if an invisible hand had grabbed her by the throat. *A special agent of the Lord Protector.* Special agent . . . or secret weapon.

"*Dar Dia,* but I'm a fool," she whispered to Father Tully in Irish. "I *knew* about him, and never even realized."

"What do you mean?"

She told him about the letter Curran had stolen, months ago in Galway. "The letter mentioned Hawkins," she concluded. "Not by name, but I should have realized when he first came to Clonmuir." Furious with herself, she pressed her fist to her mouth to spare Father Tully from her curses.

Suspicion hooded Tate's pale eyes as he read and reread the paper. He seemed torn between beating the truth out of Hawkins and ingratiating himself to an intimate of Oliver Cromwell.

Caitlin voted for the beating.

"I must say, it does look irregular, you in the company of an Irish slut and a popish cleric."

One corner of Hawkins's mouth glided up in a dangerous half smile. His gaze slid pointedly over Tate. "Believe me, Captain, I've been in worse company."

The men stared at each other across the wall of Hawkins's implacability. Finally he blew out his breath. "The woman's tired, Captain. Surely you don't want it said that you withheld hospitality to a female, Irish or not."

Tate jerked his head at a subaltern. "Take them below."

Clinging to Father Tully's hand, Caitlin followed the sailor to the foredeck and descended a steep ladder to a dark, damp room full of rotting rope and mildewing canvas. His face a snarl of contempt, the seaman pushed aside a pile of old sail to reveal four cramped bunks.

"You'll lodge here." He kicked at a large brass container. "Use that for puking. And other necessities."

When he left, Caitlin sank to the wooden slats of a bunk, which was inadequately covered by a thin moth-eaten mattress. She dropped her head to her hands. "Father Tully, forgive me. This whole affair is purely my doing."

He sat beside her and patted her knee with his strong, squarish hand. "Nonsense, daughter. There's none left in Ireland to resist the English. All our warriors—the great O'Donnell, Mahony and Comerford, the O'Carrolls and the Croftons —have all been forced from our shores. You held out against the *Sassenach* as long as you could."

"I'd be fighting still if I hadn't been so stupid as to trust an Englishman."

"Nay, Caitlin. Resisting the Roundheads is like throwing rocks at the moon. Now. Tell me all that's come to pass at Clonmuir. How is your father?"

She laughed humorlessly. "Daida has gone on a quest to find the priests of Ireland."

"Ah. He hasn't found Inishbofin yet."

"He probably got waylaid at a booly hut in the hills and is distilling poteen with a shepherd. I pray he's safe somewhere."

"The Lord protects children and—" Father Tully caught himself, but not before Caitlin understood.

"—and madmen?"

"Faith, I didn't mean it that way."

"I know. He abdicated as the MacBride before he left."

Father Tully's eyebrows lifted, two thick caterpillars framing eyes of the purest blue of heaven. "Did he now?"

"I was elected the MacBride in his place."

The priest gave a low whistle. "Glory be to the high saints of heaven. You always were the MacBride in fact. 'Tis fitting."

Encouraged by his ready acceptance, she felt the lid being lifted from a boiling pot. Like escaping steam, the words poured out of her. She told Father Tully of the problems between Logan and Magheen. She told him how she had nearly settled the dispute only to be thwarted by her father.

"He roasted your last bullock, you say?"

"Aye." But she felt no anger, only helpless frustration. "Daida sees Clonmuir through the frame of the past. He remembers how it was in the days of his youth, when the English were still far away and Clonmuir prospered."

She drew a deep breath, lowered her voice and continued in rapid Irish. She related her first meeting with Hawkins, the lies he had told, her naïveté in sending him on his way.

She offered the details of the raids, the capture of Hammersmith's stores, and of Hawkins.

"I should have given him to Logan. But he would have revealed my involvement with the Fianna. For the same reason, I couldn't send him back to the Roundheads." She twined her fingers in her lap. Hawkins could be telling them now. The Fianna could be ruined, and all her friends punished.

"In your grandsire's day," said the priest, "the scoundrel would have been given a drumhead trial and a speedy execution."

She shook her head. "I couldn't do that either. My will is weaker than that of my grandsire."

"Because your heart is bigger."

"But look where it's got me. A captive on an English hulk. No doubt Hawkins means to drag me before Hammersmith, and *he* won't be bothered in his conscience when he hangs me."

"Don't be so swift to judge Hawkins ill," said the priest. "Perhaps he means to help in a way you've not considered."

She gazed at him in surprise. He smiled. "The man's a Catholic—he told me so when we were escaping Inishbofin. He knows he's failed in his vocation. Still, I'll not condemn him until I discover what he's about."

Caitlin flung her arm at the cramped chamber. "Can he be about anything good?"

"Time will tell, Caitlin."

She thought of the many facets of Hawkins. She remembered his gentle touch and the feelings that poured through her when he kissed her. She remembered him laughing in the sunshine and looking more handsome than a Celtic god. She recalled his passionate claim that she should be the MacBride. He was the blank-eyed mystic, taming a stallion. He was the hot-blooded lover, bringing her desires to life, the compassionate confessor, hearing a man's last words.

"He's a sly fox," she told the priest. "He'll say anything to win your trust."

"I fear slyness far less than outright cruelty." Father Tully rubbed his fine knob of a nose.

Like an oncoming squall, certainty blasted over her. "You were mistreated at Inishbofin!"

"The Almighty doesn't make a man bear more than he's able, Caitlin."

She studied him closely, seeking signs of injury. He was gaunt and windburned. "Are you all right, Father?"

He nodded. "Aye. What the English fail to understand is that they've hardened the Irish against privation and cruelty. They thought they were giving us short rations when in sooth a day's allotment of bread was more than most of us were used to seeing in a week."

"But they did more than try to starve you."

"They may beat my flesh to the bone, but never will they touch the soul deep inside me. That belongs only to the Almighty, and no Englishman can take it from me."

Caitlin wished her faith ran as deep as Father Tully's. But she couldn't take a passive role; she had to fight back. She was too much a creature of the here and now.

"How is it that you were captured, Father?" she asked.

"Sure wasn't it odd. Day after the wedding, Lord Logan asked me to consecrate a field for the planting. As all his men-at-arms were sleeping off the nuptial toasts, I went alone. The field was deserted. I was after thinking there was no one in sight save myself and the Almighty. I'd barely uncorked my bottle of holy water when a gang of ruffians seized me."

"Englishmen?"

He hung his head and stared at the planks. "They were Irish, my girleen."

A chill trembled through Caitlin. Though she fought the recollection, she remembered Hawkins's speculation that Logan's hand had been in Father Tully's disappearance.

"There are bounty hunters everywhere," he said. "Some forty pounds British is what they got for me." Father Tully moved to another bunk. "Rest now, child. You've had a rough time."

"We've got to do something about your hair," said Wesley, sitting in the prow of the ship's pinnace and gazing at Caitlin.

"I'll not primp for Titus Hammersmith," she said, bracing herself against the swells of Galway Bay. "Let him see me as I am, as you've made me."

Wesley's skin crawled with guilt. During the voyage to Galway, he had accepted plenty of ribbing on the subject of his captive. The English seamen had chided him for having selected a recalcitrant and weather-beaten wench when there were so many soft, comely females to be had in Ireland.

Wesley had responded with sheepish grins and manly backslaps, when inside he seethed with fury and burned to demand respect for the MacBride. But for her sake, he concealed her identity, and so the sailors had no more regard for Caitlin than they would have had for a fat ewe being taken to market.

He was grateful that she had kept to her quarters. He took care not to speak to her more than was necessary, for when he did, he could not stop his voice and his eye from going tender.

Even now, in a crowded pinnace sailing to harbor in Galway, he longed to take her hands and tell her, Soon, Caitlin. Soon all will come clear. But he knew better than to hope for forgiveness.

The boat bumped the dock. The once beautiful city of Galway stood drenched in mist. The grand marble houses huddled in miserable neglect. At the fish market, a few procurement officers and army contractors milled about, dickering with fishmongers over the price of herring.

Father Tully, whom Wesley had come to admire for his good sense and fortitude, climbed onto the dock and extended his hand to Caitlin.

"I'll help the lady," a seaman said, shoving the priest aside. He grasped Caitlin by the waist, his hands deliberately finding her softer parts as he lifted her.

The instant he put her down, she lashed out with her bare foot. With reflexes quickened by the dangers of sailing, he jumped away, and she succeeded only in stumbling to her knees on the wooden planks.

A jet of pure rage spurted like distilled venom through Wesley. Caitlin scrambled to her feet. Wesley fixed an easy smile on his face, leapt onto the dock, and slammed his elbow into the seaman's ribs.

The man tottered at the edge of the dock, failed to regain his balance, and toppled into the cold waters of Galway Bay.

"Sorry, my good man," said Wesley, speaking above the laughter of his crewmates. "Haven't gotten my sea legs back to land yet."

Captain Tate and a company of musketeers accompanied Wesley, Caitlin, and Father Tully to Titus Hammersmith's residence in Little Gate Street. An aide directed them to the rear of the building, where Hammersmith stood behind a field table, paying out bounties to wolf hunters who looked as wild and dangerous as their prey.

The aide whispered in Hammersmith's ear. The commander turned, and wonder broke over his face. "Hawkins, is that you? By God, man, I thought you were dead!" He raised a distracted hand to his temple where a lock was missing from his beautiful glossy hair. The new growth resembled a bottle brush, Wesley saw with some satisfaction.

A few minutes later, Captain Tate had been dismissed with a citation for a job well done, and Wesley and his companions were accompanied by an armed guard into Hammersmith's drawing room.

Barefoot and bedraggled, Caitlin stood beside

Father Tully and gaped at the room, taking in the velvet hangings on the windows, the cut crystal service on a rosewood sideboard, the ivory Aran wool carpet.

He knew she had never set foot in a town house before. And he knew she realized that all the luxurious trappings, from the brass and etched glass lamps on the mantelpiece to the brocaded settee facing the hearth, had once belonged to an Irish family.

"And who are these . . ." Hammersmith paused a moment, studying Caitlin and Father Tully. ". . . people?"

Wesley cleared his throat. "Sir, they are—"

Caitlin slapped him on the chest and stepped forward. "I don't need an Englishman to speak for me. I'm Caitlin MacBride of Clonmuir, and this is my chaplain, Father Tully."

"The blessings of God be upon your head, sir," Father Tully said obligingly.

Hammersmith leaned over and had another murmured conversation with his aide. When the man left, the captain turned to Wesley. "I trust you have some explanation for this."

Before Wesley could answer, Caitlin strode across the carpet, set her hands on her hips, and thrust up her chin. "No, *you* must do the explaining, sir. I have been dragged from my home, pirated by your Roundheads, and held prisoner by this—this" For want of an adequate insult, she gestured furiously at Wesley.

Hammersmith glared at her in distaste. "Madam, no one speaks to me in that tone—least of all an Irish wench." He held his arm toward the doorway. "Mr. Hawkins?"

Wesley stepped into the hall and nearly collided with Edmund Ladyman. The soldier blanched, then hissed a curse through his drooping mustache.

"I'm no ghost, Ladyman," Wesley assured him grimly.

"Keep them under guard," Hammersmith instructed his men. With a wave of his hand, he gestured Ladyman into the room. "If she so much as blinks, clap her and the priest in irons." He wrinkled his nose. "Oh, and don't let her sit on the furniture."

Wesley restrained the urge to throttle his commander. Hammersmith's contempt for Caitlin was but a mild foretaste of what she would soon face.

Hammersmith stalked into his office, jerked his head to indicate that Wesley was to enter, and slammed the door.

"Damn it, Hawkins, this had better be good. If Lord Cromwell didn't have such high regard for your abilities, I'd have you transported to the Barbados where riffraff and madmen like you belong."

Wesley stood easily against a thick carved chair. "Are you finished, Captain?"

Equally sarcastic, Hammersmith made a small bow. "I await your explanation."

"It's simple enough." His plan had to work. He had to bend Hammersmith to his will. "I've captured the leader of the Fianna, and I'm ready to take ship back to England."

Hammersmith's eyebrows shot up. "You've captured the devil? God's blood, why didn't you say so right off? Where is the scoundrel, Mr. Hawkins?"

"In your drawing room."

"The priest? Impossible! The popish lout doesn't look capable of leading a flock of spring lambs much less a company of rebels. Impossible, I say."

"You're right. It's not the priest."

Red faced with frustrated confusion, Hammersmith burst out, "Enough of riddles, Hawkins. Just tell me—"

"It's the girl."

Shock, disbelief, and suspicion led the Roundhead's features through a series of contortions. "Impossible!"

"It came as a surprise to me as well." Wesley suffered a vivid memory of the night he had nearly killed Caitlin. "But it's true. I witnessed her in action the night of the Lough Corrib raid."

"None of the survivors of that raid mentioned a girl."

"She fights in a war helm with a veil."

Hammersmith rubbed his jaw. "Ladyman did say he saw you bring down a man on a black horse. He was under the impression you'd perished in the raid."

"The horseman was Caitlin MacBride."

Rocking back on his heels, Hammersmith pinched his lip between his thumb and forefinger. "Extraordinary."

"I agree. She's rather like Joan of Arc."

"Who's that?" asked Hammersmith. "Another female chieftain?"

Wesley felt a rare wistful longing to be in the company of scholars at Douai, where they not only had heard of Joan, but could tell her story in seven languages.

"Never mind."

Hammersmith steepled his fingers. "So. Since you and Ladyman are eyewitnesses to her treachery, I think we can dispense with a trial."

"I think dispensing with a trial is an excellent idea, sir."

"I'm glad you agree. Honestly, Mr. Hawkins, I confess I had my doubts about you, but we finally seem to see eye to eye on this matter. Now. I've a full schedule tomorrow. We're getting ready to send a shipment of wenches to the Indies, and—"

"A shipment of *what*?"

"Of wenches, Mr. Hawkins. Women."

"Irishwomen?"

"Of course. You don't think we'd subject good Englishwoman to transportation, do you?"

"So these women volunteered to be transported to the colonies?"

"Are you daft? Of course they didn't volunteer."

Wesley's vision swam with rage. "You're forcing them?"

Hammersmith laughed. "Forcing is just a word. Their villages are rubble; their fields bear nothing but weeds. Their men are all killed or exiled. They have no life here."

Because we took it from them, Wesley thought. And then, like pieces of a puzzle, a picture formed in his mind. His hand went to the fold of his belt, where his papers were stored, including the list of names he had purloined from Hammersmith. Now he realized it was not a census roll at all, but a receipt.

"My God," he said, barely able to govern his fury, "you *sold* them into bondage."

"That's a lie! This is a legitimate enterprise sanctioned by the Commonwealth."

"No." Wesley took a step forward. Hammersmith's hand went to the hilt of his sword. "You collected money for the women. And I doubt the Commonwealth will see a copper penny of it."

Hammersmith's color deepened. He made a dismissive gesture with his hand. "We stray from the point. I merely brought up the matter to explain why the execution can't take place until the day after tomorrow."

Wesley planted his hands on his hips. "You're not going to execute her." He was certain of it now.

"Cromwell requires only her head. From the way she behaves, I'd think you'd be grateful. Alive, she's bound to be a great deal of trouble."

"I couldn't agree with you more, captain. She does indeed promise to be trouble."

"Damn it, you're doing it again. You're talking in riddles."

"I don't mean to. Captain Hammersmith, the young lady is not to be executed." The power of his knowledge about the Roundhead's deceit swelled within him.

Hammersmith slammed a beefy fist down on the desk. "For God's sake, why the devil not?"

"Because I'm going to marry her."

"Impossible!" Caitlin stood in a stateroom of the English trading frigate *Mary Constant*. In front of her stood John Wesley Hawkins. "Sure that's the most ridiculous thing I've ever heard."

Hawkins nodded agreeably. "A few months ago I would never have believed it. But that was before I met you, Caitlin."

"Save your infernal blather. For once in your life, Mr. Hawkins, tell the truth. Just what are you about?"

"First, marrying you. Second, taking you to London. And third, returning to Clonmuir, preferably before it falls to ruins for lack of a chieftain."

"London? What the devil is this about London?"

"It's our destination."

"I won't go. Hammersmith will punish the people of Clonmuir."

"No, Caitlin. I've ensured Hammersmith's cooperation."

"I trust no *Sassenach*. You least of all."

He took her hand firmly and led her to a settle which ran beneath the stern windows. The trading vessel rode deeply in Galway Bay, her holds crammed with spoils from raids on Irish towns and strongholds. "Caitlin, you must stop playing the rebel long enough to listen."

She tossed back her tangled hair. It hadn't seen a comb since the day Wesley had pirated the hooker and kidnapped her. "I'm listening."

His eyes deepened with an emotion she could not fathom. "I came to Ireland in the secret service of the Lord Protector, Oliver Cromwell."

She leapt up in a fury, her hands forming fists. "I knew it! You sneaking *seonin*, I should have—"

He grabbed her wrists. "You're supposed to be listening, remember?"

She pushed his hands away and glared at him.

"My task was to find the leader of the Fianna and bring his head to Cromwell."

Sheer terror streaked through Caitlin. She did not allow so much as a tremor to betray her. "I see," she said coldly.

"No, Caitlin, you don't see—"

"And you think to be amusing yourself by making me your wife, and then yourself a widower."

"Of course not. Now look. Cromwell wants you stopped, and he sent me to do it. If I fail, he'll find another assassin who lacks my scruples."

"You have no scruples. You're a lying, cheating—"

"My lies will save your neck. You see, I have Cromwell's sworn statement that neither he nor his agents will bring harm to any of my kin."

"You have kin?"

He opened his mouth, closed it, and gave her a look of soul-deep pain she did not want to see.

"I doubt you do, Mr. Hawkins." She forced out the insult. "You probably crawled from beneath a rock somewhere."

His gaze shifted. In nervousness? she wondered.

"I thought it prudent to word the statement so as to include any of my kin."

"And why are you so afraid for your own life that

you would compel the devil to swear such a thing?"

"Because I had been condemned to die for my papist activities. Cromwell's Secretary of State literally snatched me from Tyburn Tree." Absently he touched his neck. She recalled the fading marks she had seen there when she had bathed him.

"So that's how it is," she said. "Cromwell promised you your life in exchange for mine." At least she understood him now. But that didn't mean she had to like him any better.

"Don't you see, Caitlin? Marriage is a way to solve both our problems."

And a way, she thought bleakly, to shatter the dream I have cherished in my heart for four years. When she thought of Alonso coming for her only to find her married to an Englishman, she wanted to weep. Yet even in her grief she recognized the humanity of Hawkins's scheme. He could have simply killed her. Most Englishmen would have.

"Assume I agree to this farce, Mr. Hawkins. It wouldn't matter anyway. Marriages between English and Irish have been outlawed."

"Titus Hammersmith made the same point. However, the marriage will be perfectly legal so long as it takes place at sea. An interesting loophole, is it not?"

"This is absurd. How can you think that marriage will transform me into some submissive Englishman's wife—"

"Who says I want a submissive wife, Cait?"

"—and stop Cromwell from doing his worst?"

He gripped her arms. "Damn it, I have to believe that."

Disconcerted by his urgency, she pulled back. "And do you really think I'll cease to fight the Roundheads?"

"Caitlin, you've tested your luck too often. You've challenged fate and won. But one day it will have to end. One day you'll be stopped by force if you don't stop on your own. We'll find a safer way to resist the Roundheads."

"We? You speak as if you intend to come back to Clonmuir."

"Indeed I do."

"Why?"

"Because England is not my country anymore. Cromwell has failed to keep the peace. He's taken freedom away from good men and women. We're at war with Spain, with the Netherlands, probably with France, too. I tried my damnedest to help King Charles back to the throne, but it's not working."

"And why should I be after caring about Charles Stuart? No English monarch has treated fairly with Ireland. Henry the Eighth gave us his bastard son as a leader. Elizabeth outlawed our faith. King James gave our lands to foreigners. Charles the First forgot we existed except to collect taxes. Why should I expect fairness from a new king?"

"Can anyone short of the devil himself do worse for Ireland than Cromwell has done?"

Painful hope rose inside her. "You seem to have switched loyalties."

He pulled her close, pressed his lips to her hair. "Aye, Cait. So it seems."

She let him hold her for a moment, enjoying against all reason the comforting feel of his arms around her. "Why go to England at all? Why do you not simply disappear into the countryside or take ship for the colonies?"

"I have to return to London."

She drew herself out of his arms. "Why?" she repeated.

New pain flickered in his eyes. "I'm bound by my word."

She turned to the stern windows and stared across the bay. In the distance wallowed a great hulk. Boatloads of people were being rowed to the huge ship. Caitlin squinted through a glare of sunlight. A feeling of dread curled in her gut. "Blessed Mary," she whispered. "Those are women."

Hawkins joined her at the windows. "Aye."

"Where have they come from? Where are they going?"

"God, Caitlin. I wish you hadn't seen this."

"Tell me. I demand to know."

"They're being transported to the Barbados to help populate the island."

"As slaves, you mean." She pressed her hand to her throat and prayed she would not be sick. But she nearly retched, for the thought of all those young women, ripped from their homes and families, made her ill.

She swung to face Hawkins. "I hate all English. And that includes you, Mr. Hawkins. You'd be miserable as my husband."

"I'm no stranger to misery."

"I will not marry you."

"Yes, you will, Caitlin."

"No proper priest would ever consent to this farce."

"Father Tully agrees with me wholly."

"That's a lie."

Before she knew what was happening, he drew her close. "You will marry me, Caitlin MacBride."

"Never."

"Then I'm afraid you'll never see Clonmuir again."

A cold shiver passed through her. "That, Mr. Hawkins, would kill me. Believe it."

"And then where would Clonmuir be? Tom Gandy alone cannot act as chieftain. Your father was no leader. Clonmuir will fall to ruins." He gestured at the hulk, the women lining the rails. "Your friends would probably be transported—those who didn't die defending their freedom."

"Oh, God," she whispered. She had no choice. *No choice*. This English scoundrel had trapped her like a vixen in a snare.

11

Mr. Hopewell, captain of the merchantman *Mary Constant*, always traveled with his wife. Younger than Caitlin and childless, the lady warbled like a lark at daybreak as she bustled around the stateroom.

"We'll surprise everyone for certain, oh my, yes. Here, the bath's ready, and I'll just find something for you to wear."

Caitlin stood in her shift in the hip bath. The fresh, scented water felt heavenly, and she wished the bath were big enough to immerse her entire body.

"Here's a silk velvet." Mrs. Hopewell pulled a garment from a chest. "It will look stunning on you, oh my, yes. See?" The orange confection, bubbling with lace and bows, resembled a floral arrangement rather than a dress.

"I'll be after wearing my own clothes, thank you." Caitlin bent to dip her hair in the water.

"Oh, but you mustn't. Your—er, what is this thing called?"

"Kirtle."

"Your kirtle is simply in tatters." She drew out another dress, this one yellow and black. The *Mary Constant* carried a seemingly endless supply of clothing and furnishings, some seized from the Irish and others confiscated from the English settlers who had embraced the cause of Irish independence. "You can't go to your own wedding looking like a beggar woman."

Caitlin scowled. It would serve Hawkins right if she did. "Mrs. Hopewell," she said, her voice cool but polite. "Those are English fashions. I know it's hard for you to understand, but I'm proud to dress as an Irishwoman."

"English fashions are so much more becoming. Like it or not, Miss MacBride, you are an English subject about to become an Englishman's wife."

Scrubbing furiously at her hair, Caitlin winced.

"It would behoove you to start dressing and behaving as an Englishwoman," chirped Mrs. Hopewell.

"Other conquered people submit to the ways of their aggressors," Caitlin said. "That's not true of the Irish. The English who came here under Elizabeth adopted our ways, our culture, our mode of dress. Now they're as Irish as a singing harp. Many of them are fighting Cromwell alongside their Celtic hosts." She scooped water over her hair. "I'll go to this marriage dressed as my mother went to hers, as her mother before her did."

But I will not have willingness in my heart as they did, she thought bleakly.

Under her breath, the little woman muttered, "Stubborn as Mr. Hopewell on the Sabbath day. Perhaps there's something . . ." She opened another chest. "These come from Castle Kellargh."

"Spoils of war." The words stung with the bile of distaste.

"I'm afraid so. But the Irish put up a fierce resistance. The army had no choice but to devastate the area. They poisoned the wells, burned fields and houses."

Caitlin fixed her hostess with a piercing stare. "And did it ever occur to you that the army left women and children homeless and starving?" She indicated the chest. "And naked?"

Mrs. Hopewell held her ground. "War is an ugliness, Miss MacBride. Innocent victims suffer. I pray that one day your countrymen will capitulate and adopt English ways."

"And why should we let our self-rule be taken away, our very faith outlawed? You're bound to be disappointed, Mrs. Hopewell. For as fervently as you pray for capitulation, we Irish plot to drive you from our shores."

Mrs. Hopewell's hand fluttered to her brow. "This discussion makes my head ache. I'll never understand you Irish. Never. Just wear whatever you like, then."

Wrapping herself in a towel, Caitlin stepped from the tub. With her heart in her throat, she inspected the plunder. To wear garments seized from blameless Irishwomen gave her pause. But wouldn't the owners of the clothes prefer to see their lovely things adorning the MacBride rather than a London lady?

Certain of the answer, she picked up a garment so beautiful and so uncompromisingly Irish that it could only have belonged to a noble countrywoman. "This will do," she said.

Wesley stood amidships on the *Mary Constant*, awaiting his bride.

A sharp wind howled in from the northwest, filled the canvas, and sang in the rigging. The ship cut a wake through muscled waves the color of smelted iron.

The wind snatched at his broad brimmed hat. He

jammed it down firmly on his head. In Galway he had bought the fine, plumed cavalier's chapeau along with a suit of clothes an exiled courtier would envy: cuffed boots, blousy fawn breeches cinched at the waist by his broad belt, a padded doublet and a buff coat of tough leather with shoulders so wide he could hardly fit through the portals of the ship. Freshly washed with soap scented by ambergris, his hair flowed like a gleaming russet cloak down his back.

He stood with his unlikely ally, Father Tully, his uneasy host, Captain Hopewell, and his unwelcome chaperon, MacKenzie.

"Fine day for a wedding," Father Tully said, clapping his chapped hands.

"Lovely," muttered Wesley. God! What was he thinking of? In order to marry Caitlin, he had blackmailed Titus Hammersmith and threatened Caitlin herself. What madness to gamble their lives and Laura's, too.

But the alternative was executing Caitlin and taking her head in a bag to Cromwell. The very idea nearly sent Wesley stumbling to the rail to spill his guts into the Celtic Sea.

The marriage would mean exile for him and Laura at Clonmuir. Wesley could not think of a place in the world he would rather live.

A nasal screech seared his ears.

Hammersmith's man, MacKenzie, gave a seraphic smile. Under his arm he held the bloated bladder of a bagpipe. "Wouldna be a weddin' without a tune or twa," he said, wiping his nose with the back of his hand. It was a great prow of a nose, painted purple and red by the broken veins of an inveterate tippler.

Hopewell's brows pinched together. "With that, Mr. MacKenzie?"

"Oh, aye. Nothin' like the fine skirl of the auld pipes, eh, Father?"

Father Tully gave a noncommittal cough.

Wesley eyed the man with interest. Stout, bow-legged, and thick-headed, MacKenzie was as Scottish as Charles Stuart.

"'Tis said the pipes were actually invented by the Irish," MacKenzie explained. "D'ye ken the legend, Father?"

"Aye, the Irish invented the contraption as a joke, and gave it to the Scots. But the dour Scots never caught on."

Neither, apparently, did MacKenzie. With a flatulent blast, he launched into an earsplitting melody.

In the midst of the cacophony, and in a swirl of salt smoke from a breaking wave, Wesley's bride emerged from a portal.

The men fell silent. The pipes whined to a halt. And John Wesley Hawkins whispered, "Help me, Jesus."

Caitlin paced slowly toward him. She wore the most extraordinary costume he had ever beheld. A tunic, white as a summer cloud, cloaked her from throat to ankle. Open-worked sleeves hugged her slim arms. Polished stones and iron studs adorned the belt that cinched her tiny waist. The large oversleeves, scalloped at the cuffs, brushed the planks as she walked. A circlet of silver crowned her head while her unbound hair flowed out like a banner of gold behind her.

She might have stepped from the pages of a legend, so strange, so ethereal, and so lethally Irish was she. She was a part of some savage druidic rite. She was a warrior, a goddess. Her terrible beauty bound Wesley in a spell of helpless fascination.

On bare feet she mounted the steps. Her face was a study of solemn melancholy as if she were a virgin making her way to a sacrificial altar. Sadness haunted the amber wells of her eyes. Vulnerability softened the corners of her mouth. She looked as if becoming his wife were eternal damnation.

He wanted to fall to his knees and beg forgiveness for forcing her. He wanted to take her by the shoulders and shake her for making him feel like a scoundrel. He wanted to crush her in a fierce embrace and vow to bring her joy.

Half expecting her to drift away on a wisp of wind, he took her hand. Together they knelt. Her fingers were icy and rough, her hand small, trembling inside his. It was a hand that wielded a sword against England, that soothed Tom Gandy's fevered brow, that passed out food to the hungry. It was the hand of Ireland.

Father Tully cleared his throat and stood before them, his feet planted wide for balance against the surging motion of the deck.

He made the sign of the cross. *"In nomine patris et filii . . ."* And then, as the wind shoved them toward England, as cormorants flew screaming through the clouds, and as the hard planks of an English frigate pressed into their knees, John Wesley Hawkins and Caitlin MacBride became husband and wife.

"You might as well talk to me, Cait," Wesley said that night. "We'll be sharing these close quarters until we reach London."

She presented her narrow, rigid back to him. Her wavy hair swung, thick and lustrous, to her waist. He imagined burying his face and hands in the silken mantle, feeling it drift across his naked chest and inhaling its wonderful fragrance. He imagined lifting it away from the nape of her neck and pressing his lips to the tender flesh hidden there.

Tortured by yearning, he tossed back a swallow of sack and clapped his pewter goblet on the table. From above decks came the incessant yowl of MacKenzie's pipes, bleating and farting and gasping for breath. The sailors, glad for any excuse to drink away the tedium of the voyage, had stopped protesting the noise hours ago and now joined in the discord.

As an agent of Cromwell, Wesley had been granted special privileges. The quarters were comfortable, low ceilinged but broad, and furnished with an alcove bunk and a bolted down table. Sighing, Wesley moved behind her. He touched her tense shoulders, his hands patiently kneading her tightened muscles.

"We will make this marriage work," he whispered. "It can mean a new start for us and for Clonmuir. In our children will mix the blood of Briton and Celt, of—"

"Stop!" She jerked away. "I may have had to marry you to save my neck, but I don't have to pretend we have a future together."

"'Tis done, Caitlin, and not even your stubbornness can undo this marriage."

She turned to him, defiance flashing in her eyes. "The English have taken our homes and our lands. Your laws forbid skilled men to ply their trades. Your soldiers burn our fields and rape our women. You snatch unsuspecting girls from their families and transport them to a hellhole where they'll be slaves to the devil."

"None of that is my doing."

She shook her fist. "But this is. You think to conquer me by forcing this marriage. It won't work, Mr. Hawkins."

"It must, or you'll die at Cromwell's hands." He took her arm. She resisted, but he pulled her toward the bed. His rampant imagination conjured an image of her lying there, arms open to receive him.

A sprig of hawthorne peeped from beneath the feather bolster. Small damp spots dotted the bleached linen sheets.

"Father Tully has blessed the marriage bed with holy water. He approves of the union, Caitlin."

"You must have threatened him, too."

"No," said Wesley in a low, rough voice. "To him, I told the truth. That I had no true vocation as a priest. He released me from my vows."

She stared at the slanting floor. "Wesley." She spoke so softly that he thought he might have imagined hearing his name on her tongue.

He brushed his finger along her cheek. "Aye, Cait?"

"I'm asking you, too, to release me from my vow."

A coldness formed around his heart. "I can't do that." To his utter chagrin, he felt a hot tear drop onto his finger. "Caitlin, don't," he begged. "This doesn't have to be such a tragedy."

With the swiftness of a recoiling spring, she drew back. Anger danced with the tears in her eyes. "Did you never wonder, you great fool, why I hadn't married?"

The coldness in his heart became an icy burn. "I didn't dare wonder for fear of spoiling my good fortune."

"I was waiting for the man I love," she flung at him. "I would have waited seven lifetimes."

The words stunned Wesley, stealing his breath. Long ago, he had considered the possibility and discounted it. Now the truth assaulted him like a rapier thrust.

"Who is it, Caitlin?" His voice was knife sharp with jealousy.

"He is Spanish, and highborn, and I'll not profane his good name by revealing it to the likes of you."

"Ha!" Wesley forced out the bluff exclamation. "Now *you're* the one with pixies in your head. Name him, Caitlin, or I'll know you conjured him out of wishful thinking."

With an angry swipe of her hand, she dashed the tears from her face. "He is Alonso Rubio, son of the grand duke of Alarcón."

Recognition slammed through Wesley. Part of the

Spanish ambassador's retinue, Rubio resided in London
and worshiped at the Catholic chapel Cromwell allowed
for foreign dignitaries. Like a man wounded in the dark,
Wesley probed his memory. He recalled a slim, courtly
gentleman of astonishing beauty and graceful demeanor.
Everything John Wesley Hawkins was not.

"And how did you meet this paragon?" he demanded.

She tossed her head. "He was on a trading vessel
bound for Connaught to take on timber. The ship
stopped for refitting at Logan Rafferty's yard in Galway."

"He gave you the stallion, didn't he?"

"Aye, and his promise to wed me, to help me
defend Clonmuir."

And what did you give him in return? Wesley
choked off the question. Instead, he snorted rudely.
"And you believed him?"

"Unlike you, he doesn't make his living by lying."

Wesley poured more wine. He needed courage for
the task ahead. It was no longer simply a matter of
winning her heart. First he had to drive out the dark
Spanish hero who dwelt there.

But not for nothing had he been a cavalier. Caitlin
had thrown down the gauntlet. With grim determination
and pounding anticipation he took up the challenge.

"Four years is a long time, my love. I'd never let
you wait so long. How can you be certain he's been
true to you?"

"He sends letters, when he can, and I answer them.
Every single one." She enunciated each word clearly.

Wesley recalled his last meeting with Cromwell.
The Lord Protector had referred to a letter from
Caitlin to a Spanish gentleman. "Your tender mis-
sives," he said bitterly, "betrayed you. Cromwell
intercepted at least one of them."

Her face paled, but the anger burned steadily in
her eyes. "Sure isn't it the English who have forced

hardships on us," she retorted. "If we were at peace, my life could go on."

"Life," he said, sinking to one knee before her, "is what has been happening to you during all those years of waiting." Intent on banishing the Spaniard from her thoughts, he took her hand and carried it to his lips. She bent her head, and the rich, untamed waves of her hair shone with reflected lamplight.

"Caitlin," he said, "you are the moon on a cloudless night, the first ray of sunshine at dawn. You're a mortal man's vision of an angel. God, Cait, I need you."

She glared down, tight lipped, regarding him with the esteem she might afford a toad. "If you need a woman that badly, I'll buy you a whore in London."

Her disdain slashed at his pride. In one swift motion he surged upward, clasped her around the waist, and pressed her to the bed. "You weren't listening, Cait. I need *you*, not a whore." He kissed her face, her neck.

Like a cat with a bad itch, she squirmed beneath him. "Get off me."

"No. I've been honest about my needs, Caitlin. It's time you were honest about your own."

"And how would you be knowing what I need?" she demanded.

"You need a man who can call forth the woman inside you. A husband who can touch your beautiful Celtic soul. A lover who can push past your distrust and make you admit the wanting in your body."

Caitlin fell still for a moment. His words whispered a seductive song through her yearning heart. A wild hunger rose in her, and it was all she could do to summon back the anger. "Get off me, you ill-mannered Goth," she said. "Or will you rape me? You English have much practice at that."

"But I don't, Cait. You know that. Look, I can't woo you with poetry. I can't overwhelm you with my virility. Good God, what must I do to win you?"

"You'll never win me, Mr. Hawkins. Get used to it."

"What's wrong with me? Am I ugly?"

She laughed without humor. "Faith, you know better than that. You're as comely as heather in springtime. When I first clapped eyes on you, I thought you a vision spun by the fey folk."

He dropped a kiss on her brow. "That's encouraging."

Caitlin knew no reason why his weight pressing on her should feel so agreeable, yet it did. In spite of everything, they were comfortable with one another. Their bodies . . . fit.

But she willed away the thought and said, "Take no encouragement from that, for the fact that you're English makes you as loathsome as a troll to me."

"Oh. Anything else?"

"Yes, since you're after asking. I find you faithless and lacking in conscience. You swore a vow before God when you entered the novitiate. Yet see how eager you are to break faith."

His thumbs circled her temples, finding the shape of her skull beneath tendrils of hair. "It wasn't right for me. I knew that even before I met you."

"How can I accept a man who tosses away pledges like so much rubbish? What of the wedding vow you made to me this very day? One day you'll decide that, too, isn't right for you."

"This is different. Caitlin, you have to believe me—"

"I believed you when you claimed you were a deserter from the Roundheads, and a few weeks later you marched against the Irish. I believed you when you said you'd help me free the priests of Ireland, and you made me your captive. Why should I believe anything you say, Mr. Hawkins?"

His hands moved to cover hers, palm to palm. He laced their fingers and held tightly. His face wore a look of aching sincerity that she did not want to see. "I swore I'd not attempt to escape when I was your prisoner, and I held true to that promise."

"Only because it served your purposes."

"Caitlin, trust me. In time, all will become clear." Wesley nearly choked with the effort to keep from confessing to her. He wanted to tell her about Laura so she would understand why he had lied, why he had forced her to marry him.

But not yet. He must not speak yet. He was too close to saving Laura to jeopardize his daughter's life. He wanted Caitlin, craved her with a desire so vivid it staggered him. But he could not trust her with his secret, for her anger was too new, too raw. Reluctantly he remembered Hester Clench, a woman he had trusted. Caitlin had more honor, but she had a temper, too. And if anyone could kindle that anger hotter, it was Oliver Cromwell. He might goad her into revealing that Wesley had betrayed his part of their bargain.

Besides, he told himself, feeling an ironic smile twist his mouth, a man did not speak of his illegitimate children on his wedding night.

"Cait." He pressed her against the bolster and nuzzled her neck. She tasted of scented soap and spindrift. The deep golden cloud of her hair cushioned his face. "I want to be in your life."

"You can't. I won't let you, Mr. Hawkins."

"I swear you will, Mrs. Hawkins."

Red blotches bloomed in her cheeks as if he had slapped her. "Don't call me by that name."

"It's your name now," he pointed out.

"I took it only to save my neck."

Instead of cooling his passion, her words merely

sharpened the challenge. His ears strained to hear her cry out in passion; his mouth hungered for the taste of her. He wanted his babe in her belly. For the utterly practical reason that even Cromwell would bring no harm to a pregnant woman. And for the utterly unbelievable reason that he adored her.

The truth of it struck him. He had gone to her with no other purpose than to use her to regain his life and his daughter. But somewhere along the way, he had lost himself in the mystical enchantment of Caitlin MacBride.

Though she didn't know it, Caitlin held his heart and his life in her sturdy hands. She had bound him in a spell of unbearable sweetness and overwhelming power. He gazed down at her, certain she would read the staggering message of love in his eyes.

"You look sick," she said. "Are you going to be sick?"

The response was so unexpected, and so very much like Caitlin, that he laughed. "No, my dear love, it's not a sickness of the gut that plagues me, but one of the heart."

"You have no heart. And I have no skills for mending one."

"You're right. I have no heart because I lost it to you."

She framed his waist with her hands. "Blarney."

He expected her to push at him, but she held still, waiting. "Caitlin, it's our wedding night. We pledged ourselves to one another and Father Tully has blessed the union. And now we must sanctify the bond with our bodies."

Her hands slid up his back, then down again. Closing his eyes, he reveled in the slow, massaging motion—until he felt the prick of a knife at his back.

"Get off me, Wesley." Her voice was strange, dark and rich, like silk gliding over steel.

Swearing, he got to his feet. She leapt up after

him. Her fist was clenched around the dagger she had stolen from his hip sheath. Holding the blade with the sharp edge turned outward and the tip pointed up, she planted her feet on the gently shifting floor. "I will not honor a pledge you forced from me."

Wesley took a step toward her. "Now, Caitlin. You know it would be a sin to break a vow made before God."

"It would also be a sin for me to kill you," she retorted, "but that won't stop me from slitting you from your gullet to your crotch. Besides, *you* broke a vow."

"But I'm a desperate man." He took another step. In all the weeks he had spent as her prisoner, she had not harmed him. He had to believe she would not harm him now.

Acting on pure instinct, he undid the row of small orb-shaped buttons that ran down the front of his doublet. She watched warily as he shrugged out of the padded garment.

"You see," he said. "I trust you. I would bare my chest to you so that nothing stands between my flesh and your steel." Lifting his hand, he found the tasseled ends of his collar tie. The *welsche* came loose and drifted to the floor. Clad in a white cambric shirt, the sleeves loose but tightly cuffed, the neckline gaping wide, he advanced another step.

"That's far enough," she warned.

He yanked the shirt over his head.

"Stop," she said. "Put that back on."

"Do you remember what I said to you that last day on the strand? Do you remember how I described all the ways I wanted to make love to you?"

She said nothing, but the furious blush that stained her face from neck to brow gave him the answer he sought.

"I still want those things, Caitlin. Very, very badly. I want to feel your bare breasts against my bare chest. I want to touch you—"

"Stop it!" She edged backward so that her hips touched the table. "I'll cut your tongue out!"

"Go ahead." In one long stride he closed the distance between them and stood inches from her.

She lifted the dagger. Her gaze fixed on his broad chest. "You have a lot of scars, Englishman. I suppose you lied about where they came from, too."

"It hardly matters now. Are you going to stab me, Caitlin? You're a warrior who knows how to wield a knife." He pointed to the muscled flesh below his ribs. "This is a good spot here. No bones to get in the way of your blade." He spread his arms wide and hoped she would not discern the wild pounding of his heart. "Here's your chance, Caitlin. Will you take it?"

The dagger swung downward. Wesley tensed, awaiting the cold slice of steel. The knife fell with a clatter to the floor.

"Thank you, Jesus," Wesley muttered. Then he reached for her.

She jumped back. "I'll scuttle your knob with my daddle, see if I don't!"

His gaze searched her, wondering if he had overlooked a second weapon. "What's a daddle?"

"This." Her hard, closed fist smashed solidly against his jaw, sending him reeling.

Bright points of pain sparkled before his eyes. The entire lower half of his face caught fire. Stumbling back against the bunk, he sank down, cradling his jaw in his hand.

Caitlin looked on with an uncertainty he had never seen in her before. He worked his jaw tentatively. Not broken. But bruised to the bone.

Anger sped like a storm through him. He adored her, yes, but she needed taming. "Good God, woman!" he burst out. "I am heartily sick of your games. Would you fight to the death to protect your hallowed virginity?"

"Men and maidenheads! You've probably swived half of England. What matter is it if I've had a man myself?"

"Ah, so the Spaniard's already had y—" He broke off, shook his head. "No. I know better, Caitlin. The first time I kissed you, I tasted your innocence." He ran his finger along the throbbing tenderness in his jaw. Cavalier's tricks, forcefulness, and logic had gained him nothing. No man would ever have Caitlin MacBride but with true love.

How could he show her what was in his heart if she wouldn't let him near her, if she clung to fanciful dreams of an elusive Spanish nobleman?

"Look, Caitlin. I'd like to make a bargain with you."

"I don't bargain with faithless Englishmen."

"Just hear me out. You claim to love this Spanish fellow, and I assume you believe he loves you."

"It's not a matter of believing, but of knowing beyond all doubt."

Wesley lifted one eyebrow. "True love? The pure, all-forgiving kind that the poets sing about?"

Her features softened with reminiscence. "Aye. Pure as the green on the hills in springtime."

"And all-forgiving?" Wesley persisted.

"Of course."

He crossed his arms over his chest. "Well. I should not like to stand in the way of a love so great as that."

For the first time, she seemed to relax, her hands opening and her shoulders sloping downward. "It's glad I am that you've decided to see reason."

"I'm glad you're glad. Take off your clothes and get in bed."

"What?"

"You heard me."

"But you said—"

"I did. Play the wife, Caitlin. Share my bed and my life—just until we settle our business with Oliver Cromwell. Then if you still taunt the angels with your towering passion for the Spaniard, I'll arrange an annulment. And then" —he let a teasing smile curve past his throbbing jaw— "you'll have the rest of your life to remember how I made you feel."

Perhaps it was a trick of the swinging lamplight, but he thought he saw her lower lip tremble. "I thought annulment was granted only in cases of consanguinity, or when a couple fails to—to—"

"Consummate the marriage. Quite right. But Father Tully will be more than willing to help us. Think of it, Caitlin. A few weeks with me, and you'll be free to pine away for Don What's-his-name. If the love you share is as deep and abiding as you say, then nothing you and I do together will change that."

"But he'd—" She snapped her mouth shut and turned away.

"He'd what? Regard you as damaged goods? Not if he loves you."

Caitlin shivered. She reached deep into the channels of her memory and sought Alonso. He hovered there, a shadowy figure, the echo of a whispered promise, the faint ineffable fragrance of masculine perfume, the tender brush of lips against her brow.

She swung back to face the Englishman. Alonso's image drifted away like a wisp of fog before a blast of wind. Now there was only John Wesley Hawkins, standing with his bare shoulder propped against a support post, his chest wearing fearsome scars like medals of honor. His long rusty hair framed a face too comely to look at. One lock fell forward, a teasing question mark in the middle of his brow.

He grinned very slowly, making a visible effort not

to wince. "Well?" he asked. "Is the MacBride not woman enough for an Englishman?"

"Of course I'm—" Caitlin couldn't continue, for at last she saw the truth he tried so desperately to conceal behind his insouciance.

John Wesley Hawkins was afraid.

Fear shone in his eyes, visible despite the deep magic of his masculine appeal and the subtle wizardry of his smile. Like a siren song his vulnerability drew her, peeled away the layers of her resistance, mocked her denials, and found the truth at the very core of her.

She wanted him.

It was for Clonmuir, she told herself as she took the first step toward him. For the sake of Clonmuir and all the people who depended on her, she would give herself to the enemy.

To her husband.

A soft gasp escaped her. She felt his arms close around her. Her cheek brushed his chest and she turned and put her lips there, for she wanted to taste him.

The essence of him filled her. Once again, the mystic Celt inside her came to life and made her a creature of sensation, not thought, a creature driven by the demands of the body, not the mind.

He was so gentle, this enemy of hers. He lifted her face and lightly traced the outline of her lips with his finger. His hands and mouth seduced her with promises no man had ever made to her before. He was a light glimmering through the darkness, as captivating and compelling as an ancient song.

His fingers manipulated the fastening of her wide belt. The absence of the cinch gave her a feeling of freedom. She became weightless, boneless, a sailing cloud. The long tunic skimmed down her shoulders and drifted to the floor. The shift of gossamer lawn that had once belonged to a great lady followed in its wake.

She embraced a man who was her enemy. But where was the shame, the fear? She felt only a breathless anticipation, and then sheer intoxication as he brought his lips to hers. The madness of desire flowed into her, driving out doubts and fears.

Before long, an uncanny feeling of urgency took hold of her, and she gripped his shoulders. The magic seemed so tenuous and fleeting that she feared one wrong move or one errant thought would shatter the spell.

"Wesley," she breathed against his mouth. "Hurry. Before I change my mind."

"My love, I want this night to last forever. I want you to remember each endless moment."

He led her to the alcove bed. A great lassitude gently dismantled her will. She relaxed against the linens, and the spots of holy water cooled her fevered skin. Her lips, slightly parted, still stung from the moist fire of his kisses.

"Cait," he said, "look at you, lying there like a goddess, awaiting me."

She reached for him but he put her hands aside, bent and placed his mouth on her throat and then moved it lower, skimming the tops of her breasts. She gasped at the unexpected heat. Arching her back, she reached upward.

She sensed a certain lazy grace in his movements, a teasing quality to his caresses. He kissed a sinuous path across her skin, his tongue flicking at, but never quite touching, the most sensitive spots. She learned to appreciate fully what he meant by an endless moment. She hung suspended, her body in a state of burning awareness, her every sense focused on his warm, wet mouth.

"Ah, for the love of God, Wesley," she whispered.

"Patience, sweetheart. You're a treasure, a jewel to be savored." With maddening slowness his mouth traced rings around her breasts. Just as she thought she would go mad, his tongue flashed out at one burning peak, bringing forth a gasp from her.

Finally, answering the terrible need he had awakened in her, he closed his mouth over her breast.

She dared to think that she had found the magic at last. She could rise no higher than this dizzying height. And yet . . . and yet . . . his hands skimmed down her torso, and she realized she had only glimpsed the very edge of wonder.

"Aye, Cait, there is more," he said, reading her thoughts. He stretched long beside her and bent to kiss her mouth. "Would you like me to show you?"

"Yes. I want to know—to feel—everything."

His hand slid up her leg, the hand of a master harp maker smoothing a perfect length of ashwood; the hand of a sorcerer conjuring a spell. She was an empty jar which he filled, drop by precious drop with a potion more powerfully intoxicating than poteen. Yet with each drop she craved more.

In the back of her mind she realized that what he was doing was extraordinary. She knew the ways of lusty men; she had heard enough tales whispered in the women's corner of the great hall. Men did not often trouble themselves to see to a woman's pleasure.

But Wesley behaved as if her satisfaction were his only goal. She absorbed his unceasing caresses as parched earth absorbs the rain. The pleasure filled her, swirled around her. She forgot to breathe. She forgot to think. She forgot he was her sworn enemy.

Drop by precious drop. The rhythm of his hand matching the pulse of her heart. Finally the passion rose up and spilled over, drenching her in a warm rain of sensation.

A long sweet sigh escaped her. She opened her eyes to find him smiling down at her. He had an odd expression on his face. It was the delight of shared pleasure, she realized, but deep in his eyes she recognized pain, as if he had shouldered a heavy burden. As if the breaking of vows truly distressed him.

"Caitlin," he said. "Touch me, I beg you."

She responded because he had asked, not demanded. Her hands made a study of his scarred and thickly muscled body. She discovered the tautness of his shoulders, the silkiness of the hair on his chest. And to her surprise, she discovered that she loved the warmth of his flesh against her palms, the rapid thudding of his heart when she lay her cheek on his chest.

So this was how a man was made. She touched his body in ways she hadn't dared to dream about. He responded with a hiss as if she had burned him.

"Cait," he said, "this is the sweetest torture I've ever endured." He pulled her into an intimate embrace, his arms supporting her back and his legs separating hers. And to think, she reflected languidly, that only a short time ago they had been twined together in the heat of battle, each intent on murdering the other.

Now her emotions flared just as high, but not with rage. She hugged him with her legs, bringing his body close. Closer.

He moved against her, his shoulders trembling and his face a mask of concentration.

Wesley battled the lust raging inside him. He forced himself to remember that Caitlin was a maiden, and that he did not want to hurt her. He pressed downward into the deep moist center of her, and then deeper still to the wisp of silk that stood between innocence and fulfillment. With one gentle stroke, the veil was swept aside by his ardor.

Her head fell back, and she smiled. The secret,

beguiling smile of a woman. He kissed her closed eyes, her cheeks, her mouth. He whispered words that had no logical meaning.

Caitlin listened with her heart. The pressure inside her built, pressing at the edges of a world that would never be the same again. He was a wizard, full of mystery and magic, and he offered a gift she hadn't known she had craved.

She lifted her hips and he began to move, long slow ripples of motion that streaked her senses with fire. She was surrounded by a mist that held no beginning and no end. No world existed beyond this small alcove; no time passed beyond this moment.

Wesley's movements quickened, and she joined him in the rhythm of a song that had no words. She surged toward a great unnameable purity and burst into the light with a cry of joy.

Wesley's voice joined hers. She felt a movement, gentle pulsations that thrust him deeper inside her and seemed to touch her soul. He buried his face in her hair and inhaled deeply.

"Caitlin." Her name blew pleasant and warm near her ear. "We are complete."

With the steadily slowing beats of her heart, the magic lost its potency. She turned her head away. "I have betrayed myself, my people—"

"No." He propped himself on an elbow. The high color in his cheeks gave him a robust look of satiation. "I won't let you say that this is wrong."

"But we're enemies—"

"Stop it." Again, the pain glimmered in his eyes. "You say I broke a holy vow, Caitlin. Contrary to what you think, I did not make the decision lightly. For three years I kept faith with that vow. I'd nearly convinced myself that I could stay chaste until the day I died. But saying our loving was wrong only cheapens it. Don't do that to us, Caitlin. Please."

"We'll speak of it no more, then." She turned away, drew up the coverlet, and reached out to embrace regret and shame. But when sleep stole over her, it was not Alonso she dreamed of, nor even Clonmuir, but her husband, John Wesley Hawkins.

12

"*Bless me, Father,* for I have sinned." Caitlin nervously made the sign of the cross.

"I am here to give you God's grace," said Father Tully. They sat together in the galley, empty of sailors now that the morning watch had taken its meal. "What is it that pains your soul?"

Caitlin laced her fingers together. She had confessed to him freely since her youth; she would not avoid his eyes now. "Father, I have committed the sin of lust."

He lifted one eyebrow. "Sure and have you now?"

"Yes. Last night. With my—with the Englishman."

"With your husband, you mean?"

"Yes, Father. I beg the Lord's forgiveness."

"Faith, not so fast. We must first establish that you have indeed committed a sin. Now, you say that on your wedding night with your new young husband, you committed the sin of lust?"

She remembered the wildness in her heart, the complete abandonment with which she accepted—welcomed—his kisses and caresses, the sweet fulfillment of their joining. "I did."

He slapped his hands on his knees. "Well, that's a grand matter indeed, my dear. I'm most happy for you."

"Happy for me? But—"

"It's not every woman who can enjoy the conjugal union. Many's the time I've comforted a new wife who has been used ill by her husband. Be glad Mr. Hawkins inspired lust rather than fear or shame."

"You don't understand, Father. I don't want to feel this way about him."

"You prefer fear and shame?"

"No, but—"

"Then accept what has happened, Caitlin." He took her hands and chafed them between his own. "Finding delight in your husband is a rare gift."

Hot anger sped through her, and she welcomed it, for anger threatened her less than the roiling sea of emotions she felt for Wesley. "And should I be delighted that he is dragging me off to London to face Cromwell?"

"He has his reasons."

"Did he tell you those reasons?"

"The man means you no harm, Caitlin. I believe he will protect you. I advise you to leave the rest in God's hands."

"Bless me, Father, for I have sinned." Wesley furtively made the sign of the cross.

"You, too?" Father Tully brushed his black hair out of his eyes. They stood at the rail and watched the gulls dive for herring. The high wind snatched at their voices, giving them privacy despite the fact that Hammersmith's man, MacKenzie, loitered nearby.

"This is not the first confession you've heard today, then?"

"On that matter, my lips are sealed."

So, Caitlin had already confessed. What had she said?

"Mr. Hawkins, would your troubles be having anything to do with that great colorful bruise on your jaw?"

Wesley touched the tender spot. "I've fallen in love with her, Father."

"And you consider love a sin? Faith, I'd call it a blessing. Have you told her?"

"Had I the tongue of a poet, she wouldn't believe me."

"You must, with care and tenderness—not just words—bind your two hearts."

"But the failure to make her love me is not what I came to confess."

"Then unburden yourself, *a chara.*"

A pleasant warmth washed through Wesley at hearing the priest call him friend. So few men in his life had. "I'm lying to her about a very important matter."

"Then tell her the truth."

"I can't. A person's life is at stake. My own and Caitlin's, of course, but there is a third innocent who will be hurt if I tell all to Caitlin. To anyone." He gazed out at the churning sea, the waves slapping down into shadowy troughs. "There is no point in telling her," he said, more to himself than to the priest. "The truth would force her to make difficult choices. Besides, she'll know soon enough."

"Would you be after speaking of another woman?" Father Tully demanded, his thick eyebrows beetling.

"No! I swear before God, it's not that."

"Let no secrets come between you and your wife. Secrets can kill a marriage quicker than poison."

Wesley studied the priest's drawn and weary face. He recognized the look of troubled sympathy, for he, too, had borne the burden of confession. Putting a hand on Father Tully's shoulder, he said, "When we make port, will you use Hammersmith's safe conduct to return to Clonmuir?"

Father Tully smiled wistfully. "Ah, and isn't it

Clonmuir that brings my soul close to heaven?"

"It's dangerous for you there. Hammersmith fears what I know about his slave trade and the taking of priests. He'll stay away from Clonmuir for now, but he's clever. Don't gamble your safety, Father."

Father Tully combed his fingers through his black hair. "A priest goes where he's needed."

Wesley envied him at that moment, envied the certainty of his calling, the knowing that he had chosen the right path. For Wesley, the way was marked with torn loyalties, self-doubt, and now the agony of frustrated love.

"You made your confession today, didn't you?" Wesley asked that night as he entered their quarters.

Caitlin bit her lip. "Father Tully abides by the seal of confession. Who told you?"

"I made a guess."

"Guess yourself to Whitehall for all I care." She chewed halfheartedly on a ship's biscuit.

"I guessed when I went to make a confession of my own," he added.

Caitlin inhaled a crumb of biscuit. Clearing her throat with difficulty, she said, "I'm sure you bent his ear for hours, then, for you're a black-hearted sinner, Mr. Hawkins."

"I'm also your husband, Mrs. Hawkins. Come here."

"No."

He sighed. "Caitlin, we wasted hours in argument last night when we could have been making love. Let's not repeat that mistake tonight, or ever again."

"Not make love ever again?" She dusted the crumbs from her skirt. "I agree completely."

"I was speaking of arguing."

"I was speaking of lovemaking."

"Good. Let's carry on with that topic." Evening light streaming through the stern windows touched his eyes, transforming the gray-green tint to the diffuse color of magic. Framed by burnished hair, the bruise on his jaw contrasted with the healthy color of his face.

"How can you deny our passion," he asked, propping his shoulder against the alcove support, "when I can look at your lovely face and see the yearning there?"

Resisting the urge to make a sign against enchantment, she planted her hands on her hips. "It's Clonmuir that I yearn for, not you. You've forced me to marry you. The union has been consummated. What more do you want from me?"

"I want you as I had you last night, full of a woman's desires, your face a picture of unguarded surprise and delight." He reached up with his hand and made a lazy trail down the post with his fingers. The simple gesture raised a havoc of disquieting emotions in Caitlin's chest.

She tried to block out Wesley's words, but her heart listened as he went on, "I want you in every way a man can want a woman, and in ways we've yet to invent. Every single day and night, Caitlin. Now, come here."

"No."

"I'll give you a son for Clonmuir."

The suggestion shot her through with fear and longing. He stepped toward her. Only pride kept her from fleeing toward the door. "I want no sons from you," she stated.

"Caitlin, don't be bitter. I care for you."

"Like a drover cares for a prize pig."

He reached out, fingered a curl that had strayed from her braid. "Don't you remember the passion, Caitlin? Don't you remember the sweetness?"

She did, and too well. His nearness scattered her thoughts. Yet at the same time she saw that he, too, seemed discomfited, and the fact somehow endeared him to her.

"You're trembling," she said.

"You make me feel too much, Caitlin. I'm not used to this."

"Then don't." She hated herself for being curious about him, for wondering about every aspect of his life and his past.

Taking her in his arms, he kissed her slowly, softly, drawing away her protests as a splinter is drawn from flesh. She leaned into him, loving the security of his arms around her, savoring the taste of him and marveling, as she had the night before, at the uncanny harmony of their bodies. He had turned her world upside down. He had taken her to heaven and to hell. And she would not have traded a moment of it for the very surety of her soul. God, if only he would disavow Cromwell, she would have a name for the things she felt when he kissed her like this. She would call it happiness.

He lifted his mouth from hers. "Caitlin."

"Yes?"

"I love you."

Not now, she wanted to scream at him. How can I believe you now? She stepped back, shaking her head slowly. "Don't say those words to me, Wesley. I can never love the man you are."

His face paled, but she forced herself to continue. "I have only contempt for a man who does Cromwell's bidding. Don't you understand, being married to you changes nothing! It's Alonso I love!"

He let go of her as if she had burned him. He stepped back, and she saw that his face had changed into a visage she had never seen before. Agony, devastation, and finally rage contorted his features. With a jolt of fear, she realized that this was the first time she had seen him truly angry. At her.

"Very well, Caitlin." His voice thrummed with carefully controlled fury. "So long as you deny what we are to one another, so long as you cling to dreams of your Spanish hero, I will leave you alone."

She should have felt relieved. She tried very hard. All she felt was a black emptiness. "I think it's for the best."

He lifted his hand, stopped himself before touching her. "Caitlin, one day you'll find the truth in your heart. And then you must come to me, for I won't reach out again."

London, June 1658

Caitlin craned her neck to peer out from beneath the canopy of the river barge. "I've never seen a paved street before. Even Galway doesn't have a paved street."

"Do you like it?" Wesley asked.

"Sure it seems a lot of trouble."

"The paving's necessary. The traffic would turn the streets into rivers of mud." Wesley settled back, trying to appear composed. The ever-present MacKenzie rode astern with the waterman. Caitlin perched on the edge of her seat like a child on her first trip to a fair. The last thing Wesley had expected after their quarrel was that they would become friends. But it had happened. Perhaps it was better this way. Safe. Reasonably comfortable so long as he kept her at arm's length.

"What building is that?" She pointed to the structure that shadowed St. Katherine's Street along the wharf.

The thin slits of windows squinted menacingly from towers and turrets. The thick walls of pale limestone and hard, coarse ragstone brought on a rush of memories that nearly made him ill. "It's the Tower of London," he said.

Her interest sharpened. "Is it, then? You mean where the poor princes were murdered? Sure and didn't Silken Thomas, our own Irish hero, wait out his last days there."

"Indeed."

"What's it like, I wonder."

"Hell on earth." Wesley averted his glance to the river, where lighters vied for position along the quays. "There are holes called oubliettes so cramped that a man can neither stand nor lie down."

Hearing the pain in his voice, Caitlin studied his pale face, his clammy hands. "How do you know this?"

"I was there."

"Visiting prisoners?"

"Caitlin, I *was* a prisoner."

A cold wind of shock swept over her. "You were?"

"Aye."

"Did they put you in an oubliette?"

"Aye."

She remembered the scars that laced his back and shoulders, the horror that, in rare unguarded moments, haunted his eyes. He had suffered for the sake of his faith, probably more severely than he had ever told her.

"Ah, Wesley." She laid her hand on his. Since they had come to an accord regarding intimacy—or the lack of it—she was more comfortable touching him. "You should have told me before."

He stared at her hand. "Don't touch me, Cait," he said in a low, gravelly voice. "Don't touch me unless you mean it."

She hesitated, liking the rough texture of his hand beneath hers, yet knowing where it would lead if she refused to obey. She drew back her hand. "I wish you'd tell me, too, how a Catholic came to be an agent of the devil Cromwell."

He leaned his head against the leather cushion. "Cromwell and I have been aquainted seven years. Since Worcester."

"Did you fight with the royalists there?"

He nodded. "When we realized the battle was lost, I was with those who helped King Charles escape. We spent a long day in an oak tree in Boscobel wood. When the searchers drew close, I gave myself up as a decoy. King Charles escaped, and so did I, eventually. I went to the seminary at Douai." He gave her a sideways glance. "Am I boring you yet?"

"If you were, I'd be after telling you directly."

A smile pulled at one side of his mouth. "I was sent back to England. I acted as both priest and royalist messenger, but by that time I was neither, Cait. I didn't know what I was. When the priest catchers finally took me, I was sentenced to die. But Cromwell's man, Thurloe, stopped the execution."

Gripping her knees, she leaned forward. "Why?"

"Because he realized I was the man Cromwell had been seeking for seven years."

"How did he know it was you?"

To her amazement, a blush crept up to the tips of his ears. "It was the women who gave me away."

"What?"

"The women." He waved his hand in impatience. "At my execution. Some of them recognized me, by sight or reputation."

Caitlin blinked, unable to envision the scene. "So why did Cromwell spare you?"

"He needed my skills as a thief taker."

She braced her hands on the arms of the seat. "You were a thief taker, then a cavalier, then a novice to the priesthood?"

"Aye."

"That's more careers than most men pursue in one lifetime."

He stared down at his hands, flexing his fingers. "I was . . . searching. Trying to find my place in the world."

Her eyes narrowed. "And you found it with Cromwell, who spared a thief taker from the gallows to take *me*."

"Aye."

As evening gathered in the last rays of the sunset, the barge bumped to a halt at Whitehall Steps. A jumble of boxy buildings loomed over the water's edge. Torches burned on each side of a doorway, and a footman came to help them disembark.

"Evenin', gov'nor," said the footman. "Pleasant voyage, was it?" He gaped at Caitlin in her soft, loose tunic. "Brought along a bit o' the Irish, did you, sir?" The footman chuckled. "Where's 'er leash, eh?"

"Around your gullet if you don't shut that great trap," Caitlin retorted.

His face as dark as a thundercloud, Wesley stepped from the barge. His booted foot landed squarely on the man's instep.

"Ouch! 'Ave a care there, sir!"

"So sorry," Wesley murmured. Reaching down, he took Caitlin's hand and helped her to the stone quay.

She ignored the hapless footman. MacKenzie led the way along a passageway past the chapel and the Great Hall, across the broad courtyard and under the palace gate, and finally into the Outer Chamber, teeming with protectoral officials, dark-clad clerics, and foreign dignitaries. She fought an urge to hold onto Wesley's arm for support. At the same time, her eyes combed the crowd. Possibly, just possibly . . .

"He wouldn't be here," Wesley muttered under his

breath. "Your grandee wouldn't mingle with commoners."

Caitlin flushed, wondering at the ease with which he read her thoughts. She gave her attention to the Great Chamber and then the Presence Chamber. Opulence shimmered in the rooms, dripped from the crown of candles suspended by a chain from the ceiling, and glowed in the sober portraits that lined the walls.

Wesley's gaze searched the busy room even more desperately than hers had. Whom did he seek? she wondered. A former lady love? For the first time, it struck her that she still knew little of his past, nothing of the people he had known.

"The Lord Protector is with his daughter Bettie, the Lady Claypole, at Hampton Court." A liveried man hurried forward, extending his hand to Wesley. "He will be back within the week."

Wesley swore under his breath.

MacKenzie blew the red bulb of his nose. "The puir lady's still ailin', is she?"

The messenger lowered his eyes. "Lost her baby son a fortnight ago. Oliver, he was called, after his grandsire."

Caitlin pressed her lips together. She did not want to think of Cromwell as human, a grandfather grieving with his daughter over a baby's death.

The official turned to Wesley. "You're guests of the Protectorate."

Two soldiers marched forward, swords slapping against their blousy trousers.

"We're not guests at all," she snapped, her heart catapulting to her throat. "We're prisoners."

For three days, Caitlin lived alone in guarded luxury. A snap of her fingers brought hot water for a bath. A nod of her head summoned a houseboy with firewood. The amount she ate at a single meal would have fed Mrs. Boyle and her entire brood.

Wesley sent a mercer, a clothier, and a seamstress. Simply to escape the stultifying boredom, Caitlin submitted to their measuring and pin sticking.

Her heart ached with loneliness as she gazed out a high window at the cold stone buildings that housed the privy apartments of the Protectorate. She longed for the wild splendor of Connemara, the sharp smell of the sea in the summer air. She missed the evenings in the hall, listening to Magheen playing the harp or Tom Gandy spinning hero tales that grew more and more improbable with each cup of smoky, rye-flavored poteen.

And finally, she admitted to herself that she missed Wesley.

He had banished her from his heart because she would not yield her own to him.

He spent his days closed in a library, a room devoted entirely to books. He met daily with protectoral officials. Sometimes she heard the sound of hearty laughter and thought bitterly that they must consider it a grand joke that Wesley had taken an Irish bride. Other times she heard voices raised in anger and wondered if they would have her head after all.

On the fourth day, the dressmaker arrived with her trunks and assistants. "The master wants you gowned straightaway."

A frisson of fear sneaked down Caitlin's spine. The summons could mean that Cromwell had arrived from Hampton Court. "I dislike these fashions."

"Ladies of quality adore my designs."

"As a game hen adores being trussed for the roasting spit," Caitlin retorted, but she gave in. The sooner Wesley dragged her before Cromwell, the sooner she could go back to Clonmuir and be done with this farce. Besides, the rebel in her wanted to meet Cromwell, wanted to face the devil who murdered Irish babies because, as he put it, "Nits make lice." She wanted to tell the Lord Protector of England to go to hell.

An hour later, Caitlin studied her wavy image in a tall standing mirror. Wicker farthingale hoops shaped an overskirt of emerald velvet, parted in the center to reveal a silk petticoat. Satin slippers with chunky high heels peeped from beneath the hem. Glittering with gold thread, the bone stiffened bodice rose in a vee from waist to shoulders. The dresser had swept her hair into a loose braid and pinned it up with shell combs.

What a stranger she looked. A *Sassenach* stranger.

A footman came to accompany her down the grand staircase to the broad foyer. Wesley stood at the bottom.

He, too, looked the stranger, dressed in loose black trousers cinched at the waist by his ornate belt, and cuffed knee boots polished to a high sheen. A flowing black cloak was drawn back to reveal a dress sword at his hip. A hat with the brim turned up jauntily on one side shadowed his face.

She caught her breath. Were she an artist, she would yearn to capture the picture he made—his easy pose, his insouciant grin, and the riveting masculinity that emanated from him. Were she a poet, she would try to shape his appeal in words—the blithe charm on the surface, the undercurrent of pain and regret in his eyes, the nearly invisible world-weary lines about his smiling mouth.

She must be losing her mind. They were enemies. Her goal was to be rid of him and find Alonso, whose memory became more distant each day she spent with Wesley.

"I'm ready," she stated.

He used one finger to tip back the brim of his hat. His expression changed from astonishment to delight, then finally to a frank lust that nearly propelled her into his arms.

Instead she fixed him with a frosty stare, swept out the door, and marched across the green quadrangle with no notion of where she was going. Wesley's long, swift strides quickly brought him to her side. "You didn't give me a chance to tell you how beautiful you look."

She smoothed her hands over her skirts. "It's the dress that's beautiful, by English standards. Devil admire me, but I'm the same as I've always been."

He reached across and cupped her face gently in his hands. "What you are, Cait, and what you have always been, is beautiful." Leaning down, he kissed her, his lips lingering over hers until she clutched at him. He pulled back, a grin playing about his lips. "I've missed you, too, Cait," he said. "But when you come back to me, I want all of you."

"Forever is a long time."

"I invited you to dine with me each evening. Why did you refuse?"

"I don't like being summoned. Besides, England puts a great weariness upon me, and the food disagrees with me."

His eyebrows clashed in concern. "Caitlin, are you ill?"

"In the way of a swallow put in a cage, perhaps," she said.

He subjected her to a long, probing stare that traveled from her face to her breasts to her belly. "Cait, could it be—"

She thrust up her chin. "I presume I'm all tricked out like this because you're taking me to see the murderer, Cromwell."

"In time." Wesley started along a path to the left. MacKenzie scudded watchfully in their wake. "And it would behoove you to refrain from calling him a murderer."

"You're right. It's too good a word for the devil."

"Caitlin, if you want to get back to Clonmuir, you'll keep your opinions to yourself and show respect." His voice dropped, and she heard real fear in his tone. "I mean that, by God. You risk both our necks with your tart tongue." He took her hand, rubbed her chilled fingers. "So cold."

"England is a cold country, even in summer."

A look of revelation passed over his face. "You're afraid, aren't you?"

"Of course I'm afraid, you great lout. What Irishwoman would not be afraid of Oliver Cromwell?"

"It's a side of you I've not seen before, not even when I abducted you, not even in the heat of battle."

"When I can meet a man on a battlefield and pit my speed and my wiles against him, I have no reason to fear. In an honest battle, God's will prevails. But I'm not used to battles of words, waged by cheaters and traitors."

"Just remember, I'm on your side. I want to protect you, and then I want you to go free."

She sensed excitement in him and wondered what he was about. "Do you, Wesley?"

No, he thought with a lurch of his heart. I want to hold you and keep you always. I want to bring you and Laura together.

But he could not speak of Laura yet. He was too close to getting her back to risk a confession now. Later, when Laura was safe in his arms and the confrontation with Oliver Cromwell was behind them, he could tell all to Caitlin.

And probably lose her for good.

They entered the privy chamber. Perfect. His timing was perfect. The scene he had orchestrated so carefully was about to unfold. God forgive my cruelty, he thought.

No, he told himself. He would not feel guilty for grinding Caitlin's dreams to dust. She needed to see the truth, to see that her ideal image of the Spaniard was false.

His hand brushed the dress sword that rode at his hip. If Caitlin's grandee dared to harm her, Wesley would take great pleasure in running the bastard through.

A shiver passed over Caitlin as she studied the men and women in the crowded room. Gowned officials, resembling crows in their black winglike cloaks and with their shiny dark eyes, stood deep in conversation. Other groups spoke in foreign tongues. Ambassadors, she realized.

Her nerves thrummed, and her gaze sharpened on a knot of dark-haired men near a marble hearth, chafing their hands near the flames. The beautifully coiffed and oiled hair, the glittering costumes, set them apart from the drab-robed English. One man held himself tall and straight, his head cocked slightly as he listened to his stocky companion.

Alonso.

Joy washed over her, as sweet and pure as sunshine. She stood riveted by the sight of him. Yet at the same time she felt Wesley tensing beside her.

Her memories of Alonso paled beside the reality. Four years had broadened his shoulders, added maturity and wisdom to his handsome features.

A sense of unreality gripped her. So close. After years of anxious waiting and unbearable yearning, she stood mere steps away from realizing her long-cherished dream.

She pressed her fists to her breastbone, felt the pounding of her heart. How would he react when he learned she had wed another? He would understand, she told herself. He would help her find a way out of the mess with Hawkins. With a guilty thrill, she prayed Alonso would not hesitate to express his jubilation at seeing her again. The one chaste kiss they had shared had sustained her for years. But now she knew the meaning of passion. Like it or not, Hawkins had given her that.

Closing her eyes, she envisioned coming together with Alonso, mouths pressing hard, bodies straining for completion . . . . Her eyes flew open and filled with tears. For the man in her vision had not been Alonso, but—

"Caitlin."

She turned at the sound of her husband's voice.

Hawkins. Damn him. He had invaded her fantasies. His frank, rough affection had overrun her dreams of Alonso as the English had razed Ireland's forests.

He gave her a gentle push in the direction of the Spaniards. "Go and greet him, Caitlin." His voice was soft, but edged by irony. "It's what you've been waiting for, isn't it?"

She hesitated. What could be his purpose in bringing her here deliberately? She decided it was not important. Smoothing her hands over the bony structure of her farthingale, she tossed Wesley a defiant look and started forward.

"Excuse me."

The four gentlemen turned to her. She was unprepared for the appreciation that lit their faces. Each smiled. Each allowed his gaze to stroke her from head to toe.

Perhaps this English frippery had a purpose after all.

Braving a rush of bashfulness, she smiled directly at Alonso. Although his gaze devoured her, no recognition flickered in his eyes. With courtly stiffness, he took her hand and bowed over it. "A pleasure beyond compare, I assure you, señorita."

The lucid thoughts streaming through Caitlin's mind surprised her. When Wesley touched her, she could not think at all. "Alonso," she whispered. "Don't you know me?"

His eyes narrowed. They were smaller than she remembered. Darker. "No, señorita. Should I?"

She stepped back, her hand going out behind her, reaching against her will for support.

For Wesley. But he stood several feet away, watching, his face unreadable.

Cheeks flaming, Caitlin ignored the curious stares of the other Spaniards. "Alonso, it's Caitlin MacBride of Clonmuir. For the love of God, do you not remember?"

His face changed. A hardness came over his features.

Questions roared through her mind. Had Alonso already learned of her marriage? Did he understand why she had been forced to break faith with him?

Yes. He must. True love knew no jealousy. True love was the essence of pure understanding, unconditional forgiveness. There had never been a love so pure as the one she and Alonso had pledged to one another that day high on the crags of Connemara.

And yet . . . what was it she had felt, in the dark when Wesley was deep inside her, and their very souls seemed to mate?

Animal passion, she insisted stubbornly. Not the soft, dreamlike emotions she felt for Alonso.

He cleared his throat. A delicate sound. A sound of polite discomfiture. "I did not expect to see you here, señorita." He bowed to his companions and said something in Spanish. Then he led her out to the long green courtyard and stopped in the shade of an ornamental yew tree.

"Alonso." His name came on a rush of breath. "I've waited so long and fought so hard. There's so much to discuss."

He seemed not to hear her. Furtive hunger shadowed his eyes. "*Dios*, but you have become a beauty!" he exclaimed.

With a cry of joy, she flung her arms around his neck.

With an oath of fury, Wesley strode across the green toward them. Caitlin jumped back. Her heart thumped at the deadly expression on her husband's face. Fury boiled in his eyes and blazed across his features. As he came forward, his hand went to the hilt of his dress sword.

"Here, sir," Alonso snapped out. "Who are you?"

"Your worst enemy," Wesley said without slackening his pace.

"Wesley, no!" Caitlin stepped in front of Alonso.

He stopped walking. Huge and powerful, he had the look of a man who had never lost a battle. His sword sliced from its sheath. "Step aside, Caitlin," he said. "Or is your lover in the habit of using a woman as a shield?"

"Never!" Alonso pushed past Caitlin. His own bright blade glittered in the sun. He stepped forward and sketched a neat challenge in the air with his sword tip. "I refuse no invitation from an English commoner."

"You'll wish you had, you Spanish bastard." Wesley lunged with his sword arm extended.

Their crossed blades made a metallic whine.

"Stop it, both of you!" Caitlin shouted, knowing

even as she spoke that they would ignore her. They were two furious champions, each intent on victory. Alonso fought with the agile precision of a well-schooled swordsman. Wesley battled with the unearthly strength and dogged will that slapped formal training in the face. In an odd way, they were well matched: Alonso's crafty quickness against Wesley's raw fury.

Alonso extended himself in a perfectly executed lunge. Wesley leapt back, bumping into a stone bench behind him. Undaunted, he made a grand backward jump and mounted the bench. He took full advantage of the added height, his wrath blazing in the face of Alonso's icy composure.

Alonso's close-playing wrist sought entrance to Wesley's broad-reaching defense. The Spaniard fenced magnificently, cold as steel, his eyes blank and pitiless. In contrast, Wesley flamed with passion.

He leapt down from the bench. By main force he battled Alonso backward across the greensward, where a crowd had quickly gathered. Alonso made an ill-timed thrust. Wesley caught the blade with the edge of his. They came together, swords crossed, chests heaving, muscles trembling with deadly effort.

"Tell me, my friend," said Wesley, panting hard, "do you make it a practice to seduce other men's wives?"

For a split second, Alonso's cold composure vanished. His jaw dropped. His grip on the hilt faltered.

Wesley's booted foot came up. In a ploy that would appall any master swordsman, he stomped on Alonso's foot.

The Spaniard cried out. Wesley plucked the sword from his hand and flung the blade away. With the same motion, he whipped his point to Alonso's throat.

"Wesley!" Caitlin rushed forward. "I beg you, don't—"

"He won't," said Alonso in a shaky voice. His eyes flooded with relief as he looked past Wesley's shoulder.

Swords drawn, Alonso's companions raced toward them. Two women wearing lacy black shawls hurried in their wake. The plump younger one carried a baby on her hip.

"Release me," said Alonso, "or my men will run you through like a sausage on a stick."

Wesley hesitated for a heartbeat, then lowered his sword. The heat of madness cooled; his anger turned in on himself. He should have exercised more self-control. He should not have surrendered to the rage that had gripped him on seeing Caitlin fling herself at the Spaniard.

The younger woman clung to Alonso and spoke in rapid Spanish, making sure he wasn't injured. In moments, Caitlin would know the truth. Wesley hated the dark satisfaction that crept over him. "I'm sure Mrs. Hawkins would be delighted to make your acquaintance," he said to the woman.

Alonso gave a hiss of anger as he looked from the Spanish woman to Caitlin. He wiped a bead of sweat from his brow, then snapped a practiced bow. "Doña Maria," he stated. "And this is little Federico. My wife and son."

Wesley would have traded his sword arm to spare Caitlin the pain he saw so clearly in her eyes. The amber jewels seemed to splinter like shards of sunlight. The color dropped from her face. Her hands clenched into fists.

But she was still the MacBride. She recovered in scant seconds. Like a queen bestowing royal favors, she nodded at her Spanish swain's wife, then swept back toward the palace.

Sheathing his sword, Wesley hurried after her. "I'm sorry. But you had to know."

She gave a bitter laugh. "You English bastard. You planned this. Is it your mission in life to hurt me, make me miserable? Do you take pleasure in my pain?"

"Caitlin, you have to feel the hurt before you can start to heal."

"Oh, spare me." She tossed her head and quickened her stride. "Don't we have an appointment with Oliver Cromwell?"

13

A long, stark corridor lined with menacing-looking pikemen opened to the equally stark privy chamber. There, at a polished table in front of a hanging that bore the arms of the Protectorate, sat Oliver Cromwell.

Caitlin stopped walking. Her face and lips paled, making her eyes appear vividly gold. Wesley tried to guess what she was feeling as she faced the man responsible for laying waste to her homeland and outlawing her faith. His legions burned crops and pillaged towns. They abducted women and children and sent them away in bondage. They hanged rebels, butchered livestock, and stole horses. They razed castles and ripped families apart.

And here he sat, holding court like a monarch. His badly barbered hair, red-brown streaked with iron, framed a face that, Wesley realized, had aged years in mere months. Peering beneath the studied cruelty of that face, he saw a man who had lost his grandchild and whose favorite daughter lay dying.

"Mr. Hawkins, come in, and bring your companion."

Cromwell gestured amiably. "You, too, Mr. Thurloe." Clad in severe Puritan black, John Thurloe entered through a side doorway.

Wesley placed his hand in the middle of Caitlin's back. "Courage, darling," he murmured under his breath.

She stiffened at his touch. Her anger over the meeting with the Spaniard burned Wesley like a glowing iron.

A retainer brought wine. The servant discreetly sipped from a cup, swirling the liquid in his mouth before swallowing and handing it with a nod to the Lord Protector. So, Cromwell worried about poisoning.

"Do sit down," invited Cromwell.

"I prefer to stand," said Wesley. "We should be able to conclude our business in a matter of minutes."

Cromwell glanced at a letter on the table in front of him. "I shall be the one to declare when—and if— our business is successfully concluded."

An ominous chill tiptoed up Wesley's spine. "You demanded that I deliver the chieftain of the Fianna. And so I have."

Cromwell and Thurloe craned their necks to see beyond the doorway. "Where is the godless cur?" demanded the Lord Protector.

Wesley slipped his arm around Caitlin's shoulders. "You're looking at her, sir."

A burst of harsh laughter exploded from Cromwell. "By the Almighty, Hawkins! I didn't think even you would stoop so low." His bright, cold eyes drifted over Caitlin. The blatant appreciation in his regard made Wesley itch to rip his face off.

"He speaks the truth." Caitlin's voice rang clear and sweet as a harp in the cavernous room. At the sound of her liquid, Irish purr, Cromwell and Thurloe exchanged a glance. She added, "I am Caitlin MacBride."

Wesley started to add "Hawkins," but Cromwell slapped his hands on the table and surged to his feet. "You're the treacherous mistress of Clonmuir?"

"Treachery is your specialty, not mine. I am also the MacBride, chief of my sept."

"You have led the Fianna on all its murderous raids?"

Fierce hatred sharpened her features. "Aye, I admit it."

"How very interesting," said Cromwell. He sighed and sat back down. Weariness carved vertical lines in his cheeks. "You realize that you face a penalty of death for breaking my laws."

Wesley felt a subtle trembling in her shoulders, but her voice was steady. "Sir, I cannot trespass against your laws because I did not submit to them."

Red patches mottled his cheeks. "All Ireland submits to me! Madam, your country will accept the law and order of my Protectorate."

"You brought no law and order to Ireland," she snapped. "You brought only greedy settlers who bleed us dry, take our lands, and charge us taxes. If that's your brand of law and order, you can keep it. Don't pollute Ireland with it."

Her loathing shone as pure and clean as a polished blade. Cromwell's answering hatred was corrupt, sullied by ambition and intolerance. "Nevertheless, I rule Ireland—and you."

"The wench has a fiery tongue, to be sure," said Thurloe. "But the Irish are born liars."

Caitlin glared at him. "And who—or what—might you be?"

Thurloe's nostrils thinned. He picked up a quill and dipped it in ink, making a notation at the bottom of a document. "Secretary of State to the Commonwealth."

She thrust up her chin. "Bully for you."

Cromwell addressed Wesley. "I presume you have proof."

"I witnessed the raid she led. So did a lieutenant named Edmund Ladyman." Wesley produced Ladyman's statement, notarized by Hammersmith. He gestured at the man who stood in the doorway. Clearly overawed by the Lord Protector, the Scotsman gave a sharp salute. "MacKenzie will attest to the authenticity of this."

Caitlin, who had looked death in the face a hundred times and laughed at it, twined her fingers together in fear.

Cromwell added the document to his papers. "There will be a trial, of course. A mere formality given the evidence. And then" —Cromwell sighed— "I'm afraid the outcome is rather distasteful. But I must make an example of you. Other Irish rebels must learn the price of murdering the English."

He raised his hand to summon a guard.

"Not so fast." Wesley's voice lashed like a black whip. "You gave your word in writing that if I brought you the leader of the Fianna, you'd not harm me or my kin."

"I fully intend to honor my word."

"Good. Then you must understand that you cannot harm Caitlin."

"Why the devil not?"

"Because she's my kin. I married her."

Thurloe dropped his quill and his jaw. Cromwell leapt up again. His wineglass fell to the floor and shattered, the red wine pooling like blood on the floor.

Wesley placed yet another paper before the Lord Protector. "There it is, sir. The special license, the witnessed certificate. She is my legal wife and my kin."

"There can be no marriage between Irish and English."

"We married on the high seas. The union is legal."

"Why, you conniving papist devil," shouted Cromwell.

The Secretary of State examined the documents. "They seem to be in order, Your Highness."

"I've registered copies with the High Court of Justice and the Commissioners. Oh, and also with Viscount Fauconberg."

Rage blazed across Cromwell's face at the mention of his son-in-law. Fauconberg had royalist leanings and plenty of influence. He'd not look kindly upon Cromwell's schemes.

With growing confidence, Wesley curved his arm around Caitlin's waist. "If you so much as let your shadow fall on this woman, you'll be exposed as a faithless breaker of promises, unworthy of the trust of the lowliest mongrel in the kingdom."

"There is no kingdom. I have made of England a Commonwealth dedicated to republican principles."

"And that's why you'll keep your word," said Wesley. "The public trust is everything, is it not? One slip, *Highness*, and you'll find every eye in England turned eastward. To a small town on the Continent. To a man called Charles Stuart."

Cromwell pounded the table. "Do not dare to utter the traitor's name in my presence!"

"But who will be called traitor if you break faith with your sworn agreement?" asked Wesley.

"You haven't stopped the Fianna, my good friend." Triumph flashed in Cromwell's eyes as he waved a letter in the air. Wesley snatched the letter. "What's this?"

"A communiqué from Titus Hammersmith, dated just eight days ago. The Fianna has struck again. And on a day when you and your whore of a wife were at sea."

"No!" said Caitlin. "That can't be."

Wesley forgot to breathe until his lungs screamed

for air. Rory Breslin, he thought. Tom Gandy. Conn O'Donnell and Liam the smith and all the others. They must have torn apart the entire west coast of Ireland searching for Caitlin. Damn them. Their loyalty had slipped a noose around their necks.

"This must be the work of a different faction," he said. "I have done my part. You can't hold me responsible for the actions of every band of rebels in Ireland."

Cromwell motioned to Thurloe. "Take Mrs. Hawkins to the outer chamber. She could use a bracing dish of tea."

Wesley stepped in front of her. "I'm not letting her out of my sight."

"Quit playing the gallant. She'll be perfectly safe with Mr. Thurloe. Besides," he added persuasively, "you and I have further business to discuss."

Knowing precisely what the Lord Protector meant, Wesley stepped aside. Shooting a last, furious look at Wesley, Caitlin left with Thurloe. The door closed with a loud thump.

Wesley whirled on Cromwell. "All right. Where is she?"

"Patience, patience, my good friend." Cromwell walked unhurriedly to a side door and tapped on the panel.

In walked Hester Clench, her black-clad arm around a child's tiny shoulders.

"*Laura.*" Rushing to her, Wesley dropped to one knee in front of her and cradled her against his chest. Her sweet pure scent flowed like a stream of sunshine through him. "Oh, my Laura." He kissed both cheeks.

She pulled back. A familiar locket winked on her chest, and sober confusion glowed in her green eyes. "Hello, Papa. You mustn't kiss me so. Auntie Clench says it's unseemly."

His arms went numb. His child extracted herself from his embrace, taking a piece of his heart with her.

"What's the matter, Laura?" he asked cautiously. She was dressed all in black, a pale little mourner regarding a corpse. "Aren't you happy to see your papa?"

"Well, I suppose so, but—"

"Laura, dear." Cromwell's voice dripped like treacle into the conversation. "Come see what I've got for you. Lively now."

Oblivious to Wesley, Laura skipped across the room and climbed into the Lord Protector's lap. "What is it, Uncle Oliver?" She pressed her hands to his quilted doublet.

"Here." He brought out a little silver bell. "Something sweet to remind you of the sweetness of our Lord Jesus."

She rang the bell, and her laughter joined its chiming. "Thank you, Uncle Oliver! I can't wait to show Miss Bettie!"

Wesley's heart sank like a rock. He shot a venomous glare at Hester Clench; then he slowly approached the table. It took all his control to keep his expression pleasant and fatherly. Inside he seethed like a volcano on the verge of eruption. The bell was one of those rung by Catholics at the consecration. Trust the bastard to turn a sacred object into a child's toy.

Seeing her seated, laughing and secure, in the Lord Protector's lap, Wesley felt his plans unravel, and panic broke in a cold sweat over him. He had to get her out of here, and fast. "Laura, darling," he said. "I've come to take you with me. We can be together again."

Instead of the joy he had expected, instead of the smile he had envisioned during the long weeks in Ireland, she clutched at Cromwell and regarded her father with apprehension. "You're taking me away? From Uncle Oliver and Auntie Clench?"

"Yes, Laura. We'll be together again."

"Oh, no, Papa. Uncle Oliver says it's not safe to wander the roads with you."

"I'll keep you safe, Laura. I swear it."

Her eyes filled with tears. "But I don't want to go! I have a skin horse and a dollhouse and my friend Lisbeth to play with at Hampton Court, and—" She pressed her face into Cromwell's doublet. "Please don't make me go away, Uncle Oliver. I want to stay with you and Auntie Clench and Miss Bettie."

Cromwell stroked her hair. "There, there, poppet. Uncle Oliver will see what he can do."

Wesley tried to deny the gentleness in the way Cromwell handled the child. He tried to deny the real affection the Lord Protector showed to Laura. But despite his reputation, despite his manipulative ways, Cromwell did possess a softness. "Run along with Mrs. Clench and she'll help you draw a nice picture to take to Miss Bettie at Hampton Court. And you can have seed cakes and oranges for tea."

Wesley thought of the crude meals he had scraped together for her over the years of running and hiding.

Laura sniffled. "Can I have honey on my cakes?"

"Of course, poppet."

She dropped from his lap and ran to Hester Clench.

"Laura . . ." said Wesley, his voice close to breaking.

Almost as an afterthought, she called, "Good-bye, Papa!" She skipped out, her father already forgotten.

Wesley shuddered with a feeling of betrayal and inadequacy. How easily he had lost his daughter's affection. "Damn your soul to hell," he whispered to Cromwell. "I'm surprised you didn't see fit to flaunt my daughter before my wife."

Cromwell rubbed his temples. "I'd not bring shame upon that child, Mr. Hawkins. And no one must know of our arrangement."

Wesley gave a bitter bark of laughter. "Ah, yes, your precious reputation once again. The public trust and all that. I've a mind to let the public know that you take children from their parents—"

"Do that," said Cromwell, each word a ball of hot lead in Wesley's gut, "and you'll never see the girl again."

"You bastard." Wesley itched to pound Cromwell's face into a pulp. "You turned her against me."

"I fulfilled her needs. As you can see, we treat the child with love and care. She's been such a comfort to my Bettie."

A comfort, thought Wesley, his panic burning hotter. For a woman who had just lost a small child. God, Lady Claypole might never let Laura go. "You're manipulating an innocent mind."

Cromwell's face chilled. "Look at the facts, man. When Mrs. Clench brought Laura here, the child was a bedraggled urchin, unwashed, ill-fed, crude of manner, and ungovernable."

Against his will, Wesley remembered nights she had fallen asleep hungry because they were on the run from priest catchers. He remembered the times they had slept in hayricks or cellars. He remembered picking lice from her hair, his clumsy mending of her clothes when she tore them. But through all the hardships, her sunny disposition had rarely dimmed. "She was a happy child," he insisted.

"She simply didn't know any other life," Cromwell said reasonably. "But thanks to Mrs. Clench and my own dear daughter, Laura has learned that there are such things as warm baths and comfortable beds. Forks and plates. Good, hearty meals."

"Creature comforts are nothing."

"That's an ignorant statement even from you. You dragged the child from pillar to post, sleeping in the rain and taking her among people of questionable character. Is it any wonder she prefers her new life?"

"It's an artificial life. She's been rewarded like a pet spaniel for performing a clever trick."

"She has been loved and comforted."

Desperate, Wesley leaned toward Cromwell's face. "She's my daughter. I want her back."

"We made a bargain, Mr. Hawkins. You subdue the Fianna. In exchange, I return Laura to you. If you breathe so much as a word about this arrangement, especially to that Irish wife of yours, the child's life is forfeit." He gestured at the communiqué from Hammersmith. "You've not yet succeeded, Mr. Hawkins. Until I receive word that the Fianna has ceased its murderous rampages, your daughter remains my hostage."

An antechamber with two thick doors separated Caitlin from Wesley and Cromwell. Under the watchful eyes of Thurloe, MacKenzie, and a half-dozen pikemen, she paced the corridor.

The revelations of the day cascaded through her mind like a spring torrent over jagged rocks. Fear and rage and confusion mocked her attempts to reason and plan.

Wesley had orchestrated the encounter with Alonso. How it must have gratified him to watch her discover that the man she had yearned for had married and sired a child.

You have to feel the hurt before you can begin to heal.

And yet the pain she felt was vague, uncentered, as if she had known all along that a marriage with Alonso was impossible, as if a chapter in her life had closed.

More significant than Alonso's betrayal was the

meeting with Cromwell. Before today, she had assumed that Cromwell and Wesley were in league against the Fianna. The meeting had shaken the foundations of her belief.

Oliver Cromwell and John Wesley Hawkins were adversaries.

The revelation filled her mind with unanswered questions. Why didn't Wesley defy the Lord Protector? He had every reason to; he had been tortured for his faith; he possessed an unshakable sense of humanity that even Caitlin couldn't deny.

Still, he had dedicated himself to stopping the Fianna.

Why?

The door of the antechamber slammed open. Caitlin was about to demand an explanation, but the words died on her lips when she saw the look on Wesley's face. It was like the day of the race, when his whole manner had changed and he had tamed the stallion. His skin was pale, his eyes hard, ice coated. Yet behind the ice, a fire blazed. She realized he hovered scant inches from losing control. His mouth was as hard and unyielding as stone.

"What is it?" she asked.

None too gently, he took her arm and hauled her toward the door. "We're going back to Clonmuir. Tonight."

The fury of his silence caught Caitlin at a loss. Five days earlier they had left London for Milford Haven and boarded a protectoral frigate bound for Galway. Two days after that they sailed the high, surging seas. The waves had the weight of an old storm in them, and the wind carried a chill not even the balmy streams of air from the west could warm.

They shared a luxurious berth and the ship's crew treated them with deference. From this Caitlin deduced that Wesley was still in Cromwell's favor. But she could discern nothing more. He neither spoke to her nor touched her. At night she slept in the cozy bunk while he made do, without complaint, on a hard wooden bench beneath the stern windows.

Pride kept her from initiating a discussion.

Fury kept him from offering an explanation.

Deadlocked, they spent pain-filled days and empty nights in bitter agony.

Desperately bored, her nerves frazzled to shreds, Caitlin sought companionship from the ship's crew.

They were foulmouthed Englishmen, but at least they spoke to her. The boatswain carved her a whistle from driftwood, and she blew a signal. Delighted by the bright sound, she laughed.

Wesley, who stood at the binnacle several paces away, flinched as if she had struck him.

The sailmaker taught her a ditty about a seal who turned human and fell in love with a mortal, only to revert forever to his original state in order to save her from drowning. Caitlin broke down and wept at the sad tale.

Seeing her tears, Wesley came running, his face gray with apprehension. Upon learning the source of her distress, he turned away with a snort of disgust.

A foremastman invited her to try her hand at climbing the rigging. Dressed again in her comfortable tunic and trews, she grasped the thick ropes and hoisted herself with ease.

The great height exaggerated the pitch of the ship. The swift and breathtaking movement gave her the sensation of flight. For a moment, she soared as free as the gulls that winged beneath a boiling mantle of clouds.

She heard Wesley's voice from below. "Get her down," he snapped to the foremastman. "And if you ever endanger her again I'll have you skelped within a bloody inch of your life."

Caitlin considered staying aloft just to spite him. But out of concern for the crewman, she descended.

That night in their cabin, she sat across the table from Wesley. She found herself watching his hands, big and rough, yet nimble in the way they twisted the stem of his wine goblet.

His silence, she realized, was making her miserable.

She resented the hold he had on her mood. She resented the fact that he could make her feel anything at all.

She glared at him. Staid and emotionless, he concentrated on the wine in his glass.

Like a too-taut harp string, her control snapped. "Wesley."

He glanced up, his eyes as blank and impenetrable as shadows.

"If you've a point to make with me, I wish you'd be after speaking up rather than sulking in silence like a child."

He jerked away from the table and surged to his feet. "Is that what you think, Caitlin? That I'm a child who's had his favorite plaything snatched away?"

She sighed. "Faith, I don't know what to think. You won't talk to me."

"Is there anything to say?" he asked quietly. "Anything that won't set us at each other's throats?"

"We're people, not a pair of snarling wolfhounds."

"Very well. What would you like to talk about?"

About the deeds of the ancients. The people of Clonmuir. The color of the sun rising over the crags.

Whirlwinds, comets, dark magic. With a painful wave of nostalgia, she reflected on matters they used to discuss with easy amiability and a deep, mutual sense of wonder.

"We could start with Alonso," she said at last.

His shoulders tensed. "Ah. A favored topic of mine indeed."

"I told you about him on our wedding night."

"Give yourself high marks for honesty."

She hated the terrible expression on his face. She hated the hurt he could not quite manage to hide. Against her will, she felt a pained tenderness toward him. Shoving aside the feeling, she stated, "You knew I loved him."

"It's easy to love a man you've not seen in four years. Every time you thought of him, your imagination added a fresh patina to his perfection."

Comprehension blazed through her. "So that's it, then. You knew I'd never find the man in the flesh as appealing as the man in my memories." She waited for his response, but he merely stared, unblinking, waiting. "You knew him," she accused. "And you didn't tell me."

"I knew him only vaguely. A lot of the London Catholics celebrated mass with foreign dignitaries. They escaped persecution that way."

"Why didn't you tell me that he was married?"

"I didn't know for certain until we reached London. Then I wanted you to see for yourself what a liar he is."

"And you contrived the most humiliating way possible for me to find out!"

"I didn't make you fling yourself into his arms."

"How considerate of you. Tell me, Wesley, did you never feel remorse at deceiving me?"

"I did, Caitlin. And I still do. Every minute of every

day." Then his expression changed, going fierce and hard. His hands shot out, and he gripped her shoulders. "I'm glad he's married, do you hear me? Damn it, Cait, I want you for myself."

His touch, and the raw honesty of his admission, awakened a reluctant sympathy in Caitlin. "For pity's sake, Wesley, why?"

"You know the answer to that," he snapped. "I'll not repeat it only to have you fling it in my face." He let go of her. "We were speaking of Alonso, were we not? Did he match the expectations you'd built up around him? Tell me, how did he explain away the fact that he was married?"

"You drew your sword and challenged him before—"

"Before you let him make adulterers of you both?" he demanded. "Would you have let him take you right then and there? Fling you on the ground in the shadow of Whitehall Palace and—"

"Stop it!" She struck him on the chest. "Alonso would never be so crass as you."

"Yes, dear Alonso. Always so honorable."

"I'm learning that honor is a relative thing." She looked away, summoning anger from the regrets that softened her will. "Why play the jealous husband, Wesley? You said that you were willing to accept that my affections will never be yours."

"That was before—" Wesley bit off the words, but his heart finished the thought. *That was before I learned how much you mean to me. Before I'd discovered the magic of loving you.*

Love. What a grand, glorious curse. Love was supposed to make a poet of a man. Of John Wesley Hawkins it had made a wretched, uncontrollable beast.

"Before what?" she prompted.

Reaching out, he took her in his arms once again.

The rage flowed out of him like foul water draining from a pond.

"Caitlin. When you kept pleading fatigue, turning aside my invitations at the palace, do you know what I thought?"

"No. But I've never understood you."

"Fatigue is so unlike you, Caitlin. But even the most energetic of women falls prey to weariness when she's pregnant."

"Pregnant!" Her hands lifted to cover her midsection.

"I thought you had conceived my baby on our wedding night."

The anger melted from her expression. "Ah, Wesley—"

"Do you know how that made me feel?"

She shook her head.

"My heart took wing, Cait. I felt so proud, I wanted to ring all the bells of London."

"You shouldn't have leapt to an unlikely conclusion."

"Unlikely? Caitlin, we made love in the deepest, richest way possible. I gave you a piece of myself, of my body and soul. Is it any wonder that I fancied my love had borne fruit?"

She cast her eyes down. "You should have asked me. You might have spared yourself the disappointment."

"I've coped with disappointment before, believe me." With an angry motion, he yanked off his doublet and shirt. "You've seen the scars. I've been tortured. Whipped, stretched, mangled. But your fatigue vanished when you saw your lover. God, Cait, it gave me a pain worse than any torture." At least under torture he could retreat from the agony. But nothing could shield his heart from Caitlin.

She said, "You knew when you forced me to wed that I didn't want you."

He touched her beneath the chin, drew her gaze up to meet his. How was it that she could embody both misty sweetness and implacable will? "What I didn't know is how much I would come to love you."

She took his hand and set it aside. "You can't love me."

"I do, Caitlin. From the very depths of my soul, I do."

"Then stop. Just stop it, now."

"Better I should stop the sun from shining." He caught her again, pressing her to his chest. The silk of her hair threaded his fingers. "Tell me you care for me."

"You've captured me. You've conquered me. What more do you want?"

"Caitlin, I want you to look at me and see no other than the man you love. I want you to feel a start of pure joy when you awaken in the morning and find me beside you. I want you to wish you could rush the sunset so that we can be together sooner."

She pressed her hands to her flaming cheeks. "You ask the impossible."

"No. By God, we could have a love such as the angels would envy if you would but let down your fierce Irish pride." With a groan of yearning he pulled her closer. "These days and nights of silence have been torture."

"Because you won't even think of compromising," she whispered, and he heard the ache of sadness in her voice. "You haven't even told me the conclusion of your business with Cromwell."

The pain burrowed deeper into his chest. "Thanks to your friends at Clonmuir, I am still obligated to Cromwell."

She lowered herself to the bed. The skin tightened across her cheeks. Her distrust was so tangible he fancied he could reach out and grasp it. She asked, "Why do you let him force you to attack my people?"

"He'll not be satisfied until the Fianna stops raiding." He held her gaze. "And I will stop it, Caitlin."

Her cheeks blanched, then flooded with livid color. He thought she might strike him and found himself wishing she would. Instead she twisted her fingers into the bedclothes. "You faithless blackguard," she said. "You profess to love me. You expect me to be fool enough to believe you. And then you propose to keep me from protecting what is mine. You call that love, Mr. Hawkins?" She raised her wide, pleading eyes to him. "If you love me, you'll turn your back on Oliver Cromwell and give your loyalty to Clonmuir."

He had seen the challenge coming. He should have been prepared. More than anything, he wished to be honest with her. *Cromwell has made a hostage of my child,* he wanted to say. *She is the lever that forces me to do his bidding.*

Wesley held the words at bay. Caitlin was a woman of compassion who took strangers into her home. For that very reason, he couldn't tell her about Laura. Her knowing could make no possible difference now; it would only manipulate her emotions further, confront her with a choice that could tear her well-guarded heart in two. He refused to make her choose between the safety of a child and the security of her people.

Besides, a confession now was too risky. One slip, and Laura was forfeit.

Would Caitlin keep faith with him? Or would she divulge the secret? Yet who could she tell?

Logan Rafferty.

She would scoff at Wesley's distrust of the Irish lord. Rafferty was overbearing, stubborn, and arrogant, but she would never believe him capable of intriguing with the Roundheads for his own gain. She was blind to Rafferty's darker side, just as she had been blind to the Spaniard's faults.

"Caitlin, I'm asking you. Help me keep the peace with Hammersmith."

She reclined and drew her knees up to her chest as if to shield herself from him. "I think I liked our silence better, Mr. Hawkins." She lay quiet, unmoving, while the water rushed past the hull and twilight slid into deep night. At some point, she drifted off to sleep.

Watching her, Wesley recalled that some postulants saw their vocations as clearly as a reflection in still water. His own calling, if it had ever existed at all, had been submerged in the murkiness of duty, frustration, and a desire to rebel.

The prior of Douai had recognized this. He had sent Wesley back to England to minister to the underground Catholics. In braving the dangers of practicing an outlawed religion, Wesley had hoped to find his vocation, shining like a beacon fire in the night.

Instead his purpose had dimmed, his loyalties had been divided among Charles Stuart, the Holy Church, and finally—irrevocably—Laura.

He smiled bitterly at the woman sleeping on the bed. At last, John Wesley Hawkins had learned the terrible joy of finding a vocation.

And then, as the frigate smashed through the waves of the cold sea, he realized what he must do.

He must prove himself to her. Mere words were not enough, for she was a woman of action. And in the proving, he would win her love.

He gazed at the uncompromising beauty of her face and suppressed a sigh. She would resist him every step of the way. She would call him names, scream at him in anger, and when she thought he wasn't looking, she would gaze at him in desire.

And he would love every minute of the fight.

14

They came to Clonmuir at night, the crew expertly heaving to at the outer banks of the rocky shoreline. Caitlin stood on deck amidships. Like a mother inspecting a babe, she probed the darkness for signs of trouble. Her heart exulted at the sight of the familiar profile, majestically intact, against the night sky.

MacKenzie clasped hands with Wesley. "Yon ship's boat is yours to keep. We'll nae be waitin' for its return."

Caitlin shot him a wry glance, understanding what the man refused to say. He feared the Irishmen of Clonmuir and would not tarry any longer than necessary.

The boat settled into the water with a resounding splash. Wesley picked up the oars and began rowing. Caitlin fixed her gaze behind him, on the huge craggy shadow of her home.

How would they receive her? When she left, she had been the MacBride, chieftain of the sept.

Now she was returning as an Englishman's bride.

"Cold?" asked Wesley.

She realized she was shivering. "No."

"I've worked up a fine sweat." He pulled off his shirt, flexed his fingers, then resumed rowing. He extended his sinewy arms forward, then drew back, plowing through the swells. His flesh was pale in the moonlight and shaped by rippling muscles. Moisture dewed his neck and chest. His face wore a look of intent concentration, as if he enjoyed physical exertion.

Reach and pull. Reach and pull. The rhythm pulsed through her veins. She tried to disregard him, tried to focus her thoughts on Clonmuir.

But against her will, her whole awareness stayed fixed on Wesley. Reach and pull. The powerful cadence held her spellbound. She remembered the feel of his arms around her, his mouth pressed to hers, the giddy delight she felt when he caressed her. It was mad to want him so, mad to feel yearning when she should loathe him.

The sweat rolled in rivulets now, coursing down the center of him, into the cuff of his wide belt. Her gaze strayed lower; she saw the fullness there and realized what it meant.

Mortified, she jerked her gaze back to his face. And was struck by the knowing charm of his smile.

I want you. Silently he mouthed the words to her.

Frustrated, Caitlin buried her face in her sleeves and did not look at him again until the boat slid ashore on the strand below Clonmuir.

"We're home, Cait," Wesley said. "Give me your hand."

His palm was hot and moist and sticky. She turned his hand over. "Blessed St. Brigid, you're bleeding."

"Bother it." Bending, he plunged his hands into the surf and winced as the saltwater bit into the broken blisters.

She would never get used to him. One moment he

acted the conqueror. The next he worked his hands raw to get her home. Guessing his motive, she said tartly, "You're in quite a hurry to flaunt your new status as my husband."

He straightened, wiping his hands on his loose breeches. "I was in a hurry to bring you here. Right here where the magic between us started."

Dawn was cresting on the horizon, gilding the lost garden of Siobhan MacBride. Slowly Caitlin approached the quiet tidal pools, the tumbled stones, the profusion of wind-raked gorse and brambles. A tide of memories washed over her.

Pluck a rose the moment the sun dies, and wish for him.

She had sought her true love. She had found Hawkins, an enemy to her people and a danger to her heart.

How could he be the one? He had been nothing but trouble since that portentious evening. And yet in spite of everything, she had never felt so alive, so . . . cherished.

She whirled to find him watching her, his eyes mysterious pools with undercurrents of passion streaming in their depths.

"You still feel it, don't you, Caitlin?" He stepped closer, heedless of the water that closed over his boots.

She opened her mouth to reply but no sound came out.

The enchantment rose through her like the borning sun bursting over the horizon. He wasn't Hawkins, but the Warrior of the Spring, reaching for a fairy maiden. His outstretched arms promised a world of passion. His deep, shadow-colored eyes pledged a splendor beyond imagining.

Don't touch me, Caitlin. His words called across the weeks to her. *Don't touch me unless you mean it.*

She could not tell who made the first move, the beguiling man or the ancient believer inside her. The cold water swirled around her ankles while his embrace bathed her in a fiery heat that banished the chill.

I mean it now, Wesley, God help me, I do.

"Caitlin," he said, his mouth soft upon hers as he spoke between kisses, "I've missed holding you close."

A sound of yearning rippled in her throat. She stretched up on tiptoe and pressed her hands to his chest. His heart hammered madly, and she realized he was not so calm or self-possessed as he appeared. Her hands moved up to frame his massive shoulders and discovered a tautness there. He was a man on the verge of explosion, a coiled spring about to be released.

A coiled snake about to strike.

But try as she might, she could read no evil into his intent. The idea that simply holding her strained the very bonds of his control gave her a heady feeling of power and delight.

She lifted her face and saw him framed by the pale sky. He plied his lips in a poem upon her mouth. The taste of him flooded her, racing through her veins and pooling with unbearable heat in the most vulnerable part of her. She pressed closer, discovering his rigidity and an answering softness deep within herself.

Ah, but she wanted him, and she was losing her powers of resistance. He plucked them away, one by one, like red berries picked from a rowan branch.

Unable to stop herself, she pressed her lips to his skin, tasting the salt-sweet flavor secreted in the hollow of his neck.

His hands slid up her torso, his thumbs gliding over her breasts. She caught her breath, then let it out slowly as warm, melting sensations poured through her. He brought her body to life with his touch, and yet he tormented her heart with dreams of what could never be.

"Cait," he whispered, his voice mingling with the hush of the waves, "London—everything—is behind us. God knows what lies ahead."

The truth of it caught at her heart. They had only this moment, suspended between their two worlds. And in his eyes glowed a promise that, if she would just open herself to him, he would show her where the stars were lit.

A slow sigh escaped her. She twined her fingers into the thick mane of his hair and drew his head down to hers. Their lips met and clung together; the shared taste of ancient pleasure intoxicated her. They tumbled to the sand, not Englishman and Irishwoman, not even husband and wife, but two searching souls desperate for the narcotic oblivion of physical ecstasy. He took her swiftly, roughly, and she cried out and returned his turbulent caresses with exultant wantonness. The frenzy left them spent, panting, a little dazed.

Something had changed between them, but Caitlin was too tired to puzzle it out. Shivering in the chill dawn, she stood and shook the sand from her clothes.

The furious barking of a dog echoed down from the cliffs. With a gasp of mortification, she stumbled back. Wesley was no Irish legend, but a conquering Englishman, Cromwell's creature. Whipping a glance over her shoulder, she spied the wolfhound, Finn, bounding toward them. The thick gray fur bristled on his back as he raced down to the strand.

His barking turned to yelps of greeting. His feathered tail drew great circles in the air. Careening through the pool, he made a leap for Wesley, placing huge paws on his chest.

"Enough, you great beast." Spluttering, Wesley pushed the dog away.

Caitlin barely acknowledged the wet tongue licking her hand. For on the cliffs high above stood a

dozen men, their feet planted on Clonmuir soil and
their weapons at the ready.

The last pulsations of pleasure ebbed away as she
climbed up to face them.

Rory Breslin swung a spiked war flail back and
forth, back and forth, with a chained, hypnotic violence. "You've had your adventure, Caitlin." His furious gaze snapped to Wesley. "*Now* can I kill him?"

She hesitated, became aware of the wind whistling
through the crags and the explosion of the surf upon
the rocks far below.

The men waited, Rory with his swinging flail, Liam
with his iron hammer, Curran with his sling; the rest
as well armed and as vengefully angry as Rory.

And before them all stood John Wesley Hawkins
with naught but the look on his face for defense.

"Well?" Rory demanded.

Yes, screamed the warrior inside Caitlin. Put him
out of my life so everything can be as before.

No, countered the yearning woman inside her, the
woman whose thighs still tingled from his loving.
Nothing can be the same, for he has transformed me.

"Put away your weapons," she said wearily.

The men exchanged looks but maintained their
combative stances. Caitlin drew herself up. Whatever
else had happened, she remained the MacBride.

"Put away your weapons," she repeated. "Now."

Rory stilled the war flail. Curran flicked the stone
from his sling. Conn put away his crossbow and the
blacksmith lowered his hammer. One by one, the others followed suit.

"He lied to us a hundred thousand times," said Rory.

"Yes, he did," Caitlin replied.

"He nearly drowned me in the cold sea," Conn
reminded her.

"Aye, that, too," Caitlin conceded.

"He abducted you."

"So he did."

Rory gave a bellow of frustration. "Then by the Blessed Virgin's sweet smile, why don't you let us avenge you?"

She glanced at Wesley. He had stood silent through the exchange, distant but respectful. Leaving, as he so often did, the decision to her. Not because he was weak, but because he respected her.

She drew a deep breath. The surf slammed down on the beach, and the sand hissed as it was drawn back to the sea. The dry grass rattled in the wind.

Then Caitlin spoke: "Because he is my husband."

Wesley sat at the round table that evening and surveyed the assortment of people in the hall. The room overflowed with newcomers who had arrived half starved during their absence. Brigid told a tinker's brood of children how she had helped to swim twenty of Clonmuir's ponies to Little Island for the high summer grazing. A group of men huddled around the central hearth and worried aloud about rebuilding the fishing fleet the English had destroyed. The few undersized mussels they had found clinging to rocks would not feed the people through the winter.

At the table, conversation was held exclusively in Irish. Wesley heard himself insulted, vilified, and denounced.

Caitlin had told, in one bitter, cathartic rush, the tale of their excursions to Inishbofin, to Galway, and to London. Her marriage to an Englishman on the deck of a ship. Her meeting with Cromwell at Whitehall Palace.

"'Tis a terrible, bad thing you've done," said Tom Gandy, facing Wesley and switching to English.

"Aye." Wesley saw no point in denying the statement.

Tom brightened. "And yet you did find the captured priests. You rescued our own Father Tully."

Wesley brooded into the fire. "One day we'll free them all."

"We, Mr. Hawkins?"

He held Gandy's gaze for a moment. "I'm charged with keeping the Fianna from raiding. But Cromwell hasn't ordered me to stay away from Inishbofin."

"So where's our good chaplain now?" Rory demanded.

Wesley took a very small sip of poteen. "I thought to find him here when we arrived. But perhaps he took my advice and stayed away."

"You'd keep the shepherd from his flock?" Conn slammed his fist down on the table.

"He was betrayed once," said Wesley. "It could happen again." He drank once more as the horrible implications of his statement found a home in the fierce hearts of his Irish family.

Rory lurched up from the table. "I'll not be listening to any more of this." One by one the men followed him to the central fire.

Caitlin stood and glared at Wesley. "Is this your purpose, then? To worry my people with your distrust?" Without waiting for an answer, she went to join Magheen, who sat wan and listless among the women. With their heads together, Caitlin's tawny waves contrasting with Magheen's pale, silky braid, the sisters spoke quietly.

Only Tom Gandy remained. His stumpy finger traced a bead of spilled ale along the surface of the table. "So," he said at length, "has it happened yet? Have you fallen in love with the girleen?"

Wesley was learning to accept Gandy's uncanny insights into the hearts and minds of people. "I think

I loved her from the first moment I saw her. Before that, I loved her, too. Before I even knew she existed outside the realm of my dreams."

"Spoken like a true cavalier."

"No, Tom. Spoken from my heart. Loving Caitlin is the only certainty in my life right now." He studied the broad, wise face, the shining eyes and smiling mouth. "You knew all along I would fall in love with her."

"Of course I knew."

"But how?"

"How does the sun know to shine? How does the dew know to mist the heaths at dawn?"

The blithe, evasive words jabbed at Wesley's temper. "Because God made it so! Damn it, Tom, these riddles of yours—"

Gandy nodded toward the women's corner and interrupted, "You see how it is with the girleen."

Caitlin's features were gilt by rushlight, her hands gently soothing Magheen's trembling shoulders. Fatigue and worry haunted her face.

Wesley sighed. "If I'm to win Caitlin's heart, I must also win the trust and respect of this household."

"The question is, which will be the harder battle?"

"No question at all," said Wesley. "The answer is Caitlin." He drummed his fingers on the table. Conditions at Clonmuir had gone from bad to worse. Magheen's natural vibrancy had dimmed to a wistful glow. More refugees had arrived with their empty hopes and frightened eyes. And, according to Curran Healy, Hammersmith had indeed managed to garrison the fort at Lough Corrib, sealing off Clonmuir's traditional eastward land routes.

"I'll take the problems one at a time," Wesley said. "How long will the stores last?"

Tom took out a stylus and notch stick. "With the

extra mouths to feed and the potato yield so poor, I'd say a week, give or take a day. Might have been more if it weren't for that tinker. Fourteen children, he has, and another in the oven."

Magheen gave a loud sob and buried her face in her hands.

"We also need to do something about that one," Tom said ruefully, "before she floods the hall with her tears. Faith, but she flings bad humors on the night."

"I have an idea that could take care of both the refugees and Magheen," said Wesley, leaning forward and lowering his voice. "Listen."

"What did you say?" Caitlin's eyebrows clashed in a frown. She had withdrawn to her chamber, and Wesley had followed her there.

"I said, I'm sleeping here with you."

"Oh, no, you're not."

"Caitlin, I'm your husband. You've proclaimed it so in front of the household. I'm only behaving as a husband should."

"Only until Father Tully can help us be done with this farce."

"What about this morning, Caitlin, on the beach?" His voice turned harsh. "Was that a farce?"

The memory warmed her cheeks. Discomfited, she walked to her three-legged dressing table and sat on the stool. "It was . . . something that shouldn't have happened."

She heard him draw an angry breath. "Damn it, Caitlin, why can't you just accept it?"

"Do you really need an answer to that?"

"No," he muttered. "Damn it."

Her mother's pedestal mirror stood before her. A

boar-bristle brush and some wooden combs lay at hand. Glancing into the mirror, she saw Wesley's face contort with a look of tension. "Something wrong?" she asked with sarcastic sweetness.

"Oh, no." He gave a dry laugh. "However, I was just thinking. If the good-night wishes of your men had been poisoned darts, I'd be convulsing on the floor in my death throes. That should make you happy."

"I could have ordered your execution any number of times. Sure it would have meant one less mouth to feed. I can't think why I didn't."

He came up behind her. In the mirror, their eyes met, hers wary and confused, his angry and pained. "Is it because—"

"I said I don't know why, so don't you be after trying to have a dance of words. I'm tired, Wesley. I'd like to go to sleep."

He picked up one of the combs. "Something's wrong here."

"One of the few honest truths I've heard you utter."

"I was speaking of your dressing table."

"And what in the name of St. Ita's stag beetle is the matter with my table?"

"It lacks pomatums and beauty pastes. Patches, perfumes, and such."

"For a man who once studied for the priesthood, you seem to know a lot about the contents of a woman's dressing table."

"I know a lot about personal vanity. And you seem to have very little of that. I wonder why, Caitlin."

"I haven't time for frippery." She pushed a stray curl behind her ear. "I've barely time to plait my hair, let alone paint my face."

"It doesn't bother you that you lack the leisure to primp?"

She remembered Alonso's reaction to her, in

English dress, hair done up and cheeks rouged. The devastating effect had given her a brief sense of power, a different sort of power than the one she wielded as the MacBride.

But Hawkins desired her whether she was dressed as an English lady or an Irish warrior.

She dodged the thought, for it flattered him. "The objects of my pride don't sit on a dressing table. I need nothing more than my sword and helm to satisfy my personal vanity."

"I understand, Cait. I do." He untied the leather thong at the end of her braid.

"What are you doing?" She tried to jerk away but his free hand held her still.

"Let me," he said softly, unweaving her braid. Their eyes met again in the mirror, distorted in the wavy glass. He took up the brush and stroked it through her hair.

"This isn't necessary," she began, but the tingle of the bristles over her scalp relaxed her, even when the brush caught a snag. With the dexterity of a fisherman mending his best seine, he separated the tangle and stroked the lock to silky smoothness.

He followed each motion of the brush with his other hand. "Your hair is so lovely. Did your mother used to brush it?"

The question brought on misty visions of bedtime tales and good-night kisses, childish prayers uttered in fervent voices, and bright linen ribbons around expertly woven braids. How simple times had been then, how sweet.

"Yes," Caitlin said finally, grieving for the loss of the evening ritual. Now, bedtime meant falling exhausted onto her pallet and awaiting a restless sleep plagued by worries.

"Bend your head down," he said. He brushed her hair forward, baring the nape of her neck. She felt his fingers unravel another tangle, felt the slide of the brush over her scalp.

Glancing through the fall of hair into the mirror, she saw that his face wore a look of deep tenderness. He was only brushing her hair, and yet the task held a sense of intimate familiarity.

He touched her neck softly, sending pixies dancing down her spine. And then his lips were there, kissing secret hollows usually concealed by her hair. His breath blew warm upon her flesh, making her shiver.

"Wesley. I think you should be stopping that for now." She shook back her hair and was annoyed to see a flush of color in her cheeks.

"Look at yourself, Cait, and tell me I've done you harm." He tilted her chin so that she caught a full view of herself in the mirror. His patient attention had given her hair a sheen like the sun on bright water, a texture like silk. The waving curls seemed fuller, glossier. More feminine.

The idea brought back thoughts of her troubles. "I suppose I should thank you." Carelessly she clubbed her hair at the nape with a bit of leather.

Annoyance flickered in Wesley's eyes but still he smiled, and his hands massaged her shoulders until the tension melted from her. "Very well," he said. "Pandering to your vanity won't gain me your heart. I should have known that."

"Yes, you should have."

He pulled up a stool and turned her to face him. "Magheen seems worse for knowing you've gone and found yourself a husband."

Caitlin smiled ruefully. "She despairs for lack of a husband, while I despair because I have one." Her eyes narrowed. "I suppose you consider yourself an expert on women."

"Were I an expert, we'd not be sitting on these

stools but lying in that bed, doing shocking things to each other."

She tried to shrug off the suggestion as lewd, but she had sampled his loving and learned that certain things were not lewd at all. "What makes you think you can help Magheen?"

"I can recognize a broken heart when I see one."

"A one-eyed badger could see her heart's been broken. I'll not applaud you for that."

"Would you applaud me for remedying the situation?"

The certainty in his voice rankled her. "It's not your problem, Wesley."

"But it is." He gripped her hands and held tight. "You need me, Caitlin. I'll prove it to you."

"Try all you wish. Magheen's too proud to pay for the privilege of being a man's wife. Even the wife of a great lord." Caitlin pulled her hands from his and rubbed her palms on the rough homespun fabric of her kirtle. "I never should have tried to keep the bride price a secret. She was bound to find out."

"And that's when she came home? When she found out about the bride price?"

"No. That's when she refused her favors to Logan."

A rueful grin tugged at one corner of his mouth. "You MacBride women."

"We have standards." She found herself struggling not to smile. And then the laughter burst from her, mirth as sweet and cleansing as water from a mountain spring. It seemed the most natural thing in the world to reach out and draw him into a hug.

"She wants to go back now, doesn't she?" He spoke the question into the cloud of her hair.

"Aye, but the stubbornness is on her. To her mind, he must want her and her alone and have no thought of cattle and booly huts."

He sat back, his hands lingering at her knees. "I think there's a way to salvage Logan's pride, find homes for some of the refugees, and get Magheen back where she belongs."

Caitlin lifted her eyebrows. "Haven't I pondered the problem for weeks, and—"

"Just listen. I want to help."

"Why?"

"Because Magheen is your sister. Because her sadness tugs at your heart. I don't want you to be sad, Cait."

She gave a bitter laugh. "Sure and haven't I been sad since the day I clapped eyes on you."

"It was evening," he corrected her. "And you didn't seem at all sad. But we were speaking of my plan for Magheen."

Caitlin realized she would not get a moment's peace until she heard him out. "Very well, Wesley. What is your plan?"

"I shall go to swear fealty to Logan Rafferty."

Surprise knocked the breath from her. "What?"

"When a man comes new into a district, he must pledge himself to the ranking lord."

"True, but—"

"Then it's only right that I do so. In the company of you and Magheen. Rory and Tom should come along as well. Oh, and that tinker and his family. They eat like horses."

She pictured Wesley striding into Logan's keep, the two men facing off, Wesley as bright as a burnished blade, Logan as dark as shadows at midnight. Never, she reflected, were two men so clearly marked to be enemies as brash Wesley Hawkins and proud Logan Rafferty.

"He'd probably cut you down before you got a word out of your mouth," she cautioned.

"I'll risk it."

"But what does swearing fealty have to do with reuniting Magheen and Logan?"

He grinned and told her.

"You're mad," she said when he'd finished, but she found herself smiling, recognizing the cleverness of his ploy. "But then, madness and determination sometimes wear the same mask, don't they?"

The day dawned bright and cool, the sky a shattering shade of blue. Wesley and Caitlin accompanied by Tom, Rory, and Magheen raced on horseback along the coast. The tinker's family walked the distance. Wesley did not want them to arrive until later.

His spirits lifted. No one rode like the Irish, in saddles so slight they seemed a mere formality, with bits so dainty a teething baby would not feel them.

Wesley rode a tall brindled pony. Why the Irish called them ponies was beyond his ken, for the mare stood taller than most hunters from Kent.

Caitlin took the lead, setting the pace at an easy canter. The stallion's hooves seemed to caress the uneven ground. Horse and rider united to become one, a creature of the wind, swifter than the kestrels that haunted the coastal bogs.

Wesley knew now where the black horse had come from, and why Caitlin treasured the beast so.

His mind jerked back to the days in London. What a fool he had been to imagine that seeing the truth about her Spanish hero would send Caitlin running to Wesley's arms. Instead, the revelation had underscored her distrust in men and made her more wary than ever.

He forced his attention to the others. Rory Breslin rode in the manner in which he did all things: hard, blunt, and uncompromising. A crevice in the terrain or a rock in the path was nothing; winning the game against

Cromwell would be easier than befriending Rory.

A distracted rider, Tom Gandy let his pony tarry behind the others while his gaze wandered over the passing landscape. Magheen rode gracefully, her ladylike mien duplicated by the smooth gait of her tall ivory pony.

Wesley absorbed the ruggedness of land and sea. Connemara might have been another world, untamed and alive with the pulsing of the waves on the shore and the song of the wind through the crags. The mountains reared to the east, great hulks of thinly wooded rock, brooding in ancient defiance at the pummeling sea.

The mist-shrouded magic of the land seeped into his soul, and he remembered something Tom had once told him. The Irish cannot be conquered. For centuries untold, Viking and Norman and English had battered her shores and tried to subdue her people. Rather than breaking the Irish to a new way of life, the victims became victors. The conquerors surrendered to the spirit of the Irish, absorbed their language and customs, and succumbed to their charm and their power.

England commanded Wesley's loyalty. She needed Charles back on the throne, needed law and sanity pulled from the quagmire of intolerance Cromwell had made of the Commonwealth.

But Ireland. No man could compromise his sentiment about the vast, wild land. One loved it, or one hated it. No one shrugged an indifferent shoulder.

Wesley watched Caitlin sailing on horseback across the heath. The wind made sport of her thick braid, unweaving her hair until the strands sailed out in a golden veil behind her.

She was the very essence of Ireland: strong, mysterious, unconquerable, her character a potent distillation of the warriors and heroes of generations. He had married her and come into her household. But he knew better than to deceive himself that he had broken her will.

With these thoughts moving his mind, he rode the remainder of the distance to Logan Rafferty's ancestral home, Brocach. The stronghold crowned a steep hill, slender Norman towers piercing the sky, thick, pitted granite walls surrounding a square keep.

Sentries spied them a quarter mile from the hilltop castle. A horn blared. Caitlin slowed her horse to a canter, and Wesley drew up beside her. He glanced back at Magheen to see her reaction to the home she had left in a rage.

She held herself like a queen, only the high color in her pretty face and her white-knuckled grip on the reins betraying her nervousness.

"I'm still after thinking this is a crazy idea," Caitlin said. "Logan is bound to see through your plan."

"If he's truly in love," said Wesley, "then he's as blind as a mole in broad daylight." He lowered his voice. "I know I am."

She lifted her chin. "I just hope you're right about Logan."

"If I am, will you swear to be appreciative?" he asked.

"In what way?"

He shrugged. "Oh, enough so as to give me a son."

Her eyes widened in surprise; then she scowled. "I give no Englishman a son."

Wesley laughed, for beneath her anger he recognized longing, and it gave him hope. "Very well. I'll settle for a daughter . . . if she looks like Magheen."

Four men-at-arms joined them on the road. They spoke little after Wesley stated their business. He occupied himself with studying the outlying lands.

The landscape seemed healthier than the empty villages and desolated fields they had passed. Far in the distance, on a narrow strip of emerald grass between the road and the sea, great brown rocks dotted the slopes. Wesley gave them only passing interest; then one of the rocks moved. With a start of astonishment, he realized he was looking at a herd of shaggy Irish cattle.

The sight was a revelation; he'd had no idea Logan was so prosperous.

To the east lay a field. Reapers had harvested the early crop and left a light brown stubble, even as a newly trimmed beard. An image flashed through Wesley's mind: other fields, burned by the Roundhead invaders. No smooth cloak of well-shorn stalks, but blackened stubble.

"Rafferty's crops weren't burned," he said to Caitlin in a low voice.

She nodded. "Logan manages the English well. He's capable of compromise. He plays the landlord now, charging rents and paying taxes."

"He sold out to the Commonwealth."

"He chose to protect his people in the best way he sees fit."

"Could you not compromise, too, Caitlin?"

Her chin lifted even higher. "I prefer the old ways. I prefer freedom."

"Don't you rebel at the unfairness of it? Rafferty lives in prosperity while you struggle just to feed your household."

"I'd have no household, should Cromwell have his way. It's not a perfect world, Wesley. Each does as he sees fit."

"But don't you prefer peace—"

"Peace is my dream," she hissed vehemently. "But fighting is my reality. I have to live with that."

Hearing the fierce words, Wesley felt a rush of love so intense that his head seemed to spin. He knew beyond all certainty that he wanted to spend his life with this woman, to watch her grow round with his children, and then to grow old and mellow as the years galloped past.

As they entered the lofty hall, he only hoped Rafferty would not see fit to spike John Wesley Hawkins through the gut.

The Lord of Brocach looked as if he'd enjoy it. Rafferty occupied a thronelike chair, the high back carved with rowan leaves and berries. As Wesley and Caitlin, followed by their party, walked the length of the hall toward him, he made no move to rise. Instead he propped an elbow on the chair arm and toyed with the ends of his braided beard. His gaze settled coldly on Caitlin and Wesley, but just for a moment. The Lord of Brocach had eyes only for his wife.

In spite of his distrust of Rafferty, Wesley felt a twinge of empathy for the Irish lord. Rafferty's dark anger failed to conceal his helpless adoration and frustrated desire, two passions with which, in recent weeks, Wesley had become unwillingly acquainted.

He reached the raised dais and bowed. "My lord."

One corner of Rafferty's mouth lifted in a mocking grin. "So you've finally come to Brocach, have you, Hawkins? As I recall, you had an invitation some weeks back."

"I've come on my own terms," Wesley said pleasantly. "As Caitlin's husband." He felt her stiffen beside him. He stifled the urge to shake her. He wanted her to feel pride, not resentment, when he announced that he was her husband.

Rafferty's face contorted with disbelief, then anger, and finally mockery. "Well, well. The lady rebel of Clonmuir has finally been brought to heel. And by an English nobody, no less. Tell me, Caitlin, what brought about this amazing development?"

"True love," Wesley said before she had a chance

to respond. "She couldn't help herself."

"My hands were tied," said Caitlin. Wesley looked at her sharply and saw a spark of amusement in her eyes.

"Well!" Magheen stepped forward and planted herself in front of Logan. "Don't be expecting such as Logan Rafferty to understand true love."

"This from a woman who abandoned her own dear husband." Logan tried to conceal his eagerness as he added, "Are you ready to come back to me, Magheen?"

Her pretty features softened with longing. "Only if you'll accept me without a dowry."

"St. Patrick preserve my immortal soul." He lifted his clasped hands toward the rough-beamed ceiling. "A man who takes a wife with no dowry is less than a man."

"A theory that bears ruminating . . . later," Wesley said. "My lord, I've come to swear fealty to you."

Rafferty lifted his eyebrows in surprise, then shot a look at Caitlin. "What trick is this? You MacBride females are full of tricks."

"No trick," Wesley cut in. "It's a sincere offer."

"Sure you're as sincere as a weasel in a dovecote."

"Look," said Wesley, "if we're to live together in this district, we'd best not be at each other's throats."

Logan waved a hand, the thick fingers weighted with rings. Reaching to his belt, he withdrew a gleaming, pointed dirk. "Let's be after it, then. On your knees, Hawkins."

While every impulse told him to rebel, Wesley knelt before the Irishman. In London Caitlin had seen his pride broken by her Spanish lover. Now again he must allow himself to be humiliated. But it was all part of his plan, he reminded himself.

She looked on gravely, but utterly without sympathy. And why should he expect sympathy from a woman he had forced into Cromwell's presence?

Because, damn it, said a mutinous voice inside him, it was time she saw the value in compromise.

"Do you swear to uphold the laws of this district and obey my rule?" Logan's black eyes danced with enjoyment.

"I so swear," said Wesley in his best bell-toned voice.

Logan extended the dirk for the customary kiss of peace. "And if you break this vow, may this blade bury itself to the haft in your heart."

His face flaming, Wesley bent over the large, rough hand. He clamped his jaw to stifle a sound of surprise.

Then, his mind boiling with suspicion, he brushed his lips over the blade. But his eyes stayed on Rafferty's signet ring: a golden rowan branch surmounted on the back of a badger.

Brocach, he thought. Irish for badger's warren. God, why hadn't he realized sooner? He straightened, schooled his features to blandness, and lifted his hand in salute. "My lord."

"Very good, Hawkins. Let us have a cup of usquebaugh, and we'll discuss the fines owed to me by Clonmuir."

"Fines?" Caitlin burst out. "What blarney is this, Logan?"

He strode to the table. He did not look at Caitlin or Magheen. "No blarney," he said. "Simply a fine I'm compelled to levy for your disobedience."

She joined him at the table and slapped her palms on the surface. "What disobedience?"

His face became a hard mask of accusation. "The Fianna."

Her face paled. "And what's that to do with me?"

"Don't waste your wind in arguing. Of course, I knew all from the start, but I waited to be sure. You were careless in that last raid." He fixed his stare on Tom Gandy. "You've a unique look on you, my friend, and you were recognized."

That last raid, thought Wesley, when the men had ridden in a rage without their leader. A feeling of protectiveness rose fierce and hot through him, and he moved to her side.

Caitlin hesitated, then sank onto a bench. "Logan, my people are starving. More exiles come every week. How can I turn away the crying babies? Hammersmith has an endless supply of stores from England."

"I'm your lord. You should have come to me."

"I did, Logan. Remember? I begged you for provisions but you refused."

"Didn't I take Magheen off your hands—"

"For a price, damn your eyes," Magheen cut in.

"—and I a lord who should have wed high nobility?" Logan's hands kept busy, handling his horn mug, rubbing the table. His eyes shifted—to the fire, to the wolfhound sleeping at his feet—everywhere but at Caitlin.

Wesley's suspicions froze into icy certainty. Suppressing his rage, he walked to Tom Gandy and dropped his voice to a whisper. "Scuttle the plan; we can't leave Magheen here. Rafferty's a traitor."

Tom started. "Sure and that's a hard accusation."

"That ring he's wearing. Titus Hammersmith has an ornament in the same design. I saw it in his office."

"Bless me, are you certain?"

"Aye, and then there's Father Tully. Didn't he disappear from Brocach?"

"Aye, but—"

"And Logan's lying about knowing of the Fianna from the start. He's got more pride than sense.

Would he really sit idle while Caitlin led raids that moved Cromwell to murder and the bards to ballads?"

"The sin upon my head, but you're right! What are you going to do, Wesley?"

"I can't carry on with the plan for Magheen. He betrayed a priest. He'd not balk at betraying his wife."

"I disagree," said Tom. "If you're right, we need her here more than ever."

"What can Magheen do?"

Tom smiled. "She's Caitlin's sister. And tell me, do you relish entirely the prospect of taking Magheen back to Clonmuir to starve with the rest of us?"

Wesley shuddered. "I still don't like it—"

"It was your idea." Tom pushed him toward the table. "All will be well. Do something terrifically clever. I'll play my part."

Wesley made what he hoped was a deferential bow. "My lord, about the fine."

"Aye, let's talk about the fine," Logan boomed.

"In payment, I offer you a skilled tinker to see to repairing your fine possessions. A good man from Wexford, very—er—prolific. You'll not find better in Ireland."

Logan's eyes narrowed in calculation. "You offer another mouth to feed."

Try sixteen, Wesley thought. "I offer an honest worker. Surely you can use him."

Logan's gaze locked with Magheen's. She stared at him implacably until he said, "Very well, I accept. But a tinker doesn't cover the amount owed by Clonmuir."

Wesley smiled. "I agree. There's something you need more than a tinker, my lord."

"And how would you be knowing what I—"

"A wife."

Logan's eyebrows crashed together like black lightning bolts. "By God, Hawkins, what kind of a scoundrel are you, to be offering a woman as payment for a fine? Damn it, I have a wife!"

"Take me and cancel the fine." Magheen braced her arms on the table and gave Logan a heaven-sent view of her bosom. Just as his eyes kindled, she stepped back. "That's our offer."

"It's preposterous. I won't hear of it."

True to the plan, Tom tapped his mug on the table. "Saints of heaven be praised, the mood has been hurled upon my tongue!"

Everyone stopped what they were doing. When a gifted bard felt the urge to relate a tale, it was a special occasion. England had outlawed the bards of Ireland, so this treat had the fine seasoning of the forbidden to sweeten it.

Logan looked torn between continuing the argument and listening to Tom. Seizing the moment, Tom stood on a bench and drew his audience in with the long sweep of his gaze.

To Wesley's surprise, Caitlin inched down the bench toward him. He felt her presence like a warm glow, a flicker of light in his heart. "I hope your plan works," she whispered.

"Caitlin, I must know. Do Logan and Magheen love truly?"

"Look at them, Wesley. Do you have to ask?"

Magheen sat across the table from Logan, staring at him with pained yearning. She had dropped her shawl. Her unbraided hair hung like a long, loose veil around her face and down her back. Rosy color suffused her cheeks. Her moist lips and blue eyes gleamed in the rushlight.

Rafferty had one elbow propped on the table. His lidded gaze clung to Magheen in silent worship.

"You're certain he'd never hurt her?"

"Of course not." She shifted away from him on the bench. "He's not like you, Wesley. He doesn't use women."

Her statement slapped him in the face like a bucket of ice water, awakening rage. "By God, Caitlin, I went on my knees before him for your sake! What else must I—"

"Hush. I'm listening to Tom."

He made himself smother the fury. Giving no sign that he understood the Gaelic, Wesley pretended great interest in the bottom of his mug and prayed Tom's powers of persuasion would weaken Rafferty's stubbornness.

The narrative came forth in hushed whispers, bursting shouts, dramatic pauses. The audience listened, enraptured, absorbing every word as grass in springtime absorbs sunlight.

"What's he saying?" Wesley asked Caitlin.

"It's the tale of Bridie McGhee. An abduction tale."

Caught up in his own recitation, Tom paced the narrow bench, gestured and contorted his face. The audience listened in a state of breath-held captivation.

"What's happening to Bridie now?" asked Wesley.

"Faith, she thinks she's lost him. She's standing on the edge of Leacht Cliff about to hurl herself over."

Tom lamented in dirgelike tones.

In an undertone, Caitlin translated, "She's calling out to Ruath, begging him to snatch her from black suicide, but he doesn't hear."

To Wesley's surprise, he noticed tears in Caitlin's eyes. She slid her hand under his beneath the table. Very gently he moved his thumb in slow circles in her palm. With absurd swiftness, his body jolted to life.

He had been indifferent to ladies of the blood

royal. He had resisted with ease the arts of talented courtesans. And yet the simple act of holding Caitlin's hand filled him with a sharp, sweet yearning that left him breathless.

It must be true love, he thought. I could die happy just holding her hand.

Her grip tightened. "Ruath has bridled a wind horse and is after saving her."

Forcing an agony of suspense on the audience, Tom described in minute detail Ruath's flight to the coast. The love-struck hero battled her kinsmen and braved a storm.

Bridie stepped off the edge of the cliff.

Magheen wailed and buried her face in her hands. Logan rushed to her side and cradled her against him. He inhaled, his face blissful and stupid from the scent of her.

Ruath sailed off the cliff after her. Just as Gandy had convinced the listeners that the lovers were falling to their deaths, Ruath scooped Bridie onto his horse. The enchanted beast landed with exquisite ease in a dark meadow.

To the glory of Ireland, Bridie and her lover lived happily ever after.

Women dabbed their eyes with their shawls. Men wiped their noses with their sleeves. Tom winked at Rafferty. "Nothing like a good abduction to prove who's master," he said.

Sensing Logan's perfect state of vulnerability, Wesley rose and announced that it was time to go. Logan had the look of a dying man about him as Magheen drew herself from his arms.

They had ridden a mile to the south when hoof-beats drummed behind them. Like a horseman from the underworld, Logan Rafferty galloped out of the twilight.

Magheen gave a shriek of both terror and triumph. Logan bore down on her. Their horses ran neck and neck, so close that their shoulders bumped. He snatched her from the saddle in a move worthy of a carnival gypsy.

Magheen screamed. And then fell silent.

Wesley's last glimpse, just before they crested a rise in the road, was of the lord and his lady embracing passionately, on a horse galloping back to Brocach.

15

"*In my born, natural life,*" said Rory, "I wouldn't have been after believing it would work." With grudging admiration, he eyed Wesley across the round table in the hall of Clonmuir. "Rafferty'll keep her, and no more talk of dowries."

"Aye," said Tom Gandy, "and Magheen will see to sending food. Well done, *a chara.*"

"It was just a matter of understanding the nature of a desperate man in love," said Wesley.

"You're such an expert," said Caitlin.

"Long on brains, after all," Rory said in Irish, "to make up for the shortness otherwise."

Force of habit had taught Wesley to ignore the recurring jibe. Into the hall came the smallholder named Darrin Mudge, a surly man who had a long-standing debt to Caitlin. Playing upon her generous nature, he had for a few years refused to pay. She had summoned him today, for he was the last of her neighbors who possessed livestock.

"Sure it's not a thing I remember." Mudge scratched his head beneath a soiled hat.

"You mean it's not convenient for you to remember," Caitlin said. "But it's past time you paid. I've mouths to feed."

"On my oath, I cannot—"

"Yes, let's talk of oaths," Wesley cut in. The smallholder's manner grated on his nerves. "Would you be willing to swear an oath that you owe no debt to Clonmuir?"

"Aye, of course, but—"

"Then listen carefully and repeat after me."

"Wesley," said Caitlin. "This is not your—"

Tom Gandy shushed her with a wave of his hand.

Thank God, thought Wesley as she closed her mouth and planted her elbows on the table. At last she seemed to accept that he might have something of value to say. "Now, Mr. Mudge," he continued. "Here is the oath. If I fail to tell God's own truth—"

"If I fail to tell God's own truth—"

"May the bloat poison my herd—"

"Eh? That be a curse, not an oath!"

Wesley fixed him with a commanding stare. "May the bloat poison my herd—"

"Ach, *musha.*" Mudge pressed his hands together. "May the bloat poison my herd—"

"—and may my fine flock of sheep be clifted—"

Mudge took a step back. "What be this curse you're trying to bring upon me, Englishman?"

"Don't argue with the husband of the MacBride!" Rory thundered.

Mudge made the sign of the cross. "—and may my fine flock of sheep—" He sent Caitlin a pleading glance. "Can this truly be in the oath?"

"You're calling on God to punish you if you don't speak the truth," Caitlin explained.

"And may the high King of Glory permit my children to get the mange," Wesley added.

"Oh God!" Mudge broke out in a fine sweat. "Bedad, I remember me now. 'Tis a debt I'll be paying you before the sun sets!" Shaken, he scurried down the length of the hall. Silence, then huge gusts of merry laughter, chased him out.

Rory scrubbed the mirth from his eyes and lifted his mug to Wesley. "Well done, by God!"

Wesley raised his own cup to acknowledge the salute; then he looked at Caitlin.

She regarded him with a bitterness that stabbed at his heart. God, would he never learn to anticipate her? He had solved the problem of the debt. But in doing so, he had usurped her authority. And it would not be the last time.

"Let's get to supper," she murmured.

The meager meal on the table could hardly be called supper. The turnip and potato soup, already thin, had been doubled by water.

In London, this type of hunger would have incited a riot. But here at Clonmuir, the people accepted deprivation with order and civility, even gratitude.

Wesley's temper took wing. Had these people been thieves or outlaws, he would have felt nothing for their plight. But they were pious folk who had done no worse than occupy a magical isle coveted by its English neighbors.

English greed made them suffer. In just a few short months, winter would come rushing upon the land, bringing starvation with the cold.

Even as a decision firmed in his mind, he ached for Caitlin. Once again, he would have to override her convictions. But surely she could not resent him any more than she already did.

"We're going on a cattle raid," he said.

Caitlin's spoon dropped with a clatter. "A cattle raid, is it?"

"That's what I said." Feeling the heat of a dozen pairs of eyes on him, Wesley explained, "We've less than a week's worth of stores. There is only the milch cow left in the byre. Mudge's payment in sheep will be gone long before Michaelmas. If we don't do something, we'll have to start slaughtering the horses."

The outraged protests came as expected.

"That's why I propose the raid." He allowed himself a look at Caitlin. He wished he could pluck the moment from time and hold it forever in his heart. Unaware of the true nature of his plan, she gazed at him with admiration shining in her eyes and a heartfelt smile sweet upon her lips.

"The Fianna will ride against the Roundheads again," she said in triumph. "Oh, Wesley, I knew you'd side with us." She frowned; he could almost see the thoughts cavorting behind her eyes. "It'll be a riskier venture than we've ever attempted since he's so well dug in at Lough Corrib, but with—"

"Caitlin, wait." He wished he didn't have to shatter her illusions. He forced himself to say, "We can't take English livestock."

Her admiration froze to anger. "I should have known."

"So whose cattle are we after raiding?" Rory demanded.

"Logan Rafferty's herd at Brocach."

Silence dropped like a wet blanket over the gathering.

"Never," said Caitlin. "You're mad if you think I'd stoop to thieving a fellow Irishman's cattle."

"He's got more cattle than a tinker has lice."

"Caitlin," said Tom, "I think you should hear Wesley out."

"Logan Rafferty is my lord and my sister's husband besides. For pity's sake, Wesley, you just swore fealty to him. Besides, Magheen's there now. She'll not be letting us starve."

"Logan might not give her a choice," Tom said.

"Rafferty's also a traitor to the Irish," Wesley added. A silence even heavier than the first descended on them. With flat regret, he told them his suspicions about Logan.

Blazing with fury, Caitlin jumped up. "None of us will be a party to any of this!"

"Now, Caitlin," said Rory. "Let's at least hear his plan."

She scowled at him. "Not you, too."

"Times are hard," Rory said. "A body has to eat."

"And you call yourself an Irish warrior," she said. "You'd steal from your lord like a common poacher instead of going to war like a proud Irishman."

"There's no harm in listening to the man. Didn't he settle Magheen and the tinker's brood, and Mudge besides."

"God, Rory, do you remember nothing? He lied to us from the moment he stepped foot in Clonmuir. Now you'll listen to him deride Logan Rafferty?"

"The lord of Brocach is rich on the *slainte* paid to him by his Irish tenants. The English haven't touched his estates. I'm after wondering why."

Caitlin felt sick with the suspicions that pushed into her mind. "Wonder all you like. I'll have no part of it."

She bolted outside, across the yard and to the wall walk looking out to sea. Traitor's Leap framed a view of the waves rushing up to the shore, flinging themselves against the rock in an explosion of translucent foam.

A cold wind gusted over her, chilling her to the marrow. But the cold in her bones was not nearly as icy as the sense of betrayal that froze her heart.

She was losing her grip on Clonmuir. The smooth-tongued Hawkins lured her people to his side. He was the high, shifting wind off the Atlantic, driving them from the old ways.

She gazed steadily at the silvery horizon. She used to stand here and think of Alonso. But even then he had seemed a distant dream, hazy and indistinct, far out of reach.

"Caitlin."

Refusing to turn, she braced her hands against the wall.

"It has to be this way, Caitlin." Wesley stepped up behind her so that she felt the warmth of him. "I cannot let the Fianna ride against the English again."

She whirled and found herself caught in his strong arms. "*You* cannot?" she demanded, pushing against his chest. "You talk as if you're the MacBride."

"No," he said. "I'll never, ever take that from you."

"Then why do you insist on this raid? For heaven's sake, Wesley, how can you live with us, break bread with us, and still give your loyalty to England?"

He pressed his lips into a thin, angry line. "I only want you to see that there is more than one way to solve our problem."

"Such as raiding a neighbor."

"Aye."

"I'll not have it, do you hear me?"

A sweet, regretful smile played about his lips. He leaned down and softly kissed her forehead; then the touch of his lips descended, closing over hers with a silkiness that she felt in places he wasn't even touching.

Calling up the strength of will that had made her the MacBride, she drew back. "You shall not dismiss me like a chastened child!"

"Cait, I don't mean to, but—"

"I say you will not raid Brocach. I forbid it. The Fianna will ride again."

"Look, Caitlin." He grasped her shoulders. "Hammersmith knows your secret now. More than ever, he'll be on the alert. The men of Clonmuir would follow you if you commanded it. They'd die for you, Caitlin, if you choose to make it come to that."

She shrank from the truth in his words. "I'll warn Logan."

"Then you'd be signing the death warrant of your men."

She bit her lip and looked away. She felt torn, her loyalty to Logan pulling against the sick truth that had planted itself implacably in her mind. A moan of frustration escaped her.

Wesley caught her chin and drew her gaze back to his. "Think about it, Caitlin. Could you bear seeing Rory betrayed by your own, maimed or killed? Or young Curran? How would you face his mother if anything happened to the lad?"

"The risk has always been there," she snapped.

"But I offer you a solution that carries very little risk."

"I won't have you stealing from the Irish. From my own sister, for heaven's sake."

"Magheen would cheer us on. Logan Rafferty has stores to spare, and you know it, Caitlin. You're his family, by God. He owes you. Besides, he has ties to the English. To Hammersmith. It would behoove us to drive a wedge between those two."

The ocean spray leapt up from the breaking waves. Somewhere in a distant part of the keep, a baby cried. Caitlin winced, weighing anguish over her people against the beliefs of a lifetime. Finally she took a deep breath of the briny air. "Do what you must, Wesley. But I'll have no part of it. The sin's upon your head."

* * *

In the deep, mysterious heart of the night, six men emerged from behind a booly hut. The cold blackness enclosed Wesley like an iron gauntlet. Burdened with halters and ropes, he led the way up the summer pastures of Brocach.

A cowherd's peat fire burned in the lee of a hill. A man sat by the embers, playing a lullaby on a whittled flute. The shaggy hulks of sleeping cattle dotted the landscape. Concealed in the shadows some yards away, the men drew into a huddle.

"St. Peter swoop my soul up to heaven," Conn whispered. "There's more cattle here than saints in my canon."

"He'd have you believing he's as poor as the rest of the district," said Wesley. "Get those helms in place."

The quiet clicking of metal buckles sounded as the men donned Roundhead garb, cuirasses and helms seized in raids. Wearing the costumes of murdered Englishmen raised cold prickles on Wesley's skin. But his plan required the disguise.

"Remember," he said, "don't hurt the cowherd or knock him senseless. We want him to see exactly what we're about. And for God's sake, don't speak unless you're sure you can sound like an Englishman."

Round iron helms bobbed in accord. In the distant hills, a wolf howled, and another answered.

Wesley begged in silent prayer for success. Even more than food for Clonmuir, he needed to prove himself to Caitlin.

"Let's go." With the stealth that in years past had gained him success as a thief taker, he crouched low and headed for the light. Booted feet crept along the pasture.

He climbed to the crest of the hill above the fire. The howling of the wolves had brought the cowherd to full alert. A robust, stocky man, he stood with his staff dug into the ground and a bog pine torch held aloft.

"Now," Wesley whispered. He leapt down onto the cowherd's back and took him in a choke hold from behind.

The man gave a grunt of surprise. He waved his arms at his attackers. Wesley eased the pressure on his throat, and the cowherd spoke brusquely. "Here now, you're not supposed to take this lot."

The statement confirmed Wesley's darkest suspicions. He tightened his grip. "Look, you Irish devil, you'll spare us a few of your cattle, and we'll spare your life."

The man made a strangled sound of accord.

"Come help me bind him, Ladyman," Wesley ordered.

Curran Healy made deft work of the task. Meanwhile, the others raced down to the pasture, haltering cattle and leading them off toward the coast.

Three hours later, dripping cold water from their swim with three dozen head of cattle, the raiders slogged ashore at a protected grazing island.

After another three hours, news came from Brocach that Rafferty's estate had been raided by Roundheads. Logan threatened a counterstrike at the garrison of Lough Corrib.

That evening, drunk to the tips of his tonsils, John Wesley Hawkins staggered into his wife's private chamber. Sounds of revelry still drifted from the hall.

Startled, Caitlin upset the ink bowl, spraying walnut ink over the letter she was writing. A letter to His Holiness the Pope himself, begging for an annulment.

The sight of Wesley made her glad the ink had spilled. Candlelight flickered over his lopsided grin. She bit her lip to scare off an answering smile.

He staggered over to her, plucked the quill from her fingers, and set it on the table. Taking both her hands, he drew her to her feet.

"Well?" he demanded. He smelled of poteen and peat smoke and salt from the long swim.

"Well what?"

He carried her forefinger to his lips and kissed it. "I've gotten your sister back to her husband where she belongs." He kissed the next finger. "I've gotten us enough beef to last th' winter." His lips moved on to her ring finger. "Rafferty's finally broken faith with th' English." He brought his mouth against the flat of her palm and buried it there, inhaling as if she held in her hand the very essence of life.

"Is it enough yet, Cait? Is it?"

Another unspoken question haunted his shadowy green eyes. *Now will you accept me as your husband?*

Part of her—the womanly part, the lonely part—wanted to shout, Yes! But another part screamed a denial.

"You overrode my wishes. You turned my men from me."

"For th' sake of Clonmuir, my love. But if it's not enough, I'll do more, I swear it. Slay dragons, brave th' fires of hell." He rubbed his hands up and down her arms. "Ah, Cait, you are intoxicating in your loveliness."

"'Tis the drink, not me."

He leaned forward. "No drink could so sweep a man's reason away like you do." His mouth drew closer and closer. Her lips tingled in anticipation of his kiss.

He hesitated, a breath, a heartbeat away.

His eyes glazed over, and he slipped to the floor, out cold almost before he hit the rushes.

Torn between rage and amusement, Caitlin shook her head.

What the devil would her husband do next?

"We're going fishing," he announced the next day. Still bleary eyed, he blinked in the smoke that pervaded the great hall. A new family had arrived from the Twelve Bens. Getting them settled in promised to take all day.

Wesley's welcoming grin brought smiles to faces not used to smiling.

Caitlin frowned at the men, who formed a half-circle around her husband. "But we've only the one curragh and the hooker. Besides, the herring aren't running."

"We're not after herring," said Rory, buckling on a sword.

"Then what would you be after fishing for?" she demanded.

Blowing her a kiss, Wesley led the way out of the hall. "Priests," he said.

"Magheen, I'm so confused." Sitting in a well-furnished solar at Brocach, Caitlin took a sip of imported tea, let the liquid slide over her tongue, then put down the cup. "One minute I think he's all I've ever desired in a husband, and the next, I feel certain he means to hand Clonmuir over to Hammersmith."

Magheen smiled sympathetically. Since returning to Logan she had grown even more beautiful—rounder, softer, draped in a veil of womanly contentment. She patted a glossy yellow curl. "How long has he been gone?"

"A week."

"Well, I'm after thinking that your feelings are natural."

"Then natural is a sickness." Caitlin took an oat cake from the tray and bit into it. The food might have been pasteboard for all she could taste it.

"You're resisting your feelings for Wesley."

"The only feeling I have for him is contempt."

Wisdom kindled in Magheen's eyes. "I think you love him."

Caitlin tried to deny it. But with a wave of sadness, she realized that everything had changed. She was no longer the girl who had lost her innocent heart to a handsome Spaniard. The sweet idealism of their youthful pledges had turned bitter.

War and privation had forced her to become hard and calculating. With a great sigh, she bade farewell to a long-cherished dream.

"Here, blow your nose." Magheen handed her a handkerchief. "I haven't seen you weep since Ma passed. You must have a bad case of it."

"Of what?" Caitlin sniffed into the fine linen.

"Of love," said Magheen. "Wasn't that what we were speaking of?"

"How can I love Wesley? He's *Sassenach*. He abducted me—"

"Logan abducted me, and I loved every minute of it."

"I'm not like you, Magheen. I can't excuse a man's actions simply because my heart tells me to."

"You'd be a lot happier if you'd listen to your heart. Tell me, did you expect to rule Clonmuir alone forever?"

"No, I thought—" She broke off. Lord, but she had not even had time to think. She stared out the window. Bristling yellow-brown hayfields rose toward the hills to the east. She turned Magheen's words over and over in her mind.

And stopped when she came to the truth.

All her reasons for abandoning her feelings for Alonso paled to weak excuses. It wasn't the years, nor even his betrayal, that had slain the dream.

It was John Wesley Hawkins.

Aye, from the first moment she had seen him walking toward her through a tangled twilit garden, he had invaded her soul.

Each time she had tried to remember her Spanish gentleman, a tall Englishman with blazing red hair and a rakish grin strode into her mind.

Each time she had tried to recall Alonso's courtly caresses, she became enveloped in memories of Wesley's frankly sensual affection.

And each time she searched her heart for the bright glow of love she had once felt for Alonso, she found only the burned-out embers of dead feelings.

I will drive him out of your heart as surely as the sun will rise. Wesley's declaration on their wedding night whispered across the weeks to her.

At the time, she had declared it a patent impossibility.

Now she realized it had been true even before she had learned of Alonso's betrayal.

God, where was Wesley now? He could get killed rescuing the priests.

"Here, you've gotten that one wringing wet," said Magheen. "Take another handkerchief, and do stop crying. This is my last one."

But Caitlin wept on, for the naive girl she had been and for the confused woman she now was.

"You need something more potent than tea." Magheen went to the sideboard and returned with a crystal decanter and a small glass. A medallion bearing the Rafferty badger hung around the neck of the decanter.

Caitlin took a large gulp of the amber liquid, then choked into the handkerchief. "What the devil is this, Magheen?"

"Brandy. Logan brought it back from Corrib."

Caitlin's heart sank, and she set aside the glass as if it contained poison. "I'd hoped Logan would return with Hammersmith's head on a pike."

"That was his intent when he set out after the cattle raid. But he and the Roundhead came to an accord, just as they did when Father Tully—" Magheen broke off. A mortified flush stained her cheeks.

"When Father Tully what?" Caitlin demanded. Her vision swam red with fury. "Damn you, Magheen, how long have you known?"

"R—right from the start. But I—oh, God, Caitlin, I'm sorry!" Sobbing, Magheen reached out with a shaking hand. "It's myself who's needing the handkerchief now."

Caitlin slapped her face.

With a yelp of pain and horror, Magheen stood and backed away. "Caitlin, you don't understand. Logan had no choice."

"He betrayed Father Tully, didn't he? He sold our chaplain to the priest catchers for the price of tea and brandy, didn't he?"

"It—it wasn't like that. Logan arranged to have him transported for his own good. The English would have put him to death. It's his brand of justice, Caitlin. It works for him."

Rage surged through Caitlin faster than the brandy. "How can you abide it, Magheen? Your husband is Hammersmith's pet spaniel. He can be bought off with a juicy bone while everyone else in Connemara starves."

Magheen sighed miserably. "But at least he keeps the peace and feeds his people."

Bleak awareness crept over Caitlin. She thought of

Wesley, a *Sassenach*, braving peril to save the Irish priests. While Magheen consorted with a traitor.

"Magheen, can't you persuade Logan to join us?" she asked. "Think how much stronger we would be if we were united."

"I'll try, Caitlin. Haven't I already promised to keep you in plenty of food for the winter? But Logan—"

"Caitlin!" A clear voice called from the outer hall. "My lady, where are you?"

She jumped and ran to the door. "Curran Healy, what the devil are you doing here?"

Apple-cheeked and grinning, panting with exertion, he doffed his caubeen and clutched it to his chest. "Come back to Clonmuir, and you'll see."

She burst into the hall and stopped to take in the scene.

Tom Gandy stood atop the round table and spoke faster than a spinning wheel.

Seated around the table, amid the "fishermen" with their windburned faces and triumphant grins, were no less than three dozen priests.

"Praise be to the Lord," whispered Caitlin. She barely felt herself putting one foot in front of the other as she moved into the hall. Near the fire, a flash of ivory caught her eyes. White hair and a white beard.

"Daida!" She ran to her father, threw her arms around his neck, and kissed him.

"Aye, 'tis back in the fine wide boozalum of Clonmuir I am, *a stor*." Seamus grinned from ear to ear. "A hundred thousand blessings upon us all."

She drank in the sight of his dear, noble face, so beautiful in its untroubled simplicity. Feeling a clash

of worry and affection, she asked, "You were at
Inishbofin?"

"Aye, that I was." He gestured grandly about the
room and raised his voice above the thunder of
conversation. "I and the great good men of God,
left to starve in that inhospitable place. But I
brought them all safely home, aye, just as I said I
would."

Someone cleared his throat. Caitlin spied Rory
Breslin nursing a mug of poteen in his large paws.
Rory said, "He had some little help in the rescuing."

"Very little," said a strong English voice. Caitlin
caught her breath at the sight of Wesley. Wind-tossed
hair and ruddy cheeks. Broad shoulders and narrow
hips. Eyes the color of moss in shadow. And a grin
that could melt butter at fifty paces.

She didn't bother to resist the smile that tugged at
her lips. Relief and tenderness glowed in her heart.

"Tell me," she said softly.

"It was all your father's doing," said Wesley.

Seamus drew himself up. Rory opened his mouth
to protest.

Wesley shot him a quelling look. "Over Brian's
loud protests, Seamus cleverly disguised himself as a
cleric and let himself be seen by a priest catcher in
Waterford. They transported him to Inishbofin, and
then it was just a matter of waiting for us to play our
part. A part that wouldn't have been possible had it
not been for Seamus."

Seamus launched into a rambling recitation of his
exploits.

Caitlin's gaze met Wesley's. She felt a sweet gen-
tling inside her, like water settling in a jar. Wesley
could have grabbed the credit for himself, but
instead allowed the proud old man his moment in
the sun.

"A toast!" Tom Gandy shouted. Mugs and glasses lifted all around the room. "To the priests of Ireland," he called. "May you never again stray from your flock."

Conn O'Donnell stood. "To the clan MacBride, for all that has been done this day."

Seamus rose. "The holy light of heaven shine upon us all. And if we can't go to paradise, may we at least die in Ireland."

Caitlin glanced at Wesley. His full-throated "Hear, hear" before he drank made her believe he truly wished it. The feeling of tenderness inside her tightened, became something stronger. Something she hesitated to acknowledge.

He motioned her to his side, then winced. She longed for him to touch her, longed to feel his strong arm around her waist and his chest against her cheek.

Instead he gave her a familiar smile that had a familiar effect. "We've got to do something about these priests," he said.

"Aye, it would be tragic indeed if they were seized again. I doubt the English would trouble themselves to send them into exile a second time."

"They'd shoot them on sight," Wesley said.

Heads together, united in their concern, they made a plan. Caitlin felt herself drawing closer to him, the weight of her office shifting, somehow, becoming lighter. In some part of her mind she knew that it was odd to be sharing her duties with this man, and yet the moment felt comfortable, as if they had done this often.

Some of the priests, they decided, would dress as fishermen and head north for Connaught where the English didn't trouble the Irish. Others would leave on foot disguised as wanderers. Still more would go to cities and lose themselves amid the crowds.

"And Father Tully?" Wesley asked at last.

"Father Tully stays," said Caitlin. "Without him, we're a rudderless ship."

"He was betrayed once. It could happen again."

"It won't."

"How can you be certain?"

"I found out who betrayed him." Caitlin took a deep breath. "You were right. It was Logan."

Certainty chiseled his features to stone. "Just as I thought. When did you decide to believe me?"

"Magheen admitted that Logan sold Tully's whereabouts to a priest catcher. He swears it's because he feared for Father Tully's life but I'll never believe that." Unthinkingly she pulled his hand into her lap. "Ah, Wesley, he's my brother by marriage. It pains my heart to think ill of him."

He lifted her hand to his lips. "It will pain more than your heart if you continue to trust him."

A shattering sound broke into their conversation. Rory had flung his mug at the wall and was advancing on Tom Gandy.

"You wouldn't dare," Rory shouted.

"Now, Rory, sure and it's a fine idea—"

"Shut your mouth, you parboiled imp!" Grasping Tom by the shoulders, Rory lifted him off the table and held him so they were eye to eye, nose to nose. Tom's legs flailed in useless protest. "We'll hear no more of your English-loving blarney, Tom Gandy," said Rory.

"Huh! You are the dumbest Goth in creation. I say we do it."

"I say we don't," Rory snarled.

"Do."

"Don't."

"Do what?" Caitlin demanded in exasperation.

Tom lifted his chin. "Make Wesley one of the Fianna."

Gasps of surprise gusted from the crowd; then a hush fell over the hall. Unable to look at Wesley, Caitlin said, "That's absurd."

"It makes perfect sense to me," Seamus called.

"There," said Tom. "You see? And put me down, you great, bad oaf."

Rory dropped him. "I'm with Caitlin. No *Sassenach* can join the Fianna."

Tom picked himself up off the floor. "I say he's earned the honor. Look all these good priests in the eye and deny it."

Rory stared at the floor.

"Tom's right." Seamus MacBride came to stand beside Wesley. "He nearly paid for the freedom of the priests with his life."

"What?" Caitlin asked.

Father Tully stepped forward, bringing a thin, gray-haired cleric with him. A chain of office glinted on his chest. Lifting his hand to point at Wesley, the bishop said, "This man took a saber cut meant for me."

Caitlin's heart dropped to her knees. "Where?" she asked Wesley.

"Just a graze." He touched his shoulder.

"What say you, Caitlin?" asked Tom. "Has he earned the right to join the Fianna?"

Yes! her heart shouted. But pride made her doubt him.

"We'll put it to a vote, as we do all clan matters," she said.

And when the voting was done, everyone save Conn and Liam voted to offer Wesley initiation.

And Caitlin, more torn and confused than ever, claimed the right to abstain.

* * *

The day began bright, cool, and lonely as usual. Wesley rose from his pallet to find that Caitlin had left him and gone about her business. Lord, what he wouldn't give to awaken with her warm in his arms, to tarry beneath the covers with that firm, silken body, to share intimate secrets and make plans for the future, to fantasize about the babies they would have.

To be fair, she had plenty to occupy her. The dispersing of the priests had taken most of her time.

Rubbing the sleep from his eyes, he went to the basin to shave. Numbed by the icy water, he barely felt the scrape of the razor or the twinge of discomfort in his shoulder.

The shave made him feel human again. He managed a smile when Curran Healy tapped on the door and entered.

"This just came." The youth handed Wesley a letter. "A courier from the east brought it." His gaze took in Wesley's bare chest and the livid gash on his upper arm. "Does that hurt?"

"Not so much."

Curran went to the door. He hesitated, turned back. "Sir?"

"Yes?"

"Good luck to you, sir." Curran left.

Wesley dressed in tight leather trews and knee boots. He pulled a plain white tunic over his head. He would endure the initiation bareheaded and bare chested, but first he would go to pray.

He broke the seal of the letter and read it.

His blood turned to ice, and a groan ripped from his throat. Cursing, he crumpled the letter and tossed it into a brazier. As he watched the paper burn, he tried to control his frustration.

Damn Cromwell. Damn Titus Hammersmith.

For a few weeks, Wesley had managed to put them from his mind. To fool himself as he had imagined he had been fooling them. Evidently Titus had decided to call his bluff about the profits gained from transporting wenches. Wesley should have known the threat wouldn't last.

Twenty Clonmuir horses, the letter had commanded. To be given over to the English cavalry.

Tomorrow.

Regrets crushed his chest. Just when he had come close to winning over Caitlin and the men of Clonmuir. Just when they were about to extend the hand of acceptance to him.

Send the horses, Clonmuir's one priceless treasure, and lose Caitlin. Ignore the order and lose Laura.

He made a fist and jammed it against his chest as if to keep his heart from tearing in two.

Then he pondered a third possibility. A way to appear to follow Hammersmith's orders while actually deceiving him. Yes, it could work. Caitlin didn't trust him yet, but the men of Clonmuir would help.

Wesley smiled and made his way to the chapel.

Kneeling before the altar, he folded his hands and raised his eyes to the smiling Virgin. An old feeling swept over him, a remnant of simpler times, when kneeling in the house of God had brought him close to a state of grace.

Caitlin skidded to a stop when she saw him. Unnoticed by Wesley, she moved silently up the side aisle and settled on a kneeler several feet away.

Lord save her soul, but he was a sight. Candle glow bathed his massive shoulders and handsome face in shades of gold. John Wesley Hawkins in action was a sight to set one's heart to pounding.

John Wesley Hawkins at prayer was a sight to stir the soul.

A pained, pleading expression transformed his rough features. Deep shadows molded the hollows below his cheekbones, giving him the aspect of a statue. And yet vibrancy glowed from him, the warmth of life rather than cold stone. His hands clasped each other, and she had a sacrilegious thought of those hands on her body, that mouth on her mouth.

Wesley spoke. "Lord Jesus, I beg you to help me. Please. Make me a part of this place. Make me a part of Caitlin. Please God, I love her so."

Caitlin's jaw dropped. She quickly slipped into the shadows of a round pillar, where she reeled with the impact of the declaration.

He had spoken to her of love before, had sworn it. But she had been skeptical, thinking it simply another of his lies.

But would he lie to the Almighty?

God, I love her so.

She pressed her back to the pillar and inhaled the subtle fragrance of burned-out incense. A feeling of joy rose through her, coursing upward like a fountain of light, bathing her heart and her mind in splendor.

She wanted to run to him, to fling her arms around his neck and cover his face with kisses.

She was the MacBride. Other men respected and obeyed her.

John Wesley Hawkins loved her.

She was inches from reaching out to him when hurrying footfalls sounded.

"Wesley, there you are." Tom Gandy rushed up the aisle. "Come, we're about to begin."

Wesley rose and turned. Caitlin caught her

breath. He looked much as he had the first time she had seen him: imposing, confident, bathed in hero-light.

Tom, too, seemed struck by his appearance. "Lord, but you're in the high state of grace. I was about to wish you luck, but I can see you'll not be needing it."

Wesley laid his arm across Tom's shoulders as they walked out. "Wish me luck anyway, my friend."

16

Wesley stood bare chested in a waist-deep hole, a plain wooden shield in one hand and an arm's length of hazel wood in the other. His hair had been intricately braided close to the scalp and woven with leather and beads.

Tom Gandy had explained in unsparing detail what must be done. Wesley had prepared for the trials to come. He had girded himself with prayers and self-confidence.

The rite smacked of paganism, and always at the back of his mind lurked the reality of Hammersmith and Cromwell. If this savage rite didn't kill him, Wesley would find himself committing the ultimate betrayal against Clonmuir and Caitlin. He prayed his plan to thwart the English would work.

Nine warriors armed with sharpened spears formed a circle around Wesley. Rory posed the greatest threat, his red hair wild and his long beard flaming on the wind.

"God's grace be with you," said Father Tully.

Wesley nodded in thanks but his eyes stayed fastened upward on the pointed weapons. A spear hurled by a brawny Irish warrior could stave him through like a spitted pig.

A stir of movement caught his eye. Caitlin joined the circle of warriors. She wore her hair loose, and a tunic bearing the golden harp of Clonmuir encased her figure. As regal as a queen and as mysterious as an angel, she regarded him solemnly.

Their gazes locked and held. And then a miracle occurred.

She smiled at him. It was a smile such as he had never seen grace the countenance of Caitlin MacBride. There was something fresh and new about it, soft as mist, compelling as a whispered endearment.

She mouthed the words "Good luck."

Wesley knew then that he would succeed.

A goatskin *bodhran* rattled. The warriors turned their backs on Wesley, measured off nine paces, and faced him.

He gripped the hazel branch and shield. Gandy shouted something in Gaelic. Nine spears sailed down at Wesley.

Time seemed to slow. The sharpened tips drove toward his heart. His shield came up to deflect them.

The sound of cracking wood burst in his ears. Wesley moved by instinct, seeming somehow to know the paths of the spears before they flew. The branch met them and turned their flight. Moments later, he found himself surrounded by broken spears and grinning faces.

Feeling as proud as he had the day he had first held Laura in his arms, Wesley climbed over spent and splintered spears. He caught Caitlin's eye and gave a jaunty salute. The peculiar glow still lighted her face. She reminded him of a woman who guarded a delicious secret. He longed to take her in his arms and kiss the mysteries from her lips.

Instead he turned his mind to the next trial, a pursuit through the murky forest. Mounted on his pony, Tom Gandy trotted along at Wesley's side. "Mind you follow the path we laid out last night," he said. "And do be remembering you'll have to jump a branch as high as your head, and pass under one level with your belt. Neither branch nor twig must disturb the weave of your lovely braids."

"I'll remember." With mock vanity, Wesley patted his hair.

"If even one of the warriors draws blood," Tom went on, "you'll fail."

The warriors girded themselves for the chase, strapping on sword belts and gripping new spears. The fire in Rory's skeptical eye seared Wesley with fortitude. "I'll outrun them," he vowed.

"Hold a minute," said Tom. "I'll be having those boots from you. You're to run the gauntlet barefoot."

Wesley drew off his boots and handed them over. The sandy earth of the yard felt soft under his feet. If anyone had told him a few months earlier that he would be running half-naked through the mountains of Connemara, he would have declared him touched in the head.

But then again, if anyone had told him he would lose his heart to an Irish warrior woman, he would have declared *himself* touched in the head.

He stopped at the fringe of woods. He sensed a magic in the moment, in the land that unfolded before him, full of sun and shadow and the secrets of warriors whose courage had been molded by half a millennium of fighting.

God, what vanity to think himself worthy of the giants who had taken their strength from the rugged land, their music from the sharp plaints of seabirds swooping over the fells, their poetry from the song of the wind through the green-draped vales.

"They were all just men," said Tom, sensing Wesley's thoughts. "Their power came from their human hearts."

Wesley nodded. Already he had begun to empty his mind, as he had learned to do long ago on the eve of battle, when the Parliamentarians and the Royalists were fated to meet at Worcester. Determination sharpened his instincts to a blade edge.

"Ready?" asked Tom.

Wesley made the sign of the cross.

Caitlin drew up on the black stallion. Bright hope danced in her eyes. "Luck be with you, Wesley," she said.

The *bodhran* drummed a rolling tattoo. Pipes whistled in crescendo and peaked at an earsplitting note.

Casting one last look at Caitlin, Wesley plunged into the forest. Sharp rocks cut into his feet. Thorny branches whipped past his face. And from behind, drawing closer, sounded the dread thunder of pursuit.

A hand ax sailed by, slicing the air dangerously close to his ear. "Jesus!" Wesley gasped.

The path rose steeper, littered with stones. Ahead loomed the alderwood branch that would test his agility.

He felt himself flagging, the agony in his bleeding feet rising like fire through his body. The branch drew closer . . . unassailable, impossibly high. A mere length of wood became the measure of his character.

He could not leap it.

In his mind's eye he saw himself slamming into the stout wood, dropping like a wounded deer, entangled in brambles and thorns. He would forfeit all, lose Caitlin and Laura.

The pain of that thought lashed at him like a spiked whip. And then a flash of blinding light cleaved through his consciousness. He was lost, sucked into a burning white nothingness.

Cantering along with the pursuing warriors, Caitlin felt fear pressing at her. Wesley had reached the limit of his strength; she could tell from the labored movements of his powerful legs and the loud sound of his breathing. She thanked God he was fleeter than any of the warriors, even Conn who won all the foot races at Beltane.

But Wesley left bright smudges of blood in his path. Winded and bleeding, the wound on his shoulder still puffy and livid, he would never make that jump.

When he was several feet in front of the branch, she noticed a change in him. His breathing evened out and he said something. His legs coiled and extended. In a leap that would have daunted the most gifted of athletes, he sailed over the branch. Caitlin blinked and shook her head. For a moment, it had seemed that a bright glow moved with him, gilding the leaves and branches in his path.

Tom Gandy cantered up beside her. "Saints of heaven, have you ever in your born and natural life seen the likes of that?"

Wesley landed on the path. He made no sound as his bloodied feet struck the rocky ground.

Tom lowered his voice. "Caitlin, did you see . . . ?" For once, the bard of Clonmuir was at a loss for words.

Before Caitlin could reply, Rory loosed a bellow and plunged after his quarry. He let fly with his spear. Without looking back, Wesley ducked. He was a man possessed by some demon and yet divinely protected; he was wild and fey, no quarry for mortals. Again Caitlin sensed some strangeness about him and at first she could not place it. And then she realized. As

Wesley ran, his feet seemed to skim the ground; his passing did not stir a single leaf or branch.

"Faith, he's not clear in his head," Tom said wonderingly.

Awe shone in the warriors' eyes. Liam chewed his thumb against evil. The back of Caitlin's neck prickled. Some unnatural spirit had taken hold of Wesley. Like Ruath of legend, he had harnessed an invisible wind horse.

The race continued another quarter mile. Wesley possessed a surging power that daunted his pursuers and baffled his observers. He seemed more than human as he dodged, ducked, and vaulted the obstacles without slackening his pace, and sped to the end of the course.

As he approached the fluttering pennon that marked the end of the gauntlet, Wesley sensed that something extraordinary had happened. The blinding whiteness of oblivion deepened to the shades of reality. The pain rushed back, screaming through his chest and shooting up his legs. With amazement he realized that the murderous course lay behind him.

He stopped at the pennon, grasped the pole, and fell to his knees. His hand came up to touch his hair. The braids lay neatly in place.

"My God," he gasped. "I made it."

"You did," cried Tom, trotting up on his pony. "Saints be praised and sinners be damned, you did it, lad!"

Caitlin arrived on the black. Her round bright eyes regarded him with a mixture of pride and awe. "How, Wesley? How did you manage?"

Gripping the pole, he drew himself up and shook his head, unable to explain.

"You're a true champion," Curran Healy crowed.

The sweat crawled in rivulets down Wesley's face

and back and shoulders. "No, Curran," he said. "I . . ." He accepted a flask from Brigid and took a drink, then spat it out. "Water? By God, what must a man do to get beer?"

The girl handed him a second flask. "Tickle your throat with this, sir," she said, her face wreathed in smiles.

Wesley drained the flask, then turned to Caitlin. "I have the oddest feeling that it was not my doing."

He heard a nervous edge to her laughter as she tossed her head. "And who then did every last one of us watch moving like the Second Coming through the woods?"

Before Wesley could answer, Rory Breslin stepped forward, tugging at his gorget and puffing with exertion. "Never in my born days have I seen the like."

"I see the hand of a wise and just God in this," Seamus declared. "He's one of us, else he'd not have survived."

"Aren't you forgetting something?" asked Rory.

Wesley sent him a lopsided grin. "Yes, that I'm mortal, after all. The Fianna asks much of a man."

"I was speaking of the poetic composition." Slipping into Irish, Rory said, "The body might be fit—though I hold certain parts of it in grave doubt—but what of the mind and tongue?"

Still in the grip of pain and guilt, Wesley reached for more beer.

"Is it true he must make songs and recitations in Irish?" Curran asked worriedly.

"Aye," said Tom Gandy. "So it be written."

The large party started back toward the stronghold. Clearing his throat, Wesley hesitated. Rory glared at him.

"Nature's call." Wesley jumped down a slope to the shelter of the bushes.

"Me, too." Rory joined him.

Wesley rolled his eyes. "God, will you not trust me to take a piss?"

"After what I saw today, I'd sooner trust the Bad One himself." Rory whistled through his teeth as he unlaced his trews.

Wesley couldn't help himself. After all his bold talk, Rory Breslin invited attention. Those who bray loudest usually had the least to bray about.

Wesley blinked. His jaw dropped. For the boastful Irishman had a member that made a full grown bullock's look like a lapdog's.

Wesley glanced away quickly. "Christ, no wonder you're not married," he muttered.

Rory chuckled. In Irish, he said, "You've good reason to be in awe of a real man. You'll not keep her happy for long with that."

Filled with a long denied yearning for retribution, Wesley took his time lacing his trews.

As he did so, he said in flawless Irish, "Pardon me, *a chara*. But I'm after thinking that ' tis not the size of the weapon that matters, but the fury of the thrust."

A ceremonial hush closed over the assembly in the hall. Flanked by Seamus and Tom, Caitlin sat at the round table. She tensed with anticipation, her nerves burning and her heart beating fast.

The last phase of the initiation was crucial. A warrior could not be accepted until he had proven the power of his mind as well as that of his body.

Seamus toyed with the ends of his beard. "Sure I'd like to see the man become one of us. But the poor soul doesn't know the Irish."

Rory took a long drink of his poteen and chuckled richly. "I'd not be after worrying myself on that, Seamus. Hawkins has the touch of the green on him."

A sadness welled up in Caitlin. She, too, wanted Wesley to succeed. How simple it would be if he gave his whole heart to Ireland. Then she would be free to open her soul to him as a wife should do.

Then she would be free to love him.

But John Wesley Hawkins was a born Englishman, and that fact would be painfully apparent when he came before the assembly and revealed that his tongue had no talent for the Irish. She felt the melancholy conviction that, after tonight, he would leave her. And she would be left with bittersweet memories of a love that she had been too stubborn, too proud to reach out and grasp with both hands.

The main door banged open to the gathering evening. Twilight had turned the world blue and cold. The distant bleating of Mudge's flock of black-faced sheep sounded with the noise of the battering sea and the song of the wind.

Wesley appeared in the doorway. The hush in the hall deepened. Caitlin caught her breath.

The torchlight magnified his size. He was, in that breath-held moment, bigger than a legend, broad of shoulder and narrow of hip, moving with clean-limbed grace down the length of the hall. He gave no sign that his torn feet pained him. The subtle surge of his ropy muscles beneath a loose white tunic drew the eye and held it captive.

His red hair, freed of the braids, fanned out in a magnificent mane around a face that, once glimpsed, could never be forgotten. The austere lines of nose and cheekbones were softened by his wide, full-lipped mouth. His eyes possessed hidden depths that urged a woman to plumb his soul and discover the miracles hidden there.

Caitlin felt the secret woman inside her stir to life. The ancient believer wanted to run forward and embrace the approaching man, to mesh herself, body and soul, with his sumptuous handsomeness and extraordinary strength.

His soft leather knee boots scuffed lightly against the flagged floor. The simple costume of tunic and trews, his waist cinched by the wide belt, gave him the look of a postulant about to take vows.

As indeed he had, Caitlin remembered with a jolt of discomfort. She pictured him lying prostrate before an altar lit by candles. And said a silent, shocked word of thanks that he had not found a vocation.

He reached the table and went down on one knee before her. Despite the obeisance, Caitlin could detect nothing even remotely humble in the man bowed down before her.

Following the dictates of tradition, she said, "Rise and tell us the poems of the ancients." She spoke in the Irish tongue and did not expect him to understand the words.

He straightened. She fought to keep her face expressionless, but the emotions shining in his eyes made indifference impossible.

What did he see when he looked at her?

God, I love her so.

He had whispered the words like a prayer in the chapel.

Now his eyes spoke the same message to her.

Her woman's heart heard and believed. A beautiful smile softened her lips. Wesley's answering smile warmed her heart.

"If I may begin," he said.

Her spirits dropped, for he spoke in English. In the language of her enemies. She forced herself to nod.

He took a step backward. His gaze moved over the entire assembly. His presence filled the room like firelight.

Wesley began to speak.

Beautiful Irish words flowed like warm honey from his throat. Every syllable, every inflection, every roll of the tongue sang like the wind through the vales of Connemara, like the cry of a bird over the heaths, like the chiming of distant church bells.

"He would have made a good priest," Tom whispered.

The entire assembly sat spellbound by his mastery, by the long grave looks he sent about the room, by the vibrating timbre of his voice.

The voice of Wesley speaking Irish, sounding like an ancient Celt.

"Faith, I'll be out of a job," Tom Gandy muttered.

Wesley told of battles won and fortunes lost, of strong women and valiant men. Of a love that was as bright and deep as the very soul of Eireann.

When the recitation ended on a vibrant, irresistible note, grown men wept. Women sighed and lifted their eyes to heaven.

"How the devil did you learn our tongue?" Conn asked wonderingly.

Wesley's unfocused stare fixed itself on the low-burning fire, as if he were looking into the very distant past. "I was fostered with Irish monks at Louvain. They put me to work at the presses, printing works in Irish that had been banned here." His shoulders drooped a fraction of an inch. "I must go, my friends. This day has taken the heart out of me." He left the hall amid a babble of amazement.

Scarcely aware of herself, Caitlin rose from the table. Tom said something but she didn't hear. The lodestone of Wesley's magnetism drew her inexorably from the hall.

Unashamed, her soul filled with a shimmering enchantment, she opened the door to their chamber and stepped inside.   * * *

He stood warming his hands at the brazier and did not turn or acknowledge her approach. His head was bent, his face grave and unreadable. Yet still that terrible, beautiful glow hovered around him, illuminating the red-gold sheen of his hair and the quiet majesty of his form.

Full of awe and longing and fear, Caitlin stepped up beside him. He made no reaction; it was as if the trials of the day had drained his energy and Caitlin's constant refusals had sapped his spirit. Aye, for months he had endured her scorn, had forgiven her distrust, had accepted her condemnations.

She prayed she had not come too late.

In silence, she went and filled a basin with water and healing herbs, setting it on the floor in front of him.

"You'll be wanting to bathe your feet," she murmured.

He lifted one brow in faint surprise, then lowered himself to a stool. He reached for the laces of his boot.

She put her hand on his wrist. "No. Let me."

The eyebrow went up a notch, but he shrugged and settled back while she removed his boot and eased his feet into the water. Her fingers moved gently over the tender and broken flesh. She winced as she remembered his wild race through the woods.

"Tell me, Cait," he said quietly. "Were you put through the ordeal, too?"

"Of course." She kept her gaze focused on the basin. "But for me—for all of us—it was different. There were allowances that weren't extended to you."

"Because I'm English."

"Aye."

He stood, wiping his feet on a towel and then going to the window, gazing out at the night. Caitlin studied his broad back, the ruddy hair curling over his neckline, the tense pressure of his hand on the embrasure.

Oh, Wesley, am I too late?

She approached him softly, hoping he would turn, hoping he would smile. And then, for the first time since a wish made on a wild rose had summoned him, she reached out.

Her arms went around him from behind. She rested her cheek against his back, heard the sharp intake of his breath and the forceful beating of his heart.

A hundred times he had begged her to let him love her.

A hundred times she had denied him.

Now the asking was up to her.

She did not know where to begin. And then she remembered his recitation in the hall, the simplicity of words sprung from a yearning heart a thousand years old. "'His touch did enslave my soul and did gild my heart with splendor . . .'"

He turned slowly, and his hands came up to grip her shoulders. "Caitlin. . . ?"

A smile hovered tentatively about her lips. "'Come, my love,'" she recited, "'move soft with me, to where the wild birds call . . .'"

"'. . . and the land reaches out to kiss the sea,'" he finished, his voice quiet and deep with wonderment.

Caitlin wound her arms around his neck and drew his head close to hers. "Aye, you are the sea, my Wesley," she whispered. "As terrible and deep and beautiful as the sea struck by God's own hand. And so here I am, coming to you, asking you . . ."

"Asking what, Caitlin?" Anger flashed in his eyes. "My God, woman, what more can I give you?"

She raised up on tiptoe and pressed her lips to his cheek. "I can only hope I'm not too late."

"Too late for what?"

"To tell you that I love you."

A sound of joy and pain and yearning burst from him. He swept her up into his arms and laid his lips on hers. They shared a deep, open-mouthed kiss, and the taste of him flooded her, probed her soul with fingers of light.

Caitlin wanted to whisper the words that were in her heart, but this was not a moment for talking. It was instead an eternity of light and darkness, a timeless moment when all things became clear.

Desire poured like warm rain through her. An answering passion flared in Wesley; she felt the bright heat emanating from her skin.

Of one heart, one soul, and one accord, they shed their clothing and stood bathed in the low golden light of the brazier.

Wesley's eyes adored her; his tender regard transported her to a realm where the past was forgotten, the future a golden promise.

"You make me feel like a wild spirit who's found a home," he whispered. He covered her breast with his hand. Her flesh sprang to vivid life, and she stepped into his caress, a begging sound escaping her lips and a heady throb of rapture moving through her.

"Wesley." She murmured his name between tastes of his lips, his throat, his shoulders. "You once said you would write poetry on my skin."

His smile moved against her temple. "Caitlin, are you asking me?"

She rested the palms of her hands on his slim, hard hips. "No, I'm begging you."

He pulled her into his arms. She reveled in his crushing embrace, in the hungry, urgent kisses he rained over her mouth, her throat, her breasts. She loved the roughness of it, the frank lust barely tempered by tenderness. Her old dreams of a stiff, courtly lover fled before the storm of his passion. This was what she wanted, what the woman inside her craved—to be swept away on a whirlwind.

She inhaled his scent; he smelled of the woods at midnight, of heather soap, and of mysterious essences unique to him alone.

He laid her on the bed linens and held back a moment, struggling visibly for control, and then he came to rest beside her. His eyes contained depths of wonder and desire and uncertainty. His hands beguiled her flesh with caresses as soft as the passing wing of a moth. His touch brought her to a state of unbearable sensitivity.

"Caitlin, *agradh*." The Irish sounded mellifluous on his tongue, strange and yet wholly right. "'Tis a miracle that you have come to me at last."

She twined her fingers in his hair. "The miracle happened ages ago when I held a rose and wished for you, and you came to me."

"Sometimes I think I was sent."

She held very still for a moment, wondering at his words. "Magic or happenstance," she said, "it matters not." And then she touched him, marveling at the way his flesh heated and leapt to life under her questing hand.

He made a strangled sound in his throat. "Jesus! Slow down, woman!"

She laughed in delight and slowed, but did not stop her caresses. "Am I a bother to you, Wesley?"

He rose up on his knees. "Yes, by God, and I love you like this. Brazen and lusty and honest. But wasn't it you who begged for poetry?"

She nodded, staring at the languid play of fire glow

over his body.

"Good," he said, "because the inspiration is on me."

His large rough hands moved with shattering tenderness over her breasts and belly and hips. She arched upward into his embrace, reaching, clinging, breathless with wanting him. His mouth followed the path of his hands, delving into warm secret places, and Caitlin was lost, no longer aware of anything beyond the undefined promise of the man wrapping her in his soft spell. She whirled like a grain of sand in an hourglass, spinning inexorably toward warmth and completion.

"Wesley," she gasped.

Her breath fanned the passion flaming through him. He felt open and raw, his nerves ragged with tension. He was not accustomed to feeling so intensely, so deeply. To loving so desperately.

He told her so in English and then in Irish. He told her with his hands and with his lips. And after a while, they spoke a secret lover's language that neither remembered learning.

He had looked at her a thousand times, and yet her eyes never ceased to startle him. The amber depths held the glow of sunshine rippling through a field of ripe wheat.

Adoration flowed through him, as warm and slow moving as a river in high summer.

"I love you, Caitlin." His hand traced the line of her thigh, from the knee upward, to find her flesh softened and ready.

"I love you," he said again and surged against her, burning for her but aware every moment that she was fragile, that he did not want to hurt her.

"Then show me, Wesley. Show me."

His kisses fell like soft rain upon her upturned

face. He pressed himself into her moist cleft, and then deeper still to the silken depths that embraced him with a pulsing heat.

She made a small sound in her throat. He moved to pull back, but she arched toward him, her hands clutching his shoulders and her lips reaching for his.

Her sweet sigh gusted over him like a blessing. He felt her rising, saw her eyes flutter shut, saw her lips part in surprise and delight.

Her rapture was a subtle rhythm that probed an answering throb in him. A vast pulse of bliss ran through his body, and he spent himself with a feeling of utter contentment. Release had claimed his body, but, like sunlight stealing through the greenwood vales of Connemara, Caitlin MacBride had invaded his soul. He had been transformed, linked heart and mind to his lovely Irish warlord.

He kissed her long and hard and tried to beat back the thoughts that came upon him, thoughts of the betrayal he must commit before dawn broke over the horizon.

He should tell her.

Tell her he intended to give Clonmuir horses to Titus Hammersmith.

She would freeze her heart to him more quickly than a sudden frost. If he explained his plan to thwart the Roundheads, she might forgive him. But, as the MacBride, she would insist on participating. And that he could not let her do. The mission was too dangerous. He had not won her heart only to lose her in battle.

He would act in secret with the men who were now loyal to him. Caitlin need never know the horses had disappeared in the first place.

He need never test the fragile bond of their new love.

For Laura, he must betray Caitlin just one more time.

"Wesley." She looked at him through half-lidded eyes, a slumbrous smile of contentment soft upon her lips. "That was splendid. Poetry, it was."

Fatigue spread through him. The day had been long, the trial arduous and emotionally draining. Tomorrow would bring more trials, he thought, kissing a curl of golden hair at her temple. He shaped his body around hers and marveled at the fact that he could not remember sleeping any other way.

He had come a long way from his hanging at Tyburn Tree. But if tomorrow went as he'd planned, he would soon be home. Like the folding wings of an angel, sleep closed over him.

Caitlin felt him relax in her arms. "I love you," she whispered, knowing she had spoken too late, for he was oblivious to her pledge. But she didn't mind, for they had all their tomorrows ahead of them.

And tomorrow she would stare into his deep, mysterious, shadowy eyes and tell him a hundred more times that she loved him.

But in the morning he was gone.

17

Tugging a plain tunic over her head, Caitlin hurried into the hall. The women sat around the table breaking their fast with Brocach beef and small beer.

"Where is Wesley?" she asked.

Aileen Breslin gave her a motherly smile. "This be the first morning you've even thought to ask about your husband. I'm after thinking it's about time. Praise the blessed saints, both the daughters of Clonmuir are happily wed."

A blush stole to Caitlin's cheeks but the sensation pleasured her, for the warmth echoed the splendor she had felt in the dark moments of the night, when Wesley had held her close and whispered that he loved her.

"Well? Have you seen him?"

The women looked at one another and shrugged. Caitlin frowned. "Then where are the others?"

"Sure they've all gone off to fetch back the island stallions for the breeding," said Aileen.

Caitlin pursed her lips. She had always enjoyed taking part in the annual rite. Each spring, they swam

Connemara ponies to a high green island for grazing on the rich salt grass. Later, they brought the stallions back to breed with the mares. The process was exciting and dangerous, and Caitlin loved it. Yet after last night nothing could dim her pleasure in simply being alive. "Even Daida?" she asked.

Aileen nodded. "Aye, even himself."

Caitlin wandered out into the yard to check the weather. A fine warm rain misted her face. Feeling a presence beside her, she saw that Brigid had joined her.

Caitlin smiled. "Soft day," she remarked.

"Aye." Brigid chewed her lip. "My lady?"

"Yes, Brigid?"

The girl stabbed her bare toe into the damp ground. "You know how I'm always wont to be sleeping in the loft over the stables?"

"Aye, you've a fine affection for the ponies. You put me in mind of myself when I was young."

"Well, my lady, just before dawn I did be hearing something that wasn't meant for my ears."

Caitlin smoothed back the girl's glossy black hair. "And what might that be, my girleen?"

Brigid took a deep breath. "Well, 'twas your husband and Rory talking together. They argued some. Your man didn't want you taking part in the swimming of the horses today."

A cool shadow passed over Caitlin's heart but she laughed, discounting the premonition. "Sure he's playing the typical husband. Much too protective. I shall set him right when he returns."

Brigid's thin shoulders relaxed. "Aye, my lady, I've no doubt you will."

Just then, Logan Rafferty galloped through the gate. A wrathful expression darkened his face.

Caitlin ran to meet him. "Logan, what's wrong? Is it Magheen, or—"

He waved a hand to silence her. A purse of coins jingled at his belt. "Magheen's fine, and the fright of Brocach for her biting tongue."

Caitlin cast her eyes down, thinking of the cattle raid. "Then what is it?"

"Where's your husband, Caitlin?"

His taunting tone touched off a shiver of nervousness. "He and the men are off collecting the island stallions."

Logan tossed his large head, his eyes shining and his hair an ebony mane. "Caitlin, I do think myself that your husband has betrayed you."

As Logan explained his suspicions, the shadow over Caitlin's heart hardened to black ice.

"You're sure this will work?" Rory, Wesley, and the men of Clonmuir climbed over a spill of rocks at the edge of the island.

"No." Grim apprehension pervaded Wesley, and he forgot the aching burn of his muscles. He had given himself no time to recover from the initiation, and still less time to enjoy the new sense of peace he had found with Caitlin. "We could lose the stallions and our bloody lives as well."

Rory scratched his thick red beard. "Then why gamble?"

For Laura, thought Wesley with a lump in his throat. Fighting to hide his gnawing sense of desperation, he scowled. "Because we have the chance to take Hammersmith prisoner and acquire an English ship as well."

"We should've brought Caitlin into this," Rory grumbled. "She knows the ways of the *Sassenach*."

"She's also my daughter, and a hothead where the Roundheads are concerned." Seamus MacBride drew himself up to his full height. "I agree with Wesley. She's better off not knowing until the deed is done."

The men squatted in a circle around Wesley to review the plan. He sketched an outline of the island in the dirt. "The frigate will anchor here, where the cove waters are deepest. They'll lower a ramp to bring the horses into the hold. We'll swim the horses out to the ramp and drive them aboard."

He glanced up, studied the circle of rough masculine faces—the faces of men he longed to hear call him friend. Rory touched the hand ax strapped to his thigh. Liam the smith flexed his thick right arm, which Wesley had broken in battle. In his silent way, Liam seemed to offer forgiveness. Conn and Tom busied themselves with inspecting the blades of their daggers. Father Tully and Seamus held their spiked steel maces with obvious distaste. Curran laboriously counted out the round stones he had collected for his sling.

God, he's only a lad, Wesley thought. Misgivings bored deeper and deeper into his spirits.

"And after the boarding?" Rory prompted, jabbing Wesley in the ribs.

"After that, we'll have only our speed and our fighting skills to rely on."

"Who'll be after nabbing Hammersmith?" asked Tom.

"I will." Wesley touched the knife tucked into his belt. "The rest of you will subdue his men—the soldiers first, for they'll put up a fight. As for the sailors, they'd sooner take our bribes than our steel."

A fierce smile slashed through Rory's beard. "'Twill be high sport, nudging all those tight-pants bastards overboard."

An answering grin appeared on Wesley's face. "And then we sail for Clonmuir with our own horses in the frigate." And Hammersmith as his bargaining chip. A prisoner to trade for Laura.

Anticipation of seeing Caitlin's face warmed his earlier sense of dread. Soon there would be no more secrets, no more guilt. What a prize he would bring her.

Caitlin prayed she would not be too late. The swift black stallion, galloping with breath-stealing speed along the beaten road to Galway, assured her she would be on time.

The haziest of plans occupied her thoughts, and a cache of gold provided by the most unlikely of sources weighted her pocket. She almost smiled, remembering Logan's downcast eyes, his clenched fist as he held out the heavy purse and said, "Magheen has convinced me. This is long overdue."

Caitlin would buy or steal a dory and row out to the frigate. Then she would set fire to the ship and pray to God she escaped before the Roundheads detected her.

She had scuttled Commonwealth ships in the past. But the Fianna had always been there to help her. Now they were busy helping Wesley.

Helping him hand over Clonmuir horses to her sworn enemy.

Why?

Logan had not been able to help her puzzle that out. Wesley must hold some threat over their heads, something to do with her. Some stitched-up tale; she had let herself forget what a smooth liar he was. Why else would her own men betray her?

Her mind shied like a skittish yearling from thoughts of the night before. She could not bear to remember how completely she had surrendered to Wesley—heart and mind, body and soul. In the arms of her enemy she had found rapture; she had whispered that she loved him. It was unthinkable. She should have learned her lesson from Alonso's treachery.

Sweating in the armor she wore beneath her surcoat, she stopped at the Claddagh, a fishing village at the outskirts of the city. A family watched her fearfully from the doorway of a thatched stone house. Living in the shadow of an English-held town had dampened the natural hospitality of the Irish.

Speaking in Irish, she held out a gold coin and said, "I need to board my horse."

An elderly man, his face bearing the weather-beaten stamp of the fishing trade, edged out into the yard, snatched her coin, and gaped at the amount.

"I'll give you this much again when I return." Caitlin pressed her palm to the stallion's damp neck, then handed the reins to the fisherman.

The horse bridled, his rolled-back eyes glaring at the stranger. The man took a cautious step back.

"If I don't return, take him to Castle Clonmuir—for another reward, of course. The girl called Brigid will see to it."

She sent a last look at the black, then walked the rest of the way to Galway. A short time and several silver shillings later, she brought her curragh alongside the frigate in Galway Bay. With the hood of her tunic concealing her hair and face, she prayed that she resembled a lone fisherman.

She had just lit the first bog pine torch when she heard a thumping sound. A grappling hook snagged the hull of the curragh, tearing into the leather as two sailors pulled the line taut.

With the sharp taste of fear in her mouth, Caitlin sawed at the thick rope with her knife. But within seconds, a swarm of Roundheads had descended, dragging her up a rope ladder and depositing her on the deck of the frigate.

Titus Hammersmith came running. His hand shot out and captured her arm, his thick fingers biting into her flesh. She tried to wrench away, and her hood fell back.

"Well, well," he said, relishing every word, "'tis young Caitlin of Clonmuir come for a visit."

"He's taking a long time with the anchoring," whispered a voice beside Wesley.

"Shut your trap, Tom Gandy," snapped Rory. "Noise carries across water."

Wesley gritted his teeth. He heard the grunting of the stallions tethered at the shore. Half wild from their freedom on the island, the horses had made the capture an exhausting affair.

His hands rode at his hips, his fingers toying with his hidden knife. "Make sure your weapons are concealed," he reminded the men. "If we rouse their suspicions, things will go ill with us."

Rory shifted his weight from foot to foot. "Faith, but I don't like the feel of this mace near my tender parts."

Tom Gandy rotated his shoulders, wincing at the tightness of the leather straps that bound his crossbow to his back.

With a grinding of heavy chains, the ramp of the frigate lowered into the water.

And then, resplendent in his Roundhead livery and flanked by two armed guards, Titus Hammersmith appeared at the top rail. The Roundhead's glorious curls bobbed in the orange light of the sunset. Triumph wreathed his cruel, handsome face.

The urge to attack leapt up in Wesley. He forced himself to wave calmly.

"Well done, Mr. Hawkins," called Hammersmith,

eyeing the skittish horses. "I knew you'd come through for the Commonwealth."

"My pleasure." Wesley forced a grin.

Hammersmith's gaze raked the gathering of Irishmen. "So many of you," he remarked.

Wesley shrugged. "These itinerant Irish aren't as efficient as the Fianna. It'll take the lot of us to swim the horses out."

"Carry on, then," said Hammersmith.

Each Irishman mounted, cursing at the nipping and bucking of the half-wild stallions. They took the bridles of the others and waded the horses until the water deepened and they were swimming. The chill Atlantic swirled around Wesley, but he ignored the discomfort and set his sights on reaching the ramp.

His horse's hooves thumped against the submerged portion of the ramp; then the animal lurched clumsily up the wide, notched incline. The smells of saltwater and horse pervaded the air. With water streaming from his chest to his feet, Wesley dismounted and hauled on the tethers of the animals he led.

Soldiers waited to stable the horses in the hold. With a vicious snapping of teeth, a burr-infested skewbald shooed back the nearest Englishman.

"They have spirit." Wesley reached for Tom Gandy's hand to help the small man up the ramp. "It's from being in the wild all spring. 'Tis best you hood them for the stabling."

Cursing vividly, the soldiers called for rags to bind the eyes of the unwieldy horses. Each moment was an agony as Wesley helped bring the rest of the animals aboard. Rory came last, struggling up the ramp while the chains groaned ominously under the weight of the warrior and three horses.

Their eyes met; Wesley gave the slightest of nods. Rory drew a Spanish stiletto from his belt and jabbed the slender blade into the rump of the last horse.

An equine scream ripped through the air. The horse's panic infected the others, and within seconds, the hold rocked with terrified animals and cursing soldiers.

Ducking past a shrieking stallion, Wesley mounted a series of ladders to the top deck where Hammersmith stood.

The Roundhead captain turned at the sound of Wesley's squishing footfalls. A knowing gleam lit his eyes.

The eyes of a chess player about to say checkmate.

A cold finger of apprehension caressed Wesley's spine. Ignoring it, he lunged. Swift as lightning, his arm shot out and crooked itself across Hammersmith's windpipe.

A clutch of soldiers ran forward. With a lurch of his stomach, Wesley recognized Edmund Ladyman.

"Not another step closer," Wesley snapped out, "or your commander waters the deck with his blood."

Swords drawn, the guards stood still.

With a gasp of shock and an oath of rage, Hammersmith butted his elbow into Wesley's ribs. Wesley pressed the edge of his knife to Hammersmith's throat, just above the plate gorget. The very place where the rope of Tyburn had once burned Wesley.

"There now," he said with quiet finality. "I'll have none of that."

Hammersmith held himself motionless. "I suppose we should hear what Mr. Hawkins wants." He spoke with admirable composure, but tiny vibrations of fear thrummed in his voice.

Aware of his captive's strong body, Wesley held fast with a grip of steel. "I want you to follow some simple instructions, Captain. First, evacuate the ship. And then pray to God I don't kill you as my friends and I sail off with our horses."

"Sail off? You'd abandon us on this island?"

"Your men, not you. The men will soon become as wild and rangy as the horses. It might do the comfort-loving bastards some good. But you, my friend, are coming to Clonmuir with me, and you'll stay there until Cromwell meets my demands."

As stiff as a stone column, Hammersmith asked, "Why? For God's sake, Hawkins, you're an Englishman."

"No." Wesley raised his voice over the thumping hooves and cursing men. The truth flamed in his soul. "I am not Irish by birth, but by conviction."

Hammersmith motioned to the guards with his eyes. "You know what to do."

The soldiers hurried off. Moments later, they reappeared. Ladyman held a loaded musket.

The other man held Caitlin.

Biting blue oaths streamed from her as she struggled. The evening wind whipped the tawny banner of her hair. Ladyman aimed the musket at her head.

"My God." Wesley blinked, then shook his head as if to banish the vision. The deck listed from the force of a swell.

Hammersmith gave a tight smile. "Now, about your knife . . ."

Wesley dropped the weapon. A dizzying blur of action wheeled around him. With bellows of rage, a tide of angry Irishmen came roaring up from the hold.

Hammersmith pivoted, slicing the air with his sword. Wesley ducked, feeling the wind on the back of his neck.

Ladyman's musket went off. A cloud of yellowish smoke enveloped Caitlin.

English and Irish filled the deck. The gut-deep explosions of muskets mingled with roars of pain and the clash of steel. Moving through a fog of rage and sulphur smoke, Wesley found Tom Gandy's loaded crossbow on the deck. Gandy was nowhere in sight.

An ax in one hand and a hammer in the other, Rory fought two Englishmen on the ladder between decks. A musket ball slammed into him with a wet slapping sound.

Out of his mind with fear, Wesley raced toward the bow where he had last seen Caitlin.

A shout stopped him. Hammersmith appeared at the rail on the high afterdeck.

Cold to the very heart of him and aware that all was lost—Caitlin, Laura, life itself—Wesley took aim with the crossbow.

Choking and half blinded by the smoke of musket fire, Caitlin twisted in the arms of her captor. He laughed and squeezed her breasts. He was used to women who did not know how to fight.

She kneed him in the groin. Hard.

He fell, gasping and puking, to the deck.

She jumped over him, shoved aside Ladyman and his spent musket, and stumbled across the deck. Her ears rang from the exploding shots. A foul cloud of yellow-gray fog enveloped the deck. Arrows whined through the rigging, thudding into wood and sometimes into men. Ducking low, Caitlin fought her way over coiled ropes, intending to leap over the aft rail to freedom.

Fury and regret blazed in her heart. Fury at herself, for not trusting Wesley, and regret that her husband had not confided his plans to her.

She reached the high afterdeck. The smoke was thick here, rising from the deck. She reached for the rail.

And found herself once again in the grip of Titus Hammersmith.

* * *

Wesley felt his mind empty as he prepared for the kill. The Roundhead captain made a perfect target. Screaming commands from on high, his buff coat flapping around him and smoke billowing up from the decks, Hammersmith was a fat roebuck.

Filled with cold purpose, Wesley pulled the trigger of the crossbow. In the same tiny slice of time, Hammersmith's arm shot into the mist. He yanked something—someone—toward him.

Caitlin!

"No!" screamed Wesley. *"No! Jesus, God, no!"*

The crossbow bolt thudded into her chest. She reeled back and dropped out of sight.

"You sorry fool," Hammersmith barked in triumph. "You killed your own wife!"

Night sounds rose in a screeching, croaking chorus over the island. The pop of the campfire punctuated the eerie sounds. Rory Breslin groaned and swore. He had pried the musket ball out of his shoulder but the wound had become inflamed. The others lay about, exhausted, none wounded so badly as Rory. The overwhelming numbers of English had driven them overboard and they had swum to the island.

Wesley stared unseeing into the heart of the fire. His body felt stiff and his mind agonizingly alive. Punishing himself like a flagellant, he relived the scene over and over again.

The sharp bolt triggered by his own hand, driving through the smoke-filled air. Caitlin bursting through the thick fog, straight into the path of the bolt. The deadly missile embedding itself in her chest. The look of utter shock on her face just before she fell. Titus Hammersmith's taunt, Wesley's own screams of rage and denial. The impassioned curses of the Irishmen, swimming for their lives in a hail of musketry. Their cries of rage and impotence as the English set sail.

Now here they lay, still weak from the shock of seeing Caitlin killed before their eyes.

How could everything have gone so wrong?

Wesley tried to pray. Failed. Praying was for men who still believed, who still hoped. All hope had died in John Wesley Hawkins.

Faintly he heard snatches of conversation among the men. Seamus MacBride's voice trembled with grief. "Aye, my Caitlin was too good for this world. Sure and the great God carried her to heaven on wings of light."

Murmurs of sympathy rippled through the gathering. Someone asked, "Where could Tom Gandy have got his wee self off to?"

"Sure no one's seen him since the start of the battle."

"I'm after thinking he's dead, too."

Rory nudged Wesley. "'Tis a shock to be sure, but we saw how it was, all that smoke and us as wild as berserkers and the *Sassenach* shooting off like crazy. May God forgive you, for it was a pure and natural accident."

Wesley continued staring into the fire, seeing the color of Caitlin's eyes in the golden flames, the gloss of her hair in the glowing embers. He heard her voice in the keening of the wind and the shush of the waves on the shore. He felt her touch like the ghostly echo of a dream, and deep in the heart of him he couldn't accept that she was gone.

He moved through the task of hauling out their hidden curraghs, and the men murmured their admiration for his stoicism. But Wesley knew better. The rage and sorrow inside him brimmed higher and higher, and soon he would not be able to contain himself. Soon the fury would burst forth with fearsome strength, wreaking vengeance without mercy upon the race of men who had been responsible for Caitlin's death.

Driven by the rage that ruled him, Wesley threw himself, heart and soul, into revenge. He had no room in himself for softness. He could not smile at a posy offered by a shy child. He could not pray during Father Tully's night-long vigil for the souls of Caitlin and Tom. He could not commiserate with Magheen who, as soon as she heard the news, came to Clonmuir and sobbed out her grief until she lay weak and spent on the chapel floor.

Instead, Wesley coldly plotted campaigns designed to kill and maim and plunder.

He felt a flash of some feeling—he wasn't sure what—when Logan came to fetch Magheen. Rafferty was uncharacteristically subdued, guilt in his shining jet-colored eyes as he offered money and food to the refugees who still streamed to Clonmuir.

The first week, the men rode out in a daring raid to the heart of English-held Galway. Wesley felt a cold relish when, through the slit of his antique visor, he saw the astonished fright of the Roundheads, surprised in the dead of night. Crossbow bolts whirred through the darkness and thumped into English flesh.

Sometimes the fighting became a blurred dream. He would find himself holding a bloody sword, but with no memory of killing. At these times he caught the men regarding him with something like wonder. And afterward, he reached for a rosary to put himself into dreamless sleep with the clicking of the beads.

During an ambush on the road between Galway and Lough Corrib, Wesley captured an Englishman he recognized from Hammersmith's household. Before slitting the man's throat, he learned that Hammersmith had gone to England.

Now there was truly no hope of getting Laura back, either. The knowledge did not throw him into paroxysms of fury, for Caitlin had taken all his love and tenderness into eternity with her. He had nothing left to give Laura now.

He could not let himself think of his daughter, clad in Puritan black, laughing in Cromwell's lap.

The second week, a fisherman from the Claddagh arrived with Caitlin's beloved black stallion in tow. Wesley was in the yard, pacing up and down as he planned another raid.

The visitor stopped and stared. Wesley saw himself reflected in the man's apprehensive face. His hair unkempt, his half-grown beard straggly, his clothing dirty and his eyes wild, he knew he made a formidable sight.

The man handed over the horse. "She said there'd be a reward."

Wesley jerked his head toward Seamus, who sat beneath an alder tree poring over his book of hours. "See the MacBride." The visitor hurried away.

The high gloss of the stallion's blue-toned coat gleamed in the afternoon sun.

And Wesley, who had not shed a tear since seeing his wife fall from the shot loosed by his own hand, buried his face in the magnificent horse's neck and wept. The sobs rose from a bottomless well of sorrow inside him, erupting with a violence that made men remove their caps and children dive for their mothers' skirts.

But the great outpouring brought Wesley no comfort. A sound of rage tore from his throat. He vaulted onto the horse and savagely kicked its flanks. Having no handhold save the inky mane, he bent low over the neck and rode at the horse's caprice.

They streaked across fields and fens, jumped stone fences and thundered along the strand, sand and surf flying up and stinging his face while he worked the horse into a high lather.

He came to the forgotten garden where he and Caitlin had first met. Tumbled rocks and spiny green brambles formed ugly bracelets around the tidal pools. Breathing fast, he dropped from the horse and let it wander away.

It was what Tom Gandy would call a clarion day, the sun bright and the sky hard and clean. And still the place seemed to pulsate with enchantment. Magic hung in the very air he breathed. Secrets wafted on the voice of the wind.

Wesley sank to his knees and dug his fingers into the damp sand. "No," he bellowed. "Caitlin, you cannot be gone!"

But she was, borne to heaven where she would no doubt strike fear into the hearts of the angels.

The day stretched into evening, and evening into twilight. He lay on the sand, pondering the hopelessness of his lot. Hammersmith was gone to England to report Wesley's treachery to Cromwell.

Wesley remembered the Lord Protector's gentleness with Laura, the way the implacable eyes softened and the murderous hands soothed. Deep inside Wesley lived the certainty that even Oliver Cromwell would show mercy and give Laura a gentle upbringing. The Puritans were a harsh lot, but they looked after their own. And Cromwell, so recently deprived of his favorite grandson, clearly considered Laura his own.

All that was left to Wesley was the fight. Only in the teeth of a life-and-death struggle did he feel himself truly alive, pulsing with a lust for revenge.

The stars came out, and the brightest one burned its incandescence deeply into his mind, rousing memories of the day of Caitlin's inauguration. Then, the MacBride had seemed eternal. And surely she was! She could not be gone. She had only been transformed into a higher state of existence.

Like the brightest star.

London, August 1658

"Oh, my dear, this simply won't do at all." Lord Protector Oliver Cromwell strode into the cell of the Brick Tower, overlooking the moat on the north side of the Tower of London. He crossed the room to stand beside the leather-sprung cot. "You haven't touched your supper. You haven't eaten for days. I took such pains to have delicate fare sent to you."

The cot creaked as Caitlin stirred to life. She struck out with her arm and swept the laden tray to the floor.

"I'll not be after choking myself on your English pig swill!"

Unperturbed by her outburst, Cromwell waved back the huge, blond-haired man who had stepped inside behind him. "Mr. Bull, bring wine for the lady and me."

Caitlin caught the giant's eye. Thaddeus Bull had delivered the meal, and with it a blown glass vial which she fingered in the pocket of her apron.

Moments later, Cromwell poured pale yellow sack into two pewter goblets. Drawing a stool to the cot, he set the cups on the table. She drew back her hand to fling the cups away.

"I wouldn't, Mrs. Hawkins," he said. "You might find you'll need a drink."

I might at that, thought Caitlin, her fingers tightening on the vial. She lowered her other arm.

"You sorely try my patience," he said. "My daughter Bettie is not ten days in her grave, and I've been making myself ill with all the travel between Hampton Court and London."

Caitlin's view of the Lord Protector was colored by hatred, but she noted the gray lines of grief framing his mouth, the slight tremor in his voice as he spoke his daughter's name. So, she thought uncomfortably, the monster had a heart after all.

"My condolences on the death of your daughter," she said through stiff lips. "But you'll not have my pity on your illness."

"I'm not asking for it," he snapped. He looked past her, and his eyes softened. "God's will be done," he murmured, more to himself than to her. "At least I have Laura."

Caitlin had no interest in the man's mutterings. "Why are you here?"

"You were duly tried today."

His words cut a swath through her control. "Tried, was I?" she demanded. "And what manner of justice is it that puts a body to trial, and she not even present to give a defense?"

"The same manner of justice you showed to the English you murdered," he shot back. "Are you interested in hearing the outcome?"

Caitlin tried to resist her sudden longing for the wine, but the lure of the sack proved too great. She snatched one of the goblets and took a sip while Cromwell did the same. "Go on."

"The High Court of Justice has convicted you of treason, murder, theft, and the practicing of the outlawed popish faith."

Caitlin took another sip of wine. The smooth Spanish sack failed to thaw the frozen wasteland of her heart. "I cannot be guilty of breaking your laws, for I do not claim England as my sovereign country."

He shrugged, the chain of office moving on his shoulders. "The Council decrees that you are to be hanged, drawn, and quartered."

Horror erupted in her brain. "You cannot harm me! You signed a statement protecting the kin of John Wesley Hawkins."

"He broke faith with me!" Cromwell burst out. "I'm no longer under any obligation to him."

"Faith, faith, faith," Caitlin burst out. "I do not understand the word anymore. Whose faith, yours or God's? And which God, yours or Wesley's?"

"You add blasphemy to your crimes, woman!"

Caitlin stared implacably at the Lord Protector, noting with distaste the bulbous shape of his ruby nose, noting with a tremor of fear the bright cruelty in his eyes. Yet her mind wandered far away.

Back to Ireland. Back to Wesley.

She should have trusted him. She should have believed her own heart that told her he would never, ever betray her.

During the long days of the voyage to London, she had pieced together the truth. Wesley never meant to give the horses to Hammersmith. He and the men of Clonmuir had planned an ambush.

The raid would have worked if she had not interfered and gotten herself captured.

Wesley, why didn't you tell me?

Because she would not have trusted him. Too late, she knew the truth. Too late, she knew she loved him. Had loved him from that first spellbound moment when she had wished for him on a white rose. She adored him with a painful, pitiless intensity that mocked every naive idea she had ever had about the love between a man and a woman.

Now their love would never have a chance to flower. And that was the greatest tragedy of all.

Her hand came up to touch the healing bruise just below her collarbone. Wesley's arrow had struck the breastplate beneath her tunic. The impact had knocked her off her feet but the injury had been slight.

No doubt Wesley believed he had slain her. Another tragedy that would never be resolved.

". . . no reason at all to delay carrying out the sentence," Cromwell was saying.

Caitlin dragged her mind to the present. "When?" she forced herself to ask.

"Tomorrow." He refilled both their wine cups.

Caitlin's fingers sneaked again into the folds of the rough shift she wore. She felt the vial and remembered Bull's words.

You won't want to endure the torture, he had whispered, his large, blunt-featured face alight with a twisted compassion. *Spare yourself the agony with Dr. Bate's remedy.* Bull had instructed her to dissolve the powder in a cup of liquid. One sip alone would rob him of his duty.

Her soul recoiled at the thought of taking her own life. But the brutal alternative brought her to a decision.

She dropped to her knees in front of Cromwell. "Please, Your Highness," she pleaded, although the words tasted as sour as vomit in her mouth. "I beg you, spare me!" She pressed the hem of his cloak to her lips. "For the love of God, please!" She caught at the chain of office that spanned his shoulders.

He shoved her back. The chain came loose and fell to the floor. "Groveling ill becomes an Irish chieftain. Sit down!"

She meekly obeyed.

He bent to retrieve the chain.

She unstoppered the vial and dashed the contents

into her wine cup. Her unsteady hand made the vial clink against the rim of the cup. She winced, certain he would notice. But as he groped around on the floor, the powder fizzed briefly; then the granules disappeared. She tucked the empty vial back into the pocket of her apron.

Cromwell straightened, scowling at the broken link of the chain. "Hawkins should have heeded me, by God. Now he'll lose all. All!" Gaining control of himself, he feigned a regretful look. "Pity about the child, though."

Shock slammed into Caitlin's chest. "Child? What child?"

"You mean he didn't tell you about Laura?" A mysterious smile lifted the corners of his mouth. "I must've scared him more than I thought." He rubbed his chin. "Still, that would be like Hawkins, not wanting to use Laura to manipulate your sympathies—as if there were any such thing in your heathen soul."

Swallowing back apprehension, she asked, "Who is Laura?"

"Why, his poor little daughter. Nigh on four years old, she is, darling mite. In his preaching days he dragged the child on his treacherous errands, passing her off as an orphan and himself as a priest, when his true purpose was to incite the people against me. Poor little motherless mite. When Hawkins was arrested, he entrusted her to a godly woman who had the wisdom to bring the girl directly to me."

"Arrested?" The information was coming too fast at her. For a moment she forgot the dread contents of her wine cup. "Wesley was arrested?"

"Aye, and sentenced to death." Cromwell chuckled unpleasantly. "Funny, but he was to die as a priest, and he never really was one. He very nearly did die, but I found a way for him to serve the Commonwealth."

Suddenly all became clear to Caitlin. Shadows of doubt and mistrust were swept away by brilliant rays of truth and comprehension. "To stop the Fianna," she concluded bitterly. "That was why he obeyed you. Because you held his daughter hostage."

Filled with fresh misery, Caitlin buried her face in her sleeves and pressed hard to hold back the tears. Wesley had been pledged to the Church. And yet he had fathered a child.

Motherless, Cromwell had said. But who had the woman been? Wife? Mistress? Had he loved her? More mysteries, thought Caitlin. More unanswered questions.

She heard Cromwell lift his cup, then set it back on the table. Remembering her purpose, she raised her head from her arms. "And what," she asked cuttingly, "do you have in store for the child? Torture for her as well?"

"It suits your narrow view to see a monster in me," Cromwell shot back. "I, who brought order to chaos." He clasped his hands as if wrestling his own anger. "In truth," he began calmly, "I've taken a liking to the babe. The good widow Clench is raising Laura up properly now. Now that Bettie's gone, I shall have to think further about Laura's place in my life."

Dear God, thought Caitlin, I have cost Wesley his child.

She grabbed the stem of her goblet. She was about to commit the ultimate sin, the sin for which there could be no redemption—to condemn her own soul to eternal damnation.

No. Damnation was giving in to Oliver Cromwell. Damnation was never being able to tell Wesley again that she loved him.

With a strange smile on his face, Cromwell lifted his goblet. "A toast, is it?" he asked, his voice full of irony.

Caitlin smiled back. "If my soul doesn't go to heaven, then at least may it come to rest in Ireland."

Cromwell laughed. "I'd sooner burn in hell." He drained his glass.

"More's the pity for you, sir." Caitlin clasped an image of Wesley to her heart, said a silent prayer, and drank to the bottom of the goblet.

18

Wesley faced Logan Rafferty across the round table in the hall at Clonmuir. Rafferty slammed his gloved hand on the table with a resounding thump. "Damn you, Hawkins. This hell-bent raiding has got to stop!"

Their gazes clashed; gray ice met black fire. "Why, my lord?" Wesley asked with the venom of sarcasm in his voice. "Is it interfering with your English alliance?"

Gasps rose from the people in the hall. Rafferty's nostrils flared. His ruddy face darkened two shades. "Sure that's a foul accusation, *seonin*."

"You told Caitlin what you thought we were about with the horses," Wesley stated. "My wife would be alive were it not for your treachery."

Logan's dark red flush drained into his beard. "You lie, Englishman!"

"It's God's truth and no mistake," said a small, tremulous voice from the middle of the hall. "I heard him tell her." Logan swung around just as Aileen Breslin clapped her hand over the mouth of young Brigid.

"The females of Clonmuir start their busybody ways at a tender age," Logan snarled. He turned back, spreading his arms wide. "And how was I to be knowing what you'd planned? Sure it looked to any man as if you were going to hand over the horses."

"How did you know anything of the plan in the first place?" Wesley demanded. "No one here told you."

"It is my business to know such things."

"Your business is with Titus Hammersmith. He's the one who told you." Each damning word dropped like a cold stone from Wesley's lips.

Logan went completely still, save for the agitated rising and falling of his massive chest. "You fling me a direct challenge, *Sassenach*." Very deliberately, he sank his teeth into the middle finger of his leather gauntlet and tugged, baring his hand with its heavy Celtic rings.

He struck Wesley across the face with the glove. The stinging slap to his pride resounded in the silence of the hall. Bellowing an oath, Wesley sprang from the bench. Rory and Liam grabbed Wesley's arms to keep him from throttling Rafferty where he stood.

Logan's challenging gaze streaked over Wesley. "Choose your weapon, Hawkins. I'll choose the time and place."

Breathing hard, Wesley hesitated, his gaze sweeping the residents and refugees who populated the hall. They depended on him now. He had to temper his desire for revenge with their need for peace in the district.

While Wesley debated his options, Curran Healy burst through the main door. Pale faced, his hair coated with mist, he skidded to a stop at the high table. Wesley took one look at the youth's round, frightened eyes and forgot Logan

Rafferty. "What news from Galway, Curran?"

"'Tis Titus Hammersmith, sir. He's back from England."

An iron fist of hatred closed in Wesley's stomach. "And?"

Curran knotted his fingers. "He's brought reinforcements. L-lots of 'em. Sir, he plans to lay siege to Clonmuir."

In the Tower of London, they were alone. The Lord Protector of England and the MacBride of Clonmuir. Caitlin stared across the table at Oliver Cromwell and waited for the poison to sear her insides. She braced herself for the sharp griping pain in her gut, the thickening of her tongue, the pounding in her head.

But so far the only poison she felt was the lethal evil of hatred. She decided to tell him so; for herself, and for all the people of Ireland.

"You are a great, bad man," she stated. "'Tis you who deserves to die, not me. Your English justice mocks the Republican ideals you claim to embrace."

"Impertinent wench." Sweat pearled on his brow even though the thick walls of the room held in the chill.

"You call yourself Lord Protector, but whom have you protected? Widows and orphans? There are plenty of those in Ireland, for you've killed all the men."

He mopped his brow. "It's called war," he said, irony heavy in his voice.

She gave a bark of laughter. "I've seen babies spitted on English pikes. I've seen women forced to eat the flesh of rotting corpses just to keep from starving. You claim the Irish as your subjects, but look me in the eye and tell me you've protected them."

His wary gaze met hers. Dampness shone on his pasty face. "You Irish rebelled. You deserve no mercy!"

"You call yourself God's Englishman, and yet you have the blood of thousands on your hands. You are the father of all murders and treacheries. You took away our priests; you'll burn in hell for that. Cursed be every breath you take, Oliver Cromwell, to the very last of your days!"

Cromwell lurched to his feet. "You're a witch! By God—" His face contorted, his eyes bulging. A low, strangled cry rumbled from his throat. He dropped like a felled tree to the floor. A rusty mutter escaped his lips. His body stiffened, back arching and limbs trembling.

Caitlin watched, gratified that she'd struck a chord of conscience in the English monster. An instant later, though, foreboding tiptoed over her. She snatched both wine cups and held them to the light from the brazier.

Her goblet shone clean. In Cromwell's cup, tiny grains clung to the sides.

"Sweet Mary Mother of God," she whispered. "The devil drank the poison." Cromwell had guessed correctly about the poisoning, but, ever suspicious, he had thought the powder had gone into his own drink. Thinking to outsmart her, he had switched the goblets.

In horror—and a fierce, undeniable sense of satisfaction—she backed away from the sick, convulsing man.

Running to the door, she found it locked.

Her mind worked feverishly. What would she do if she were discovered alone here with the Lord Protector of England dead at her feet?

She heard a sound from outside. It was the click of a key tumbling a lock.

* * *

Six wheel-mounted heavy cannon trundled through the deserted village of Clonmuir. The inhabitants had all fled to the stronghold. In the near silence of a ceaseless hissing rain, the Roundheads dug trenches out of range of Irish crossbows.

Wesley watched in dread and frustration as Englishmen carried stout pavises to shield the gun crews from Irish bolts and arrows. Their fiercest weapons were rendered useless, as useless as hoping they had a chance. The men of Clonmuir had, in lightning raids, felled scores of Englishman. But for each man eliminated, more came to take his place. The stronghold was surrounded save for the portion that faced the sea. By that route, Wesley had sent the women and children and horses to Brocach. Logan Rafferty had proven himself faithless, but his wife Magheen was a MacBride. She would care for the refugees.

The men waited in sodden silence. The mantle of leadership weighed heavy on Wesley's shoulders. Then the English guns spoke.

The walls of Clonmuir started to crumble.

Her heart hammered, but Caitlin planted her feet, held her head high, and waited. She would make no excuses, offer no denials.

The cell door swung open. Her remorseless stare greeted the visitor.

And then an astonished smile lit her face. A handsome cavalier's hat, with plumes nodding over a familiar elfin face, reached just to her waist.

"Tom Gandy!" The jubilant cry burst from her. She bent and hugged him.

"Hist there!" he said. "No time for that, though sure I'm hard to resist. Come away with me, Caitlin, and quickly." He gave a cursory glance at Cromwell who lay, moaning softly, on the floor. "What ails him?"

"Crimes against Ireland," she said curtly. "And his own distrust. Can we get past the guards?"

He lifted one eyebrow. Fatigue deepened the folds of his eyes. "Can the poteen get past the tonsils of an Irishman?" He grabbed her hand and drew her into the stairwell.

The hulking figure of the executioner, Thaddeus Bull, stood there. At his feet lay the personal life-guards of the Lord Protector. The huge man loomed over the unconscious guards. He did not look at Caitlin as he spoke. "I never could abide the torturing of women," he explained. "Hurry now, I'd best get the Lord Protector to a physick. The way's clear to the river."

"Bless you, sir." Caitlin hastened down the stairs after Tom. "The Tower of London is the last place I'd expect to find a decent Englishman."

Tom mopped his brow. "Lord, it took half the ale in London and most of the stories I know to get that great ox to cooperate."

Moments later they leapt into a lighter boat and rowed out to the middle of the inky Thames. The stale smell of river water hung in the air.

"Tom," she asked, when at last she dared to believe she was free, "how did you come to be here?"

"It's a long story, *a stor*."

"Magic, Tom?"

His eyes gleamed like fairy fire in the darkness. "So you're after believing in magic again?"

"I do now," she said fervently. In her mind's eye she saw a beautiful man, walking toward her out of the sunset. She heard the smooth music of his voice, felt the tender caress of his smiling regard, and the devastating joy of his embrace. Wesley. Oh, Wesley. Please God, don't let us be too late.

She put her hands on Tom's arm, stopping him in midstroke. "Tom, wait. Cromwell told me that Wesley has a daughter. We can't leave London without her. I'd never forgive myself if we did. She's the reason he did . . . all that he did." She watched Tom closely, expecting a shocked reaction.

He merely patted her hand. "Not to worry. I know all about the wee girleen."

A familiar sense of wonder swept over her. "Magic again?"

"Give me a little credit for brains and cunning, Caitlin."

"Well, how can we find Laura?"

"She's waiting with a good Catholic lady at Milford Haven. That port's just fourteen miles from our dear Ireland."

Caitlin took the oars and threw all her energy into rowing. They passed freight barges laden with bundled goods, small skiffs tugging at their cables, punts docked along the quays for the night. Lanterns on poles made bright pools on the surface of the water. "Tom, you're a sorcerer."

"If I were that, we'd be at Milford Haven already. As it is, we've a long hard ride ahead of us."

"Are we there yet?"

The single-masted pinnace nosed up the west coast of Ireland. The vessel had been appropriated by Daisy Lane, Tom's "good Catholic woman." Daisy's entire family had been seized by priest catchers. She had been left with nothing save her muscular two-hundred-pound body and a burning desire for revenge.

"Almost, Laura," Caitlin said in answer to the question. She held Wesley's daughter in her lap and wondered for the thousandth time at the miracle of her. Her stepdaughter. Saints in heaven, she was a mother. The idea ignited a queer ache in her chest.

No wonder the Lord Protector had been so taken with the child. Laura was astoundingly beautiful. Freckles dusted her creamy skin. Her rose-gold hair tumbled in waves down her back. Her great wide eyes reminded Caitlin so poignantly of Wesley that she nearly wept each time she looked at the girl.

Wesley's love child. Daisy Lane had, through methods Caitlin preferred not to contemplate, wrested information from Laura's former nurse. The woman called Hester Clench had accused Wesley of breaking his vows with Annabel Pym of Lincoln. The birth had killed Annabel, and her family had rejected the baby.

Holding Laura gave Caitlin a sense of kinship with the hapless Miss Pym. She felt no resentment, only determination to protect the child, to perform the duties Annabel hadn't lived to fulfill.

Laura sniffed. "I'm cold."

"I know, *a storin*." Caitlin tucked a shawl more securely around the child.

"You talk funny."

"So you've said. I talk like my mother and her mother before her, to the time before time."

"I miss Uncle Oliver. He used to let me sit at the end of Miss Bettie's bed while he read from the Good Book."

Caitlin refused to contemplate the image of Oliver Cromwell, reading aloud to his dying daughter. "It's a natural thing to miss the people who showed you kindness, Laura." Caitlin had to force out the words.

Laura poked out her lower lip. "Are we there yet?" she asked again.

Caitlin handed her a bit of biscuit. "Soon, sweet girleen. You'll be with your daida soon."

"My what?"

"Your papa."

The tiny chin trembled. "Auntie Clench and Uncle Oliver said he was a very bad man. They said he was a papist who dragged me through the mires of sin. They said I'd never have to go with him again."

"That was wrong of them," Caitlin said gently.

"But they said—"

Caitlin gave her a gentle shake. "Laura, sometimes grown-up people tell lies. You were lied to about your papa. He didn't drag you through the mires of sin. Surely you remember what your life with him was like."

Laura chewed her lip thoughtfully, then brightened. "Oh, 'twas exciting sometimes! We played hide and seek, and I had to be very, very quiet. And I was never afraid of the dark."

Caitlin smiled, knowing Wesley had made a game of hiding in priest holes and abandoned crofts. "There'll be lots more fun times like that, sweetheart. Wait until you see the horses at Clonmuir. Your father and I will take you on a pony ride."

"It's been such a very long time," Laura mused. "What if I don't remember my papa? What if he doesn't remember me?"

Caitlin rested her chin on the child's head, delighting in the silky feel of her hair. Her daughter. "He has never forgotten you, Laura. He's worked for months so you can be together. He loves you." So much, she thought. So much that he had gone against his principles to do Cromwell's bidding. So much, she thought with a wrench of pain, that he had feared to tell her about the child.

Because he had too much honor to force her to choose between his beloved child and her convictions. And because he did not trust her.

"And why should he be after trusting you?" Tom Gandy demanded as if she had spoken aloud. "You rebuffed him, denied him your heart."

"I've changed, Tom," Caitlin stated, with love rising like the sun in her heart. She kissed the top of Laura's head. "We'll be a family, and all will come right with us now."

But as they rounded the rocky point, and Clonmuir hove into view, she felt a sense of dread so strong that she quivered in fear.

"The scourge of hell be upon us," Tom muttered in Irish under his breath. A smudge of black smoke hovered in the clear blue sky over the keep, obscuring the watchtowers. Thunder rumbled across the water.

Caitlin clutched Laura tighter. "Clonmuir's under attack!"

Daisy surged to her feet, her bulk causing the pinnace to list. "God, let me at those tight-pants bastards!"

Tom Gandy passed the tiller to her and tacked northward.

"What the devil are you doing?" asked Caitlin.

"We'll not go scudding into that vipers' nest with just the three of us and the poor wee girleen. We're going to Brocach." With grim finality, he set the course.

"Not there! Logan's a traitor. Wasn't it he who betrayed Father Tully, and then convinced me that Wesley meant to give Clonmuir horses to Hammersmith?"

"'Tis time his lordship proved his faith with the Irish, then."

The fresh wind carried them swiftly northward.

Blessed Mary, thought Caitlin. What if Wesley were slain? She winced at the notion that he would never again hold his daughter in his arms, never again hear Caitlin declare that she loved him.

Logan's watchmen must have heralded the arrival, for Magheen herself came running down to the landing to greet them.

"Caitlin! Saints in heaven be praised, you're alive!" Laughing and sobbing, Magheen hugged her tightly.

"What of Wesley?" Caitlin demanded, bracing herself for the worst.

"Still holding out at Clonmuir, God willing." Magheen hoisted Laura onto her hip. "And who is this wee pretty?"

As they made their way to the hall, Caitlin gave hasty explanations. Then, full of fury and fear, she planted herself in front of Logan, who sat in his thronelike chair on the dais.

Staring at her as if she were a ghost, he jammed his thumb into his mouth, chewing it to ward off enchantment.

"Feeling guilty, Logan?" Caitlin taunted. "Aye, I'm back, come to haunt a traitor."

He yanked his thumb free. "*Arrah,* it's redeemed I'm wanting to be. Sure haven't I done my best. For two weeks I've been sending runners to your husband advising him to seek terms. But the madness is at him. The only way he'll lay down his arms is with his life—and the life of every fool who fights at his side."

Caitlin closed her eyes, picturing Wesley battling the English legions. For her. For Clonmuir. For Ireland.

Magheen stepped up beside Caitlin. "And I've been telling you for two weeks that some things,

Logan Rafferty, are worth dying for." She tugged at
Caitlin's sleeve. "Come. Wesley sent us Clonmuir's
horses so the English would find no prize if they managed to breach the walls."

Caitlin blinked. "The black?"

"Of course."

Logan shot to his feet. "By God, woman! I forbid
you to go to Clonmuir."

Magheen tossed her head. "I take no orders from a
coward."

Thirty minutes later, wearing breastplates and
helms from Logan's armory, Caitlin, Magheen, Daisy,
and Tom rode hard for Clonmuir. They had left Laura
in the indulgent care of Aileen Breslin, and Logan in a
state of blind shock.

They had gone only a short distance when the
thunder of pursuit sounded behind them. Caitlin
whipped a glance back.

Logan and a company of men-at-arms came on in a
flurry of dust, the particles aglow with the hues of the
sunset. Weapons rode at their hips, and banners fluttered over their heads.

"Stop," said Caitlin to her companions. "Let's hear
what he has to say."

Logan drew up between Caitlin and Magheen.
He handed Caitlin a swatch of black silk. "You forgot something, my lady. Veil yourself with this."

Hope rose in Caitlin's chest as she recognized the
golden harp of Clonmuir embroidered on the fabric.
"Thank you, brother-in-law." She secured the veil so
that the silk flowed down her back.

Logan turned to Magheen, reached out and
touched her arm with a gauntleted hand. "And I
forgot something as well, my love. I forgot my
place in the world, my sacred duty as your husband
and as an Irishman."

Of one mind and one purpose, gilded by the light of sunset, the Irish surged forward.

Logan lifted his fist to the sky. "Fianna and Eire-ann!"

Evening closed over Clonmuir, but this night the Roundheads did not retreat to the abandoned houses of the town.

With a twist of cold dread, Wesley knew the reason.

The Roundheads had battered a huge breach in the wall—an opening wide enough to admit six horsemen riding abreast. Logan had been badgering Wesley for days to seek terms. Staring at the breach, Wesley was tempted. Then a memory intruded, Caitlin's voice, fierce with conviction: *Clonmuir is my home. I'd defend it until the last stone is torn from my dying hands.* He knew what her decision would be. He would not fail her by giving in.

His arms ached from twisting the cranequins of his big crossbow. The few muskets and the small cache of gunpowder had been spent early in the siege. The war flails, hammers, axes, and swords were of little use against the distant cannons.

As night fell, the English soldiers flowed like black shadows toward Clonmuir. Wesley took aim with his crossbow and pulled the trigger. A man screamed and fell.

For you, Caitlin. Wesley glanced at the first bright star of evening. For you.

Seamus MacBride and Father Tully worked a cata-pult. With the wind whipping his beard, the elder MacBride resembled a wizard. They strapped a rock in place. Father Tully blessed it. Seamus loosed the hoisting rope from the windlass. The rock sailed over the wall and felled two Englishmen.

Conn and Curran made good use of their yew long-bows, bringing down soldiers as quickly as they could shoot.

But it wasn't enough, Wesley thought frantically. A swarm of Roundheads funneled into the breach.

"To the yard!" he yelled, flinging down his cross-bow and drawing his heavy broadsword.

Fiery Irish curses roared from the men. Swords and axes, hammers and war flails made from grain-threshing tools, appeared in their hands. Wesley leapt down from the wall walk.

His mind emptied. He knew only the numbing reverberation of sword blows, only the clang of steel, only the searing heat of hopeless hatred.

But the enemy came on, streaming in nightmare waves across the yard. Torches ignited the thatched outbuildings. Screaming shadows streaked through the darkness. Irish curses trumpeted from hoarse throats while the English fought in weird, single-minded silence.

Mounted soldiers and warriors on foot harried Wesley from all sides. He felt his strength seeping like sweat into the bloodied ground. Stealing glimpses through the smoke and flame, he saw Rory, a sense-less heap in the mud. Father Tully and Seamus des-perately tried to repulse four men armed with plug bayonets.

And then, riding a low tide of despair, Wesley saw Titus Hammersmith enter through the main gate. With his sausagelike curls bobbing beneath the edge of his helm, the Roundhead commander rode a bay war-horse toward the guard tower.

Curran Healy had sprung from concealment near the tower to sling a stone at a foot soldier.

Riding with icy precision, Hammersmith bore

down on the unsuspecting boy. Wesley bolted across the yard.

"Over here, Titus!" he bellowed, waving his arms to call attention to himself. "Or have you sunk to butchering children?"

Hammersmith checked his horse and turned while Curran melted back into the shadows. A musketball whined past Wesley's head. A warrior encased in siege armor stepped in his way. Furious, Wesley held his sword in a two handed grip and swung out. The bone-shattering impact nearly tore the blade from Wesley's hand, but left no more than a dent in the armor.

A curse of frustration had barely escaped his lips when a sledgehammer swung out of nowhere. With a clang like the clapper striking a great bell, the hammer clubbed the warrior on the top of his helmeted head. He fell without a sound, and Liam the smith gave Wesley a raised fist of victory.

Wesley ran through the smoke, jumping the body of a fallen wolfhound. Reaching Hammersmith, he swung out with his sword, slicing the stirrup. Hammersmith slid off-balance. Seizing the moment, Wesley dragged him from the saddle.

Hammersmith coiled into a ball on the ground. His booted feet exploded in a blur of motion, catching Wesley in the chest and sending him reeling back. In one graceful motion, Hammersmith surged to his feet.

"Aye, catch your breath, my lad," Hammersmith taunted, "for I'll give you a fight you won't soon forget." Gripping his sword in both hands, he hacked at Wesley.

Wesley stumbled backward, trying to buy time to catch his breath.

"You'd run from me?" Hammersmith goaded.

"What would your dear wife think of that, Hawkins?" Seeing the furious look on Wesley's face, he drove the insult deeper. "Aye, we all had her on her dying breath, my friend, and a sorry lay she was by then!"

Wesley felt something inside him snap. He no longer cared that he could hardly breathe, that his sword hilt slipped like a channel trout in his sweaty grip. He no longer cared whether he lived or died. But first, he intended to kill.

The Roundhead commander's well-aimed blade hissed through the air toward Wesley's head.

Wesley ducked and returned the strike. Irish curses streamed from him as if he had been born speaking the tongue.

Hammersmith fought quietly, straitlaced and unimaginative, in the manner of Cromwell's army. He emitted no soul-deep calls of triumph or despair, gave no heartening battle cries, invoked neither saint nor monarch.

In a deadly calm corner of his mind, Wesley pitied him. Hammersmith had never known true passion, while Wesley had learned to commit his whole heart and soul—and soon his life—to a cause. Caitlin had given him that. In return, he would give her memory the death of Titus Hammersmith.

Wesley brought his sword up and out to meet a new strike. The impact reverberated numbingly up his arm. He heard a metallic clatter. His sword felt strangely light.

Hammersmith had broken it in two.

"Yield, Hawkins," Hammersmith ordered. "Yield, and pray I remember you're still an Englishman."

"Call a retreat," Wesley countered, surprising himself with the clear strength of his own voice. "Retreat, and beg God you die an easy death."

Hammersmith said no more, but came on with rhythmic swings of his sword, a reaper felling a bloody harvest with his scythe. Wesley fended off blows with the stub of his sword. Hammersmith backed him step by step to the wall. Wesley's circle of awareness tightened until he saw only the gleaming blade swinging like a pendulum, its razor edge coming closer and closer, kissing his heart with death.

"Oh, Jesus," he wheezed through his teeth. "God have mercy on my soul." Wesley ducked beneath a whizzing blow and felt the cool wind on his neck. He waited for the bright light of oblivion to close over him.

But he remained alone in this world to face the thrusts of his enemy's sword.

Hammersmith lunged. Wesley twisted to one side. The blade ripped through his tunic, through the leather of his cuirass.

Hot pain seared his chest. Jumping backward up two steps toward the walk, he prayed for the light, the pulse of mystic power that would receive his agony. Only a faint glimmer penetrated the urgency of the moment.

The English blade slashed out. Wesley backed up three more steps. Four. Five. The soothing light retreated to a pinpoint.

"Not now, for Christ's sake! Not now!" Wesley eluded blow after blow, his lungs aching with exertion.

"My God," Wesley begged, "who—what *are* you?"

I am you. A last flicker, and the light vanished. Forever. The finality of it stung like a small, secret death in his soul.

"No! Come back, I—"

"By God, you're a madman!" Hammersmith

pressed on, stronger than ever, closing in for the kill.

Wesley reached the wall walk. He could hear the roar and crash and hiss of the sea far below the cliffs. The stiff wind buffeted his back.

Below, the yard rang with clanging weapons and screaming horses and bellowing men. The Irish battle cries had dissolved into mindless bellows of pain.

"Do you hear that?" Hammersmith demanded. "They're dying! Yield, and I'll consider being merciful."

"You really don't understand, do you, Titus?" With new fervor, plumbed from some inner well of strength, Wesley spoke through his teeth. "To an Irishman, death in battle is a greater mercy than surrendering to scum like you."

Hammersmith's sword made a clean arc toward Wesley's neck. The blade slammed against his gorget. The force of the blow nearly choked him. The pain rang through his neck, his head, his vitals.

The white light did not come to take it away. At last Wesley understood why the gentle priest inside him had left. It was time for them both to die.

He did not know why he bothered to ward off still more blows with his broken sword. He did not know why he bothered to duck and twist and feint from side to side.

All was lost. Caitlin. Laura. And now Clonmuir.

Hammersmith's sword struck the wall. A flurry of sparks briefly lit the air, illuminating his adversary's face. And in that face Wesley saw the destruction of Ireland.

He must not die alone. A few more steps, and they would reach Traitor's Leap, the sheer drop to the sea. Together, he and Hammersmith would plunge into eternity.

Out of the corner of his eye, Wesley spotted movement. Ducking beneath a blow, he thrust upward with his half blade. Too short. The jagged end snagged in Hammersmith's blousy trousers.

Shadows rippled across the yard. A keening wind tore the shroud of clouds from the rising moon.

At that precise moment Wesley spied, in silvery splendor, a silk-veiled warrior on a magnificent black stallion, sailing through the main gate.

Good God, had he died and gone to heaven already?

Hammersmith made a driving thrust. Wesley moved aside. Instinct, not thought, directed his movements now.

For his heart, his mind, and his soul were focused entirely on the lithe warrior.

On Caitlin.

She was a rainbow cleaving through a sky of boiling clouds, a vision of light in the darkness of his soul. She was a miracle. Wesley glowed inside like a pilgrim whose faith had been restored. He dared not question what marvel had brought her here with a small army at her back. He knew only that he was not alone. All was not lost.

Renewed power surged like wildfire through him. "You sorry son of a bitch," he said to Titus.

With cold rationality he maneuvered himself along the embattled parapet between two embrasures. He waited calmly for the next thrust. Hammersmith had him cornered. His death was a certainty. But for Caitlin he could do one last deed. He could escort Hammersmith to his death. He pictured them struggling, falling together, the terrifying flight to the jagged rocks below and the sea that offered the ultimate oblivion, the sea that had brought him to Caitlin.

Bending low, he threw aside his broken sword and

made a beckoning motion with his hands. "Aye, come to me, Titus. Don't let steel get in the way of our fight."

"You tempt me with the prospect of an easy brawl. But I'm a soldier and not given to foolish games."

"You invented the word foolish, Titus. All of Ireland laughs at you."

With a bellow of rage, Hammersmith lunged. His blade scored a deep furrow in Wesley's cuirass. Seizing the hilt of the weapon, Wesley ripped it from Hammersmith's grip and flung it away with a clatter.

Possessed by a final surge of strength, he held fast to Hammersmith and made for the top of the wall.

"You're mad." Hammersmith's voice shook.

"It hardly matters now." Wesley shoved Hammersmith toward the edge.

The Roundhead's eyes rolled back in fear. He clung like a limpet to Wesley. "Please, I beg you—"

"Plead with the devil, for I'm taking you to hell with me."

Hammersmith hooked his thumbs into Wesley's windpipe and pressed hard.

The two of them teetered on the precipice. Stars of pain shattered in Wesley's head. Consciousness ebbed. He knew he had only seconds to act.

He pulled up his knee and pushed it against Hammersmith's chest.

Still clinging to Wesley, Hammersmith flew over the wall. Wesley felt a rush of wind, a weird, momentary weightlessness. Terror and regret and love streaked through his mind in those final moments.

Then a hand grabbed him by the seat of his trews. The leather ripped. The tendons in Wesley's arms stretched taut from the weight of Hammersmith. He pounded the Roundhead's clinging hands against the wall. Hammersmith screamed in terror. His body tumbled down, wheeling hundreds of feet below into blackness.

"And where do you think you're off too, *a chara*?" said a familiar and completely unexpected voice.

Blinking in confusion, Wesley leaned out to peer over the wall. The rushing surf outlined the thrusting rocks of the shoreline. The sea had already swallowed her sacrificial offering.

Turning back to his rescuer, Wesley doubled his fists. "You were too late to save him, Logan. Now, about that challenge . . ." But fatigue and fear weakened his knees, and he stumbled.

Logan Rafferty threw back his head and shouted with laughter. His braided beard shone silver in the moonlight. "Time was, I might have taken advantage of your state." He extended his hand, helped Wesley to his feet, and jammed a dented helmet on his head. "I didn't come to save Hammersmith, but to right a grievous wrong. Let's finish this, my friend."

Adjusting the helm, Wesley blinked in disbelief. Then, with a cry of jubilation, he staggered down the stairs to the yard, snatched up a sword from the mud, and rushed to join the fighting.

And found little fighting to be had.

With his hammer upraised, Liam chased five Roundheads out of the yard. Rory had revived; Wesley heard his hellish war cries through the smoke. He fought alongside a giant blond woman Wesley did not recognize. Seamus unleashed a pack of wolfhounds on the Roundhead cavalry. Father Tully grabbed a dagger from a rabid-looking Englishman. He swiftly made the sign of the cross over the man, then slit his throat.

Tom Gandy—Gandy, for God's sake, looking like a deadly Cupid—calmly shot off arrows from the gate tower. Wielding a charred broom, Magheen chased, with age-old fervor, a stray soldier.

And then there was Caitlin. Lovely as the moon, graceful as the wind, she rode down panicked soldiers, herding them out of the yard with expert arcs of her sword. Her task accomplished, she gave a great whoop of triumph.

Pure love flooded Wesley's heart. He wrenched off his helm and flung it away. Spying him, Caitlin did the same. Her tawny hair rippled like hammered gold. Her eyes shone brighter than the stars of midsummer night.

The stars of eternity.

His throat clogged with words he could not speak. He grasped her about the waist and lifted her from the saddle. The shells of their breastplates clashed as they came together. They were kissing—hard, desperately, joyfully—before her feet touched the ground.

"Caitlin. You've come back to me."

"Aye, my Wesley. This time, forever."

"But how—"

She pressed her fingers to his lips. "Tom Gandy will tell it better than I. And I've the rest of my life to be making explanations. For now, my darling Wesley, I'll be after saying just one thing to you."

He tasted the damp tendrils of hair at her temple. "And what is that?"

"I love you. *Dia linn!*" Her kisses rained upon his astonished face. "I love you!"

"That's three things," he said shakily.

She laughed with a sweet, pure joy that nearly brought him to his knees. "And before the night is gone, it'll be a thousand more." She turned and loosed the cinch of the black's saddle. From out of nowhere Brigid came and lugged the saddle away.

Brigid? But Wesley had ordered the women and

children of Clonmuir to take shelter with Magheen at Brocach. Another mystery. Another miracle.

"Come ride with me." Caitlin swung gracefully onto the black. "There's work aplenty to be done here, but all can wait."

Wesley mounted behind her. The black grunted and settled beneath the added weight. As they rode toward the gate, Logan Rafferty doffed his hat, his arm encircling his beaming wife. He handed a flask to Rory Breslin who shared it with the blond Amazon. Tom Gandy began ordering people to see to the wounded, strip the corpses, and set the yard to rights.

Caitlin urged the black to a gallop. As it shot through the gate, she gave a fierce yell. A few straggling Englishmen hit the ground and rolled into a ditch for cover.

Caitlin's laughter trilled across the silvery landscape. To Wesley's surprise, faint gray glimmered over the hills to the east. The battle had devoured most of the night.

He reveled in the feel of Caitlin's healthy young body clasped to his, in the song of her mirth on the wind.

They came to the strand, where milky light illuminated the tangled garden. Caitlin dismounted, waited for Wesley, and then slapped the black on the rump. "Go on, Sean," she said. "Sure you've earned a bit of a rest."

The horse trotted off.

A chill of shock froze Wesley. "Sean? But that's Irish for John."

"Aye, I've finally named him. 'Twas Tom Gandy's suggestion. Do you like it?"

He blinked. Tom's uncanny choice nagged at strange memories in his head. "Yes, but you said—"

"I said a lot of things. A lot of blarney-brained, ill-considered things." She bent and pulled off her boots one by one, then clapped them together to clean off the dust. "And sure I'll be saying many more in the fine long years to come. Can you live with my sharp tongue, Wesley?"

He took her by the shoulders, his hands filling themselves with the miracle of her living flesh. In a voice hoarse with emotion, he said, "Caitlin, I would die without every part of you."

She turned her head into the lee of his shoulder. "Wesley, I must tell you—"

"What, love?"

"It's about your—" She broke off, studying his face, and her expression deepened with raw desire. She rose to kiss his cheek. "Later, my darling. Haven't I earned a moment or two alone with my hus—" Her body stiffened when she spied the center of the garden. "What's this?" Moving away from him, she went to inspect a carved stone.

"Something I made for you. When I thought you'd—" He stopped and swallowed, unable to shape the horror into speech.

Caitlin bent to inspect the low stone chiseled in the shape of a harp. The Irish epitaph read, *For Caitlin, the MacBride of Clonmuir, gone with the tide to a heavenly shore.* A rose bush had been planted at its base. A single white blossom pushed past the thorns.

"'Tis wondrous," she said softly, reaching out to touch the stone. She turned her pain-filled face up to his. "God, Wesley, when I think of how you suffered—"

"Don't think of it," he interrupted. "Think only of the joy we have now, Caitlin."

They kissed again, their mouths sliding slowly and

languorously together while their hands worked feverishly at buckles and fastenings, until breast-plates and undertunics lay on the sand.

Wesley laughed shakily. "I never imagined I'd have to disarm my wife just to make love to her."

They broke apart and he went down on his knees before her, tenderly divesting her of her trews. Her legs were thinner than he remembered. Questions crowded his throat, but he stopped himself. Not now. Not yet.

Leaving his own clothes draped over a rock, he took her hand. "Come into the sea with me, my love, to wash us clean of the battle," he said.

Hand in hand, they waded in. The surf swirled around his knees and her thighs. Shivery warmth flowed through him.

Her hair made a veil over her shoulders and breasts. The wind lifted the tawny drapery from her creamy neck and bosom. Moving like a willow stirred by the wind, she came against him, their skin burning at the contact.

"Do you feel it, Caitlin?" he whispered against her damp, salty cheek. "Do you feel our love, like a brand upon the flesh?"

"It hurts, sometimes," she admitted. "But some-times I want it to."

Nodding in understanding, he crushed her to his chest. Their love was born of a thousand hurts. The agony of desire was a sweet reminder of their triumph.

He took her face between his hands and kissed her deeply. Her fingers skimmed over him in a caress of silken subtlety.

Bound by an ancient enchantment, they waded deeper to where the restless waves lifted them, surged them together as if nature itself demanded their completion. The sting of salt honed passion to a sharp edge.

With a cry of exultation she wrapped her arms around his neck and her legs around his waist. He cupped her buttocks and, gazing into her face, found his home. The sensation made his ears ring with passion. He forced himself to stand very still, resisting the buffeting of the surf. They had been too long apart; he did not want to hurry their reunion.

Trembling with the effort of control, Wesley kissed her lips, her throat, her breasts, and the taste of her mingled with the tang of the great wide sea, an elixir more potent than fairy nectar. Caitlin's legs tightened, and she began to move.

Wesley groaned and threw back his head. Their bodies beating with the rhythm of the sea, they mated like wild creatures. He held nothing back, for he knew the woman in his arms was strong enough to accept his fierce, consuming love. In each thrust he poured all the passion, anger, sorrow, and joy that had been in his heart since he had first met her. In return, she offered hungry, biting kisses, wild cries of abandonment, and love words so precious that he felt buoyant, free, capable of anything.

The waves carried them up to the shore, where the surf pulled at the sand and made a bed of foam for their love-fevered bodies. Caitlin's eyes swept open. In them Wesley saw the mysteries of her, and knew his wife was the rarest woman in the world.

"Wesley," she said, "I love you." Like a rising wave, her body arched upward. The tremors of her response pulled at him like the sea tugging at the sand beneath them.

"Caitlin." He shouted her name to the wind. His final thrust drove into her, deep as the sea, deep as midnight, deep as the love pouring through his soul.

His rapture crested and another cry broke from his throat.

Spent, they lay still joined while passion ebbed in gentle pulsations, leaving a glowing warmth, the warmth of knowing that all would come right at last.

Almost all. Burying his face in her damp, tangled hair, Wesley thought of Laura. Anguish invaded his contentment. What had Cromwell done with his daughter?

The time had come to tell Caitlin everything. She loved him. Nothing he could tell her would change that.

Propping his elbows on each side of her face, he gave her a lingering kiss. Her eyelashes were spiky with saltwater and perhaps tears. The colors of the coming dawn suffused her cheeks.

"Caitlin. There is something I must tell you."

"Ah, Wesley, you can tell me anything."

"I have a daughter who—"

"I know."

"—has been in my care for three years, but—"

"I know."

"—taken from me when I was arrested for—"

"I *know*. Is it deaf you are, John Wesley Hawkins?"

At last her words penetrated his painful rush of speech. He stared at her in astonishment. "How do you know about Laura?"

"I discovered the truth the second time I went to London."

"London? Christ, you went to London?"

"And where do you think I've been, *amaden*?" She laughed at his confusion. "Taking the waters in Bath?"

With a lithe, rippling movement, she rose from the surf and dove beneath the waves to wash away the sand. Wesley gazed in pain and wonder at her sleek, darting form. Didn't his beloved care about Laura? Perhaps it wasn't fair to expect her to. Yet she was so caring with other children.

She emerged from the water and tossed back her streaming hair. "Wesley, your only problem is how you'll cease being a stranger to the wee girleen."

"It's not that simple."

"Aye, it is. Get dressed and come with me."

19

"*Papa!*" *A small figure ran* across the yard of Clonmuir. Then she stood still, glancing back uncertainly at Aileen Breslin.

Wesley stopped in his tracks. He blinked. Twice. Three times. He looked from Caitlin's smiling face to the red-haired sprite twisting her tiny fingers into her apron.

Oh, God. Laura. She'd grown taller. Her hair hung longer down her back. It seemed only yesterday that she had been a cherubic baby, cuddled in his arms, so sweet and trusting. And now she stood before him, a little girl with a mind of her own, fearful, uncertain . . .

And then he was running, feeling his daughter's presence like a warm breeze through his soul. He caught her in his arms, swung her around, and clasped her to his chest. "Laura." The tautness in his throat choked off any more words.

He detected the faint stiffness of hesitation in her, and his heart constricted. "Oh Laura . . ."

Caitlin's strong hand clasped his shoulder. "Sure

and she's had plenty of adventures for such a wee one." Bending, she placed a kiss on Laura's head. "Haven't you, *a storin*?"

Laura nodded gravely. Her little hand fit itself into his.

In Irish, Caitlin said, "Wesley, she's too young for scars."

He willed himself to believe it. And then he did believe it, for Laura moved closer yet, laying her cheek to his chest. Having her in his arms again brought the whole world back in focus, made sense of the months of turmoil that had gone before. His heart brimmed over, full of love and joy and awe for his daughter—and his wife.

"I came on a sailing boat to see you." Laura pulled back to study him. Her small hand brushed his whiskers, and she made a face. "Papa, why are you crying?"

He laughed and rubbed unabashedly at his face. "I'm just so happy to see you again, poppet."

She nodded, looking sage beyond her years. "At first I didn't want to leave Hampton Court, but wee Tom and Caitlin said you needed me."

"And so I do, my treasure," he murmured, kissing the top of her head and inhaling her familiar fragrance.

"Brigid showed me the ponies, Papa. And Caitlin said I could have one for my very own."

His tongue felt thick and clumsy. "Of course you can."

Laura glanced across the yard where noisy children, home from Brocach, played with a litter of piglets. Only the crumbled wall and small mounds of straw placed here and there to soak up the blood gave evidence of the battle that had taken place. Piglets? Wesley rubbed his eyes. Where had they gotten meat on the hoof?

"I like it here, Papa," Laura said. "Aileen says I don't have to wear shoes anymore, and I like being near the sea. Do you like this place?"

He looked over her head at Caitlin. "Oh, aye, Laura. Aye, I surely do. And we shall stay here forever, or so long as we're welcome."

"That's forever," said Caitlin.

Laura squirmed to the ground. "Can I go play now?" Without waiting for an answer, she sped off toward the group of children. In a moment of blind panic, Wesley started after her.

"Let her go, Wesley." Caitlin's soft voice stopped him. "You have all your life to hold her now."

"That's the truth," said Tom Gandy, coming forward with a spritely step. "Cromwell won't be getting his hands on her—or any other bairn—ever again. Nor will you be subject to arrest, Caitlin." He gave an impish grin. "The old devil died, you see."

Caitlin made the sign of the cross. "Blessed Mary, then the poison finished him."

"It was more likely the bog sickness," Tom said over his shoulder as he walked away. "He caught it in Ireland."

"Poison?" Confusion buzzed in Wesley's ears. Then he listened, gape-mouthed, as Caitlin told of her capture, her imprisonment at the Tower, and her fateful interview with the Lord Protector on the eve of her execution.

He buried his face in his hands, trying to banish the images of her ordeal.

"It's all right now, my Wesley," she finished.

He looked up, then stretched out his hand. She took it, and together they walked across the yard, past Rory Breslin, who was making calf eyes at the buxom Englishwoman, Daisy Lane; past Father Tully who was tearing charred thatch from the spring house; past Conn and Curran and all the people of Clonmuir who had fought half the night and spent the other half clearing away the stains and rubble of the battle.

When they came to Magheen and Logan, they stopped. Behind the lord and lady of Brocach was a train of carts stuffed to the rails with bags of grain. Drovers from Brocach tried to keep order amid the sheep and pigs and cows in the bawn.

Wesley's gaze locked with Logan's.

Logan stuck out his large hand. "It's a grand day for the mending of hearts."

Wesley clasped the proffered hand. "Aye, my lord. It certainly is that."

Magheen and Caitlin let out their breath in a burst of relief. Magheen gestured at the carts. "This is just the beginning. You have only to state your needs, and we'll help."

Seamus strolled up, buckling on a sword belt. "Ah, Rafferty, I see you got some manners on you at last."

"Aye, sir."

"None of this sir business," said Seamus. "You'll call me your da now."

"Daida?" asked Caitlin, eyeing his antique armor. "What are you up to?"

"Another quest, and a grand one this time. Brian and I are off to France to join Charles of the Stuarts. Tom says he's returning to the throne. I hear one of his mistresses is going to bring him back to the True Faith."

His daughters shook their heads as he walked away, his old armor creaking. Logan went to oversee the unloading of the supplies.

With their hearts united and their world at peace, Wesley and Caitlin made their way up the stone steps to the wall walk. Already the English had abandoned the village, and people were returning to their houses.

A chill scudded over Wesley as he looked down the west wall. The shore was empty save for the weed-draped crags. "I battled Titus Hammersmith here," he said. "He went to hell by way of Traitor's Leap." The tide had sucked the body out to sea, just as the events of the night had leached the evil from Clonmuir.

"You gave the murderer no more than he deserved," she said. Wesley stepped behind Caitlin and pulled her against his chest. "At last," he said, breathing in the sea scent of her hair, "at last I feel you are truly my wife."

"I'm still the MacBride." A smile he could not see sweetened her voice.

"And so you shall always be. Chieftain of the sept." He lifted her hair and kissed her neck. "And mistress of my heart."

She sighed, the motion lifting her breasts and dropping them into his waiting hands. "Ah, Wesley, I thought there was no more magic in Ireland. But you've proven me wrong. Thank God we lost never a soul last night."

He closed his eyes, thought a moment. "There was one loss."

She stiffened. "Who?"

"You don't know him. Or perhaps you know him very well."

"I don't understand."

"I'm not sure I do, either. It was someone who . . . lived inside me. I can think of no other way to explain. He . . . was a priest, a stranger who had the vocation I could never find with the church. When I was tortured, he came forth and accepted the pain for me."

She made a sound of confusion in her throat, and he went on. "He helped me pass the initiation."

"Aye, you did seem charmed during the ordeal." He heard no surprise or disbelief in her voice.

"It wasn't really me, but this other part of me, this Father John." Wesley rested his chin on her head and gazed out at the dazzling golden line where the risen sun struck the sea. "Aye, and I never knew it until last night."

She shuddered a little. "What happened last night?"

He held her closer against him. "During the battle, he came to me. Not to fight for me as he had in the past, but to bid me farewell. He vowed I didn't need him anymore. And he was right."

She laid her hands over his. "I should call you a madman, but I cannot. There were times when you seemed strange to me, not yourself at all. That first time I bathed you. And when you tamed the black. Perhaps it was the stranger I was seeing."

She turned in his arms. "I don't see a stranger now, but the man I shall love for all my days and longer, into forever."

"We've much work to do," he reminded her.

"And much love to make."

He smiled. Together they watched the breeze rippling through the green-clad hills. "Caitlin, men will always try to conquer Ireland."

"And the Irish will always resist."

"Always." He skimmed his fingers delicately over the rise of her cheekbones, loving the softness of her skin. "And she will always rush out to greet her invaders, grab them to her breast and fill them with the fine, soft essence of the land. In that way, Ireland will endure."

"How wise you sound—for a tight pants, that is."

"It's a wisdom I learned from you and your people. I came here to conquer you. And here I stay, a willing prisoner of your heart."

She reached up to kiss him. Pure as rain, love flowed across the bond. All around them, the great heart of Clonmuir beat in the breast of the wild and vital land.

The sea crashed over the rocks; dogs barked and men shouted in the yard, but for Caitlin and Wesley there was a stillness. She drew back, and her hand tenderly brushed his face. "Do you feel it, Wesley? Do you feel the magic?"

"Aye," he breathed into her salt-dusted hair. "It's all around me, Cait, but most especially, here in my arms." As he bent to kiss his wife, the mist of enchantment rolled forth to fold them in gossamer softness, to sweep them away to the long, shining years ahead.

Afterword

Oliver Cromwell's sudden collapse on August 17, 1658 did indeed lead to accusations of poison. Years later, Dr. George Bate hinted at his own involvement in the deed. Cromwell succumbed, presumably to malaria, on September 3, 1658. His son, Richard, proved a weak successor, and in 1660, King Charles II was restored to the throne.

The priests exiled to Inishbofin were not actually released until the Restoration. For centuries after, Connemara in the west of Ireland remained a haven for independent, Gaelic-speaking Catholics.

COMING NEXT MONTH

SONG OF THE NIGHTINGALE by Constance O'Banyon
A mesmerizing historical romance from bestselling author Constance O'Banyon. This enchanting love story sweeps from the drawing rooms of London to the battlefields of Waterloo as a beautiful woman fights for her family's honor and finds her one true love.

LOVE WITH A WARM COWBOY by Lenore Carroll
When her boyfriend returns form a trip abroad with a Croatian bride, Barbara Door is crushed. She heads for a friend's dude ranch in Wyoming to find confidence, adventure, and love with a warm cowboy. A sassy, moving story for all modern women.

SWEET IVY'S GOLD by Paula Paul
Award-winning author Paula Paul brings the Old West back to life in this winsome turn-of-the-century romance about a feisty young woman who sets up a gambling parlor in a small gold-mining town in Colorado. Adventure and true love abound when she meets Langdon Runnels.

THIEF OF HEARTS by Penelope Thomas
From the author of *Master Of Blackwood* and *Passion's Child* comes a story of love and intrigue in 17th century England. Forced to flee her village home after accidentally killing a local squire in self-defense, Damorna Milfield seeks refuge in London. She is rescued by mysterious "Lord Quent," a charming but duplicitous man-about-town, who teaches Damorna the art of deception and love.

SUNBURST by Suzanne Ellison
A sweeping tale of love and adventure in the Mohave Desert and the Sierra Nevada. Bostonian beauty Mandy Henderson goes out west in search of her fiancé, Rodney Potter, who has disappeared while doing survey work for the railroad. Drew Robelard, a handsome army captain, is assigned to help Mandy find Rodney, but he actually has his own secret agenda.

PRIVATE LIES by Carol Cail
The lighthearted adventures of a young woman reporter who sets out to investigate her boss's death and ends up solving a different crime, discovering unexpected romance along the way.

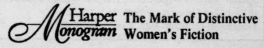

Harper Monogram **The Mark of Distinctive Women's Fiction**

ANALISE

Analise Caldwell was the reigning belle of New Orleans. Disguised as a Confederate soldier, Union major Mark Schaeffer captured the Rebel beauty's heart as part of his mission. Stunned by his deception, Analise swore never to yield to the caresses of this Yankee spy...until he delivered an ultimatum.

ROSEWOOD

Millicent Hayes had lived all her life amid the lush woodland of Emmetsville, Texas. Bound by her duty to her crippled brother, the dark-haired innocent had never known desire...until a handsome stranger moved in next door.

BONDS OF LOVE

Katherine Devereaux was a willful, defiant beauty who had yet to meet her match in any man—until the winds of war swept the Union innocent into the arms of Confederate Captain Matthew Hampton.

LIGHT AND SHADOW

The day nobleman Jason Somerville broke into her rooms and swept her away to his ancestral estate, Carolyn Mabry began living a dangerous charade. Posing as her twin sister, Jason's wife, Carolyn thought she was helping her gentle twin. Instead she found herself drawn to the man she had so seductively deceived.

CRYSTAL HEART

A seductive beauty, Lady Lettice Kenton swore never to give her heart to any man—until she met the rugged American rebel Charles Murdock. Together on a ship bound for America, they shared a perfect passion, but danger awaited them on the shores of Boston Harbor.